Praise for *In the Dark*

"A tense exploration of manipulation and betrayal . . . A solid psychological thriller with carefully developed characters and disturbing, cleverly masked revelations that will appeal to fans of Tana French and Sophie Hannah." —*Booklist*

"Your next riveting, twisty read!"
—Shari Lapena, *New York Times* bestselling author of *The Couple Next Door*

"*In the Dark* kept me up into the late hours. Clever and wonderfully complex."
—Jane Corry, bestselling author of *My Husband's Wife*

"A classy, agile, fresh, unpredictable, and utterly compelling gift of a book: hats off!"
—Nicci French, author of the Frieda Klein series

"This is a real gripper of a read and hugely satisfying."
—Peter James, author of the Roy Grace series

Praise for *Close to Home*

"Hunter does a masterly job of building tension and keeping the reader guessing to the very end." —*Publishers Weekly*

"This well-written psychological drama will keep you guessing until the very end." —*Book Reporter*

PENGUIN BOOKS

IN THE DARK

CARA HUNTER lives and works in Oxford. She also studied for a degree and PhD in English literature at Oxford University.

IN THE DARK

CARA HUNTER

PENGUIN BOOKS

PENGUIN BOOKS

An imprint of Penguin Random House LLC
penguinrandomhouse.com

First published in Penguin Books (UK) 2018
Published in Penguin Books (USA) 2019

LIBRARY OF CONGRESS CATALOGING-IN-PUBLICATION DATA
Names: Hunter, Cara, author.
Title: In the dark / Cara Hunter.
Description: New York : Penguin Books, 2019. | Series: DI Adam Fawley ; 2
Identifiers: LCCN 2018037216 (print) | LCCN 2018038983 (ebook) |
ISBN 9781524704858 (ebook) | ISBN 9780143131069 (paperback)
Subjects: | BISAC: FICTION / Suspense. | FICTION / Mystery & Detective /
Police Procedural. | GSAFD: Suspense fiction. | Mystery fiction.
Classification: LCC PR6108.U588 (ebook) | LCC PR6108.U588 I5 2019 (print) |
DDC 823/.92—dc23
LC record available at https://lccn.loc.gov/2018037216

Printed in the United States of America
1 3 5 7 9 10 8 6 4 2

Set in Garamond MT Pro

For 'Burke and Heath'
For many happy days

IN THE DARK

Prologue

She opens her eyes to darkness as close as a blindfold. To the heaviness of old dank air that hasn't been breathed for a long time.

Her other senses lurch awake. The dripping silence, the cold, the smell. Mildew and something else she can't yet place, something animal and fetid. She moves her fingers, feeling grit and wet under her jeans. It's coming back to her now – how she got here, why this happened.

How could she have been so stupid.

She stifles the acid rush of panic and tries to sit up, but the movement defeats her. She fills her lungs and shouts, flinging echoes against the walls. Shouts and shouts and shouts until her throat is raw.

But no one comes. Because no one can hear.

She closes her eyes again, feeling hot angry tears seeping down her face. She is rigid with outrage and recrimination and conscious of little else until, in terror, she feels the first sharp little feet start to move across her skin.

Someone said, didn't they, that April is the cruellest month. Well, whoever it was, they weren't a detective. Cruelty can happen any time – I know, I've seen it. But the cold and the dark somehow dull the edge. Sunlight and birdsong and blue skies can be brutal in this job. Perhaps it's the contrast that does it. Death and hope.

This story starts with hope. May 1st; the first day of spring – real spring. And if you've ever been to Oxford, you'll know: it's all or nothing in this place – when it rains the stone is piss-coloured, but in the light, when the colleges look like they've been carved from cloud, there is no more beautiful place on earth. And I'm just a cynical old copper.

As for May Morning, well, that's the city at its most eccentric, its most defiantly 'itself'. Pagan and Christian and a bit mad, and it's hard to tell, a lot of the time, which is which. Choirboys singing in the sunrise on the top of a tower. Hurdy-gurdy bands jostling the all-night burger vans. The pubs open at 6 a.m., and half the student population is still pissed from the night before. Even the sober citizens of North Oxford turn out en masse with flowers in their hair (and you think I'm joking). There were over 25,000 people there last year. One of them was a bloke dressed as a tree. I think you get the picture.

So, one way or another it's a big day in the police calendar. But it's a long straw on the uniform roster, not a short one. The early start can be a bit of a killer, but there's rarely any trouble, and we get plied with coffee and bacon sandwiches. Or at least we were, the last time I did it. But that was when I was still in uniform. Before I became a detective; before I made DI.

But this year, it's different. This year, it's not just the early start that's the killer.

*   *   *

By the time Mark Sexton reaches the house he's nearly an hour late. It should have been a clear run at that time of the morning but the traffic on the M40 was nose to tail, and the queue backed up all the way down the Banbury Road. And when he turns into Frampton Road there's a builder's truck blocking his drive. Sexton curses, slams the Cayenne into reverse and screeches backwards. Then he flings the car door open and steps out on to the street, narrowly missing a splatter of sick on the tarmac. He looks down in distaste, checking his shoes. What is it with this bloody city this morning? He locks the car, strides up to the front door, then digs into his pockets, looking for his keys. At least the scaffolding's gone up now. The sale took far longer than expected, but it should still be done by Christmas, if they're lucky. He lost out on an auction for a place on the far side of the Woodstock Road, and had to up his bid to get this one, but by the time he's finished, it'll be a bloody gold mine. The rest of the housing market might be treading water, but what with the Chinese and the Russians, prices just never seem to go down in this city. Only an hour from London and a top-notch private school for the boys only three streets away. His wife didn't like the idea of semi-detached but he told her, just look at it – it's bloody enormous. Genuine Victorian, four storeys above ground and a basement he plans to fit out as a state-of-the-art wine cellar and home cinema complex (not that he's told his wife that yet). And only some old git living next door – he's not going to be having many all-night parties, now is he. And yes, his garden is a bit of a state, but they can always stick up some trellis. The landscape designer said something about pleached trees. A grand a pop but it's instant cover. Though even that won't solve the problem out the front. He glances across at the rusting Cortina propped up on bricks outside number 33 and the three bicycles chained to a tree; the pile of rotting pallets and the black plastic sacks spilling empty beer cans on to the pavement. They were there the last time he came, two weeks ago. He'd shoved a note through the door asking the old git to get them moved. Clearly, he hasn't.

The door opens. It's Tim Knight, his architect, a roll of plans in hand. He smiles broadly and waves his client in.

'Mr Sexton – good to see you again. I think you're going to be pleased with the progress we've made.'

'I bloody well hope so,' says Sexton, with heavy irony. 'This morning can't get much worse.'

'Let's start at the top.'

The two men head up, their footsteps booming on the stripped wood. Upstairs, local radio is on full volume and there are builders in most of the rooms. Two plasterers on the top floor, a plumber in the en-suite bathroom and a specialist window restorer working on the sashes. One or two of the workmen glance over at Sexton but he doesn't make eye contact. He's got his tablet out and is annotating every job, and querying most of them.

They end up in the extension out at the back, where the old brick lean-to has been knocked down and a huge double-height glass and metal space is being built in its stead. Beyond the trees sloping down at the bottom of the garden they can just see the Georgian elegance of Crescent Square. Sexton wishes he could have afforded one of those, but hey, the market's gone up 5 per cent since he bought this place, so he's not complaining. He gets the architect to take him through the plans for the kitchen ('Jesus, you don't get much for sixty grand, do you? They don't even throw in a sodding dishwasher'), then he turns, looking for the door to the cellar stairs.

Knight looks a little apprehensive.

'Ah, I was coming to that. There's been a bit of a hitch on the cellar.'

Sexton's eyes narrow. 'What do you mean, *hitch*?'

'Trevor rang me yesterday. They've hit an issue with the party wall. We may need a proper legal agreement before we can fix it – whatever we do will affect next door.'

Sexton makes a face. 'Oh for fuck's sake, we can't afford to get the bloody lawyers involved. What sort of a sodding problem?'

'They started taking off the plaster so they could chase in the new cabling but some of the brickwork was in a pretty bad way. God knows how long it's been since Mrs Pardew went down there.'

'Stupid old bat,' mutters Sexton, which Knight decides to ignore. This is a very lucrative job.

'Anyway,' he says, 'I'm afraid one of the young lads didn't realize quick enough what he was dealing with. Don't worry, though, we're going to get the structural engineer in tomorrow –'

But Sexton is already pushing past him. 'Let me see for my bloody self.'

The light bulb on the cellar stairs flickers bleakly as the two of them make their way down. The whole place reeks of mildew.

'Mind where you're treading,' says Knight, 'some of these steps aren't safe. You could break your neck down here in the dark.'

'Have you got a torch?' calls Sexton, a few yards ahead. 'I can't see a bloody thing.'

Knight passes one down and Sexton snaps it on. He can see the problem straight away. Paint is blistering from what's left of the old yellowing plaster and, underneath, most of the bricks are crumbling with dry grey mould. There's a crack as wide as his finger from floor to ceiling that wasn't there before.

'Christ, are we going to have to underpin the whole bloody house? How come the surveyor missed this?'

Knight looks apologetic. 'Mrs Pardew had units all along that wall. He wouldn't have been able to get behind them.'

'And more to the point, how come no one was monitoring that stupid little tosser who's taken lumps out of my fucking wall –'

He picks up one of the builder's tools from the floor and starts poking at the bricks. The architect steps forward. 'Seriously, I wouldn't do that –'

A brick falls away, then another, and then a chunk of masonry slips and crashes into dust at their feet. This time, Sexton's shoes don't escape the mess, but he doesn't notice. He's staring, mouth open, at the wall.

There's a hole, perhaps two inches wide.

And in the gloom beyond, a face.

*   *   *

At the St Aldate's police station newly promoted Detective Sergeant Gareth Quinn is on his second coffee and his third round of toast, his expensive tie flipped over one shoulder to keep it out of the crumbs. The expensive tie that goes with the expensive suit and the general aura of being just a bit too smart to be an ordinary copper. And that's smart in both senses of the word, needless to say. The rest of the CID office is half empty; just Chris Gislingham and Verity Everett have arrived so far. The team don't have a big case right now and DI Fawley is out all day at a conference, so it's the rare indulgence of a late start followed by the always-enticing prospect of catching up with the paperwork.

There's a moment, dust floating in the sun slanting through the blinds, the rustle of Quinn's newspaper, the smell of coffee. And then the phone rings. It's 9.17.

Quinn reaches over and picks it up.

'CID.' Then, 'Shit. You sure?'

Gislingham and Everett look up. Gislingham, who's always described as 'sturdy' and 'solid', and not just because he's getting a bit chunky round the middle. Gislingham, who – unlike Quinn – hasn't made DS and, given his age, probably won't now. But don't judge him on that. Every CID team needs a Gislingham, and if you were drowning, he's the one you'd want on the other end of the rope. As for Everett, she's someone else you can't afford to judge on appearances: she may look like Miss Marple must have done at thirty-five, but she's every bit as relentless. Or as Gislingham always puts it, Ev was definitely a bloodhound in a previous life.

Quinn's still talking into the phone. 'And there's definitely no answer next door? OK. No – we're on it. Tell uniform to meet us there, and make sure they bring at least one female officer.'

Gislingham's already reaching for his jacket. Quinn puts the phone down and takes a last bite of his toast as he gets to his feet. 'That was the switchboard. Someone called from Frampton Road – says there's a girl in the cellar next door.'

'In the *cellar*?' says Everett, her eyes widening.

'Someone knocked through the wall by mistake. There's an old bloke living in the house, apparently. But they can't raise him.'

'Oh fuck.'

'Yup. That's about the size of it.'

When they pull up outside the house a crowd is already gathering. Some of them are clearly the builders from number 31, glad of any excuse to stop working that won't get them more shit from Sexton; others are probably neighbours, and there's a scatter of revellers with flowers in their hats and cans of lager in hand who look decidedly the worse for wear. The slightly surreal atmosphere isn't helped by the life-size plastic cow pulled up by the kerb, draped in a floral tablecloth with daffodils round its horns. A couple of Morris men have started an impromptu performance on the pavement.

'Blimey,' says Gislingham as Quinn switches off the engine. 'Do you think we can get them for parking that thing without a permit?'

They get out and walk across the road, just as two patrol cars draw up on the other side. One of the women in the crowd wolf whistles at Quinn and falls about laughing when he turns to look at her. Three uniformed officers join them from the cars. One of them has a battering ram; the female officer is Erica Somer. Gislingham spots a glance between her and Quinn, and sees the smile in her eyes at his embarrassment. So that's how it is, he thinks. He'd suspected those two might have a thing going. Like he said to Janet the other night, he's caught the two of them at the coffee machine together far too many times to be just coincidence. Not that he can blame Quinn – she's a looker all right, even in uniform and sensible shoes. He just hopes she doesn't expect too much: if Quinn was a dog, no one would call him Fido.

'Do we know the name of the old man who lives here?' asks Quinn.

'A Mr William Harper, Sarge,' says Somer. 'We've called the paramedics, just in case there really is a girl there.'

'I know what I bloody well saw.'

Quinn turns. A man in the sort of suit Quinn would buy if he had the money. Slim cut, silk weave, and a claret satin lining that glares with a purple check shirt and a pink spotted tie. He has 'City' written all over him. As well as 'Very Pissed Off'.

'Look,' the man says, 'how long is all this going to take? I have a meeting with my lawyer at three and if the traffic's as bad getting back –'

'Sorry, sir, and you are?'

'Mark Sexton. Next door – I own it.'

'So you were the one who called us?'

'Yeah, that was me. I was down in the cellar with my architect and part of the wall gave way. There's a girl in there. I know what I saw and, unlike this rabble, I'm not half-cut. Ask Knight – he saw it too.'

'Right,' says Quinn, gesturing the officer with the battering ram up to the door. 'Let's get on with it. And get that lot on the pavement under control too, will you? It's like something out of the fucking *Wicker Man* out here.'

As Quinn moves away Sexton calls him back. 'Hey – what about my bloody builders – when can they get back in?'

Quinn ignores him, but as Gislingham passes he taps him on the shoulder. 'Sorry, mate,' Gislingham says cheerily, 'that posh refurb is just going to have to wait.'

On the front step, Quinn pounds on the door. 'Mr Harper! Thames Valley Police. If you're in there, please open the door or we will be forced to break it down.'

Silence.

'OK,' says Quinn, nodding to the uniformed officer. 'Do it.'

The door is tougher than it looks, considering the state of the rest of the house, but the hinges splinter at the third blow. Someone in the crowd cheers tipsily; the rest press forward, straining to see.

Quinn and Gislingham go in, and pull the door to behind them.

Inside the house, all is still. They can still hear the bells of the Morris dancers, and flies are buzzing somewhere in the stale air. The place clearly hasn't been decorated for decades; paper is peeling off the walls and the ceilings are sagging and blotched with brown stains. There are newspapers scattered across the floor.

Quinn moves slowly down the hall, the old boards creaking, his shoes scuffing against the paper. 'Is there anyone here? Mr Harper? It's the police.'

And then he hears it. A whimpering noise. Close. He stands a moment, trying to work out where it's coming from, then darts forward and throws open a door under the stairs.

There's an old man sitting on the toilet dressed only in a vest. Tufts of wiry black hair cling to his scalp and shoulders. His underpants are round his ankles and his penis and testicles hang limply between his legs. He cowers away from Quinn, still mumbling, his bony fingers gripping the toilet seat. He's filthy, and there's shit on the floor.

Somer calls from the doorstep. 'DS Quinn? The medics have arrived if you need them.'

'Thank Christ for that – get them in here, will you?'

Somer stands back to let two men in green overalls come through the door. One squats down in front of the old man. 'Mr Harper? There's no need to be anxious. Let's just take a look at you.'

Quinn motions to Gislingham and they back off towards the kitchen.

Gislingham whistles as the door swings open. 'Someone call the V&A.'

An ancient gas cooker, 1970s brown-and-orange tiling, a metal sink. A Formica table with four unmatched chairs. And every single surface piled with dirty crockery and empty beer bottles and half-finished food cans alive with flies. All the windows are shut and the lino under their feet sticks to their shoes. There's a glass door with a beaded curtain leading to a conservatory, and another door which must lead down to the cellar. It's locked but there's a bunch of keys on a nail. Gislingham seizes them, his fingers fumbling, and it takes three attempts to find the one that fits, but even though the key is rusted it turns without jamming. He pulls the door open and flicks on the light, then stands aside, letting Quinn go first. They make their way down slowly, step by step, the neon strip hissing over their heads.

'Hello? Is there anyone down here?'

The light is drab, but it's enough for them to see. The cellar is empty. Cardboard boxes, black plastic sacks, an old lampstand, a tin bath filled with junk. But apart from that, nothing.

They stand there, staring at each other, their hearts pounding so loudly they can barely hear. Then, 'What was that?' whispers Gislingham. 'Sounds like scratching. Rats?'

Quinn starts involuntarily, scanning the ground at his feet; if there's one thing he can't stand, it's bloody rats.

Gislingham looks around again, his eyes adjusting, wishing he'd brought the torch from the car. 'What's that over there?'

He pushes his way through the boxes and realizes suddenly that the cellar is much bigger than they thought.

'Quinn – there's another door here. Can you give me a hand?'

He tries the door but it won't move. There's a bolt at the top and Quinn eventually manages to yank it across, but the bloody door still won't budge.

'It must be locked,' says Gislingham. 'Do you still have those keys?'

It's even worse finding the right one in the half-light, but they do it. Then they put their shoulders to the door and it slowly shunts forward until a wave of foul air hits them and they have to put their hands to their mouths to face the stench.

A young woman is lying on the concrete floor at their feet, wearing a pair of jeans ripped at the knees and a ragged cardigan that was probably yellow once. Her mouth is open and her eyes closed. Her skin is dead white in the sallow glare.

But there's something else. Something nothing prepared them for.

Sitting by her, pulling at her hair.

A child.

*   *   *

And where was I when all this happened? I'd love to say it was something gritty and impressive like Special Branch liaison or anti-terrorism, but the dreary truth was a training course in Warwick. 'Community Policing in the 21st Century'. Inspectors and above; aren't we the lucky ones. What with the death by PowerPoint and the stupid o'clock early start, I was beginning to think the uniforms on the May Morning stint had decidedly the better deal. But then I got the call. Followed swiftly by an exasperated frown from the officious organizer person who'd insisted we turn our phones off, and an audible sigh when I duck out into the corridor. She's probably worrying I'll never come back.

'They've taken the girl to the John Rad,' says Quinn. 'She's in a pretty bad way – she's obviously not eaten for some time and she's severely dehydrated. There was one bottle of water left in the room, but I suspect she's been giving most of it to the kid. The medics will be able to tell us more after they've done a proper examination.'

'And the boy?'

'Still not saying anything. But, Christ, he can't be much more than two – what's he going to be able to tell us anyway? Poor little sod wouldn't let Gis or me anywhere near him, so Somer went in the ambulance. We arrested Harper at the scene, but when we tried to get him out of the house he started kicking and being abusive. Alzheimer's, I'm guessing.'

'Look, I know I don't need to say this, but if Harper is a vulnerable adult we'll have to play this one by the book.'

'I know. We have it covered. I called Social Services. And not just for him. That kid's going to need help too.'

There's a silence and I suspect we're both thinking the same thing.

It's quite possible we're dealing with a child who's known nothing else – who was born down there. In the dark.

'OK,' I say. 'I'm leaving now. I'll be there by noon.'

* * *

BBC Midlands Today

Monday 1 May 2017 | Last updated at 11:21

BREAKING: Girl and toddler found in cellar in North Oxford

Reports are coming through of the discovery of a young woman and a small child, thought to be her son, in the basement of a house on Frampton Road, North Oxford. Building work is underway next door, which led this morning to the discovery of the girl, apparently locked in the cellar. The girl has not been named, and Thames Valley Police have not as yet issued a statement.

More news on this as we get it.

---

* * *

11.27 a.m. At the Kidlington witness suite, Gislingham is watching Harper on the video link. He's got a shirt and trousers on now, and is sitting hunched over the sofa. There's a social worker beside him on a hard-backed chair, talking to him intently, and a woman from the Mental Health team watching from a few feet away. Harper seems restless – he's moving about, jigging one leg up and down – but they can tell, even without the sound on, that he's coherent. At least for now. He's eyeing the social worker tetchily, waving away what he says with a stiff and withered hand.

The door opens and Gislingham turns to see Quinn, who comes over, chucks a file on the table and leans against the desk. 'Everett's gone straight to the hospital, so she'll interview the girl as soon as they let us. Eric –' He flushes. 'PC Somer's gone back to Frampton Road to coordinate the house-to-house. And Challow's gone in with the forensics team.'

He makes a note on the file then tucks his pen behind his ear. The way he does. Then he nods towards the video screen. 'Anything?'

Gislingham shakes his head. 'His social worker's been in there half an hour. Name's Ross, Derek Ross. I'm sure I've come across him before. Any news on when Fawley will be back?'

Quinn checks his watch. 'About twelvish. But he said we should get started, if the doctor and Social Services are OK with that. There's a lawyer on her way too. Social worker's covering his arse. I suppose you can't blame him.'

'Belt *and* braces, eh,' says Gislingham drily. 'But they're sure he's OK to be interviewed?'

'Apparently he has lucid intervals and we can question him then, but if he starts to lose it we'll have to back off.'

Gislingham stares at the screen for a moment. There's a line of spit hanging from the old man's chin; it's been there at least ten minutes but he hasn't wiped it away. 'You think he did it – that he was even up to it?'

Quinn's face is grim. 'If that kid really was born down there, then yes, absolutely. I know Harper looks pathetic now, but two or three years ago? He could have been completely different. And it was that man who committed this crime – not the sad old sod in there.'

Gislingham shivers, even though the room is stifling, and Quinn glances across. 'What, someone walk on your grave?'

'I was just thinking, he didn't get like this overnight, did he? This has been going on for months. Years, even. And she wouldn't have known. That he was starting to lose it, I mean. She's trapped down there, out of sight – I bet he'd started forgetting she was even there. The food starts running out, then the water – she has the kid to think about – and even if she screams the old man can't hear her –'

Quinn shakes his head. 'Jesus. We got there just in time.'

On the screen, Derek Ross gets to his feet and moves out of shot. A moment later the door opens and he appears.

Gislingham gets up. 'So you're his social worker, then?'

Ross nods. 'For the last couple of years or so.'

'So you knew about the dementia?'

'He was formally diagnosed a few months back but I suspect it's been coming on for a lot longer than that. But you know as well as I do how unpredictable that is – how it goes in fits and starts. I've been worried lately that it might have started to accelerate. He's had a few falls and he burned himself on the cooker a year or so back.'

'And he's drinking, isn't he? I mean, you can smell it on him.'

Ross takes a deep breath. 'Yes. That has become rather a problem of late. But I just can't believe he could do anything like this – anything so terrible –'

Quinn's not convinced. 'None of us really knows what we're capable of.'

'But in the state he's in –'

'Look,' says Quinn; there's a hardness to his voice now. 'The doctor says it's OK to question him, and she should know. As for charges, well, that's another matter, and the CPS will have their say as and when we get to that stage. But there was a girl and a child locked in that cellar, and we *have* to find out how they got there. You do see that, don't you, Mr Ross?'

Ross hesitates, then nods. 'Can I sit in? He does know me – it might help. He can be a bit – difficult. As you're about to find out.'

'Right,' says Quinn, collecting his papers.

The three men move towards the door, but Ross stops suddenly and puts a hand on Quinn's arm. 'Go easy, won't you?'

Quinn looks at him, then raises an eyebrow. 'Like he did, on that girl?'

*   *   *

Interview with Isabel Fielding, conducted at 17 Frampton Road, Oxford
1 May 2017, 11.15 a.m.
In attendance, PC E. Somer

ES: How long have you lived here, Mrs Fielding?
IF: Only a couple of years. It's a college house. My husband is a don at Wadham.
ES: So do you know Mr Harper – the gentleman at number 33?
IF: Well, not to speak to. Soon after we moved in he came over in a bit of a state and asked if we'd seen the cover for his car. Apparently it had gone missing. It was a bit odd since his car isn't exactly going anywhere. But we thought he was just a bit, you know, eccentric. There's a lot of it about. Around here, I mean. Lots of 'characters'. Some of

them used to be academics, so they've lived
here for donkey's years. I think a lot of them
just get to the purple and cats stage and say
to hell with it.

ES: 'Purple and cats'?

IF: You know – that poem. 'When I get old I'm going
to wear purple', or whatever it is. You know,
when you get to the age when you just don't care.

ES: And Mr Harper - he didn't care?

IF: You see him wandering about. Talking to
himself. Wearing odd clothes. Mittens in July.
Pyjamas in the street. That sort of thing. But
he's basically harmless.

[*pause*]

I'm sorry, that came out wrong – I mean –

ES: It's all right, Mrs Fielding. I know what
you mean.

*   *   *

'So, Mr Harper, my name is Detective Sergeant Gareth
Quinn, and my colleague here is Detective Constable Chris
Gislingham. You already know Derek Ross and this lady is
going to act as your lawyer.'

The woman at the far end of the table looks up briefly, but
Harper doesn't react. He doesn't appear to have registered
her presence at all.

'So, Mr Harper, you were arrested at 10.15 a.m. on suspicion of kidnap and false imprisonment. You were cautioned,
and your rights were explained to you, which you said you
understood. We are now going to conduct a formal interview, which is being recorded.'

'That means they're filming this, Bill,' says Ross. 'Do you understand?'

The old man's eyes narrow. 'Of course I understand. I'm not a bloody idiot. And it's *Dr* Harper to you, boy.'

Quinn glances at Ross, who nods. 'Dr Harper taught at Birmingham University until 1998. Sociology.'

Gislingham sees Quinn flush slightly; three times in one morning, must be some kind of record.

Quinn flips open his file. 'I believe you've lived at your current address since 1976? Even though you were actually working in Birmingham?'

Harper looks at him as if he's being deliberately dense. 'Birmingham is a shithole.'

'And you moved here in 1976?'

'Bollocks. December 11th 1975,' says Harper. 'My wife's birthday.'

'Dr Harper's first wife died in 1999,' says Ross quickly. 'He married again in 2001, but unfortunately the second Mrs Harper died in a car accident in 2010.'

'Stupid cow,' says Harper loudly. 'Pissed. Pissed as a fart.'

Ross glances at the lawyer; he looks embarrassed. 'The coroner found that Mrs Harper had raised levels of alcohol in her blood at the time of the accident.'

'Does Dr Harper have any children?'

Harper reaches out and taps the table in front of Quinn. 'Talk to me, boy. Talk to *me*. Not that idiot.'

Quinn turns to him. 'Well, do you?'

Harper makes a face. 'Annie. Fat cow.'

Quinn picks up his pen. 'Your daughter is called Annie?'

'No,' interrupts Ross. 'Bill gets a bit confused. Annie was his neighbour at number forty-eight. A very nice woman, apparently. She used to pop in and make sure Bill was OK, but she moved to Canada in 2014 to be closer to her son.'

'She wants to scrape, the silly cow. Told her I wouldn't have one of those things in the house.'

Quinn looks at Ross.

'He means "Skype". But he won't use a computer so that was a non-starter.'

'No other family?'

Ross looks blank. 'Not that I know of.'

*   *   *

'There's definitely a son – blow me if I can remember his name.'

Somer is on the doorstep at number 7, and has been for the last fifteen minutes. She's wishing, now, that she'd taken up the offer of tea, but if she had she might have been here all day – Mrs Gibson has scarcely yet drawn breath.

'A son, you think?' says Somer, flicking back through her notes. 'No one else has mentioned him.'

'Well, that doesn't surprise me. People round here – don't like to "get involved". Not like when I was growing up. In those days you looked after each other – everyone knew who their neighbours were. I haven't got a clue who half these yuppies are.'

'But you're sure there's definitely a son?'

'John – that's it! I knew I'd remember eventually. Haven't seen him around here in a while, though. Middle-aged chap. Grey hair.'

Somer makes a note. 'And when do you think you last saw him?'

There's a noise in the hall behind and Mrs Gibson turns to make a shooing sound before pulling the door a bit closer. 'Sorry, dear. Bloody cat, always tries to get out the front if I let her. She has a flap round the back, but you know what cats are like – always want to do what they're not supposed to and Siamese are even worse –'

'Mr Harper's son, Mrs Gibson?'

'Oh yes, well, now you come to mention it, I think it could have been a couple of years.'

'And does Mr Harper have any other visitors that you know of?'

Mrs Gibson makes a face. 'Well, there's that social worker, I suppose. Fat lot of use he is.'

*   *   *

Quinn takes a deep breath. Harper looks at him. 'What is it, boy? Spit it out, for fuck's sake. Don't just sit there looking like you're trying to shit.'

Even the lawyer is looking embarrassed now.

'Dr Harper, do you know why the police came to your house this morning?'

Harper sits back. 'Haven't a fucking clue. Probably that arsehole next door complaining about the bins. Wanker.'

'Mr Sexton did call us, but it wasn't about the bins. He was down in his cellar this morning and part of the wall gave way.'

Harper looks from Quinn to Gislingham, and then back again. 'So bloody what? Wanker.'

Quinn and Gislingham exchange a glance. They've both been in enough interrogations to know that this is the moment. Very few guilty people – even the best and most practised liars – can control their bodies so well they give no sign. Whether a flicker in the eyes, a sudden twitch of the hands, there's almost always something. But not now. Harper's face is blank – no careful withdrawal, no attempt to brazen it out. Nothing.

'And I don't have a fucking TV.'

Quinn stares at him. 'I'm sorry?'

Harper sits forward. 'Moron. *I don't have a fucking TV.*'

Ross glances at Quinn nervously. 'I think what Dr Harper is trying to say is that he doesn't need a TV licence. He thinks that's why you've brought him here.'

Harper turns on Ross. 'Don't tell me what I think. Fucking moron. Don't know your arse from your tits.'

'Dr Harper,' says Gislingham. 'There was a young woman in your cellar. That's why you're here. It's nothing to do with your TV licence.'

Harper lurches forward, poking his finger in Gislingham's face. *'I don't have a fucking TV.'*

Quinn sees the look of alarm in Ross's eyes; this is starting to get out of hand. 'Dr Harper,' he says. 'There was a girl in your cellar. *What was she doing there?*'

Harper sits back. He looks from one of the officers to the other. For the first time, he looks shifty. Gislingham opens his file and takes out the photo he took of the girl. He turns it to face Harper. 'This is the girl. What's her name?'

Harper leers at him. 'Annie. Fat cow.'

Ross is shaking his head. 'That's not Annie, Bill. You know that's not Annie.'

Harper isn't looking at the photo.

'Dr Harper,' insists Gislingham. 'We need you to look at the picture.'

'Priscilla,' says Harper, spitting saliva down his chin. 'Always was a looker. Evil cow. Swanning about the house with her tits out.'

Ross looks desperate. 'It's not Priscilla either. You know it's not.'

Harper reaches out a clawed hand, and without dropping

his eyes from Gislingham's face, sweeps the picture off the table, along with Gislingham's phone, which clatters against the wall and falls in pieces on the floor.

'What the hell did you do that for?' shouts Gislingham, half out of his chair.

'Dr Harper,' says Quinn, his teeth clenched now, 'this young woman is currently in the John Radcliffe hospital, where the doctors will be giving her a full medical examination. As soon as she is able to talk, we will find out who she is, and how she came to be locked in the basement of your house. This is your chance to tell us what happened. Do you get that? Do you get how *serious* this is?'

Harper leans forward and spits in his face. 'Fuck you. Do you hear me, *fuck you*!'

There is a terrible pause. Gislingham dare not look at Quinn. Then he hears him get something out of his pocket and looks up to see him wiping his face.

'I think we should stop now, officer,' says the lawyer. 'Don't you?'

'Interview terminated at 11.37,' says Quinn, with icy calmness. 'Dr Harper will now be taken to the custody suite and held in the cells —'

'Oh, for heaven's sake,' says Ross, 'surely you can see he's in no fit state for that?'

'Mr Harper,' says Quinn coolly, collecting his papers and stacking them with exaggerated care, 'may well present a danger to the public, as well as to himself. And in any case his house is now a crime scene. He can't go back there.'

Quinn gets up and strides towards the door, but Ross is at his heels, following him out into the corridor.

'I'll find him somewhere to stay,' he says, 'a care home — somewhere we could keep an eye on him —'

Quinn turns so suddenly that the two of them are barely inches apart. '*Keep an eye on him?*' he hisses. 'Is that what you've been doing all these months – *keeping an eye on him?*'

Ross backs off, his face white. 'Look –'

But Quinn isn't letting up. 'How long do you think she's been down there, eh? Her and that kid? Two years, *three*? And all that time, you've been going to that house, *keeping an eye on him*, week in, week out. You're the only sodding person who *was* going in there. Are you seriously telling me you *didn't know*?' He drills his finger into Ross's chest. 'If you ask me, it's not just Harper we should be arresting. You have some *very* serious questions to answer, *Mr Ross*. This is way beyond professional negligence –'

Ross has his hands up, fending Quinn off. 'Do you have *any idea* how many clients I have? How much paperwork I have to do? What with that and the traffic I'm lucky if I get fifteen minutes a visit. It's as much as I can do to check he's been eating and isn't sitting in his own shit. If you think I get time to pop round doing a house inspection too then you're in cloud bloody cuckoo land.'

'You never heard *anything* – never saw *anything*?'

'Quinn,' says Gislingham, who's now standing in the doorway.

'I've never been in that sodding basement,' insists Ross. 'I never even knew he *had* one –'

Quinn's red in the face now. 'You're seriously asking me to believe that?'

'*Quinn*,' says Gislingham, urgent. And when Quinn ignores him he reaches for his shoulder and forces him round. There's someone coming along the corridor towards them.

It's Fawley.

*   *   *

At Frampton Road, Alan Challow walks down the path to
the front door and stops for a moment to let the uniformed
officer lift the tape barring the entrance. It's the hottest day
of the year so far and he's sweating in his protective suit.
The crowd at the end of the drive is more than twice the size
it was and its character has changed. Most of the May Morning stragglers have gone and the builders have called it a day,
too. One or two neighbours still linger, but the majority of
the onlookers now are either looking for a morbid thrill or a
good story. Or both: at least half of them are hacks.

In the kitchen at the back, two of Challow's forensics team
are dusting the room for prints. One of them nods to Challow and pulls down her mask to speak to him. There's a line
of sweat across her upper lip. 'This is one of those times
when you're actually grateful to be wearing one of these.
Christ knows when anyone last cleaned properly in here.'

'Where's the cellar?'

She points. 'Behind you. We've rigged up some better
lighting. Which only serves to make it worse.' She shrugs
grimly. 'But you know that.'

Challow makes a face; he's been doing this job twenty-
five years. He ducks slightly to avoid the lamp now strung
over the top of the cellar stairs and makes his way down,
throwing giant juddering shadows across the bare brick
walls. At the bottom, two more forensics officers are waiting
for him, staring round at the accumulated junk.

'OK,' says Challow, 'I know it's a pain in the arse but we
need to get all this lot back to base. Where was the girl?'

'Through there.'

Challow moves to the inner room. An arc light is throwing a merciless brilliance over the filthy floor, the dirty bedding, the macerator toilet standing in a pool of evil-smelling waste. More boxes of junk. There's a cardboard pallet that once held bottles of water, but there's only one left, and though a plastic sack is bursting with packaging and empty tins, there's no sign of any food. And in the far corner, a child's bed, curled like a mouse nest.

'Right,' says Challow eventually, into the silence, 'we need to take all this stuff away too.'

One of the officers walks over to the crack in the dividing wall. Some bricks are broken and the mortar's been dug out.

'Alan,' she says after a moment, turning back to Challow, 'look.'

Challow joins her, then bends closer. The damp plaster is streaked with red smears.

'Jesus,' he says eventually. 'She was trying to claw her way out.'

*   *   *

I haven't seen Derek Ross since the Daisy Mason case. He'd sat in with her brother when we questioned him, so one way or another I saw a lot of Ross back then. It was less than a year ago but to look at him you'd think it was five. He's lost more hair, gained more weight, and there's a tic under his right eye. But I suspect Quinn may have something to do with that.

'DS Quinn,' I say, turning to him. 'Why don't you go and get us all a coffee. And I don't mean from the machine.'

Quinn looks at me, opens his mouth and closes it again.

'Sir, I –' he begins, but Gislingham touches him on the elbow.

'Come on, I'll give you a hand.'

It's as good a thumbnail of these two as you're likely to get: Gis, who has always been exceptionally good at knowing when to stop digging; and Quinn, who carries his own set of shovels.

I take Ross into the office next door. The screen is on mute now but still shows the interview room. The lawyer is on her feet, getting ready to leave, and Harper is huddled sideways on the chair with his knees clutched against his chest. He looks very small, and very old, and very scared.

I put a cup of water down in front of Ross. Then I take a seat opposite and push it a little further back. He has large dank patches under his arms and the atmosphere can best be described as 'tangy'. Take it from me, you don't want to get that close.

'How have you been?'

He glances up at me. 'So-so,' he says, wary.

I sit back. 'So tell me about Harper.'

He stiffens, just a little. 'Am I some sort of suspect?'

'You're an important witness. You must know that.'

He sighs. 'Yes, I suppose so. What do you want to know?'

'You told my officers you only went in once a week. How long has that been going on?'

'Two years. Perhaps a bit more. I'd need to check the file.'

'And you don't stay long?'

He takes a gulp of the water; some of it spills over on to his trousers but he doesn't seem to notice. 'I can't – I don't get the bloody time. Seriously, there's nothing I'd like more than to sit there for an hour and crap on about the weather, but with the budget cuts we've had –'

'I wasn't accusing you.'

'That DS of yours did.'

'I'm sorry about that. But you have to remember – he saw the state that girl was in. Not to mention the child. And if he was finding it hard to see how you could have been going there all that time and not known she was there, well, I can't say I blame him. To be honest, I'm struggling with that myself.'

Because despite what I just said, I'm a hair's breadth from questioning him as a suspect. And until I'm absolutely sure he isn't, Harper's going to need someone else to sit in with him. It's going to be difficult enough getting a conviction on this one; the last thing I need is a botched investigation.

Ross rakes a hand through his hair. What he has left of it. 'Look, those houses have thick walls. I'm not surprised I didn't hear anything.'

'You never went down there?'

He looks me straight in the eye. 'Like I said, I didn't even know he had a cellar. I thought that door was just a cupboard.'

'What about upstairs?'

He shakes his head. 'Bill's been pretty much living on the ground floor ever since I've known him.'

'But he can actually get up and down the stairs?'

'If he has to – but he doesn't much. Annie sorted out a bed in the front room before she left, and there's a bath out the back in the lean-to. It's pretty basic but it does. I dread to think what state the upstairs is in now. It must be years since anyone went up there. Probably not since Priscilla died.'

'No cleaner – doesn't the Council send someone?'

'We tried that, but Bill just shouted abuse at her. She refused to come back. I wipe a cloth around a bit and shove bleach down the bog. But there's a limit to what anyone can do in the time I've got.'

'What about food – shopping? Do you do that too?'

'When they took his driving licence away I got a local elderly charity to organize him a regular supermarket delivery.
That was about eighteen months ago. There's a standing
order back to his bank account. He has plenty of money.
Well, not "plenty" perhaps, but enough.'

'Why doesn't he move out? That house must be worth a
fortune. Even in that state.'

Ross makes a face. 'The tosser next door paid over three
million. But Bill refuses to go into a home. Even though his
arthritis has got worse the last month or so, and the doctor's
going to put him on medication for the Alzheimer's and
he'll need to be monitored to make sure he's taking it properly. There's no way I can do that. If he stays in that house on
his own it's only a matter of time before there's some sort of
an accident. Like I said, he's already burned himself once.'

'Did he know you wanted him to move?'

Derek takes a deep breath. 'Yes, he did. I sat down with
him about six weeks ago and tried to explain it all. I'm afraid
he didn't take it at all well. He got violent – started yelling at
me, throwing things. So I backed off. I was planning to talk
to him again this week. A place has just become available at
Newstead House, in Witney. It's one of the better ones. But
God only knows what's going to happen now.'

There's a pause. He finishes his water. I pour him more.

'Has it occurred to you,' I say, carefully, 'that one reason
why he didn't want to move is because of the girl?'

Ross's face goes white and he puts the water down.

'He couldn't leave that house with her still there, because
she'd be found. And he couldn't let her go, for exactly the
same reason.'

'So what was he going to do?'

I shrug. 'I don't know. I was hoping you might –'

There's a commotion suddenly, in the corridor outside, and Gislingham bangs the door open.

'Boss,' he says, 'I think –'

But I'm already pushing past him.

In the room next door, two constables are trying to re-strain Harper. It's scarcely believable it's the same man – he's clawing at their faces, kicking out, yelling at a female officer.

'*Cunt!*'

The woman is visibly shaken. And I know her – she's no rookie. There's a scratch on her cheek and the front of her uniform is soaked.

'I just gave him a cup of tea,' she stammers. 'He said it was too hot – that I was trying to burn him – I wasn't – really, I wasn't –'

'I know. Look, go and sit down for a bit. And get some-one to look at that cut.'

Her hand goes to her face. 'I didn't even realize –'

'I think it's just a scratch. But get it looked at anyway.'

She nods, and as I follow her out of the room, Harper lurches at her again. '*Cunt!* It's her you should be arresting, you moron – tried to fucking scald me. *Evil cow!*'

Ross is staring at the screen when I go back next door, and I stand there for a moment, watching him watching.

'So which is the real Bill Harper?' I ask at last. 'The one who was cowering like a frightened child or the one who just attacked one of my officers?'

Ross shakes his head. 'It's the disease. That's what it does.'

'Perhaps. Or perhaps all the disease is doing is breaking down the self-control he used to have. Perhaps he always was angry but he didn't let it get out of hand. He knew how to manage it. Hide it, even.'

Ross had turned to look at me, but suddenly he's not meeting my gaze. There's something going on here – something he's not telling me.

I let the silence lengthen. Then take a step closer. 'What is it, Derek?'

He glances at me, then away. His face is flushed.

'What else is William Harper hiding?'

*   *   *

At the John Radcliffe hospital, DC Verity Everett has been waiting for over two hours. Most people hate hospitals, but she trained as a nurse before switching to the police, and places like this never unnerve her. She actually finds the atmosphere rather comforting – even in an emergency, people here know what they're supposed to do, where they're supposed to be. The white coats, the white noise, it's all strangely soothing. And what with the slightly overheated corridor and how badly she's been sleeping lately, it's no surprise she's struggling to stay awake, even on the hard plastic chair. In fact, she must have been nodding because the touch on her arm lurches her head backwards and she jolts upright.

'DC Everett?'

She opens her eyes. The doctor's face is kind. Concerned.

'Are you OK?'

She shakes herself awake. Her neck is aching.

'Yes, I'm fine. Sorry. Must have dozed off for a minute.'

The doctor smiles. He's very good-looking. Think Idris Elba with a stethoscope.

'Rather more than a minute, I think. But there was no reason to disturb you.'

'How is she?'

'I don't have much news, I'm afraid. As the paramedics suspected, she's badly dehydrated and very undernourished. I don't think there's anything else seriously wrong, but she became very distressed earlier, so we decided not to do a full examination just yet. It might do more harm than good at this stage. We sedated her, so she can sleep.'

Everett gets up stiffly from the plastic chair and walks the few steps to the window giving on to the girl's room. She feels about a hundred years old. In the room beyond the glass, the girl is lying still on the bed, her long dark hair tangled across the pillow and the blanket clutched in her hand. There are deep shadows round her eyes and her features have shrunk against the bone, but Everett can tell she was pretty. *Is* pretty.

'And the boy?' she asks, turning back to the doctor.

'The paediatrician is with him now. As far as we can tell he's in surprisingly good shape. Considering.'

Everett looks back at the girl. 'Did she say anything? A name? How long she'd been there? Anything at all?'

He shakes his head. 'Sorry.'

'When will I be able to talk to her? It's really important.'

'I know. But my patient's well-being has to be my first priority. We're just going to have to wait.'

'But she's going to be all right?'

He comes to the window and looks at Everett's anxious face. 'To be honest, it's her mental health I'm more worried about. After what that girl's been through, sleep is the best thing she can possibly have. After that, well, we'll just have to see.'

* * *

'Derek – talk to me – if there's something you saw, something that could help us –'

He glances up at me. He's gripping the cup so hard the plastic suddenly snaps. Water lurches over his hands and down his trousers.

'OK,' he says eventually, wiping himself down. 'It was about six months ago. December, I think. One of the neighbours said she'd seen him in the street with only his slippers so I had a look round to see if I could find his shoes. He'd started losing things, putting them down and forgetting where they were – I assumed they were probably under the bed.'

'And were they?'

He shakes his head. 'No. But I did find a box. Magazines, mostly.'

I don't need a hint. 'Porn?'

He hesitates, then nods. 'Hard stuff. Bondage. S&M. Torture. Or at least that's what it looked like. I wasn't exactly poring over it.'

Like Harper must have done. Not that Ross says that.

There's a silence. It's no surprise he was wary of telling me.

'Where do you think he got it?' I say at last.

He shrugs. 'Not off the web, that I do know. But you can probably get that sort of stuff from the small ads in girly magazines if you look hard enough. He was still going down the shops on and off, back then.'

'Is the box still there?'

'Probably. I just shoved it back where I found it. If he noticed he never mentioned it. But even accepting he had that sort of – of – taste – it's a hell of a long way from looking at dodgy magazines to abducting a girl and locking her in the bloody cellar.'

Personally, I'm not so sure. I've seen the wreckage of dementia too, and I wonder again about those months when the disease first took hold, and no one, not even Harper, knew it was there. When he still had his willpower, his physical strength, but his personality had started to shrink back and harden. Did he really turn into a completely different man or just a colder, crueller version of the one he was before?

I get up and go out to the corridor, leaving Ross alone. Gis is at the water cooler and comes over.

'Anything?' he asks.

'Not much. Ross says he found a stash of hardcore porn in the house a few months back, so get on to Challow and make sure they check over the whole place, not just the cellar and the ground floor. It's possible there's other stuff in there.'

'Right.'

'And let's start checking Harper's background. Speak to the university where he worked — 1998 isn't that long ago, there must be someone who remembers him.'

* * *

Phone interview with Louise Foley, Human
Resources Manager, Birmingham University
1 May 2017, 1.47 p.m.
On the call, DC C. Gislingham

CG: Sorry to bother you on a bank holiday but
      we're hoping you might be able to give us some
      information about William Harper. I think he
      taught at Birmingham until the late nineties?
LF: Yes, that's right. I wasn't here then myself
      but I do know Dr Harper was part of the Social
      Sciences faculty. His specialist subject was

game theory. Apparently he wrote quite a
famous article on role-playing games. I
believe it was quite ahead of its time.

CG: So apart from what he'd do on *Mastermind*, what
else can you tell me?

LF: He retired in 1998. That's a long time ago,
Constable.

CG: I know, but it's not prehistoric either, is it?
I mean, you had computers back then. You must
have some sort of records.

LF: Of course, but there's a limit to what I can
tell you. I have to comply with our internal
policy on data protection. You of all people
would surely understand that. Do you have Dr
Harper's consent to release his personal
information?

CG: No, but as I'm sure you know, I don't actually
need his consent if the information requested
is pursuant to the apprehension or prosecution
of an offender. Data Protection Act, section
29(3). If you want to look it up.

LF: What's he done? I mean, he must have done
something. You wouldn't be taking all this
trouble for a parking ticket, now would you –
[*pause*]
Wait a minute – it's not that case on the news
is it – that girl in the cellar? That bloke
must be about the same age –

CG: I'm afraid I'm not at liberty to discuss that,
Miss Foley. Perhaps you could just email over
the relevant files – that would save everyone a
lot of time.

LF: I would need permission from the university's
     HR Director to do that. But if you have
     specific questions now I can try to
     answer them.

CG: [*pause*]
     OK. Perhaps you can start by telling me why he
     left when he did.

LF: I'm sorry?

CG: Well, if my O level maths serves me right,
     he'd have been fifty-seven in 1998. What's the
     usual retirement age for academics – sixty-
     five, seventy?

LF: [*pause*]
     Looking at the file, it appears it was agreed
     by all parties that Dr Harper would take early
     retirement.

CG: Right. So what was the real reason?

LF: I don't know what you mean –

CG: Come on, Miss Foley, you know as well as I do
     that that's HR bullshit speak for 'we had to
     get rid of him'.

LF: [*pause*]
     I'm afraid that's all I'm prepared to say. I
     will speak to the director and get his
     permission to send you the file. But you should
     be aware that he's in China at the moment. It
     may take some time to reach him.

CG: Best I let you get on with it then.

*   *   *

BBC Midlands Today
Monday 1 May 2017 | Last updated at 14:52

Girl and child in Oxford basement: Police issue statement

Thames Valley Police have issued a brief statement about the girl and small boy found in a cellar in Frampton Road, Oxford, earlier this morning. They have confirmed that a young woman has been taken to the John Radcliffe Hospital, and that she and a child are being assessed by medical staff and Social Services. The identity of the young woman has not been released, and although it is reported that the child is her son, this has not yet been confirmed. Those who witnessed events at the house say she appeared to be conscious when paramedics placed her in the ambulance.

Neighbours have told the BBC that the house in question is owned by a Mr William Harper, who has lived in the area for at least twenty years. Mr Harper was seen leaving the house this morning in the company of police officers, in a state of some distress.

*   *   *

In the upper storeys of 33 Frampton Road, all the curtains are drawn. Dust hangs in the air and cobwebs blur the corners. Something's been chewing the stair carpet and Nina Mukerjee, the forensics officer, steps carefully round a scatter of beady droppings, then stops in the doorway of the master bedroom. There's no linen on the bed, just a bare mattress with a large musty stain in the centre. On the wall on the right there's an ornate glass display cabinet with nothing in it, and the dressing table is cluttered with lipstick, perfume, a pot of face cream left open and dried to cement, and a scatter of tissues still marked with a faded red mouth.

A second officer joins the woman at the door. 'Blimey,' he says. 'It's like the *Mary Celeste*.'

'Or Miss Havisham. That film always gives me the creeps.'

'When did the second wife die again?'

'2010. Car crash.'

The man looks around, then walks over to the bedside table and runs a gloved finger across a surface thick with dust. 'I'm prepared to bet he's not been in here since.'

'Grief takes some people that way. They can't bring themselves to throw anything out. My gran was like that. Took years to persuade her to get rid of my grandad's stuff. Even all that time later she said it still felt like sacrilege.'

The man gestures towards a photo frame lying face down on the bedside table. He picks the picture up and looks at it, then turns it towards his colleague. 'There's one like this downstairs. Attractive. Not my type, personally. But attractive.'

Priscilla Harper is looking straight into the camera, one hand on her hip, one eyebrow arched. She looks confident, self-possessed. And very high maintenance.

Nina walks over and opens the wardrobe, pulling out items at random. A low-cut scarlet evening gown, a cashmere coat with a fur collar, a pale green blouse with a ruffled neck.

'This is real silk. She had expensive taste.'

The man comes over and takes a look. 'Pity about the moths. Otherwise you could have flogged the lot on eBay.'

Nina makes a face at him – 'Thanks for that, Clive' – then

pushes the clothes back into place. 'Do CID really want us to bag up all this stuff? We'll be here all week.'

'I think it was porn Fawley was interested in. So for now, I think we can make do with checking there isn't a case full of bondage gear under the bed and leave it at that. I'll check round upstairs. But by the looks of it the top floor's pretty much empty. Just a metal bedstead in one room and a stack of old copies of the *Daily Telegraph*.'

Nina goes over to the bedside table and pulls open the drawer to a rattle of white plastic bottles.

'Blimey, that's quite a stash,' says Clive as she opens an evidence bag and starts to take them out. The labels are all in the name of Priscilla Harper; most of them are sleeping pills.

'Did you find any papers downstairs?' she asks.

'Apart from the porn, you mean? There's a desk full of letters and old bills though I doubt any of it will be much use. But we're boxing it all up just in case. The cellar's pretty much clear now.'

Nina shudders. 'I can't get it out of my head. Those scratch marks in the plaster. The state of mind she must have been in to do that. It doesn't bear thinking about.'

'I think she could hear them.'

She turns to him. 'What do you mean?'

His face is grim. 'Think about it. That house next door had been lived in by the same old biddy since the eighties. But suddenly, a few weeks ago, the workmen move in. There were people in there for the first time in years. That's what she was doing. She could hear them.'

*   *   *

3.15 p.m. Given the issues we're facing in questioning Harper, I've decided not to interview him again until we've talked to the girl. And she's still sedated. No one's expecting to get anything out of the boy, and forensics will need a few hours yet to come up with preliminary findings. All of which means that, right now, I have the Super on my back, a press office in crisis and a full team of people with a lot of nervous energy and nothing to do with it. Gislingham is trying to track down anyone who worked with Harper in the 1990s, someone else is on to the supermarket to see if we can speak to the delivery people and Baxter is checking Missing Persons for anyone who looks remotely like the girl. It's a job with his name on – he doesn't need to dig that deep to find his inner geek – but when I look in on him an hour later there's a weary frown line across his brow.

'No luck?'

He glances up at me. 'Sod all. We don't have a name, we don't know where she came from, we don't know how long she was down there. We don't even know if she was ever reported missing. I could spend a month on this thing and get nowhere. Even facial recognition can't find someone who isn't there.'

*   *   *

Sent: Mon 01/05/2017, 15.45 GMT
From: AnnieGHargreavesMontreal@hotmail.com
To: D.Ross@SocialServices.ox.gov.uk

Subject: Bill

Thanks for the email. I'm staring at the news right now and there are pictures of Frampton Road – even on Canadian TV. They're comparing it to that man in Austria who kept his daughter in the cellar all those years. But Bill – doing something like that? He was always a bit of a bolshie sod but he wasn't violent. And I never knew Priscilla but as far as I can tell he's never even had a relationship with a woman since. If he did he never told me. And OK, a shrink might just say I'm being naive and people like him are very good at hiding it, but surely there would have been some sort of sign? Sorry – I'm probably not making much sense. It's early here and I still can't quite believe it. I probably sound like those people the press interview at times like this who stand there saying inane things like 'he seemed like such a quiet bloke'. Just let me know if there's anything I can do.

*   *   *

Somer is round the corner in Chinnor Place. From where she's standing she can see the forensics team carrying out boxes from 33 Frampton Road and loading them into the van. There are two TV vans parked on the other side of the road. She steps forward again and rings the bell for a third time. It seems this house is empty, though from the bikes and the number of bins and its general state it's probably student digs. One of the few like it left round here. Thirty years ago these houses were dinosaurs. No one wanted them: too big, too difficult to maintain. Most of them were split up into bedsits or picked up cheap by crammers or university departments. Not any more. Now they're gradually turning back into the family homes the Victorian developers built them to be, complete with suitable quarters for live-in staff. Mark Sexton is only the latest example of a much bigger trend.

She rings one last time, and is just about to turn and walk away when the door finally opens. He's about twenty, ginger hair, rubbing the back of his neck and yawning; it looks like he's just got out of bed. There's a line of empty bottles leading down the hall and a smell of stale beer. He takes one look at Somer and does a pantomime start.

'Shit.'

Somer smiles. 'PC Erica Somer, Thames Valley Police.'

The boy swallows. 'Have those old farts been complaining about the noise again? Seriously, it really wasn't that loud –'

'It's not that, Mr –'

'Danny. Danny Abrahams.'

'OK, Danny. It's about the house in the next road. Number thirty-three. Do you know the man who lives there – Mr Harper?'

He scratches his neck again. His skin is blotched and red. 'Is that the nutter?'

'Do you know him?'

He shakes his head. 'Just wanders about talking to himself. Gave us a four-pack of lager once. Seems all right.'

Somer gets out her phone and shows him a picture of the girl. 'What about this young woman – have you ever seen her?'

The boy peers at the screen. 'No idea.'

'Are any of your flatmates in?'

'Not sure. Haven't seen anyone. Probably in the library. Finals. You know.'

She puts the phone away and hands him a card. 'If any of them have any information about Mr Harper please ask them to call this number.'

'What's he done – started flashing the local biddies?'

'What makes you say that?'

The lad flushes bright red. 'Nothing. I just thought –'

'If you could just pass on the message.'

She turns on her heel and leaves him standing there on

the step, wondering what all that was about. A state of igno-
rance that lasts approximately a minute and a half, after he
shuts the door and gets out his mobile.

'Shit,' he says as he scrolls down the news feed. 'Shit
shit shit.'

*   *   *

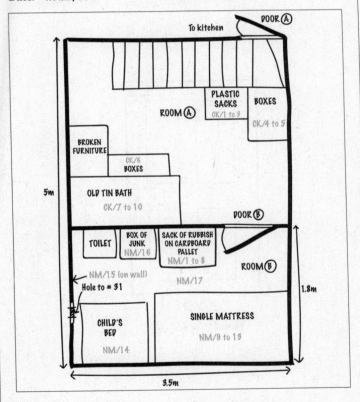

FORENSIC INVESTIGATION UNIT
Scenes of Crime Sketch

Address: 33 Frampton Road, OX2

Case Reference: KE2308/17J

NOT TO SCALE

CSIs: Alan Challow, Nina Mukerjee, Clive Keating

Date: 1st May 2017   **Time:** 10:00 hrs

To kitchen   DOOR Ⓐ

PLASTIC SACKS
CK/1 to 3

BOXES
CK/4 to 5

ROOM Ⓐ

BROKEN FURNITURE

CK/6
BOXES

OLD TIN BATH
CK/7 to 10

5m

DOOR Ⓑ

TOILET

BOX OF JUNK
NM/16

SACK OF RUBBISH ON CARDBOARD PALLET
NM/1 to 8

ROOM Ⓑ

NM/15 (on wall)
Hole to # 31

NM/17

1.8m

CHILD'S BED
NM/14

SINGLE MATTRESS
NM/9 to 13

3.5m

Signed: CSI 1808 JJ GETHINS   **Date:** 1ST MAY 2017

Page 1 of 2   **RESTRICTED (when complete)**   FIU/SCR/03

FORENSIC INVESTIGATION UNIT
Scenes of Crime Sketch

Address: 33 Frampton Road, OX2

Case Reference: KE2308/17J

NOT TO SCALE

CSIs: Alan Challow, Nina Mukerjee, Clive Keating

Date: 1st May 2017   **Time:** 10:00 hrs

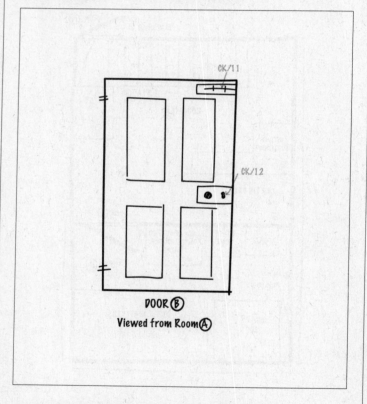

CK/11

CK/12

DOOR Ⓑ
Viewed from Room Ⓐ

EVIDENCE KEY

CK/1 to 3	Assortment of empty packets recovered for chemical fingerprint enhancement from plastic sacks next to stairs in Cellar, Room A.
CK/4 to 5	Partial fingerprints lifted from tape sealing a box recovered next to stairs in Cellar, Room A.
CK/6	Fingerprints lifted from glossy cardboard box flap recovered in Cellar, Room A.
CK/7 to 10	Fingerprints lifted from multiple external surfaces of items recovered from an old tin bath in Cellar, Room A.
CK/11	Partial fingerprint lifted from locking bolt on Cellar Door B (exterior, Room A side).
CK/12	Partial fingerprints lifted from set of keys in locking mechanism of Cellar Door B (exterior, Room A side).
NM/1 to 5	Assortment of empty packets, food boxes and containers recovered for chemical fingerprint enhancement from a sack of rubbish in Cellar, Room B.
NM/6 to 8	Fingerprints lifted from empty plastic containers recovered from a sack of rubbish in Cellar, Room B.
NM/9	Dark pillow case with white staining (presumptive test positive for saliva) recovered from single mattress in Cellar, Room B.
NM/10	Grey bed sheet with multiple white staining (presumptive test positive for semen and saliva) recovered from single mattress in Cellar, Room B.
NM/11	White duvet with red staining (presumptive test positive for blood) recovered from single mattress in Cellar, Room B.
NM/12 to 13	Female underwear with white staining (presumptive test positive for semen) recovered from single mattress in Cellar, Room B.
NM/14	Piece of bedding with small red stain (presumptive test positive for blood) recovered from child's bed in Cellar, Room B.
NM/15	Wet and dry swabs of red smears (presumptive test positive for blood) from neighbouring wall in Cellar, Room B.
NM/16	Box of miscellaneous items including several old books from Cellar, Room B.
NM/17	Torch containing dead batteries from Cellar, Room B.

*   *   *

I'm in the canteen buying a sandwich when DC Baxter finds me.

'I think I've got something,' he says, slightly out of breath. His wife tells him he has to take the stairs; it's the only proper exercise he ever gets.

'The girl?'

'No. Harper. I gave up on Missing Persons but while I was at it I thought it was worth running Harper's name through the system.'

'And?'

'No convictions. Not even speeding. And if he's a kerb-

crawler we haven't caught him doing it. But I did find two
call-outs to the house in Frampton Road. One in 2002 and
one in 2004. No charges brought and the notes are a bit
sketchy but it was clearly a domestic.'

'Who was the attending officer?'

'Jim Nicholls, both times.'

'See if you can track him down. From what I remember
he retired to Devon. But HR must have an address. Get him
to give me a call.'

*   *   *

Shit man did u see the news? – that bloke
down the road. He's some sort of psycho.
Locked some girl in his bloody cellar. Police
just came. Wondered if I shd tell them

Fuck no way. Last thing we need. Just
keep shtum right?
Did u recog the girl?

No never seen her b4

Well then so just shut the fuck up OK?

*   *   *

'Bill Harper? Now that is a blast from the past.'

Russell Todd is the fourth former colleague of Harper's
that Gislingham's called, and the results so far have been
dead, dead, and forgetful, in that order. But Todd is not just
alive and well, he's talkative too.

'So you remember him then?' says Gislingham, trying not to get his hopes up.

'Oh yes. Knew him quite well for a while, but it's some years ago now. Why do you ask?'

'What can you tell me about him?'

There's a long exhalation at the other end. 'We-e-ll,' says Todd, 'wasn't exactly top notch. Academically, I mean. Not that he thought that himself, of course. In fact he probably considered ending up at Brum was decidedly infra dig, but his wife came from somewhere round there so that may have decided it. Buying that house in Oxford always struck me as classic denial. But he was solid enough. Knew his stuff. In fact, he did write one article that caused quite a stir –'

'Is this the role-playing thing?'

'Ah, you know about that, do you? Between you and me, it was a bit of a case of "right place at the right time". I mean, the thinking was nothing very original, but Bill hit on the idea of applying it to internet games. Or whatever those things are called. This was back in 1997, so the web was really only just getting going. All of a sudden he was quite the thing.'

Todd's tone has become increasingly waspish, and Gislingham detects a distinct whiff of peer envy. These academics, always stabbing each other in the back. He wonders in passing how many people would ever have considered Todd 'top notch'.

'Anyway,' continues Todd, 'after toiling in the dustier foothills of academe for the best part of thirty years, dear old Bill suddenly finds himself being courted by the likes of Stanford and MIT. There was even a rumour of Harvard.'

'So what happened?'

Todd laughs, not very pleasantly. He's starting to get up

Gislingham's nose. 'It was positively Shakespearean. The hero brought low at the very moment of his triumph. The house was up for sale, the bags all but packed, and suddenly – *bang*. It all comes crashing down around his ears. Or perhaps another part of his anatomy would be a more apt metaphor. In the circumstances.'

'I can guess,' says Gislingham.

Todd is clearly amused. 'Yes, I'm afraid Bill got caught with his pecker in the honeypot. It was all hushed up, of course, but you couldn't see the Americans for dust. Married man meddling with the students goes down *very* badly over there. Rather prudish about such things, the Yanks.'

'Have you kept in touch with him since?'

'Can't say I have. I did hear his wife had died. Breast cancer, I think. I don't know if he worked again. She had some money, the wife, so he may not have needed to.'

'And was that the only time? I mean, did he have a reputation for harassing his students?'

'Oh no, that was the thing – it was quite out of character. The irony was that if the authorities had wanted to make an example of someone there were several far more flagrant *dragueurs* they could have picked on – on both sides of the house. It wasn't like it is now with lawsuits at the drop of your trousers.'

The good old days of harass at will; Gislingham mouths 'wanker' at the phone.

'If anything,' continues Todd, 'Bill was on the strait-laced side of straight. If you take my meaning. It just goes to show you never can tell.'

'No,' says Gislingham through gritted teeth. 'You can't.'

* * *

American Journal of Social and Cognitive Sciences
Volume 12, number 3, Fall 1998

Dungeons and Damsels:
Role-Playing Games on the World-Wide Web

William M. Harper, PhD,
University of Birmingham

Abstract

This article looks at the potential for multi-participant role-playing games (RPGs) on the electronic telecommunications network known as the World-Wide Web. While very few enthusiasts yet have access to this technology, the capability exists to allow multiple players to interact in real time via computer terminals, across geographies and time zones. The article explores the cognitive and psycho-social implications of this 'remote gaming', including issues such as the impact of anonymous computer 'personae' on trust among players, and the effect on their decision-making processes. It also examines the possible neurological consequences of prolonged exposure to a violent 'virtual' world, including the erosion of empathy, an increase in interpersonal aggression, and the illusion of personal omnipotence.

* * *

It's shortly after 4.00 p.m., and Everett is standing with one of the nurses, looking through a glass partition at the boy.

The blinds in the room are down and he's sitting alone in a playpen in the middle of the floor, staring at a pile of toys. Bricks, an aeroplane, a red and green train. Every now and then he reaches out and touches one of them. His dark hair hangs in curls, like a girl's. There's a woman sitting in the room with him, but she's chosen the chair in the furthest corner.

'He still won't let anyone near him?'

The woman shakes her head. There's a badge on her uniform that says STAFF NURSE JENNY KINGSLEY. 'Poor lamb. The doctor checked him over and we've done some tests but we're keeping it to the minimum for the moment. We don't want to distress him any more than absolutely necessary. Especially after his mother reacted the way she did.'

She sees the question in Everett's eyes. 'We took him to her after we'd cleaned him up, but as soon as she saw him she started screaming. And I mean *really* screaming. And then the boy went completely rigid and he was screaming too. They had to sedate her in the end. That's why we brought him back down here. That sort of stress – it's not going to do either of them any good.'

'Has he said anything?'

'No. We're not even sure if he *can* speak. The environment he was in – what he must have witnessed – it wouldn't be that surprising if his development had been affected.'

Everett turns again to the window. The boy looks up and, for a few brief seconds, the two of them are gazing at each other. He has dark eyes, a slight flush to his cheeks. Then he turns his back and curls up against the side of the playpen, putting his arm over his face.

'He's been doing that a lot,' says the nurse. 'Could just be that he's adjusting to the light, but his eyes might have been damaged from being in the dark for so long. It's better to be safe than sorry. That's why we've drawn the blinds.'

Everett watches a moment. 'You just want to give him a cuddle and make it all go away.'

Jenny Kingsley sighs. 'I know. It's enough to break your heart.'

*   *   *

We have the first case meeting at 5.00 p.m. When I get to the incident room the team is gathering and Quinn is pinning up what little we have. A picture of the house, a photo of the girl, a street map. Something that basic would normally be Gis's job, but I suspect Quinn wants to be seen doing something useful.

'Right, everyone,' he begins, 'Everett's still at the John Rad waiting to speak to the girl, but we've no idea how long that's going to take.'

'So we're going on the basis that the kid is Harper's?' asks one of the DCs at the back.

'Yes,' says Quinn. 'That's the working assumption.'

'So why not do a DNA test? That'd prove conclusively that he raped the girl.'

'That's more complicated than it sounds,' I say, intervening, 'given the girl's in no state to give her permission. But I've spoken to Social Services and they're on the case. And in the meantime we're testing the bedding in the cellar. If we're lucky, that'll give us what we need.'

I nod to Quinn.

'Right,' he says. 'Thus far the house-to-house in Frampton Road hasn't turned up anything useful. Apparently Harper's a well-known local nutter but no one we've spoken to thinks he's actually dangerous. One of the neighbours in-sists he has a son called John, but we know he doesn't. So either the old lady's mistaken –'

'Not another daft old bat,' someone mutters. Someone else laughs.

'– or there *is* someone called John who used to visit Harper even though he's not his son. So we're going to have to find out who that is and track them down, even if only to eliminate them. And let's remember that even if this "John" was going in there, he may not have known what was going on. We can't afford to jump to conclusions.'

'What, like you did, with that social worker?'

I don't catch who says it but no one's laughing this time. Quinn is staring at his feet. There's an awkward pause, but I'm not going to dig him out of this one. It's Gislingham, of all people, who comes to the rescue. Though to be fair, those two do seem to have settled their differences of late. After Quinn made DS it was guerrilla warfare for a while, but perhaps fatherhood has mellowed Gislingham. Or just worn him out. I know how that feels.

'I spoke to Birmingham Uni,' Gislingham says, 'and one of Harper's old colleagues there. Harper definitely had an affair with a student in the nineties. But that's all. Nothing deviant as far as I can tell. But I'm still waiting for the full file – that might tell us more. Though there is an article he wrote back in the nineties about role-playing online and how it can make people think violence is OK because none of it's real. "Dungeons and Damsels" it was called, which is more than a bit bloody spooky, if you ask me.'

'And the supermarket – has anyone got through to them?'

'I did,' says a DC at the back. 'They've spoken to the de-livery guys who do that run and they can't tell us anything.

They just unload the carrier bags in the hall each time. Apparently Harper wasn't one for making conversation.'

'So on that basis,' says Quinn, 'the next job is to extend the house-to-house, in the hopes someone might recognize the girl, and/or know something about this John bloke.'

He steps back and points to the map he's pinned up, and starts talking through exactly which streets they're going to canvass next. But I'm not listening. I'm staring at the board, realizing for the first time what should have struck me hours ago. I get up and walk over to the map and stand there. I can hear the room fall silent behind me.

'Remind me what number Frampton Road Harper lives at?'

'Thirty-three,' says Quinn, frowning slightly. 'Why?'

I pick the pen up and mark number thirty-three, then draw a line south-east.

'I thought so.'

Quinn is still frowning. 'Thought what?'

'Harper's house is directly behind Crescent Square. Eighty-one Crescent Square, to be precise.'

I turn round. Some of them clearly don't have a clue what I'm getting at. Though, to be fair, not all this team were working here then. But Gislingham was, and I see realization dawn.

'Hang on,' he says. 'Wasn't that where Hannah Gardiner lived?'

And now the recognition is immediate. The name is like a shot in the vein; all of a sudden, the room is clamouring with questions.

'Not that woman who went missing – the one they never found?'

'When was that again? Two years ago?'

'Shit, do you think there could be a connection?'

Quinn looks at me, a question in his eyes. 'Coincidence?' he says quietly.

I look again at the map, at the photograph of the girl, and I remember Hannah Gardiner's face pinned to a board just like this, month after month, until we eventually took it down. She wasn't that much older than this girl is now.

'I don't believe in coincidences,' I say.

*　　*　　*

```
Channel:        Mystery Central
Programme:      Great Unsolved Crimes
Episode:        The Disappearance of Hannah Gardiner
First shown:    09/12/2016


Panoramic shot of Oxford skyline, dawn, summer

                    VOICEOVER

        Ever since Inspector Morse, TV viewers across
        the world have seen Oxford's dreaming spires as
        the perfect setting for the perfect murder. But
        all those dark tales of killing in the quads
        bear little resemblance to real life in this
        beautiful and prosperous city, where the crime
        rate is low, and unsolved homicides are almost
        unheard of.

        But in summer 2015, all that was about to change.
        The city's police force was about to be baffled by
        a mystery as strange as any case Morse ever
        confronted. A mystery that was destined to
        become one of Britain's most notorious
        unexplained crimes.

Wide shot of Crescent Square, bikes against railings, cat
walking across road, mother and small boy on scooter

                    VOICEOVER

        The story starts here, in leafy North Oxford, one
        of the most affluent and attractive suburbs of the
        city. It was here that 25-year-old Hannah
        Gardiner, her husband Rob and their little son
        Toby took an apartment in the autumn of 2013.

Family snapshot of Gardiners, gradual close-up; reconstruction
of small boy playing with a ball in a garden
```

VOICEOVER

Hannah had been a journalist in London when she
met Rob, and after he got a job at an Oxford-
based biotech company, the family took up
residence in a sunny first-floor apartment with
access to a pretty shared garden where Toby
could play.

Interview: Backdrop - interior

BETH DYER, HANNAH'S FRIEND

Hannah was really excited about moving to Oxford.
It was a really happy time for her. It just
seemed like everything was coming together. And
when she got the job at BBC Oxford she was just
over the moon - we all went out to celebrate.

Footage of Hannah talking to camera on BBC local news

VOICEOVER

Hannah soon made a reputation for herself
covering some of the city's most controversial
stories.

Interview: Backdrop - BBC Oxford office

CHARLIE CATES, SENIOR EDITOR, BBC OXFORD

Hannah was always first in line to take on the
difficult issues. She did several pieces on
homelessness in Oxford, and a series on the
postcode lottery in infertility treatment that
got some traction at a national level. She was
passionate about her work and she was in
journalism for all the right reasons.

Shot of MDJ Property Developments offices

VOICEOVER

In early 2015 Hannah took on her most challenging
assignment yet, when local property developer
Malcolm Jervis submitted a proposal to build a
big new housing estate some miles outside the
city.

Tracking shot of protest camp, banners, people chanting

VOICEOVER

Local resistance to Jervis's new plan was fierce,
both from residents and environmental
campaigners, who set up a protest camp near the
proposed building site.

*Panoramic view of fields, finishing with Wittenham Clumps;
atmospheric shot with racing clouds and shadows*

VOICEOVER

Many people were concerned about the location of
the new estate in the midst of unspoiled
countryside, and within a few hundred yards of a
site of special historical significance, known as
the Wittenham Clumps.

Shot of hollow on Castle Hill

VOICEOVER

The hills command views of the Oxfordshire
countryside for miles around and are rich in
folklore. Castle Hill once boasted an Iron Age
fort, and near the summit there's a hollow, known
for centuries as the Money Pit.

Cut to shot of raven with night sky and moon

VOICEOVER

A hoard of treasure is said to be buried there,
guarded by a ghostly raven.

Close-up: cuckoo in tree

VOICEOVER

And not far away there's a grove of trees called
the Cuckoo Pen. Legend has it that if a cuckoo
can be trapped in this grove, summer will
never end.

[cuckoo call]

Aerial shot of excavation

VOICEOVER

In the spring of 2015 a new archaeological
excavation had started on Castle Hill, and in
early June, Hannah herself was the first to break
the news of a gruesome find.

BBC Oxford footage taken at Wittenham Clumps

HANNAH GARDINER

I'm told that the skeletons of three women have
been found in a shallow grave, a few yards behind
me, beyond those trees. They were found face down
with their skulls broken, and from the position
of the bones, had probably had their hands tied.
The bodies are thought to date from the late Iron
Age, or around 50 AD. The archaeologists here are
refusing to speculate about what this highly
unusual burial position might signify, but some
with a knowledge of pagan rituals are suggesting
that it may relate to the so-called 'Triple
Goddess', who is often depicted in the form of
three sisters. The discovery of animal bones,

including several birds, may also be significant.
This is Hannah Gardiner, for BBC Oxford news.

Shot of skeletons in pit

VOICEOVER

Within days of the find, lurid stories had started
to circulate that the women had in fact been the
victims of human sacrifice, and this only added
to the strange and highly charged atmosphere
that prevailed in the days leading up to that
Midsummer Day.

Reconstruction: Shot of calendar, with kitchen scene in background. Calendar has date of Wednesday June 24 circled

VOICEOVER

For the Gardiner family, June 24 2015 started
like any other day. Rob got up early to travel to
a meeting in Reading, and Hannah also made an
early start.

*Reconstruction: 'Hannah' getting into orange Mini Clubman car,
and strapping small boy in car seat. She has a dark brown
ponytail and a navy quilted anorak.*

VOICEOVER

She'd been conducting interviews at the protest
camp the previous week, and she'd managed to
persuade Malcolm Jervis to meet her at the site
and film an interview. Her usual childminder was
unwell, so Hannah had to take Toby with her. She
left the house at around 7.30 a.m. to drive to
Wittenham, and Rob had already departed fifteen
minutes before, heading into Oxford to catch a
train to the nearby town of Reading.

*Reconstruction: 'Rob' on phone looking anxious, pacing up and
down*

VOICEOVER

At 11.15 Rob tried to call Hannah during a break
in his meeting, but got no answer. So it wasn't
till he got home mid-afternoon that he realised
something was wrong. There was a message on the
answerphone from the cameraman Hannah was due to
meet at the site, wanting to know why she never
turned up. Rob tried Hannah's mobile again, and
when there was still no reply he called the
police. Little did he know then, but his son Toby
had already been found. Alone.

Reconstruction: buggy and toy in undergrowth

VOICEOVER

A walker had noticed the empty buggy in the
Money Pit as early as 9.30, but it was another

hour before Toby was found, hiding in the
undergrowth, terrified, clutching his toy bird.

*BBC footage: Mini car at Clumps, with police presence and crime-
scene tape*

VOICEOVER

A huge search is mounted, but no trace of Hannah
can be found. The police have no leads.

Interview: Backdrop - interior

DETECTIVE SUPERINTENDENT ALASTAIR OSBOURNE,
THAMES VALLEY POLICE

There was no forensic evidence in the car or on
the buggy that shed any light on what had
happened to Hannah. We made exhaustive enquiries
in the Wittenham area, and although several
people came forward to say they'd seen Hannah
and Toby that morning, we were no nearer finding
out what had befallen her.

Reconstruction: Close-up of computer screens and files

VOICEOVER

Rob Gardiner was quickly eliminated as a
potential suspect, and the police then turned
their attention to anyone who might have had a
motive to harm Hannah.

After examining her laptop they found evidence
that she was about to expose questionable
financial dealings on the part of MDJ Property
Developments. The police interviewed Malcolm
Jervis, but he had a watertight alibi. He had
been delayed that morning, and only arrived at
Wittenham at 9.45.

Reconstruction: Twitter feed

VOICEOVER

Meanwhile, speculation was mounting on social
media that Hannah had been murdered in some sort
of Satanic ritual connected with the Clumps. The
police issued several statements denying there
was anything to suggest an occult motive but
that didn't stop the rumours.

*BBC footage of protest camp, yurts, people chained to trees,
dogs among the rubbish, small children running about naked*

VOICEOVER

In this fevered atmosphere, attention inevitably
started to focus on the protest camp at the
site, which had been swelled by numbers of New
Age travellers who'd come to celebrate
Midsummer's Eve.

And as it turned out, there <u>was</u> a link with the camp, just not the one the bloggers and Twitter activists had been suggesting.

Interview: Backdrop – interior

DETECTIVE SUPERINTENDENT ALASTAIR OSBOURNE, THAMES VALLEY POLICE

Three months after Hannah's disappearance, a man named Reginald Shore was arrested for an attempted sexual assault on a young woman in Warwick. A police search of his house turned up a bracelet identical to one Hannah Gardiner owned.

DNA analysis subsequently proved that it was indeed hers, and under cross-examination Shore admitted that he had been at the Wittenham camp in the summer. In subsequent interviews, other witnesses were able to corroborate that he had spoken to Hannah when she visited the camp in late May.

Shot of bracelet

VOICEOVER

Shore claimed he found the bracelet at the camp, and didn't know who it belonged to. The UK's Crown Prosecution Service considered the evidence, but concluded that the case against him was not strong enough to put before a jury, especially in the absence of a body.

Mugshot of Reginald Shore

VOICEOVER

Shore was subsequently convicted of the attempted assault on the second young woman, and jailed for three years. His family contended that the sentence passed by the judge was heavier than it should have been, because of the publicity surrounding the Hannah Gardiner case.

As it turned out, Shore served less than a year of his sentence. When he was diagnosed with terminal lung cancer in 2016 he was released on compassionate grounds.

Hannah Gardiner has never been found.

Will we ever find out what really happened?

Will the Clumps ever give up their secret?

Moody shot of Wittenham Clumps by moonlight.

Freeze-frame

ends

'So tell us what the press didn't know,' says Quinn.

I press pause on the DVD player and turn to face the team.

'We suspected that Toby had somehow got free from the buggy and crawled away into the bushes. That's why it took so long to find him. He also had a head injury, though we couldn't establish for certain if it was the result of a blow or just a fall. But we never released that fact to the media.'

There's a silence. They're picturing it, imagining what that must have been like. I don't need to. I was there when we found him. I can still hear his screams.

'And he couldn't tell you anything?' asks one of the DCs. 'Did the kid not remember what happened?'

I shake my head. 'He wasn't even three, he'd had a blow to the head. He was completely traumatized. Nothing he said made much sense.'

'So we still have no idea how he ended up in that Pit place?'

'Our theory was that Hannah took him up there for a walk after she got the text from Jervis's PA saying he'd been delayed.'

I used to do that with Jake when he was that age. When he couldn't settle or he'd had a bad dream and didn't want to go back to bed. He loved the motion of the stroller. I'd walk the empty streets in the middle of the night. Just him, and me, and the odd prowling silent cat.

But I push that memory away.

'And we know she definitely got that text, do we?' Quinn; and on point.

'Well,' says Gislingham, 'we know it was definitely sent but we never found her phone so there's no way of knowing whether she opened it or not.' He sighs. 'To be honest, the whole thing was a nightmare. All the usual loonies came out of the woodwork – you can imagine – psychics, mediums, the whole bloody nine yards. There was even some old bat who got herself into the *Oxford Mail* – said the bracelet had a pagan design on it – some sort of three-pointed star thing. Kept on and on that the number three was the key to the whole case and, just you wait, she'd be proved right in the end –'

His voice tails off as he catches sight of the photo of the house. 'Shit. It had to be sodding thirty-three, didn't it.'

'There was one other thing we didn't tell the press,' I continue. 'The Gardiners' home life wasn't nearly as idyllic as that programme would have you believe.'

'I remember,' says Gislingham. 'There'd been a lot of tension with Rob's ex – she obviously resented Hannah for breaking up the relationship. There'd been some pretty nasty stuff on Facebook.'

'Did she have an alibi?' asks Quinn.

'The ex?' I say. 'Yes, she checked out. She was in Manchester that day. Lucky for her – we'd have been all over her otherwise.'

Gislingham looks thoughtful. 'Looking at that video again after all this time, the one that stands out for me is Beth Dyer. Didn't she drop some pretty heavy hints in interview that Rob might have been having an affair?'

'She did. But she didn't have any actual evidence. Just him "looking a bit odd" or "like he had something to hide". There were no unexplained phone calls, nothing like that – we checked. And his alibi was rock solid. His train left Oxford at 7.57 that morning, and we knew Hannah was alive at 6.50 because she left a voicemail for the childminder. And she used the landline so we knew she was in Crescent Square. So there simply wasn't time for Rob to kill his wife, take the car to Wittenham, dump it and get back to Oxford in time for that train.'

'But in any case,' says Quinn, 'even if either Rob or the ex had a motive for getting rid of Hannah, what about the kid?'

'Which is exactly the conclusion Osbourne came to. Even if the timings had added up, it was hard to see Rob Gardiner leaving his son alone up there.'

'So that's why everything pointed to Shore?' says Quinn.

There's a pause. They're all looking at me. They expect me to say how we did our best to make the case stick but the CPS wouldn't go with it. How we still believe we got our man.

But I don't.

'So,' says Quinn eventually. 'You had your doubts, even then.'

I look back at the TV screen. At the freeze-frame of the Clumps. Black birds against a pale sky.

'We interviewed everyone who was at the protest camp that day. No one mentioned seeing Shore until after his name came out in connection to the Warwick assault, and that was months later.'

'Doesn't mean he wasn't there.'

'No, but we couldn't prove he was either. Not definitively. He claimed he was miles away at the time, but couldn't produce any witnesses to back him up. We know he was at the camp that summer, and the bracelet we found in his house definitely was Hannah's –'

'– but you don't think he actually did it,' says Quinn.

'Osbourne was convinced he was guilty. And he was in charge of the case.'

There's a silence. He's retired now but Al Osbourne was one of the legends of Thames Valley. Great copper, and a genuinely nice bloke too, and believe me those two things don't always go together. More than one person in this station owes a crucial leg-up in their career to him, me included. And even though we never convicted Shore for Hannah Gardiner there's always been a tacit understanding that the case was closed. Reopening it now is going to make a lot of waves.

I take a deep breath. 'Look, I'll be honest with you. I did have my doubts about Shore. He never struck me as a killer, and on top of that, this was a very organized crime. I'm not saying it was planned – Hannah could have been a completely random victim. But it was certainly covered up very carefully afterwards. No forensics – no DNA – nothing. I just couldn't see Shore doing that. He isn't bright enough, for a start. That's why he got caught in Warwick. I always thought we were missing something – some fact or clue we overlooked or didn't uncover. But we never found it.'

'Not till now,' says Gislingham softly.

'No,' I say, looking back again at the screen. 'Because that's the one possibility we never really considered – that Hannah never left Oxford at all. That whatever happened to her, happened here.'

'But in that case, how the hell –'

'I know. How the hell did Toby get to Wittenham Clumps?'

'Right,' says Quinn into the silence. 'I'll warn the press office. Because if we've made the connection with the Gardiner case, the hacks soon will too. We need to get out ahead of this one, guys.'

'Too late,' says Gislingham grimly, looking at his phone. 'They've got there already.'

* * *

The young woman opens the window and stands there a moment breathing the warm air. The honeysuckle growing up the wall is already in flower. Behind her, she can hear the little boy chattering away to his teddy bear as he has his tea, and, turned down low, the sound of the early evening news on the TV in the kitchen. Somewhere further away, a man's voice talking animatedly on the phone.

'Pippa!' calls the little boy. 'Look at the TV! That's the house with all those bikes outside!'

The young woman goes back into the kitchen, picking up a discarded panda on the way, and joins the little boy at the table. On the screen, a reporter is standing in front of a police tape, gesturing backwards towards the scene behind him. There are several police cars with their lights flashing, and an ambulance. The headline running along the bottom of the screen says: *BREAKING: Oxford cellar girl: New questions raised about the Hannah Gardiner case.* No, she thinks, please no. Not after all this time. Not now that things are finally working out. She puts an arm round the little boy, smelling the sweet artificial shampoo scent of him.

'Shall we show Daddy?' says the little boy, twisting to look up at her. There's a dark pink scar on his temple.

'No, Toby,' says the young woman, her face anxious. 'Not yet. We don't want to disturb him. He's happy where he is.'

* * *

Oxford Mail

1st May 2017

OXFORD'S OWN 'FRITZL CASE': HOW COULD IT HAPPEN HERE?

By Mark Leverton

North Oxford residents are still in shock after the discovery earlier today of a young woman and a toddler in the cellar of a house in Frampton Road. It's not yet clear how long she had been there, but parallels are already being drawn with the infamous 'Fritzl case', in which an Austrian man imprisoned his daughter for 24 years in the basement of his home and raped her repeatedly, resulting in the birth of seven children. Elisabeth Fritzl was only discovered when one of her children fell dangerously ill. Josef Fritzl had constructed a sophisticated underground prison for his daughter, behind eight locked doors, but there is no suggestion yet of any such construction in Frampton Road. Many concerned residents are already asking how the girl could have been concealed down there without anyone knowing.

'It's horrific,' said Sally Browne, who lives nearby with her three children, 'how could anyone do something like that and no one realise? There was apparently a social worker or someone coming to the house, so I don't see how they couldn't have known.'

Other residents are also questioning the role of Social Services, and that too may have tragic echoes of the Fritzl case, where social workers regularly visited the Fritzl home and yet saw nothing to arouse their suspicions, despite the fact that Fritzl claimed to have discovered three of his daughter's babies as 'foundlings' on his doorstep.

The owner of the Frampton Road house has been named locally as a Mr William Harper, an elderly man who lives on his own. No one we spoke to had had any dealings with Mr Harper, though he was apparently seen being taken away by police earlier today.

Neither Thames Valley Police nor the Social Services department have yet issued a statement. The girl and her child are said to be receiving medical attention in the John Radcliffe hospital.

Do you live in Frampton Road or know anything about this story? If so we'd like to hear from you – you can email or tweet us.

154 comments

VinegarJim1955

That's what Tory cuts does for you. No money for proper care

RickeyMooney

Not surprised no one noticed anything – those people round there, they don't give a sh*t about anyone else

MistySong

This is just awful – I can't believe it could happen in such a quiet place. Makes you worry about all the female students living alone.

> **VinegarJim1955**
>
> But she wasn't a student was she? Couldn't have been – if she was they'd have been looking for her the minute she disappeared and it'd have been all over the papers. Makes me sick.

Fateregretful77

I used to be a social worker and I know the pressure they're under these days. You don't get anything like enough time to spend with clients. And I've also had experience of dealing with Thames Valley Police and I think they do a fabulous job. Check your facts before you start accusing people

*   *   *

Tuesday morning. 8.45. The door is opened by a young woman in a white shirt and a cotton skirt. She makes you think of words like 'fresh' and 'crisp' and I suddenly feel rather worn and grubby about the edges. It's happening a lot these days.

'Yes?' she says.

'I'm DI Adam Fawley and this is DC Chris Gislingham. Thames Valley Police. Is Mr Gardiner in?'

Her face says it all. 'Oh God. It's Hannah, isn't it.' She puts her hand to her mouth. 'When I saw the news yesterday, I just knew –'

Gislingham and I exchange a glance. 'And you are?'

'Pippa. Pippa Walker. I'm the childminder. Nanny. You know.'

I remember her now. I never met her during the original investigation, but I remember the name.

'You knew Hannah, didn't you – you were their childminder back then too?'

Her eyes fill with tears and she nods. 'She was really nice to me. I never stop thinking about it. If I hadn't been so ill she'd never have had Toby with her that day and everything might have been different.'

'Can we come in?'

'Sorry, yes. It's through here.'

We follow her down the hall to the sitting room. Sunlight through tall windows, giving over the square. More windows behind looking over the garden. Cool yellow walls. Black-and-white framed prints. Every surface strewn with toys. Teddies, model cars, a train set. And on the mantelpiece, photos. Hannah and Toby, Rob and Toby on a little tricycle, the three of them on a beach somewhere. Sunlight and happiness.

'Sorry about the mess,' says the girl, picking things up distractedly. 'Rob's in his study. I'll go and get him.'

After she's gone I walk over to the rear window and look across. I can see the back of Frampton Road. Through the trees, the roof of William Harper's shed is just visible. There are some large black birds pecking noisily at something dead in the long grass and four magpies skulking like assassins in the tree above. When I was a child you rarely got beyond 'one for sorrow', but now the bloody things are everywhere.

'Blimey,' says Gislingham, moving a stuffed toy cat and sitting down. 'So I've got all this to look forward to, have I?'

He grins, and then wonders if he's been tactless. Everyone

does that. No one knows what to say to the parents of a dead child. It should make me better at dealing with situations like this, but somehow it never does.

'You've found her, haven't you?'

Rob Gardiner is standing in the doorway. His face is white. He's changed since I last saw him. His dark blond hair used to be cut short at the sides but now he has a pony-tail and one of those beards that invades your whole neck. I suppose these techy types can get away with it. But my wife would be making a face by now, if she was here.

'Mr Gardiner? I'm DI Adam Fawley —'

'I know. You were here last time. You and that man Osbourne.'

'Why don't you sit down.'

'Policemen only ever say that when it's bad news.'

He comes further into the room and I gesture towards the chair. He hesitates, then sits, but on the edge of the seat.

'So have you? Found her?'

'No. We haven't found your wife.'

'But you've got a new lead, haven't you? It said on the news. This bloke — the one with the girl in his cellar — the Fritzl bloke.'

The young woman comes forward from the door and puts her hand on Gardiner's shoulder. He doesn't acknowledge the gesture. After a moment he moves, very slightly, and she takes her hand away.

There's no point prevaricating. 'Yes, we are looking at a possible connection with a house in Frampton Road.'

Gardiner gets up and walks over to the window. 'Jesus, I can actually *see* that bloody house from here.'

He turns on me suddenly. 'How come you didn't find this man before? Back in 2015, I mean, when she disappeared? Didn't you question him then?'

'We had no reason to, at the time. Everything pointed to your wife having disappeared at Wittenham. It wasn't just that we found Toby there – there was no alien DNA or prints in the car.'

'What about those people who said they saw her? Were they just making it up, getting off on it? I mean, there are people like that, aren't there?'

I'm shaking my head. 'No. I'm sure that didn't happen in this case. I spoke to several of the witnesses myself.'

He's still pacing, raking his hand through his hair, then he stops suddenly and rounds on me. 'But this bloke you've arrested now – it's definitely him – he's the bastard who took Hannah?'

'Enquiries are still progressing. I wish there was more I could say, I really do, but I'm sure you understand. We do have to be sure, and right now, we're not. That's why we're here. Did your wife ever mention someone called William Harper?'

'That's his name, is it – this bloke?'

'Did she know anyone in Frampton Road?'

He takes a deep breath. 'No, not as far as I know.'

'Could she have met him through the BBC? Perhaps interviewed him – for a news story?'

Gardiner looks blank. 'I can check her laptop, but the name isn't ringing any bells.'

We went through that laptop ourselves two years ago. Every damn file, every bloody email. If there'd been a reference to Harper in there I think we'd have found it, and living so close we'd have followed it up. But all the same, it's worth checking.

'Look,' says Gardiner, 'the only reason I can think of why she'd have been in Frampton Road was if she'd had to park there. It gets really congested round here and sometimes that's the nearest she could leave the car. Those houses have drives, so it's usually a bit clearer.'

And suddenly, there it is. The answer. That fact I always thought we'd missed.

'Do you remember whether she definitely parked there that day?' I'm trying not to sound too eager about it, but I can see from Gislingham's face that he's clocked it too.

Gardiner hesitates. 'No. But I know she definitely didn't park outside here the night before. I had to go down and help her bring in some shopping when she got home. But I don't know for certain where the car was.'

I make to get up, but he hasn't finished.

'So does this — this — *pervert* take women *and* children? Women who have kids with them?' I see the girl looking at him anxiously. 'Is that it? That's his "thing"? Because the news said there was a child in that cellar as well. A little boy — just like my Toby.'

'To be honest, Mr Gardiner, we don't know. It's possible the child was born down there. But the girl is still too distressed to talk to us, so we don't yet know exactly what happened.'

He swallows, looks away.

'Your son is alive,' I say softly. 'Alive and safe. That's what matters now.'

When we get to the front door, Gislingham says he needs to use the bathroom and the girl goes to show him where it is. We stand there, Gardiner and me, not knowing what to say.

'You were on that other case, weren't you?' he says eventually. 'Last year. That little girl that went missing. Daisy something.'

'Yes.'

'That didn't have a happy ending either, did it.'

It's a statement, not a question, which is perhaps just as well. 'Don't you have a kid too? Am I remembering that right?'

This time I know I need to answer but Gislingham's arrival saves me.

'Right, boss,' he says, hitching his trousers.

I turn to Gardiner. 'We will, of course, keep you informed about the investigation. And please do let me know if you find any reference to Harper on Hannah's laptop. And obviously as soon as there is any −'

'I want to see her,' he says abruptly. 'If you find her, I want to see her.'

I didn't want him to ask. I was praying he wouldn't.

I shake my head. 'That's really not a good idea. It's best −'

'I want to see her,' he says, his voice breaking. 'She was my *wife*.' He's struggling to keep from weeping, right there, in front of me.

I take a step closer. 'Really. Don't do that. Remember her as she was. All those lovely photos. That's what Hannah would have wanted.'

He stares at me, and I will him to understand. *Don't put an image in your head you can't forget. I know. I've done it. And I can't take it back.*

He swallows, then nods. And I see the relief on the girl's face.

Back in the car, Gislingham yanks out the seat belt and straps himself in. 'What do you think − is he banging her or not?'

I start the engine. 'You don't even know she's a live-in.'

And in any case, it is two years. The poor sod deserves some chance at moving on. I know how hard that can be. Separating yourself from the past without abandoning it. Without feeling guilty every time you smile.

But Gislingham's shaking his head. 'Well, I reckon if he's not now he soon will be. She's definitely up for it if you ask me. In fact, I wouldn't kick her out of bed myself.'

I put the car in gear. 'I thought you were supposed to be a happily married man.'

He grins at me. 'But it doesn't hurt to look, does it?'

When we get back to St Aldate's, Baxter has dragged a clean whiteboard into the incident room and is carefully transcribing the original timeline from the case file.

6.50	Hannah leaves voicemail for childminder
7.20	Rob leaves on bike
7.30?	Hannah leaves
7.55	Text to Hannah from Jervis's PA, putting i/v back to 9.30
7.57	Rob's train leaves Oxford
8.35	Childminder's flatmate leaves message saying she's ill
8.45 – 9.15	Sightings of Hannah and buggy at Wittenham
8.46	Rob at Reading station (CCTV)
9.30	Witness sees empty buggy in Money Pit
10.30	Toby Gardiner found

When he's finished he stands back and snaps the top back on the marker pen.

'So,' he says, turning to the rest of the team, 'assuming she never got to Wittenham at all, where does that leave us?'

'With one hell of a big question mark over all those sightings, for a start,' says Quinn drily.

I've been thinking about that all the way back from Crescent Square; all those witnesses who came forward, just trying to help. And every last one of them mistaken.

'There were a lot of people up there that day,' says Baxter, scanning the statements. 'Parents, kids, dogs. There could easily have been someone who looked a bit like Hannah from a distance. None of them saw her that close up and she wasn't wearing anything very distinctive.'

'So this woman they saw, whoever she was, why didn't she come forward?' asks Quinn. 'It was all over the press and the internet for weeks – four or five appeals for witnesses. If you were there that day and looked a bit like her, wouldn't you have got in touch with the police?'

Baxter doesn't look convinced. 'Could have been a tourist. A foreigner. Or someone who just didn't want to get involved – didn't want the hassle.'

'Personally,' I say, 'I'm more interested in the dog that didn't bark.'

I see Erica Somer smile at that, but the others are slower.

'Oh,' says Everett, after a moment. 'You mean like in *Sherlock Holmes*?'

I nod. 'I can easily see someone mistaking another young woman for Hannah. It's William Harper who's the real question mark. If he abducted Hannah off the street in Frampton Road, then dumped her car and her son in Wittenham, wouldn't someone have remembered seeing him? I mean, an old man alone with a baby buggy?'

Baxter is still leafing through the file. 'One of the witnesses mentions seeing grandparents with kids, so it's possible he didn't stand out. But we only asked people if they saw Hannah. We didn't ask who else they saw.'

'Right,' I say, 'so let's get back in touch with the eyewitnesses and ask them. See if they remember anyone resembling Harper.'

Quinn nods and makes a note.

'OK,' I continue. 'We established there wasn't enough time for Gardiner to get to Wittenham and back if Hannah was still alive at 6.50, but what about Harper – could he have done it?'

Everett considers. 'If Hannah left the flat at 7.30, she must have met Harper no later than 7.45. He could have found some pretext to lure her into the house, then struck her from behind. And once she was unconscious all he had to do was tie her up and leave her there. That wouldn't have taken that long. I reckon he could have been on the road to Wittenham by 8.15, which means he'd have been there by 8.45 or so. So yes, he could have done it.'

'Was Harper still driving back then?' asks Baxter. Not much gets past him.

'According to the social worker, yes.'

'So how did he get back to Oxford? Without the car, I mean.'

Gislingham shrugs. 'Bus? He's got all day, after all. There's no one looking for him. No one at home to ask him where he's been. And all the time in the world to get rid of the body.'

'After he'd finished with her,' says Everett darkly. 'He could have kept her alive for days, for all we know.'

'There's still an issue, though, isn't there, sir?' Somer this time. 'There was no unexplained DNA in Hannah's car. I suppose this man Harper *could* have driven it and left no trace, but that's not easy.'

She's done her homework. I'm beginning to think we should get this woman into CID.

'Boiler suit?' says Gislingham. 'One of those plastic sheets garages put on the seat?'

I turn to Quinn. 'Call Challow and tell him we need to

search the Frampton Road house for a possible body. And for anything Harper might have worn to cover his tracks.'

As people are filing out I catch Baxter's eye.

'I want you to look for any unsolved disappearances of young women and small children in the last ten years.'

He shoots me a glance and I see his brain working, but he doesn't say anything. He knows when to keep his mouth shut; it's one reason why I like him.

'Focus on Oxford and Birmingham to start with, then widen the search fifty miles at a time. And then go back another ten years.'

He nods. 'On the kids, is it boys *and* girls you want, or just boys?'

I'm halfway out of the room but the question pulls me up short. I turn, still thinking.

'Just boys. For now.'

* * *

When I take a seat opposite Bryan Gow half an hour later I can tell at once he's read this morning's news. We're in the café in the Covered Market. Crowds are pushing past outside, stopping to look in the coffee merchant's opposite and at the rack of vintage postcards outside the shop next door. *Dig for Victory*, *Guinness is Good For You*, *Keep Calm and Carry On*. God, I hate that bloody thing.

'I was wondering when you'd call,' says Gow, folding his paper. 'You're lucky to catch me – I've got a conference in Aberdeen tomorrow.'

I wonder in passing what the collective noun for profilers would be. A 'composite', perhaps.

He pushes his plate away. He never could resist a full English, especially if I'm paying.

'It's this man Harper you want to talk about, I take it?'

The waitress plonks two cups in front of us, slopping coffee into the saucers.

'It's a difficult one,' Gow continues, picking up his spoon and reaching for the sugar. 'The Alzheimer's – it's going to make getting a conviction very tricky. But I assume you know that.'

'That's not why I'm here. When we found the girl, it seemed fairly straightforward –'

Gow raises an eyebrow, then goes back to stirring his coffee.

'What I meant was that the motivation seemed fairly straightforward. And we initially assumed the child was born down there – like that case in Austria – Josef Fritzl.'

'In fact, the woman Fritzl imprisoned was his own daughter, so that case would actually be very different. Psychologically speaking, of course. Though I don't expect such nuances from mere policemen. But from what you say, you've decided it's not so straightforward after all.'

'It was something Hannah's husband said. He asked me if Harper had a thing for abducting young women with their children. Whether that's why he targeted Hannah. Only for some reason he changed his mind and decided to dump Toby. Possibly to put us off the scent. But if that's true, it would put a completely different timeline on the cellar case – we've been assuming the child is Harper's, but what if the girl was kidnapped *with* the boy?'

'I imagine you're doing a DNA test?'

I nod. 'It's a bit more complicated than it'd normally be, but yes.'

Gow puts down his spoon. 'So in the meantime what you want to know is how common it would be for a sexual predator to do that – to abduct young women with small children.'

Over Gow's shoulder I can see a family looking in the window of the specialty cake shop. Two little blond boys have their noses pressed against the glass, and their mother is clearly trying to get them to decide which one they want. The chocolate dragon or the red Spider-Man or the Thomas the Tank Engine. We got Jake's ninth birthday cake from that shop. It had a unicorn with a golden horn. He loved unicorns.

'I've never come across one.'

I turn back to Gow, my head still full of unicorns.

'Sorry?'

'A sexual predator who targets both women and children. It's almost unheard of. I can do some digging about in the published case material, but I don't think I can recall a single instance. When women have been abducted along with a child it's because the child was in the wrong place at the wrong time: it was the *woman* who was the target. You know as well as I do that paedophiles are often married or in long-term relationships, but they don't abduct women. They abduct children. In fact,' he says, picking up his coffee, 'there's only one possibility I can think of that would make any sense.'

'And that is?'

'That you're not looking at the same man. Two different predators, in other words. One of them a paedophile, the other a sexual sadist. But working together. Sharing the risk, dividing the spoils.'

As if they were so much carrion. It's enough to make your blood run cold. But so many of the question marks would disappear if William Harper had an accomplice. It would explain why no one saw an old man alone with a buggy that day. In fact, it might even mean Harper was never there at all. The person who dumped the buggy could have been someone else entirely. Someone completely under the radar. Nameless. Faceless. Unknown.

Gow puts the cup down. 'Is there any evidence there was someone else in the house? Someone who could have visited, even if they didn't live there?'

Derek Ross, I think, before pushing the thought away.

'Not so far. Most of the neighbours claim they never saw anyone.'

Gow makes a face. 'In that part of Oxford? I bet they bloody didn't. I wouldn't take that as any kind of proof.'

'There was one old lady who insisted there was someone. But we've dismissed it because she said it was Harper's son and we know he doesn't have one.'

Gow picks up his cup again. 'I'd check that out again if I were you. The old buzzard might not be as gaga as you think.'

* * *

Challow gathers the forensics team together in the kitchen. 'Looks like the to-do list just got rather longer so I hope no one has a hot date planned for later. CID, in their infinite wisdom, now suspect there could be a link between this house and the disappearance of Hannah Gardiner in 2015. So until we've completely eliminated that possibility we have to work on the basis that we could be standing in the middle of a murder scene. Or a burial site. Or, indeed, both.'

Nina takes a deep breath. She remembers the Hannah

Gardiner case. She did the search on the car. The packet of mints in the glovebox, the juice stains on the child seat, the screwed-up petrol receipts. All the detritus of life that becomes so unbearable when someone has gone.

Challow is still talking. 'If we're looking for a grave, the cellar's a non-starter. You couldn't take up the concrete down there without some pretty hefty tools and there's no sign of that sort of disturbance. So where next – the garden?'

'Actually, I don't think so,' says Nina. 'It's too exposed – too dangerous. You couldn't get away with digging a hole that big without risking one of the neighbours seeing.'

She walks over and pushes through the bead curtain to the conservatory. The glass inside is greened and the only thing alive is the creeper growing through the breaks in the windowpanes. The shelves of pots hold nothing but decay. Fossilized geraniums. Yellowed tomato plants. There's a smell of damp and old earth. The rush matting on the floor is black with mildew and coming apart.

She goes up to the window and wipes a space in the murky glass, then stands there for a moment, looking down the garden.

'What about that?' she says, pointing. 'That summerhouse or shed or whatever it is.'

The two men join her. The grass outside is knee-high, and thick with nettles and dock leaves. There's a pile of dirty white plastic garden furniture, most of it upside down, and heaps of dead scrub where someone's had a go at cutting back the undergrowth and left it where it fell. Right at the bottom, by the fence, there's a large brick shed, with a tiled roof almost submerged in ivy. Several of the windows are broken.

'See what I mean?' she says.

They see it even more clearly when they get there. The slope of the garden is steeper than it looks and the shed is resting on a raised base.

'I think,' she says, reaching through the broken glass to unlatch the door, 'that we may well find there's a cavity under these boards.'

Inside, there are shelves crowded with old pots of paint and weedkiller, and a pile of rusting garden tools. An ancient wasps' nest is rotting under the eaves and, hanging from a nail, an old boiler suit splashed with stains.

Challow stamps his foot, hearing the hollow echo underneath. 'I think you're right.'

He lifts a corner of the matting. Dirt and grit cascade down, woodlice run in all directions.

'Once in a while,' he says, looking up at them, 'we just get lucky.'

It's a trapdoor.

* * *

'You can see her now. Though I'm not sure how much use it's going to be.'

The nurse holds open the door of the family room and waits for Everett to join her, then the two of them walk together down the corridor. An old man with a walking frame, two doctors with clipboards, posters about hand hygiene and healthy eating and how to spot the signs of a stroke. The room is at the far end and the girl is sitting up in the bed in a hospital gown. And for once, the cliché is true: her face is scarcely darker than the sheet she's pulled up tight against her chest. She looks bleached, somehow. Not just her skin but her eyes, even her hair. Like there's a fine film of dust over her. There are cold sores around her mouth.

When she sees Everett she starts backwards, her eyes widening.

'I'll just be outside,' says the nurse gently, pulling the door to behind her.

Everett waits a moment, then gestures to the chair. 'Do you mind if I sit down?'

The girl says nothing. Her eyes follow Everett as she pulls the chair further away from the bed and sits down. There's six foot of floor between them.

'Can you tell me your name?' she asks gently.

The girl is still staring at her.

'We know you've been through something terrible. We just want to find out what happened. Who did this to you.'

The girl grips the sheet a little tighter. Her fingernails are broken and dirty.

'I know it's hard – I do. And the last thing I want to do is make it worse. But we really do need your help.'

The girl closes her eyes.

'Do you remember how it happened? How you ended up in that place?'

There are tears now. Seeping out from under her eyelids and slowly down her face.

They sit in silence for a few moments, hearing the murmur of the hospital around them. Footsteps, the clank of trolleys, voices. The ping of the lift.

'I've seen your little boy,' says Everett at last. 'They say he's doing well.'

The girl opens her eyes.

'He's a lovely child. What's his name?'

The girl starts shaking her head, clearly terrified, and a moment later she's screaming and shrinking back in the bed and nurses are rushing in and Everett is out in the corridor on the wrong side of a closed door.

*

It takes twenty minutes and an injection to calm the girl down. Everett is sitting on a chair in the corridor when the doctor emerges from the room. He pulls up another chair and sits down next to her.

'What happened back there?' she says. 'What did I do?'

He takes a deep breath. 'The psychiatrist thinks she may be suffering from PTSD. To be honest, it would be more surprising if she wasn't. It's not uncommon for people in a situation like hers to repress the memory of what happened to them. It's the brain going into survival mode. Shutting down something that's just too painful to deal with. So when you asked her about the child you were forcing her to confront what she's been through, and she simply couldn't cope. I'm afraid it could be some time before she'll be able to talk about it.'

'How long do you think she'll need?'

'There's no way of knowing. Perhaps hours. Perhaps weeks. Possibly never.'

Everett leans forward and puts her head in her hands. 'Shit, I really fucked up, didn't I?'

He looks at her kindly. 'There was nothing wrong with your intentions. Don't be too hard on yourself.'

She feels his hand on her shoulder. The warmth of his flesh through her shirt. And then he's gone.

* * *

The cavity under the trapdoor is no more than two feet deep, and beneath it the ground is just earth and rubble. Challow lies down on the floor and shines a torch through the opening.

'Yup, there's definitely something down there. Nina – do

you want to give it a try? I'm a bit too dimensionally challenged for this one.'

He levers himself back up and watches as Nina climbs down into the space, then gets down on her hands and knees. He passes her the torch and she disappears out of view.

'Mind the rats,' calls Challow cheerfully.

Down in the cavity Nina makes a face: now he tells me. She trains the torch beam around, left to right and back again. There are scuttling noises and the gleam of small eyes in the dark. Then she gasps as the torch beam collides with something only inches from her face. Something sharp and black and very long dead. Thin feet scratching at the empty air. Cavernous eyes like a Halloween ghost. Then she breathes again as she gets her perspective. It's just a bird. Probably a crow.

But further over, perhaps six feet away, the torch is picking up something else.

No skull this time, no dried-out bones. Nothing more horrific than a rolled-up blanket. The horror is in her own imagination. In what she knows that blanket hides.

She swallows, her throat dry, and not just with the dust. 'There's something here,' she calls up. 'It's sealed with packing tape. But it's the right size.'

She crawls backwards, scraping her head against the floor above, and clambers back out.

'I think we need to get these boards up,' she says, wiping her hands against her suit.

'OK,' says Challow, getting to his feet. 'And make sure we tag them as we go. We'll need to know exactly what was where, and we need to fingerprint this whole area too.'

'And hadn't you better call the pathologist?'

'He's on his way.'

* * *

In his office in Canary Wharf, Mark Sexton is on the phone to his lawyer. Thirteen floors below, the Thames moves sluggishly towards the sea, and three miles due west, the Shard glints in the sun. The TV screen in the corner is on mute, but he can still see the rolling headlines running across the bottom. And the pictures of the Frampton Road house. And not just that house but the one next door, *his* house.

'I can't believe they don't fucking *know*. I mean, how long does a sodding forensic search take?'

The lawyer demurs. 'It's not really my area. Though I know a Criminal QC I could ask. That's criminal with a large "c", of course.' He laughs.

Sexton's clearly not in the mood for semantics. 'Just get on to those Thames Valley tossers again, will you? The builders have already said if they can't get back in by the end of the week they'll either have to charge me for sitting on their arses or start another job. And we all know what'll happen in that case – I won't see them again for six fucking weeks while they piss about with someone's sodding kitchen extension.'

'I'm not sure it'll be much use –'

'Just do it. What the fuck else do I pay you for?'

Sexton slams down the phone and stares again at the TV screen. They're clearly doing a reprise of the Hannah Gardiner disappearance; some lank-haired psychic is on reminding the world at large how she predicted the number three would hold the key to the case, and a montage of two-year-old headlines is fading in and out: *Was missing girl abducted by Satanic cult? Midsummer mystery deepens as police deny evidence of pagan rite. Toddler found near site of human sacrifice.*

Sexton puts his head in his hands; that's all I fucking need.

* * *

'We thought we'd wait for you before we opened it,' says the pathologist. 'And it isn't even your birthday.'

His name is Colin Boddie. And yes, I know, that's not funny. Only it is; of course it is. He's heard the gags so many times he's developed his own brand of pathological humour to go with it. It can sound crass, if you don't know him, but it's just a form of carapace. A way to keep the horror at bay. And what they've got here – despite the daylight and all the busy professional apparatus – is still the stuff of nightmares.

People in the houses either side were leaning out of their windows as we walked down the garden. Odds-on, some bastard has put a picture on bloody Twitter by now.

Inside the shed there's a gaping hole in the floor. And around it, us. Forensics, Gislingham and Quinn. And now me. Boddie bends down carefully and cuts away the rotten blanket and the tape. First one side, and then the other. We all know what we are going to see, but it's a clench to the gut all the same. It's lying head down, so we can't see the face. Thanks be to God for small mercies. But there are still the shreds of livid purple and green skin shrunk against the ribcage. The clawing hands. The lower legs reduced to gnawed and whitened bone.

'As you can see, there's been partial mummification of the remains,' says Boddie evenly. 'Not that surprising given that the body was well wrapped, and there'd have been ventilation under this floor. Though it looks like the bottom of the blanket wasn't very well sealed as we're missing most of the smaller bones in the feet and ankles. That's probably down to rats. There are clear signs of rodent infestation all over this area.'

I glance up to see Quinn making a face.

'The cadaver is definitely female,' continues Boddie. 'And a fair amount of the hair remains as well, as you can see.' He bends down and looks closer, parting the matted strands with a plastic pen. 'As for cause of death, I can see what appears to be significant blunt force trauma to the parietal bone. Though I'll have to get her on the table to be sure.'

'Could she have survived something like that?' asks Gislingham, his face pale.

Boddie considers. 'She'd have been knocked unconscious, without question. But possibly not killed outright. Look.' He crouches down again and points at something caught about the withered wrists. 'I think you'll find that's a cable tie. That could suggest she died some time after the initial blow.'

I remember what Everett said; about Harper tying her up and leaving her there while he went to dump her child and her car. Because he'd have wanted her alive, for when he got back. For what he wanted to do to her.

'Is there any way of knowing how long she survived?'

Boddie shakes his head. 'I doubt it. Could have been hours. Days, even.'

'Jesus,' says Gislingham under his breath.

Boddie straightens up. 'There's a lot of decomp underneath, but all the same I'm pretty sure she didn't die here. On this blanket, I mean. There'd have been an absolute slew of blood and brain tissue.'

I sometimes wish Boddie wasn't quite so good with words.

'And she was naked, by the way. Wrapped up like this, some of the clothes would have survived, but there's nothing here.'

Gislingham isn't the only one who's gone pale now. We're all playing versions of the same scene in our heads. Waking up with your hands tied. Stripped. In pain. Knowing that it was only a matter of time.

'Why would the killer do that – was it sexual?'

'Either that or they wanted to humiliate her. Either way you're looking at a very nasty piece of work.'

As if we didn't know.

'Right,' says Challow briskly. 'If you lot can clear the area, we'll bring the photographer back in and start packing up all this stuff.'

* * *

BBC News

Tuesday 2 May 2017 | Last updated at 15:23

BREAKING: Body found in Oxford cellar case

The BBC has learned that a body has been found at the house in North Oxford where a girl and a small boy were discovered yesterday morning. Forensics personnel have been seen removing human remains from the garden, which are believed to be those of a woman. Speculation is mounting that officers could have discovered the body of the BBC journalist Hannah Gardiner, 27, who disappeared at Wittenham on Midsummer's Day two years ago, and whose 2-year-old son, Toby, was subsequently found nearby.

Hannah was last seen by her husband, Rob, at their flat in Crescent Square on the morning of 24 June 2015, on her way to cover a story at the Wittenham Clumps protest camp. The fact that her Mini Clubman was in the adjacent car park, along with several apparent sightings and the discovery of Toby Gardiner, led police to believe she had disappeared in the Wittenham area.

Reginald Shore, a protester at the site who was subsequently jailed for a sexual assault in Warwick, was questioned extensively about Hannah's disappearance, but no charges were ever brought. His son, Matthew, is now writing a book about the case, and said this morning, 'My father was the victim of a witch-hunt by Thames Valley Police, spearheaded by Detective Superintendent Alastair Osbourne. We will now be renewing our calls for my father's conviction to be overturned and for the Independent Police Complaints Commission to investigate the handling of the Hannah Gardiner case. Her family deserve to know the truth, and I will be doing everything I can personally to make sure that happens.'

Thames Valley Police have declined to comment, but confirmed that a statement will be issued 'in due course'. Detective Superintendent Osbourne retired from the force in December 2015.

* * *

Boddie calls me at 8.00 p.m. I was half thinking of going home, half thinking of just ordering Chinese at the desk. But I end up in the mortuary. That's how this job goes sometimes. I call Alex on the way to let her know, and then remember she's out with some old college friends tonight. So it looks like it was Chinese, either way.

It's 8.45 when I park at the hospital and the day is darkening. Clouds are rolling in from the west and as I walk across to the entrance I feel the first spots of rain.

In the morgue, the body is laid out carefully on a metal table.

'I've sent some of the bones for DNA,' says Boddie, rinsing his hands in the sink. 'And forensics have taken the blanket for analysis.'

'Anything more on cause of death?'

Boddie goes over to the body and points out the indentations on the skull. 'There were definitely two separate blows. The first struck her here, and probably knocked her unconscious. Then here – can you see? – the damage is much more extensive. That's what actually killed her, and the weapon definitely had some sort of edge to it. The first blow probably wouldn't have bled very much, but the second certainly would have.'

You know, I think I'll pass on that Chinese, after all.

He straightens up. 'I believe you've already requested Hannah Gardiner's dental records?'

I nod. 'And Challow is going through the house, but they haven't found anything yet.'

'Well, take it from me, if she died there, you'll know about it.'

The wind is rising outside. The first whip of rain against the glass.

'You said to come alone,' I say, after a moment. 'Why?'

'I didn't see it until we started to lift the bones.' He reaches to a side table and picks up a metal tray. 'I found this under the skull.'

A strip of desiccated grey plastic. Duct tape.

'So she was gagged.'

He nods. 'Bound *and* gagged. So you see why I thought you shouldn't bring anyone else.'

He can see from my face that I don't.

'Come on, Fawley – hands tied, face down, a broken skull? You're going to have to think carefully about how much of that you release to the press. Because the hacks are going to work out very quickly that it's exactly like those bodies they found on Wittenham Clumps.'

'Shit.'

'Quite. And I don't know about you, but what we've got here is horrific enough; we really don't need more headlines screaming human sacrifice.'

* * *

Chris Gislingham pushes open his front door with his foot; he'd use his hands only he has three carrier bags in each one. Nappies, wipes, baby powder – how can such a small helpless creature need so much stuff?

'I'm home,' he calls.

'We're in here.'

Gislingham dumps the bags in the kitchen and goes through into the sitting room where his wife, Janet, is sitting cradling their son. She looks both exhausted and ecstatic – something Gislingham has got used to over the last few months: neither of them got much sleep last night. When he bends to kiss his son, Billy smells of baby powder and biscuits, and stares up wide-eyed at his father, who strokes his head gently, then sits down next to them on the sofa.

'Good day?' he says.

'That nice health visitor came to see us, didn't she, Billy?

And she said how well you'd grown.' She drops a kiss on the baby's brow, and he reaches out a chubby hand to catch her hair.

'I thought you were going shopping with your sister? Wasn't that today?'

'Billy was a bit sniffly, so I decided not to. It wasn't worth the risk. I can go another time.'

Gislingham tries to recall the last time his wife actually left the house. It's been getting more pronounced lately, and he wonders if – or when – he should start to worry.

'You need fresh air too, you know,' he says, trying to keep his tone light. 'Perhaps we can go and feed the ducks at the weekend? You'd like that, wouldn't you, Billy boy?' He tickles his son under the chin and the little boy squeals with delight.

'We'll see,' says Janet vaguely. 'Depends what the weather's like.'

'Talking of which, it's like bloody Barbados in here,' says Gislingham, loosening his tie. 'I thought we turned off the heating?'

'It was a bit chilly this afternoon so I put it back on.'

It's not worth the risk. She doesn't need to say it. After ten years of trying, and a premature birth that nearly ended in tragedy, protecting Billy, keeping Billy warm, monitoring Billy's weight and height and strength and every little development, is all she cares about. Her life barely has room for anything else, certainly not for much in the way of cooking.

'Pizza again?' says Gislingham eventually.

'In the fridge,' replies Janet distractedly, adjusting the baby's position slightly. 'Can you put a bottle in to warm too?'

Gislingham levers himself up and goes back out to the kitchen. Most of what's in the fridge is pureed, mashed or milk, but he dislodges the box of pizza where it's frozen against the back and puts it in the microwave, then switches on the bottle warmer. When he goes back into the sitting room five minutes later, Janet is leaning back against the sofa, her eyes closed.

Gislingham lifts his baby son gently from his wife's arms and props him against his shoulder. 'OK, Billy boy, what do you say you and me go and have a quiet bevvy.'

*   *   *

Alex gets in at midnight. She assumes I'm in bed, because the sitting-room lights are off, and so, for a few fleeting seconds, I can watch her when she thinks she's alone. She drops her bag by the front door and stands a moment, looking at herself in the mirror. She's beautiful, my wife; she always has been. She never enters a room without people noticing. The dark hair, those eyes that are violet in some light, and almost turquoise in others. And she's taller than me in high heels and it doesn't bother me, in case you were wondering. But her looks have never made her happy. And now, I watch as she puts her hands to her face, smooths the lines from her eyes, lifts her chinline, turning her head first one way then the other. And she must have glimpsed me in the mirror because she turns suddenly, a slight flush to her cheek.

'Adam? You scared the life out of me. What are you doing sitting in the dark?'

I pick up my glass and finish what's left of the Merlot. 'Just thinking.'

She comes in and perches on the arm of the sofa opposite me. 'Tough day?'

I nod. 'I'm on the Frampton Road case.'

She nods slowly. 'I saw the news. Is it as bad as it sounds?'

'Worse. We found a body at the house this afternoon. We think it's Hannah Gardiner. But the press don't know that yet.'

'Have you told her husband?'

'Not yet. I'm waiting for a positive ID. I don't want to open up all that for him again unless I'm sure.'

'How's the girl?'

'Traumatized, according to Everett. Not speaking. Doesn't appear to know her own name or even that she has a child. Started screaming just at the sight of him.'

There's a silence. Alex looks down at her hands. I know what she's thinking – I know only too well. How could anyone who had a child possibly forget it? How could anyone who lost a child not yearn to have another? I wonder if she'll raise it again. Her pain, her need, and what she thinks is the answer.

'How was your evening?' I ask into the unspoken words.

'Fine. It was just me and Emma in the end.'

'Not sure I know her.'

'You don't. I haven't seen her in years. She works for the Council. In the Family Placement team.'

She's not meeting my gaze now.

'So, what, she finds homes for kids? Adoptions, fostering?'

'Mmm.'

She's still not looking at me.

I take a deep breath. 'Alex, this wasn't a college get-together at all, was it? It was only ever you and this Emma woman.'

She's fiddling with the handle of her handbag now. 'Look, I just wanted to get some more information. Find out what it involves.'

'Even though you know what I think. Even though we agreed –'

She raises her eyes to my face. Eyes full of tears. '*We* didn't agree. *You* agreed. I know how you feel about it, but what about how *I* feel? While we had Jake it didn't matter so much that I didn't have any more, but when we lost him –' Her voice breaks and she struggles for composure. 'When we lost him, it was – unbearable. And not just because he died but because part of *me* died too. The part that was a mother – that put someone else first. I want that back. Can't you understand?'

'Of course I can. What do you take me for?'

'Then why are you refusing to even think about it? Emma was telling me about the kids she has to deal with – desperate for love – crying out for the sort of stability and support we could give them –'

I get up and pick up the glass and bottle and head into the kitchen, where I start to stack the dishwasher. When I look up five minutes later she's standing in the doorway.

'Are you afraid you might love another child more than Jake? Because if it's that then I get it, I really do.'

I straighten up and lean against the worktop. 'It's not that. You know it's not.'

She comes closer and puts her hand on my arm, tentatively, as if she fears rejection. 'It wasn't your fault,' she says softly. 'Just because he – because he died – it doesn't mean we were bad parents.'

How many times have I said the same thing to her, this last year. I wonder how we ended up here, that she feels she needs to say it to me.

I turn towards her and take her in my arms, holding her tight against me so I can feel her breathing, her heart beating.

'I love you.'

'I know,' she whispers.

'No, I mean, I love *you*. It's enough. I don't need another

child to — I don't know, make me whole or give me a pur-
pose in life. You, me, work, this. It's enough.'

Later, in bed, listening to her breathing, looking through the
curtains at the dark blue sky that still hasn't lost its light, I
wonder if I lied. Not by commission, perhaps, but omission.
I don't want to adopt a child, but not because the life I have
is sufficient. It's because the idea terrifies me. Like betting
your whole existence on a gigantic lucky dip. Nurture is
strong, but blood is stronger. My mother and father have
never told me they're not my biological parents, but I know,
I've known for years. I found the papers in my father's desk
when I was ten. I had to look up some of the words, but I
worked it out. And suddenly everything seemed to fit. Not
looking like them, and as I got older, not thinking much like
them either. Feeling like a misfit in my own life. And waiting, month after month and year after year until I knew it
was never coming, for the moment when they'd tell me. If I
said all this to Alex she'd say at once that we'd do it differ-
ently. That we'd be modern and open and truthful. That patterns don't need to be repeated. That most adopted kids are
happy and well-adjusted and make a success of their lives.
Perhaps they do. Or perhaps, like me, they just don't talk
about it.

When I wake at 7.00 the bed is empty beside me. Alex is in
the kitchen, fully dressed and about to leave.

'You're up early.'

'I have to drop off my car,' she says, pretending to be busy
with the coffee machine. 'It's in for a service. Don't you remember?'

'Do you want me to pick you up tonight?'

'Won't you be too busy – the case and everything?'

'Possibly. But let's assume I can and I'll email you if there's a problem.'

'OK.' She smiles fleetingly, kisses me on the cheek and snatches up her keys. 'See you later then.'

*   *   *

'Still no ID on the body yet. Apparently there's a hold-up with the dental records. There's no blood visible on the boiler suit found in the shed though they'll test it for DNA just in case. But it's probably a long shot – if Harper did wear something like that to drive Hannah's car he probably got rid of it years ago.'

Quinn's in my office, updating me. Tablet in hand, as usual. I don't know how he managed before he got that thing.

'Ev's back at the hospital. Nothing yet from Jim Nicholls. Looks like he's probably on holiday but we're still trying. And the Super's been on twice already about when we can hold a press conference. I've said you'll get back to him.' There's a pause, then, 'Did you know Matthew Shore was writing a book?'

'No. But he's hardly likely to tell us, is he.'

'Have you spoken to Osbourne?'

I shake my head. 'I tried last night, but all I got was voicemail.'

'Is it worth us trying to talk to Matthew Shore? I mean, if he's been doing his own research he might have come up with something – he's looked at all this more recently than we have –'

He's pissing me off now. 'Look, Quinn, forget it. Trust me, if he'd found anything we'd have known about it. He's a nasty piece of work, and if we talk to him now he'll find some way to use that against us. Understood?'

He's staring at his list again and I force him to look at me. 'Quinn? Did you hear me?'

Quinn glances up, then back at the tablet. 'Sure. No problem. So that just leaves Harper. His lawyer's just arrived and I've asked the custody sergeant to bring him up to Interview One.'

I finish my coffee and make a face; whatever they do to that machine, the output doesn't get any better. 'Find Gis and get him to sit in with me.'

Quinn steals a look at me as I pick up my jacket from the back of the chair. I'm not punishing him, but I don't mind him worrying I might be. For a day or two.

* * *

Interview with Dr William Harper, conducted at
St Aldate's Police Station, Oxford
3 May 2017, 9.30 a.m.
In attendance, DI A. Fawley, DC C. Gislingham,
Mrs J. Reid (solicitor), Ms K. Eddings (Mental
Health team)

AF: Dr Harper, I am Detective Inspector Adam
     Fawley. I'm leading the investigation relating
     to the young woman and child we found in your
     cellar on Monday morning. Ms Eddings is from
     the Mental Health team and Mrs Reid is here as
     your lawyer. They're here to protect your
     interests. Do you understand?
WH: Haven't a fucking clue what you're talking
     about.

AF: You're confused about Mrs Reid's role?

WH: Do I look like a moron? I know what a bloody solicitor is.

AF: So it was the other things I said – about the girl and the child?

WH: How many more times? *I don't know what you're crapping on about.*

AF: You're saying there was no young woman or child in your cellar?

WH: If there was, I never saw 'em.

AF: So how do you imagine they came to be there?

WH: Haven't got a fucking clue. Probably pikeys. They live like pigs. Cellar would be a fucking luxury.

AF: Dr Harper, there is no evidence the young woman came from the Roma community. And even if she did, how could she have got into your cellar without you knowing?

WH: Search me. You seem to be the one with all the bloody answers.

AF: The door to the cellar room was locked from the outside.

WH: Bit of a poser for you, then, isn't it? Smartarse git.
    [*pause*]

AF: Dr Harper, yesterday afternoon, members of the Thames Valley forensics team conducted a detailed search of your house and discovered a body concealed under the floor of the shed. An adult female. Can you tell me how it got there?

WH: No bloody idea, ask me another.

JR: [*intervening*]
    This is serious, Dr Harper. You need to answer
    the inspector's questions.

WH: Fuck off, you ugly cow.
    [*pause*]

AF: So let's be clear – you're telling us that you
    can't explain either why a corpse was found
    buried under the floor in your shed or how a
    young woman and a child came to be locked in
    the cellar? That's what you're asking us to
    believe?

WH: Why do you keep repeating yourself? Are you
    mentally subnormal or what?

CG: [*passing across a photograph*]
    Dr Harper, this is a picture of a young woman
    called Hannah Gardiner. She disappeared two
    years ago. Have you ever seen her before?

WH: [*pushing away the picture*]
    No.

CG: [*passing across a second picture*]
    What about this girl? This is the girl we
    found in your cellar. It's the picture I showed
    you yesterday.

WH: They're all the same. Evil cows.

CG: Sorry, are you saying that you recognize her
    or that you don't?

WH: Frigid cows making you beg for it. That slut
    Priscilla. I told her – sod off back where you
    came from, you evil cow.

KE: I'm sorry, Inspector, but I think he's
    getting confused again. Priscilla is his dead
    wife.

AF: Please look at the pictures, Dr Harper. Have
      you ever seen either of these young women?
WH: [*rocking backwards and forwards*]
      Evil cows. Spiteful little tarts.
KE: I think we'd better stop now.

*   *   *

Sent: Weds 03/05/2017, 11.35   **Importance: High**
From: AlanChallowCSI@ThamesValley.police.uk
To: DIAdamFawley@ThamesValley.police.uk,
      CID@ThamesValley.police.uk
CC: Colin.Boddie@ouh.nhs.uk

Subject: Case no JG2114/14R Gardiner, H

This is to confirm the dental records have come through.
The body at Frampton Road is definitely Hannah Gardiner.

*   *   *

'Adam? It's Alastair Osbourne. I saw the news.'

Even though I called him first, I've still been dreading
him phoning me back.

'It's her, isn't it? Hannah Gardiner?'

'Yes, it's her. I'm sorry, sir.'

Some habits die hard. Like respect.

'I assume that man Harper is the prime suspect?' he continues. 'UAU?'

UAU. Unless And Until. Unless and until we rule him
out. Unless and until we find another suspect. Or that accomplice we still don't know exists.

'For now, yes.'

'How's Rob Gardiner holding up?'

'As well as you'd expect. I mean, he must have been expecting this, but it will still be a shock.'

There's a pause at the other end of the line.

'I owe you an apology, Adam.'

'No –'

'I do,' he says emphatically. 'You were never convinced about Shore, and you wanted to widen the search beyond Wittenham. I overruled you on both. I was wrong. And now it looks like this monster has done it again –'

'If it's any consolation, sir, that girl could have been in Harper's cellar long before Hannah died.'

*   *   *

Everett can hear the noise halfway down the corridor. It's the play area at the children's ward; toys and games and pictures in happy primary colours of elephants and giraffes and monkeys, but now the walls are running with something that for one wild and appalling moment looks like blood. The boy is in the middle of the room, screaming. One of the toy trains is in pieces and three other children are cowering behind the chairs, crying. A little girl has a cut on her cheek. A nursing assistant is on her hands and knees trying to mop up a dark red stain on the lino.

The nursing assistant looks up. 'It's just Ribena, honest. And I swear I only left them alone for five minutes – Jane didn't come in today and we're run off our feet –'

'I suppose he's never encountered other children before,' says Everett. 'He literally doesn't know what to do with them.'

Nurse Kingsley hurries over to the girl. 'How did Amy get this cut?'

'I ran back in here as soon as I heard the screaming. Amy was on the floor and the boy was on top of her.'

The boy is silent now, but his face is flushed and his cheeks are covered with tears. Kingsley makes a tentative move towards him but he backs away.

'It was a nightmare on the ward last night,' says the nursing assistant wearily. 'He screamed the place down for almost an hour till he got so exhausted he curled up under the bed. We tried to coax him out but he wasn't having it. We just left him there in the end.'

Jenny shakes her head, at a loss. 'I'll speak to Social Services again. My heart goes out to him, it really does, but sick children need their sleep.'

The boy stares at her for a moment, then drops suddenly on to all fours and crawls away into the corner. The three women watch in silence as he smears his hand along the wall and starts to suck the congealing juice from his fingers.

'Christ,' says Everett after a moment. 'Do you think that's what he had to do?'

Jenny Kingsley glances across at her. 'You mean, in the cellar?'

'Think about it. The water's running low, the walls are damp —'

The nursing assistant puts her hand to her mouth. And then, in the silence, Everett's phone goes.

It's a text. From Fawley.

> Ask the doctors to check the boy again.
> Need to rule out possible sexual abuse.

*   *   *

THAMES VALLEY POLICE
Statement of Witness

Date: *25 June 2015*

Name: *Sarah Wall*   D.O.B.   *13/11/66*

Address: *32 Northmoor Close, Dorchester-on-Thames*

Occupation: *Freelance accountant*

I was walking my dog on Wittenham Clumps on Wednesday morning. I go most days so I recognise most of the regulars. There were more people about than usual on a Wednesday – it was Midsummer Eve the night before so a lot of the travellers from the camp were still about. And there were quite a few other people too. Students. Some families with children. Grandparents. I remember several buggies. I headed up towards Castle Hill past a couple of joggers I recognised and another person who walks a dog like mine. We stopped for a chat. That must have been just before 9 am. Then I got a call and had to turn back so I could deal with something for a client. It was when I was going down to the road that I saw the young woman with the buggy. She was quite a long way away, with her back to me, but she had dark hair in a ponytail and a jacket that was either black or dark blue. And some sort of backpack. I didn't see which direction she took after that. But when I walked past the car park there was definitely an orange Mini Clubman there. It was quite distinctive – the colour, I mean.

Signed: *Sarah Wall*

THAMES VALLEY POLICE
Statement of Witness

Date: 25 June 2015

Name: Martina Brownlee   D.O.B.   9/10/95

Address: Oxford Brookes, student halls

Occupation: Student

We were up all night and I was still a bit pissed tbh but I definitely saw her. She was on the path. The kid was asleep and she was bent over him. I didn't get close enough to talk to her, but I'm deffo sure it was her. I clocked the jacket – it's from Zara. One of my mates has one. Not sure what time it was. Maybe 8.45?

Signed: Martina Brownlee

THAMES VALLEY POLICE
Statement of Witness

Date: 25 June 2015

Name: Henry Nash   D.O.B. 22/12/51

Address: Yew Cottage, Wittenham Road, Appleford

Occupation: Teacher (retired)

I walk on Wittenham Clumps most mornings. I got there about 9.25 yesterday. There was definitely an orange Mini Clubman in the car park by then but I didn't see it arrive. I made my way up to Castle Hill, and went round by the Poem Tree — what's left of it. A bit further on I noticed something brightly coloured in the area they call the Money Pit. It was a child's buggy. Green. Just sitting there, as if the parents had parked it for a moment. I waited for a few minutes but there was no one around so I came back down. I knocked at the visitor centre place and let them know what I'd seen. I only wish I'd thought to look around a bit more. I might have found that poor little boy if I had. As I was passing the car park I saw a black Jaguar had arrived and there was a man I now know to be Malcolm Jervis sitting in the back seat with the door open. He was on his mobile, shouting at someone. I kept well clear.

Signed: Henry Nash

At St Aldate's, Quinn is going through the file on Hannah Gardiner. Uniform have spent all morning tracking down the witnesses who were at Wittenham that day, but so far they've turned up nothing. No one remembers an elderly man alone with a buggy, and no one has picked out William Harper from an array of similar digital images. What Quinn's now looking for is any sighting of Hannah in Crescent Square or Frampton Road, after she left her flat and went to collect her car. If Harper did kill her he must have been out in the street, and in the middle of June, it would have been broad daylight at that time of the morning. Surely someone would have seen? A commuter – even an early school run? But according to the file, there's nothing – absolutely nothing. He's making a note to issue a new appeal for witnesses, when the phone rings. It's Challow.

'Fingerprint results, hot off the press.'

Quinn picks up his pen. 'OK, hit me.'

'Those in the kitchen and downstairs bog are mostly Harper's, but there are several from Derek Ross, which tallies with what he told us. Also several other unidentified sets, none of which are in the national fingerprint database.'

'And the cellar?'

'Harper's again, and some I assume are the girl's. We'll check that, obviously. None from Ross this time, though there are some which match one of the unidentified sets from the kitchen. But there were two very clear prints on the bolt to the inner door. Database says they belong to an extremely shady character name of Gareth Sebastian Quinn.'

'Haha, very funny.'

'Seriously, though, there weren't any other prints on that bolt apart from yours, so it looks like it could have been wiped down. We also found a couple of partials in the shed that could be a match for the unidentified prints in the cellar room, though it's only a five-point match at best, so don't even bother asking the CPS to run with that.'

Quinn sits forward in his chair. 'But it's possible someone else was involved both times?'

'Don't get carried away. There's no way of knowing how old those prints are. Could be some innocent plumber. The bloke who fitted the lav. Or unblocked the sink. We've started processing the rest of the house for a possible murder scene, but thus far we've come up empty.'

'Nothing on the DNA?'

'Not yet. Don't worry, I'll make sure you're the first to know.'

After Quinn puts the phone down he wonders for a moment about that last comment. Was it as pointed as it sounded or is he just getting paranoid? The trouble with Challow is that pointed is his default mode, so it's hard to tell when he is, in fact, making a point. Fuck it, he thinks, picking up the phone and dialling Erica.

'Fawley wants us to interview that woman at number seven again — what was her name? Gibson, yeah, that's the one. See if we can get a better description of that bloke she thought was Harper's son. Can you get that organized?' He listens, then smiles. 'And no, *PC Somer*, that wasn't the only reason I was calling. I was wondering if you fancy a drink tonight? To discuss the case, of course.' He smiles again, broader this time. 'Yeah, and that too.'

*   *   *

'I only found two similar cases. And I had to go back over fifteen years to find those.'

I'm leaning over Baxter's shoulder, staring at the screen. The room is stifling. The temperature's suddenly risen and the ancient HVAC system in the station isn't designed to turn on a sixpence. All the computers crowded in here aren't helping, either. Baxter mops the back of his neck with a handkerchief.

'Here you are,' he says, tapping the keyboard. 'Bryony Evans, twenty-four, reported missing on 29th March 2001 along with her two-year-old son, Ewan. Last seen outside a supermarket near her home in Bristol.'

The picture is slightly blurred, probably taken at a party; there are Christmas decorations in the background. She looks younger than twenty-four. Hair in corkscrew curls. Smiling, but not with her eyes.

'Apparently the family had been worried about her state of mind for several weeks before she disappeared. They said she was depressed – struggling to find a job and stuck at home with the kid. They'd wanted her to go to the doctor but she kept refusing.'

'So they thought it was suicide?'

'Looks like Avon and Somerset agreed. There was a thorough inquiry – there are forty-odd statements on file – but no one ever found any evidence of an abduction. No suggestion of any sort of foul play. Inquest returned an open verdict.'

'It's pretty bloody rare for no body to be found – not after all this time. Not if it was suicide.'

Baxter considers. 'Bristol's on the coast. She could have just walked into the sea.'

'With the kid in tow? Really?'

He shrugs. 'It's possible. OK, not *likely*. But possible.'

'What about the other one?'

'Ah, this one's closer to home.'

He pulls up another file. 1999. Joanna Karim and her son,

Mehdi. She was twenty-six, he was five. And they lived in Abingdon. Baxter sees my interest kindling and rushes to douse it.

'Before you get too excited, this was one of those contested custody cases. The husband was Iranian. I spoke to the SIO who handled it and he said the kid was almost certainly smuggled back to Tehran by his father. They suspected he got rid of the wife too, but they never found enough evidence to bring charges, and by then the bastard had left the country. So yeah, it looks like a double disappearance, but I think it's actually two entirely separate crimes.'

I sit down next to him. 'OK. Even if these aren't connected, we still have a set of unidentified fingerprints in that cellar.'

'But like Challow said, it could just be the plumber.'

'You're a betting man, aren't you, Baxter?'

He flushes; he didn't realize I knew.

'Well, I wouldn't exactly say *betting* as such –'

'You do the football – the horses – I hear you're pretty good at it, too.'

'Well, I've won a bit,' he says guardedly. 'Now and again.'

'So what are the odds, do you think? That those prints are the plumber's?'

His face changes. He's not embarrassed now, he's calculating.

'Twenty-five to one. And that's a gift.'

*   *   *

'DC Gislingham? It's Louise Foley.'

It takes him a moment to remember who she is. Which doesn't go unnoticed.

'Birmingham University?' she says drily. 'Remember? You asked me about disclosing Dr Harper's file?'

'Ah, right, yes. Hold on, let me grab a pen. OK, shoot.'

'I've spoken to the head of department and he's author-ized me to send you a copy of the relevant papers. I'll be emailing them to you today.'

'Can you give me the headlines? You know – the basics?'

She sighs, unnecessarily loudly. 'It's nothing like as salacious as you appear to be hoping. There was a relationship with a student, but she never made a complaint. There was no – *coercion* involved. Indeed, some of the girl's friends suggested that it was more a case of her pursuing him, than the other way round. But nonetheless Dr Harper was married at the time, and such relationships are prohibited under university regula-tions, so it was agreed that it was in everyone's best interests if he took early retirement. You'll find all this in the file.'

'OK,' says Gislingham, tossing his pen back on the desk. 'Just one more question – what was the girl's name?'

'Cunningham. Priscilla Cunningham.'

* * *

All the windows are open in the flat at Crescent Square. The breeze lifts the long white nets and there's the sound of chil-dren playing in a garden a few doors away. The thud of a trampoline, squeals, a ball bouncing. All the children seem to be boys.

Pippa Walker goes to the door of the study and stands there a moment, watching. It's the third time she's done it in the last hour. Rob Gardiner is at the desk, staring at a laptop. The floor is covered with old notebooks, Post-its, piles of paper. He looks up at the girl, irritated.

'Haven't you got something to do? Play with Toby or something?'

'He's asleep. You've been in here hours. Surely you must have been through all that stuff before.'

'Well, I'm going through it again. *OK?*'

She shifts her position slightly. 'I thought you were working today.'

'I was. I changed my mind. Not that it's any business of yours.'

'I'm just worried about you, Rob. It's not a good idea – digging all this up again –'

She bites her lip, but it's too late.

He looks at her heavily. 'My wife was missing for two years. Her body has just been found in the most bloody awful circumstances, and the police have asked me to look through her notes again, in case there's anything in them that might help convict the bastard who did it. So I'm very sorry if *digging all this up again* doesn't meet with your approval, but I for one want to see that shit rot in jail. And if you don't like it, then go and do something else. Read a bloody book for a change.'

Her face is scarlet. 'I'm sorry. I didn't mean – you know I didn't –'

'Frankly, I don't give a toss what you meant. Just leave me alone.'

And he gets up and slams the door.

*   *   *

The team meeting is at 5.00 p.m. It doesn't take long. To sum up:

- The student Harper had an affair with ended up as his second wife. And yes, he was married at the

time, but all that makes him is an adulterous shit, not a psychopath.
- The fingerprints in the cellar could suggest the involvement of another as yet unknown perpetrator. Absolutely sod all leads on who that might be.
- No forensic evidence at the house allowing us to identify a murder scene, so there's still a possibility she was killed somewhere else, and by someone else.
- DNA results: still waiting. To quote Challow, 'I'm not a bloody miracle worker.'
- The girl: still sedated and/or not talking. The boy: ditto.
- Press conference: put off till tomorrow because I haven't got a bloody clue what to tell them.

If I sound pissed off, that's because I am. Keep calm and carry on. Yeah, right.

*   *   *

Elspeth Gibson drinks a lot of tea. Erica Somer has already had two cups and they're no way near done yet. She's already spotted the forensic artist checking his watch. The cat is sitting on the arm of the chair staring at them, its paws folded like a fishwife. It's clearly severely miffed at this outrageous usurpation of its usual seating arrangements.

'So you think the man you saw talking to Dr Harper was definitely in his fifties?'

'Oh yes, dear. The way he dressed, for one thing. No one wears clothes like that any more.'

'Like what, exactly?'

'Oh, you know. Neckties. Tweed jackets. Young people wouldn't be seen dead in that sort of thing, would they? It's all T-shirts and those jeans with the crotch around their knees. And tattoos.' She shudders and reaches for the teapot again.

The forensic artist quickly covers his cup. 'No more for me, thanks.'

Somer leans over and looks at the e-fit on the tablet. The clothes may be their best bet, in the end, because otherwise this could be a picture of just about any late-middle-aged man in Oxford. Tallish, greyish hair, heavyish build. More 'ish' than anything else, in fact.

'Was there something that stood out about him? No scars or anything like that? Perhaps the way he walked?'

Mrs Gibson considers. 'No,' she says eventually. 'Can't say that there was.'

'And his voice – anything different about that?'

'Well, I only spoke to him once or twice and it was some time ago, but he definitely sounded educated, if you know what I mean. Certainly not common.'

'No accent at all?'

'Now you come to mention it there may have been a bit of a Brummie twang. Though my guess is he'd tried to get rid of it. But when people are angry something like that often slips out –'

'Angry? I'm sorry, Mrs Gibson, I don't follow.'

'Didn't I tell you? It was that time I heard them arguing. He was obviously very upset.'

'You heard them *arguing*? You never mentioned that before – when was this?'

Mrs Gibson stops, pot in hand. 'Lord, it must have been at least three years ago. Perhaps more. Time gets so treacherous when you get to my age – things you think were a few months ago turn out to be years –'

Somer sits forward a little. 'What exactly were they arguing about? Do you remember?'

Mrs Gibson looks perplexed. 'I'm not sure I can tell you. I only heard them because I happened to be walking past at the time and they were on the doorstep. I remember this man John saying something about the old man's will. That's why I thought he was his son. But it was then I heard the twang. It was only one or two words, but I suppose I was a bit more attuned to it than most, with my husband coming from there. Funny – I never thought about that before.'

'And you definitely think his name was John?'

'Oh yes, dear. No doubt about that. Now, more tea?'

*   *   *

Even though I said I'd pick Alex up she still looks surprised to actually see me. She works in that building you can see from the ring road. The one with the spiky thing on the roof. One of the wags in the station calls it Minas Morgul. Leering down the Botley Road in mockery of the spires. It has a great view, though. And an extensive car park. Which is where I'm sat, watching the door.

She comes out with two other people I don't recognize. A woman in her thirties in a green suit, and a man, closer to Alex's age. Tall. Dark. Not unlike me. The woman in green talks to them a moment then heads off to her car. Alex and the man linger. It's not chit-chat, I can tell that. Her face is earnest, his thoughtful. Their heads are a tiny bit closer together than they need to be. He gestures with his hands a lot. He's establishing himself – his status, his expertise. In this job, you get good at body language. At assessing people with the sound on mute.

I watch as they part. He doesn't touch her. But, then again, she knows I'm watching. Perhaps he does too.

'Who was that?' I say as she opens the car door and gets in.

She glances across at me, then turns to find her seat belt. 'David Jenkins. He's in the Family team.'

'It looked pretty intense, whatever it was.'

She gives me that 'don't tell me you're jealous' look. 'I was just asking his advice, that's all.'

I'm not sure that's any better. But like Gis, I know when to stop digging.

We pull out into the traffic and I head for the ring road.

'Do you mind if we stop off at the John Rad? I want to look in on the girl.'

'OK, no problem. I didn't think you'd be here this early anyway.'

'I wouldn't be, if we'd made any progress. If there was something useful I could be doing instead.'

She looks across, then away again at the fields.

'Sorry. That didn't come out the way I meant.'

She waves her hand in dismissal, but she doesn't turn her head. She knows when to drop it, too.

When we get to the hospital, she surprises me by deciding to come in.

'Are you sure? I know how much you hate hospitals.'

'It's still better than twiddling my thumbs out here.'

On the third floor, I'm met by Everett and a doctor who looks like he's straight out of *Casualty*. Or whatever they call that thing these days.

'Titus Jackson,' he says, shaking my hand. 'I'm afraid I can't tell you much more than I've already told DC Everett. The young woman has definitely given birth but shows no signs of recent sexual violence – no vaginal or other bruising.'

'Is she still sedated?'

'No. But she hasn't yet said anything.'

'Can I see her?'

He hesitates. 'Only for a few minutes, and only one at a time, please. She's in a very fragile state, mentally. She becomes extremely distressed when anyone gets too close, especially men, so please bear that in mind.'

'I have dealt with rape victims before.'

'I don't doubt you have, but this is rather more than just that.'

I nod; I know he's right. 'And the child?'

'My colleagues in Paediatrics carried out another examination as you requested and there's nothing to suggest sexual abuse. But I'm sure I don't need to tell you that some of the things those people do to children don't leave physical signs.'

'You're right. You don't need to tell me.'

I turn to Alex.

'It's fine,' she says, anticipating me. 'I'll wait here.'

'I can show you the waiting room,' says Everett. 'It's just along the corridor.'

When I get to the girl's room I do what everyone else must have done. I stop at the window and I look at her. And then I feel ashamed. Like a voyeur. And I wonder how she feels about being here. Whether these four walls are just another type of prison – it's caring, this time, but it's still confinement. Her eyes are open, but though the room looks out on trees and grass and green things she can't have seen for God knows how long, she's staring at the ceiling. At the blank repeating tiles.

I knock on the door and she starts, sitting up quickly in the bed. I open the door slowly and step inside, but I take care not to move any closer. All the while her eyes follow me.

'I'm a police officer. My name is Adam.'

There's some sort of reaction to that, but I'm not sure I could define what.

'I think you saw my colleague. DC Everett. Verity.'

Definitely a reaction now.

'We're all really concerned about you. You've had a terrible time.'

Her lip trembles and she clutches at the blanket.

I reach into my jacket and pull out a piece of paper.

'I know you haven't said anything about it, and perhaps you can't. That's OK. I understand. But I was wondering if perhaps you could write it down? Anything you remember – anything that might help us?'

She's staring at me, but she's not frightened. At least I don't think so. I take a pen from my pocket and move slowly towards the bed, ready to retreat if she reacts. But she doesn't flinch, she just watches.

I place the paper and pen slowly on the bedside table, perhaps a foot from her hand, then back off to the door.

It's another five minutes before she touches them. Five minutes of silent patience on my part, which is not a talent of mine, but I can do it if the stakes are high enough. And this time, they are.

She puts out a hand and pulls the paper towards her. Then the pen. And then, as if it's a task she doesn't do often and has lost the knack for, she takes it in her hand and writes. It's slow but it can't be much more than a word. Then she holds out the paper to me, and I can see the strain in her eyes. The tears only just suppressed.

Five letters.

Vicky

When I go back down the corridor, Everett is waiting. I can see her react to the look on my face.

'Did she say something?'

'No,' I reply, showing her the paper. 'But we have a name.'

'Is that all — nothing else?'

I'm about to say that it's still a bloody sight more than she's managed to get so far. But I stop myself just in time, and then I'm irritated that I'm irritated. It's hardly Ev's fault, after all.

'Afraid not. I asked, but she was starting to get distressed. And then that doctor friend of yours arrived and kicked me out. Nicely, of course.'

I might be mistaken, but I think she's actually blushing.

'Look, I'm on my way home, but can you get on to Baxter and ask him to check Missing Persons for girls called Vicky?' I look around. 'And do you happen to know where my wife is?'

'She went downstairs. She wanted to see the little boy.'

It's not just Alex who hates hospitals. I remember bringing Jake here when he fell off a swing in the playground and got a bump on his forehead the size of an egg. He must have been three. Perhaps four. We sat in A&E for an hour while every conceivable catastrophic brain-damage scenario spun through my head, and then a brisk, overworked nurse took one look at him, gave him some Calpol and sent us home.

The bump went pretty quickly; the memory of the panic didn't. And later, much later, after he started hurting himself, we came here again. When we had to. Enduring the sideways glances from nurses, and the doctors taking us aside, and the explanations, and the calls to the GP to check that we weren't lying — that she knew all about it and it was under control. As if something so terrible could ever be 'under control'. And all the time, Jake's white face, his anxious eyes.

'I'm sorry, Daddy.'

'It's OK,' Alex would whisper, rocking him gently, kissing his hair, 'it's OK.'

I think, afterwards, that this explains it. That memory in my head as I push open the door to the children's ward and round the corner into the room.

The way she's holding him.

The dark hair.

His body curled into hers.

The tenderness.

I don't know how long it is I stand there. Long enough for the nurse to join me, in silence, and watch.

'It's like a miracle,' she says softly, after a long moment.

I turn to her. I know it's not Jake. Of course it isn't. *I know that*. But for a moment — just a moment —

'He just went to her, straight away. With everyone else, he screams and fights like you wouldn't believe. But with your wife — well, you can see for yourself.'

My eyes meet Alex's and she smiles, her hand slowly stroking the boy's long dark curls.

'It's OK,' she whispers, 'it's OK.'

And I don't know if it's the boy she's talking to. Or me.

* * *

The world of wyrd

(from the Anglo-Saxon 'wyrd' meaning fate or doom)

A Blog about the spooky, the paranormal and the unexplained

POSTED 03/05/17

Death and the raven – the Wittenham riddle deepens

Many of you will remember the strange case of the disappearance of Hannah Gardiner, back in 2015. If not you can read my original post here. It struck me at the time, because Hannah had broken the news of the discovery of sacrificial remains at Wittenham only a few months before. And then she disappears herself, and her little boy and his stuffed bird (note that) were discovered in the Money Pit, where legend has it that a huge raven guards a mysterious treasure (note that too – I'll come back to it). For those of you who haven't been there, Wittenham is an amazing place – criss-crossed by ley lines, and you can almost feel the presence of ancestral voices. So personally I'm not surprised at all that human sacrifice took place there, including women who had been tied up and thrown into the pit, and then had the backs of their skulls beaten in.

The reason to bring all this up again now is that my sources tell me there are some truly spooky similarities between those ancient corpses, and the position Hannah's own body was found in. Word is that Hannah was tied up too, and died of a *head wound to the back of the skull.* Creepy, eh? There was even a *dead black bird near the corpse.* Coincidence? Don't you believe it. The police aren't confirming anything, but well, they wouldn't would they?

So what is all this about ravens, I hear you say. Well, the fearsome Irish goddess Morrígan is closely associated with crows and ravens, especially in her role as prophet of doom and violent death (read my post on her here, and you can see her here in her other incarnation, as 'the three Morrígna' – the three terrifying sisters Badb ('crow'), Macha and Nemain). Anyone who knows anything about Celtic religion will also know that ravens had a central role in ritual practice. Raven calls were thought to bring messages from the underworld, and they were often killed as propitiatory offerings to the gods, especially to ensure fertility. Ravens have also been found in Dark Age human burial pits – there were bird skeletons in those graves at Wittenham too. So who knows what old gods Hannah Gardiner disturbed when she was up there in the weeks before she died, and the sacrificial graves were desecrated. Who knows what she might have seen and why she needed to be silenced. Only her son can tell us and, to this day, his father has never allowed him to be interviewed.

I suspect we'll hear more of this story in the next few days. Watch this space, guys . . .

@WorldofWyrdBlog

Leave a comment here

* * *

'It would only be for a few days.'

'No. *Absolutely not*. It's an insane idea, Alex — you know it is. I don't know why you're even considering it.'

But I do, of course I do. She looks at me, caught between fury and pleading.

'Adam, he's just a little boy. A terrified, lonely, overwhelmed little boy. He's been through the most appalling experience which we don't even know the worst of yet, and his *own mother's* rejecting him. Is it any wonder he's not coping — years in the dark and now' — she gestures around, at the ward, the trolleys, the people — 'all *this*. He just needs a couple of days of peace and quiet in a safe place. Away from all this sensory overload.'

'That's what Social Services are *for* — it's not up to us, for God's sake. For all you know, they've already got somewhere lined up.'

'They haven't. The nurses told me. They're really struggling because there are too many children and not enough people willing to take them. And it's only an emergency placement — just *a few days* —'

'Even if that's true they're not going to hand him over to any Tom, Dick or Harry who happens to be passing — there are regulations — rules — you need to be approved. That sort of thing can take months —'

She raises a hand. 'I spoke to Emma. She says it's not exactly by the book, but she could make an exception for us. With you being a police officer and her knowing me for so long, she could log it as what they call a "private placement" — because it would just be for *a couple of days*. And I know your parents are coming over soon but he probably won't even be there by then and even if he is they would understand — I know they would.'

She's pleading now, and she knows I won't be able to bear that. Any more than she can bear to do it.

'What about work — I'd have to get it cleared for a start

and I can't see Harrison agreeing. And even if he did, I can't take time off – not at the moment – you know I can't –'

'I can,' she says quickly. 'I haven't got much on and I can work from home. Just like I used to before.'

When we had Jake.

The words boom silently in the air.

'We have that lovely room,' she says quietly, not looking at me. 'Everything he could need.'

But that just makes it worse. The thought of another child in Jake's bed. With Jake's things.

I swallow hard.

'I don't want to. I'm sorry, but I just don't want to. Please don't push this.'

She puts her hand on my arm and forces me to turn and look at the child. He's sitting under the table in the corner of the playroom, staring at me, his thumb in his mouth. Just like Jake did. It's unbearable.

Alex comes closer. I can feel the heat from her body. 'Please, Adam,' she whispers. 'If not for him, for me?'

*   *   *

Quinn opens his eyes and stares at the ceiling, then rolls over and slides his hand down Erica Somer's naked back. He always did think she had a great arse. She twists her head to look at him and he smiles. She looks fantastically dishevelled and he starts to feel horny all over again. It's something about the contrast between how controlled she is in uniform and how uninhibited out of it. Not to mention the immense pleasure in getting her from the one state to the other . . .

'I meant to ask,' she says, propping herself up on one elbow. 'Was it you or Gislingham who talked to that academic in Birmingham?'

Quinn runs a finger down her spine. Right now, frankly, the case can go fuck itself. He tries to roll her over but she pushes him away.

'No, seriously, I meant to ask you earlier but it slipped my mind.'

'Really, it can wait –'

'No – it's important – was it you or Gis?'

Quinn gives up and flops on his back.

'It was Gis. Said the bloke was a real arsehole.'

'But wasn't there something about Harper's first wife coming from Birmingham?'

'Yeah, that rings a bell. Why?'

'Mrs Gibson – at number seven. She said she thought the bloke who visited Harper had a bit of a Birmingham accent. So I was wondering – even if she's wrong about him being Harper's son, perhaps he was still related. But to the wife, rather than Harper? A nephew, perhaps, something like that?'

Quinn levers himself up. 'Actually, you might have a point there. Have a look first thing – if she had any male relatives the right age it won't take that long to find them.'

'You want me to do it? You don't want to get Gis on it instead?'

He reaches out and takes a lock of her hair in his fingers, twirling it round, gently at first, then gradually tighter, pulling her face towards him.

'No,' he says, his voice dropping. 'It's your idea – why shouldn't you get the credit. But there is something I would like you to do for me. And this is definitely not one for bloody Gislingham.'

'Well,' she says archly as she slips her hand under the sheets, 'if that's an order from a superior officer . . .'

'Oh yes,' he says gruffly, feeling her tongue on his skin, 'abso-fucking-lutely.'

* * *

Midnight. A pool of yellow light and the low murmur of voices at the nurses' station.

Vicky is curled up tight in her bed. She is sobbing her heart out, her fist clenched against her mouth so that she makes no noise. And all the while, her eyes never leave the picture one of the nurses has propped on the bedside cupboard.

It's a photo of her son.

* * *

I get in early on Thursday morning, but when I get to the incident room Quinn's already there, pinning up the task list. And whistling. I look daggers at him until he stops.

'Sorry, boss. Just in a good mood, that's all.'

I haven't worked with him all these months without knowing what that means. But at least he isn't in yesterday's shirt. Whoever she is, this one's getting invited back to his place.

'The press conference is at noon,' I say, 'so if there's anything I can tell them beyond fatuous remarks about enquiries progressing then I want to know about it, pronto. Especially the DNA. What about Harper?'

'Being monitored every fifteen minutes. Custody sergeant says he sleeps most of the time. Or he just sits there, mumbling to himself. We spoke to his doctor and she's offered to come in this afternoon, just to be on the safe side.'

'Right. Good. I'm heading back to the hospital again to talk to the girl. If we're lucky, she may be up to telling us what happened. Or at the very least identifying Harper. And then we'll be able to charge him. Has Baxter found anything in Missing Persons?'

'Not yet. But it all depends whether she was ever –'

'– reported missing. Yes. I do know that, Quinn. Anything else?'

'A couple of possibilities but nothing concrete. I'll let you know. You'll be back here, will you, after you've seen the girl?'

'Actually, no. I may have to go home briefly.'

He's looking at me; he knows there's something.

'The boy – he may be staying with us for a while. Just until Vicky's back on her feet. Social Services are struggling to find him a placement.'

Back on her feet? What sort of crap phrase is that?

Quinn is staring at me. 'And your wife, she's OK with that?'

'Actually, she suggested it. She was with me last night at the John Rad, and the boy really took to her. I cleared it with Harrison – he thinks it might be useful. If the boy starts to trust Alex, perhaps he might talk to her. Assuming he can.'

Fawley's first law of policing? Liars overkill. And I just gave Quinn three reasons why I think this is a good idea.

Shit.

'Right,' says Quinn, deciding – for once – that discretion is the better course.

'Assuming it all goes ahead I'll go back to the house and get him settled in, and then I'll be back by twelve. So you pick things up in the meantime, OK?'

He nods. 'Right, boss. No problem.'

* * *

Phone interview with Sergeant Jim Nicholls (retired)

4 May 2017, 9.12 a.m.

On the call, DS G. Quinn

JN: I was after Adam Fawley, but the switchboard
     said he isn't in?

GQ: Don't worry, you can talk to me - I know what
     it's about.

JN: Something about those call-outs in
     Frampton Road, wasn't it - about ten years
     back?

GQ: Actually one in 2002, and one in 2004.

JN: Christ, is it really that long? Suppose it
     must be. I've been retired at least five now.
     Can't remember the last time I spoke to anyone
     at Thames Valley.

GQ: What do you remember about the call-outs?
     There isn't much in the notes. Certainly no
     mention of charges.

JN: There never were any. Neither of them wanted
     that. And yes, I do remember it - it wasn't
     your usual domestic. Not by a long way.

GQ: Go on.

JN: Well, it was the address for a start. Frampton
     Road. I mean, it's not exactly Blackbird Leys,
     is it? Don't think I can remember anyone being
     called to a domestic round there, the whole
     time I was on the force.

GQ: I don't know, that sort are probably just a
     bit subtler about it, that's all.

JN: But it wasn't just that. It was what we found
     when we got there. The neighbour who called
     said they'd been yelling on and off all
     evening but once it got past midnight she
     finally rang us.

GQ: And?

JN: It was the wife who opened the door. I don't
     know about you but when I was on the job it
     was usually the blokes did that - most of them
     tried to get rid of us without letting us in.
     Pretended it was all a fuss about nothing. You
     know the drill. Anyway, not this time. She
     looked a bit flushed but otherwise OK. Had this
     silky negligee thing on. Quite a looker
     actually.

GQ: So what did she say?

JN: Well, she came over all embarrassed and said
     it must be that she and her husband had been a
     bit more 'exuberant' than usual in the bedroom
     department. Said the old lady next door was a
     bit of a prude and easily shocked. Batted her
     eyelashes a bit.

GQ: What did the husband say?

JN: That's where it got interesting. I was all for
     letting it go at that but the WPC - or
     whatever we're supposed to call them now - she
     insisted on seeing him as well. So Mrs Harper,
     she goes back in and then there's a bit of a
     wait, and finally he appears. Face all bruised
     down one side and the beginnings of one hell
     of a black eye.

GQ: So *she* had been hitting *him*?

JN: He didn't say so. In fact, he said he'd
     walked into a door that afternoon. As if we
     were going to believe that. And he claimed
     the noise was exactly what the wife said it
     was. Basically backed up her story 100 per
     cent. Even used some of the same words. That

stuff about the neighbour being a bit of a
prude.

GQ: But you didn't believe him?

JN: Course not. I didn't come down in the last
shower of rain. I didn't believe a word of it.
Not then, and certainly not when the same
thing happened a year or so later. Said he'd
slipped on the stairs that time, but you don't
get the sort of bruises he had by doing that.
I reckon she'd gone for him with something. A
frying pan, maybe.

GQ: Or a hammer?

JN: It wasn't the first thing that came to mind.
What makes you say that?

GQ: Nothing. Forget it. So he never explicitly said
his wife was attacking him?

JN: Nope. I made sure I got him on his own the
second time, just to give him the chance to
talk to me without her earwigging, but he just
kept up all the same nonsense about it being
over-vigorous rumpy-pumpy. He actually used
that word. Rumpy-pumpy.

GQ: Jesus.

JN: To be honest I felt sorry for the poor old
bastard. I mean, she was a sexy bit of stuff
all right, but Christ, I wouldn't have touched
her with a barge pole. I think she was
screwing around too. That car accident? I
remember that happening — Priscilla's not the
sort of name you forget. And yes, she was way
over the limit, but what you might not know is
there was another bloke in the car and it was

pretty obvious what they'd been doing. Her knickers were under the back seat. Still, the worm's turned now.

GQ: I'm sorry?

JN: I saw the news. It's the same Harper, isn't it - the bloke with the girl in the cellar? Must be.

GQ: Yes, it's the same. We're just trying to fill in the gaps.

JN: Perhaps he just thinks it's his turn.

GQ: His *turn*?

JN: You know. Revenge. He can't take it out on his wife any more so he takes it out on women in general. Not that I want to interfere, of course.

GQ: [*pause*]
    No. That's been really useful. Thanks.

JN: Always happy to help. Say hello to Fawley for me, won't you? By the way, how's that boy of his - Jake? Fawley used to spoil him rotten but you could hardly blame him - not when they'd been trying for one as long as they had. Gorgeous kid, too. Looked just like his mother.

* * *

'How is Vicky this morning?'

Titus Jackson tucks his pen into the pocket of his white coat.

'Progress is slow, Inspector, but at least we're not going backwards. I assume you want to see her again?'

'There's only so long we can hold William Harper before

we charge him. I need to be sure what happened before I do that.'

'I understand.'

He walks with me down the corridor, and when we reach the door he stops and turns to me, something clearly on his mind.

'Nurse Kingsley said you and your wife may be fostering the little boy?'

'It's not "fostering".'

I suspect I may have said that a bit too quickly, because I see his frown deepen a little.

'Just giving him somewhere to sleep for a few days. Social Services are struggling.'

'It's very kind of you.'

'It's not me, it's my –' I stop, but it's too late.

He considers me. 'You're not so sure, yourself?'

I take a deep breath. 'No. If I'm really honest.' I look him in the eyes. He has kind eyes. 'Just over a year ago, we lost our own son. He was ten. He took his own life. He'd been suffering from depression. We did everything we could – but –'

There's a stone in my throat.

Jackson reaches out and touches my arm, just for a moment. 'I am more sorry than I can say.'

I force myself to speak. 'It's been really hard on my wife – well, both of us. But especially her. She wants another child but, you know, at her age –'

He nods. 'I see.'

'She's been pressuring me to think about adoption, but I'm just not sure. And now there's this little boy who has nowhere to go –'

He watches me, quietly. Not judging. 'And you have discussed it all – you and your wife?'

'Last night, when we got home, all she wanted to talk about was plans and arrangements. Every time I raised anything else all she kept on saying was it was just for a few days. That he'd be going back to his mother before we knew it.'

'Let's hope that's true.'

'Why, don't you think so?'

'Vicky is making progress, but it's slow, and we have to think of the child as well. We brought him up to see her again yesterday but she just turned her face to the wall.'

'The officers who found them said they thought she'd been giving the food and water to the boy rather than having it herself – surely that must mean something?'

He shakes his head sadly. 'Not wanting him to die is one thing; having normal maternal feelings for him is something else altogether. There's a barrier between her and that child, Inspector. Not a bond. You don't need to be a psychiatrist to work out why.'

He reaches for the door handle. 'Shall we go in?'

This time, she definitely recognizes me. She sits up in the bed and there's the shadow of a smile.

'How are you, Vicky?'

Half a nod.

'There are some questions I'd like to ask, and some things I need to tell you. Is that OK?'

She hesitates, then lifts her hand towards the chair.

I move forward slowly and sit down. She shrinks back in the bed, but only a little.

'Are you able to tell us what happened to you?'

She looks away from me and shakes her head.

'OK, that's fine. I understand. But if you remember anything, you can just write it down for me like you did last night. OK?'

She looks at me again.

'The other thing I wanted to tell you is that we're going to put a picture of you in the newspapers. There must be some-one out there who knows you – someone who loves you and has probably been looking for you all this time. There's been stories about you all over the papers and the internet –'

I stop because I have to – because her eyes are wide and she's shaking her head, and then as Jackson starts forward she seizes the paper I brought and gouges it in huge violent strag-gling letters.

NO NO NO

* * *

BBC News

Thursday 4 May 2017 | Last updated at 11:34

BREAKING: New appeal for witnesses in Hannah Gardiner disappearance

Thames Valley Police have issued a new appeal for witnesses in relation to the disappearance of Hannah Gardiner in June 2015. Hannah was previously thought to have disappeared on Wittenham Clumps on the morning of 24 June, but police are now asking for anyone who saw her in Oxford that morning to come forward, especially anyone who saw her near her flat in Crescent Square, or talking to anyone in that area. This would appear to corroborate local reports that Hannah's body was found in the garden of a Frampton Road house yesterday morning.

They have also asked any young women who were walking with a child in a buggy at Wittenham Clumps that morning to make themselves known to the police, if they have not done so already.

Thames Valley has still not released the identity of the young woman and small boy found in the cellar at the same Frampton Road property. A press conference is scheduled for later today.

Anyone with information about either case should contact the Thames Valley Police incident room on 01865 0966552.

* * *

'All ready, then?'

I'm really hating the sound of my own voice. The false brightness. It's that tone nurses use when they ask you to 'pop on' a hospital gown or 'slip off' your trousers. I can't believe Alex isn't giving me one of her looks but it's the measure of her absorption in the child that she doesn't appear to notice.

The boy is standing between us, his arm round her leg, and in the other hand, the grimy toy they said he had with him in the cellar. The one he won't let go. He's wearing clothes I recognize. Clothes Alex must have kept, all these years. I don't really want to think about that. He twists his head to look up at her and she reaches down a hand to caress his hair.

'We've got everything we need, so yes, I think we're ready.' Her voice sounds as strained as mine. But for a different reason. She is brittle with happiness.

I reach out a hand to the boy, but he shrinks back and Alex says quickly, 'It's OK. He just needs a bit of space.'

She crouches down. 'I'm going to carry you – is that OK?'

Apparently it is, because he offers no resistance, and the three of us make our way out to the car, where she straps him into the car seat I didn't think we still had.

I was expecting him to react to the sound of the engine, but he seems remarkably unperturbed. As we pull out into the traffic I try to think of something to say. But Alex gets there first.

'I wish I knew what to call him,' she says. 'We can't call him "boy" or "child" all week.'

I shrug. 'Hopefully Vicky will be able to speak to us in the next day or two. She'll tell us his name.'

'If she actually *gave* him one,' says Alex, turning to look at the boy in the back. 'If she's so traumatized that she's blocking the whole thing out, she may never have bonded with him at all. Giving a child a name, it's all part of that – it's how you signal your relationship. I think she's in deep denial that he's even hers. And, frankly, who can blame her – it must be tough, trying to love the child of your rapist –'

'We don't know that's what happened, Alex. Not definitively. You're a lawyer. You know better than to jump to those sorts of conclusions.'

It wasn't meant to sound patronizing, but it does. Her eyes lock with mine a moment, but she's the first to look away.

We grind to a halt as the traffic narrows to one lane. The roadworks on this stretch seem to have been going on for months.

'You said "all week".'

'Sorry?' she says.

'Just now, you said we couldn't call him "boy" all week. I thought it was just going to be for a few days.'

She's not looking at me. 'It will be. Probably. But with your parents coming —'

'That's *next month* —'

'I think we should warn them, just in case.'

'Warn?'

'Don't be difficult, Adam. You know very well what I mean.'

I do. I just wish I didn't.

*   *   *

'In the case of the young woman and child found in the cellar, all I can say at this stage is that enquiries are progressing.'

The press conference is packed and my general level of stress and irritation hasn't been helped by the fact that I forgot we were holding this at the Kidlington media centre and only got here with ten minutes to spare. I look down the rows of faces and see a lot I don't recognize. The nationals, no doubt; we haven't had this much media interest since the Daisy Mason case. That was hardly surprising — an eight-year-old girl abducted from her own garden. But right now, the wheels are going round but I've run out of road. One of the hacks in the front row is muttering that he doesn't know why we bothered getting them in here at all if that's all we've got to tell them.

'What about DNA?' asks a woman at the back. 'I can't believe you still haven't established who the father of that child is. I thought you could get results in a few hours these days?'

'Testing has improved, certainly, but it still takes time. And DNA will only be able to tell us so much. We need to talk to the young woman herself, and she's still not able to speak to us. I'm sure you can appreciate that she's in a very distressed state.'

'Have you got a pic yet?' asks the man from the *Oxford Mail*. 'The neighbours said you had one – that you were showing it to people and asking if anyone recognized her.'

'We're not releasing a photo at this time.'

'Well, what about a bleeding name then? A shot of the kid? Something – *any*thing?'

'The investigation is at a critical stage. I'm sure you can appreciate –'

'Yeah, yeah. I've heard it all before.'

'OK,' says the woman at the back. 'What about this new appeal for witnesses in the Hannah Gardiner case? That means you're linking the two, right?'

I open my mouth then close it again. What bloody appeal for witnesses?

'If it's slipped your mind, Inspector,' she says, 'I have the statement here.' She smiles at me then scrolls down her tablet. '"*Thames Valley Police are appealing for anyone who saw Hannah Gardiner on the morning of 24 June 2015, in the vicinity of Crescent Square, Oxford, to contact the incident room at St Aldate's police station, especially if they saw her talking to anyone in the area.*" Etc., etc., etc.' She holds the tablet up. 'This *is* from your team, I take it?'

'Yes –'

'So you *are* linking the cases. That means the body you found in that garden must be Hannah's and that man Harper must be suspected of killing her. That's right, isn't it? I mean, I'm not missing something blindingly obvious here?'

'I'm not in a position to comment –'

'I read somewhere,' says the old lag at the front, 'that there was a dead raven buried with the body – some sort of pagan ritual thing. Care to comment, Inspector? Or is that something else you're "not releasing"?'

'Yes, I will happily comment on that. There has never been any connection whatsoever between satanism or paganism and the Hannah Gardiner case, and there isn't one now.'

'So was there a sodding bird or wasn't there?'

The woman interrupts him. 'So you *are* reopening the case,' she says quickly. 'We can quote you on that?'

'We're not reopening it because it was never closed –'

'I'll take that as a *yes* then.'

'– and at this stage of the investigation we are not able to say any more than I've told you already. We owe it to the families of the victims –'

'What about the family of the wrongly accused? What do you owe them, Detective Inspector Fawley?'

The voice comes from somewhere at the back. People turn to look as he gets to his feet, and a buzz starts as they recognize him.

Matthew Shore.

How the hell did he get in here?

'So, do you have an answer for me? I mean, you were on the Hannah Gardiner case, weren't you?'

'This is a press conference, Mr Shore.'

'And I'm a member of the press.' He holds up a pass. 'Look, it says so, right here. So I say again – and I think that's the third time, incidentally – what about my father? What about a man you victimized and harassed, even though you had no evidence –'

I can feel Harrison's stress levels rising; this is going out live on the BBC news channel, and the bloke from Sky has his phone out videoing it.

'Look, Mr Shore, this is neither the time nor the place.'

'So when exactly *is* the right bloody time and place? I've

been trying to talk to Thames Valley Police for months – all I get is the brush-off.'

'We never charged your father in relation to the Hannah Gardiner case. The sentence he served was for an entirely different offence.'

'Yeah, but he'd never have even been convicted if his face hadn't been all over the bloody papers for months, never mind getting three sodding years – there's no way that was a fair trial –'

Harrison clears his throat. 'That's not something we can comment on, Mr Shore. You will have to take it up with the Crown Prosecution Service.'

'And you think I haven't?' he says, sardonic. 'They're no better than you. There's no justice in this bloody country – no bloody accountability. You all just clear up each other's mess –'

Harrison gets to his feet. 'Thank you very much, ladies and gentlemen. Further statements will be issued as appropriate. Good afternoon.'

The first person I see outside is Quinn. He must have been at the back. He makes a face. 'I'd like to know how Shore got in. I'll get Gis on it.'

'What *I'd* like to know is who the fuck issued that appeal for witnesses? Was it you?'

He hesitates, clearly trying to decide whether to balls it out or fess up.

'The hacks were going to link the cases whatever we did so I thought it was worth seeing if all this new publicity jogged someone's memory –'

Which is actually a very good point. Not that I'm in the mood to say so.

'Even though you know I promised Gardiner he would have time to warn Hannah's parents? Even though you know damn well you should check something like that with me first?'

'But you said –'

'I said to keep an eye on things –'

'You actually said "pick things up" –'

'– I did *not* say make significant decisions without asking me. I was only at the John Rad, for fuck's sake, not the bloody moon – you could have called – texted.'

He's gone very red now, and I realize – too late – that Gislingham is standing a few yards away. I shouldn't bollock Quinn in front of lower ranks. You just don't.

'I thought,' says Quinn, lowering his voice, 'that you'd prefer me not to disturb you. What with the kid and your wife and everything.'

And everything.

You're already thinking 'classic transference', and you're not wrong. But knowing it and doing something about it aren't the same. And now – not for the first time – I wonder whether my real problem with Quinn is that he's too much like me. Apart from the flashy dress sense and the serial shagging, of course.

'OK,' I say eventually. 'Go and see Gardiner and apologize.'

'Can't I just call him?'

'No. You can't. And get Challow moving on those bloody DNA results.' And then I take a deep breath and turn round. 'What do you want, Gislingham?'

He looks embarrassed. 'Sorry to barge in, boss, but the incident room has just taken a call after the news broadcast. It was from Beth Dyer.'

*   *   *

Quinn was right; it doesn't take long. By lunchtime, Erica
Somer has tracked down both a nephew and a niece of the
first Mrs William Harper. But when she goes to the incident
room to look for Quinn, what she finds is Fawley. He's
standing staring at the pinboard. The photos. The map. The
images of the two young women and the two young boys.
The living and the dead. He seems lost in thought. Absent.

'Sorry, sir,' she says, still slightly unsure around him. 'I
was looking for the DS –'

He turns to look at her, but it's a few seconds, she can tell,
before he actually registers who she is.

'PC Somer.'

'Yes, sir.'

It's not something she could ever tell Quinn, but Fawley
is far and away the best-looking man in the station. The fact
that he seems entirely unaware of it only adds to the attrac-
tion. Quinn's exactly the opposite – he operates with some
sort of bat-like sex echo system, constantly sending out sig-
nals and seeing how they bounce back. Fawley, on the other
hand, is entirely self-contained. She doesn't have Quinn's
level of self-confidence but she usually gets some sort of
reaction from men. Not from this one though.

'I was thinking about Vicky,' he says. 'About what sort of
family she must have come from that she doesn't want them
to know she's OK.'

'She may have run away from home. Which could be why
no one reported her missing.'

He turns to stare at the girl's photo again. 'You're probably right.' Then he turns back. 'Sorry, you didn't come here
to listen to me thinking aloud. What was it?'

She holds up a piece of paper. A print-out.

'Last night,' she says, 'I suddenly had this hunch. If Harper's first wife came from Birmingham then she might still have family there. And if the "John" Mrs Gibson thought was Harper's son also had a Birmingham accent –'

He's there already. 'Then it might be a relative of the wife.'

'Right, sir. So I checked and it could be.' She hands him the paper. 'Nancy Harper had a niece and a nephew. The niece, Noreen, is a doctor's receptionist and lives in Berwick. But the nephew, Donald Walsh, teaches history at a small private school in Banbury. He's fifty-three. I'm trying to get a picture but on the face of it he fits the description.'

Fawley looks at the print-out. 'This is good work, Somer. So your theory is it wasn't John, but Don?'

'I think so, sir. It would be easy for Mrs Gibson to have heard the name wrong. I don't think her hearing is all that great.'

'So do you have an address for this Donald Walsh?'

'Yes, sir. I've tried calling, but no answer. I think someone should go up there – given it's so close. Even if he's away, we may find out something from the neighbours. How often he comes to Oxford. If he and Harper are in touch.'

'And that's why you were looking for DS Quinn? To get that arranged?'

She wills herself not to blush, but she's not sure if it works. 'Yes, sir. So he can organize someone.'

'Well, he's not going to be back for an hour or so. And DC Everett's still at the hospital, so why don't you find DC Gislingham and tell him I've OK'd it.'

'What, you mean, *I* should go?'

He looks just a tiny bit irritated now. 'With Gislingham, yes. There isn't a problem, is there?'

'No, sir.'

'Good. Let me know what you find out.'

*   *   *

Phone interview with Beth Dyer
4 May 2017, 2.12 p.m.
On the call, DC A. Baxter

AB: Miss Dyer, it's DC Andrew Baxter, Thames
    Valley. I believe you called the station after
    the press conference?

BD: Oh yes. Thanks for getting back to me.

AB: Did you have something to tell us?

BD: Yes. It's, well, it's a bit difficult.

AB: If it helps, we'll do our best to keep what
    you tell us confidential. But that rather
    depends on what it is you have to say.

BD: That policeman on the TV, Detective Inspector
    Fawley. He said that the body you found was
    Hannah.

AB: I don't believe that's yet been officially
    confirmed –

BD: But it's her, isn't it?

AB: [*pause*]
    Yes, Miss Dyer. We believe so. Mr Gardiner has
    been informed.

BD: How did he take it?

AB: I'm not able to discuss that, Miss Dyer. Was
    there anything else?

BD: Sorry, that must have sounded awful. I'm a
    bit all over the place right now. It's

just that - well, that's why I called. It was
about Rob.

AB: I see. I believe that when Mrs Gardiner
first went missing you told us you
thought her husband might be having an
affair?

BD: Yes, I did. But it's not about that. Well, not
directly.

AB: So was he having an affair or wasn't he?

BD: I don't think he was. Not then. But it started
pretty soon after. That childminder - nanny.
Whatever it is she calls herself. Pippa
something. I saw them with Toby about three
weeks ago in Summertown. I reckon they're
definitely an item - she was all over him. Men
can be so gullible.

AB: And how does this relate to the disappearance
of Mrs Gardiner?

BD: I'm getting to that. When it all happened, you
said - the police - that she'd disappeared at
Wittenham. Only now you say she never left
Oxford at all.

AB: That does appear to be the case.

BD: So how did her car get there? How did Toby get
there?

AB: Well, clearly whoever was responsible for the
death of Mrs Gardiner must have taken the car
to Wittenham, knowing that was where she was
supposed to be that day. To make us think she
was there. As a decoy.

BD: But how many people knew that - that she was
supposed to be at Wittenham?

AB: She'd arranged to do an interview at the site.
     There was a BBC crew. A number of people must
     have known.

BD: But this man Harper. At Frampton Road. The one
     you think killed her. How did he know?

AB: I'm afraid I'm not able to comment on the
     current investigation.

BD: But Rob knew, didn't he? He knew where she was
     going. And it'd make more sense that Toby was
     there, if it was Rob.

AB: I'm not quite sure what you're trying to tell
     me, Miss Dyer. Are you suggesting that Mr
     Gardiner killed his wife and abandoned his
     two-year-old son alone up there -?

BD: [becoming agitated]
     Look, there's something I didn't tell you at
     the time. A couple of weeks before it happened
     I saw Hannah. She had a mark on her face. A
     bruise. She had make-up on it but I could
     still see.

AB: Did you ask her how she got it?

BD: She said it was Toby. That he was getting to
     be a handful and had caught her face with a
     toy car by accident.

AB: Did that seem feasible to you?

BD: I suppose it could have happened like that.
     Toby was a bit hyperactive - I thought he
     might be ADHD but she told me I was being
     ridiculous. But she had definitely been
     preoccupied those last few weeks. I'm sure she
     was worried about something. And she was very
     guarded about Rob that day. I think they were

having problems. I do know she wanted another
child but he wasn't keen.

AB: Why didn't you tell us this two years ago,
Miss Dyer?

BD: The press kept saying that you had that other
suspect - the one who was at the camp. And there
were all those people who saw her there - so I
thought it couldn't be Rob. But when you
didn't charge that man, I thought -

AB: Yes?

BD: Well, to be honest I thought she might just
have left him. Rob, I mean. Made it look like
she was dead just to get away. So no one would
look for her. I saw a TV programme like that
once. One of those crime things. And her
parents live in Spain so I thought she might
have gone there.

AB: That strikes me as highly unlikely, Miss Dyer.
Abandoning her child. No passport, no
documents -

BD: I know. It sounds crazy.

AB: And wouldn't she have got in contact with you?
If not immediately, then some time later, when
the dust had settled?

BD: [pause]

AB: After all, you were her best friend, weren't
you? Or have I got that wrong?

BD: [silence]

AB: Miss Dyer?

BD: Look, if you must know, we didn't part on the
best of terms. That time I told you about - it
wasn't the last time I saw her. We had a row

after that. She claimed I was after Rob. That
I'd been flirting with him at her birthday
party.

AB: Was that true?

BD: *He* was flirting with *me*. Of course he told her
it was the other way round - well, he would,
wouldn't he. But it wasn't. And in any case
nothing *happened*. Even if he'd - even if -
[*pause*]
Look, I wouldn't have done that to Hannah. OK?

AB: I see.

BD: And all these years you never found a body. I
suppose I just wanted to believe that meant
she was alive somewhere. But now I can't.
Because now I know she's dead and I can't get
rid of the feeling that he had something to do
with it.

* * *

If there's one thing I loathe it's watching myself on TV.
Even now, after half a dozen appeals, I still can't stand it. So
when the rest of the team gather to watch the news I make
my excuses and head for the coffee shop on St Aldate's. It's
like the answer to one of those linear programming things I
was so crap at in school: large enough that you usually get a
seat, far enough from the main tourist drag that the big
chains haven't snapped it up. Which is why it amuses me,
momentarily, to see a snake of Chinese tourists coming
down the pavement towards me, following a woman holding high a bright red umbrella, marching confidently in entirely the wrong direction. Because whatever architectural

masterpiece they've been promised, they aren't going to find it down the Abingdon Road.

I'm at the counter when my phone goes. Challow.

'You want the news or the good news?'

I swear silently as I hand over a fiver to the barista; I'm not in the mood for Challow's mind games.

'Don't tell me. The DNA results.'

'Sorry. Still waiting.'

'So I assume that's the news, rather than the good news?'

'Can't you tell?'

'Look, just tell me, can't you.'

Challow laughs drily. 'Why don't you come and see for yourself?'

*   *   *

'Adam? Is that you?' The voice on the speaker is breaking up, but I recognize it straight away.

'Hold on a minute, Dad. I'm driving.'

I pull over to the side of the road and pick up the handset.

'I'm here. Is there something wrong?'

I can hear him huffing slightly. 'Why do you always assume there must be something wrong?'

'Sorry, it's just that —'

'We saw you on the news, your mother and I.'

'Oh, OK. Right.'

'You were very good.'

Somehow or other, he always rubs me up the wrong way.

'It's not some sort of "appearance", Dad — it's not about *me*.'

'I know that, Adam,' he replies. He sounds as tetchy as I do. 'What I *meant* was that you came over very well. Calm. Authoritative.'

And now I feel like a shit. As usual.

'I know you don't think we're proud of you, son, but we are. The police force wouldn't have been our first choice for you, but you've managed to make a creditable career of it.'

That's an evil little word – 'managed'. And then I tell myself that I'm imagining it – that I need to stop seizing on every possible negative inference. I'm not even sure he meant it that way.

'Look, Dad. It was great of you to call, but I have to go. I'm on my way to the lab.'

'Your mother says hello and she's looking forward to seeing you. And Alex, of course.'

And then the line goes dead.

*   *   *

As the day wears on the clouds gather and by mid-afternoon the sky is as dark as November. Slow summer rain patters in the trees in the centre of Crescent Square. Two squirrels chase each other across the grass.

In the flat, Pippa is curled up on the sofa, playing Candy Crush on her phone. She can hear Rob talking in the other room. It's Hannah's parents. She's never met them but she knows exactly what they're like. Gervase and Cassandra – even their names are up themselves.

The door to the study opens and Rob appears in the doorway. He's dressed for work, but perhaps she can change his mind. She stretches out her legs and flexes her bare feet.

'The office called,' he says, ignoring her. 'Some sort of crisis. I don't mind going in. It'll help take my mind off things.'

'How did it go – on the phone?'

A flicker of irritation at that. 'Well, what do you expect? It's hardly a social call, is it, "How's the weather, oh and by the way they found your daughter buried in some old pervert's shed."'

He walks over to pick up his car keys. 'I don't know what time I'll be back.'

'I need to talk to you.'

'Well, it'll have to wait,' he says, moving towards the door. 'I said I'd be there by four.'

'I'm pregnant.'

He turns. Looks at her. She still has the phone in her hand.

'You're pregnant.' His voice is dull. 'That's not possible.'

'Of course it's *possible*, Rob.' She flushes slightly. 'I kept wanting to tell you. There never seemed to be a good time.'

'You said you were on the pill.'

'I was. I am. Sometimes it happens. You do science – you should know.'

'That's right,' he says, his voice dangerously soft. 'I "do science". And that's how I know that that kid you're having isn't mine.'

'Of course it is – it has to be –'

'Why?' he says softly, coming towards her. 'Because you haven't slept with anyone else?'

'No,' she stammers, terrified now, 'of course I haven't.'

'You,' he says, standing over her, stabbing the air with each word, 'are *lying*.'

She flinches back at the violence in his voice. 'I don't understand.'

He smiles a horrible smile. 'No? Not worked it out yet? *I can't have children*. That clear enough for you?'

Her cheeks are bright red. She looks down at the phone – more to avoid looking at him than anything else – but it's the wrong thing to do. He reaches for it and hurls it across the room. Then he grabs her hard by the wrist and wrenches her to her feet. 'Look at me when I'm talking to you.'

His face is so close her skin is peppered with spit.

'You're hurting me –'

'So who was it? Whose brat are you trying to pass off as mine – some random student? The bloke who reads the meter? *Who?*'

He takes her by the shoulders and shakes her. 'Have you been doing it here – in *my flat*?'

'No – of course not – I wouldn't. It was only the once – it didn't mean anything –'

He laughs. Nastily. 'Yeah, right.'

'I don't love him – I love *you* –'

She bites her lip till the blood comes. There are tears now. She's pleading with him.

Rob laughs. '*Love?* You don't know the bloody meaning of the word.'

He pushes her back hard on to the sofa and walks to the door, where he turns. He watches her sobbing for a moment.

'When I get back, I don't want to find you here.'

'You can't,' she wails. 'What about Toby – who's going to pick him up? Who's going to look after him?'

'I'm perfectly able to care for my own son. Leave the keys and go. I never want to see you again.'

*   *   *

29 Lingfield Road, Banbury. Semi-detached. Neat gravelled drive. Geraniums.

'What do you think?' says Gislingham, turning off the engine.

Somer considers. 'Looks just like what it is – a school-teacher's house.'

Gislingham nods slowly. 'Can't see it featuring in a future episode of *Unsolved Crimes*, but you know what they say about still waters.'

At the gate she turns to him but he makes a gallant gesture. 'After you.'

She smiles, a trifle tightly, then reminds herself that just because most men like to stare at her backside doesn't mean Gislingham must be one of them.

At the door, she pauses then rings the bell. Then a second and a third time. Gislingham moves to the front window and squints in. Through a gap in the nets he can see a sofa and armchairs too big for the room, a coffee table with a pile of magazines, their edges neatly aligned.

'No signs of life,' he says. Somer joins him and looks in. Neat but uninspiring. Austere without elegance. They know from the records there's no official Mrs Walsh but she's beginning to suspect there's no unofficial one either.

'He obviously likes his knick-knacks,' says Gislingham, gesturing at a cupboard on the far wall. 'I mean, with those weird little shelves, that's not for books, is it?'

Somer frowns slightly. 'I'm sure I've seen something like that before.' She shakes her head. Whatever it was, it's gone.

'Shall we try the school?' says Gislingham. 'I thought it was half-term, but perhaps those posh private places have different holidays to the rest of us?'

Somer shrugs. 'You're asking the wrong person. But yes, why not. It's only ten minutes away.'

As they walk back towards the car a woman emerges from the house opposite, struggling with a pushchair and a toddler.

'I'm just going to see if she knows Walsh,' says Somer, starting towards her. 'I won't be a minute.'

Gislingham gets back in the car and digs his newspaper out of the side pocket. When a mobile starts ringing it takes him a moment to realize it's not his. And when he reaches across to the glovebox and pulls out Somer's phone the screen says 'Gareth'. He's grinning mischievously as he answers the call.

'Hello? PC Somer's phone?'

Silence. Three beats, four, five.

'*Gislingham?*'

'Yes, who's that?'

'It's Quinn. As you know bloody well.'

'Sorry, mate, didn't expect it to be you.'

Another silence. A silence eloquent with 'like hell you didn't'.

'I was just calling to see how it's going,' Quinn says eventually. 'With Walsh I mean. I didn't realize you'd gone up there too.'

'We haven't tracked him down yet. Shall I tell her you called?'

Quinn hesitates. 'No. Don't bother. I got what I was after.'

Yeah right, thinks Gislingham as he rings off. Like hell you did.

Petersham College is an Old School old school, at least from the front. Two Victorian Oxford-copy quads complete with dining hall and chapel and stained-glass windows. Gislingham parks in a bay marked 'Visitors', and they follow a large yellow sign to what announces itself as the 'Porter's Lodge'.

'Just the one then,' says Somer. 'Wonder what they do when he's off sick.'

'Sorry, I'm not with you.'

She shakes her head. 'Grammar nerd joke. Forget it.' She spent two years attempting to teach English in an inner-city comprehensive before deciding that if she was going to spend her days dealing with drugs, knives and random violence she might as well get paid to do it professionally.

The porter, meanwhile, turns out to be a 'she' not a 'he'. A middle-aged woman in a burgundy jacket and pleated skirt.

'Can I help you?' she asks, looking at them over her glasses.

They show their warrant cards. 'Could we see Mr Walsh, please? Donald Walsh?'

She leans forward over the desk and points. 'His room is in one of the new blocks – Coleridge House. Go through the archway on the far left. I could call him and let him know you're coming, if you want to tell me what it's about?'

Somer smiles at her; she's clearly gagging for a whiff of scandal. 'There's really no need. Thanks anyway.'

They make their way across the quad. A couple of boys pass them, hands in pockets. Their voices are slightly too loud; rather like their blazers. There are teachers' names listed on a board at the bottom of each staircase, and a little wooden sign that can be slid across to show 'in' or 'out'. Gislingham moves a couple, just for the hell of it.

'Blimey, they do all right for themselves here, don't they?' he says, glancing in as they pass at the leather armchairs, the shelves of books, the over-sized stone fireplaces. 'Though it beats me why people pay through the nose to send their kids to places like this. Education's education. The rest is just the bloody packaging.'

'That's the point though,' says Somer. 'It's the packaging they want.'

But once through the archway it's a very different story. A jumble of Portakabins encroaching on the staff car park and two heavy 1970s extension blocks named, rather incongruously, after Romantic poets. I bet they don't bring prospective parents in here, thinks Somer, as Gislingham pushes open the door to Coleridge House. Harsh echoes and a smell of disinfectant. Walsh's room is on the third floor and there's no lift, so they're both huffing a bit by the time they get to the door. The man who answers has a check shirt and a knitted tie and a pair of well-shined shoes. He looks very like the man Elspeth Gibson described.

'Yes?'

'DC Chris Gislingham, PC Erica Somer, Thames Valley Police. Could we have a word with you?'

He blinks, then glances back into the room. 'Actually, I'm taking an after-school class. Can you come back later?'

'We've come from Oxford,' says Gislingham. 'So no, we can't "come back later". Can we come in?'

The two men stare at each other for a few moments then Walsh steps aside. 'Of course.'

The room inside is more a classroom than a study. No leather armchairs here, just a desk, a row of hard-backed chairs, an old-fashioned blackboard and a couple of framed posters. *Madam Butterfly* at the ENO; an exhibition of Japanese artefacts at the Ashmolean. And fidgeting a little at one of the desks, a red-haired boy with an exercise book on his lap. Eleven, maybe twelve years old.

'OK, Joshua,' says Walsh, with perhaps a little too much gusto. 'It seems an unexpected *deus ex machina* has released you prematurely from the purgatory that is the repeal of the Corn Laws.'

He holds open the door and gestures to the boy. 'Off you go. But I shall want to see that prep first thing in the morning.'

The boy pauses in the doorway and looks back at Gislingham, and then he's gone. They can hear his feet clattering down the stairs.

'So,' says Walsh, moving round behind his desk in a power play that's not lost on any of them. 'What can I help you with?'

'I imagine you probably know why we're here,' begins Gislingham.

Walsh looks at him, then at Somer. 'To be perfectly honest, no.'

'It's about your uncle, or strictly speaking, your aunt's husband. William Harper.'

'Oh,' says Walsh. 'Well, I can't say I'm surprised. Though I don't know why they felt they needed to send you.'

'It's a serious matter, Mr Walsh.'

'Of course. I wasn't meaning to imply – well, you know. Just have them get in touch with me and I'll sort things out. I suppose there isn't anyone else. Not now.'

Gislingham stares at him. 'Who are you talking about, Mr Walsh?'

'The solicitors. I assume he had some. Oxford firm, is it?'

'I'm not following you.'

'About the will,' says Walsh. 'That's why you're here, isn't it? Bill's dead?'

Somer and Gislingham exchange a glance.

'You haven't seen the news? The press?'

Walsh smiles, faux-helpless. 'I'm afraid I don't have time to read newspapers. Have you any idea how much is involved in this job?'

Somer knows very well, in fact. But she's not about to tell him so.

'Look,' she says, 'I think you'd better sit down.'

* * *

'As a colleague of mine observed only this week, sometimes we just get lucky.'

I'm at the lab, standing next to Challow, looking down at a metal table spread with sheets of paper covered with lines of handwriting. Some are intact, others streaked with damp, a few reduced to pulp and completely illegible.

'What is it – some sort of journal?'

Challow nods. 'Nina found it when she went through the boxes that were in the cellar. It was stuffed down the side, presumably so the old man didn't find it. There were some old books in there and the girl's torn out the blank pages. There were a couple of old biros in the boxes too. Those orange Bic things. Looks like Harper's the sort who can never bear to throw anything away.' He gestures at the sheets. 'We've saved what we can but I think the bog on the floor above must have overflowed recently. In fact, I'm surprised that girl didn't have raging pneumonia, trapped in that bloody awful place all that time.'

He turns on an overhead lamp and brings it down so we can see more clearly.

'I've transcribed the sheets that are still intact and sent them to you as scans, and I'll do what I can to decipher the rest. You never know – it's amazing what technology can do these days.'

'Thanks, Alan.'

'Happy reading. Though on second thought, that's probably just a figure of speech too.'

*   *   *

Quinn's just about to give up when the door finally opens. Though it doesn't open very far. Enough, all the same, to register bare feet, long blonde hair, even longer legs, and a camisole that clearly doesn't have anything underneath it. A shit day is suddenly not looking quite so shit after all.

'Is Mr Gardiner in?'

She shakes her head. She has one of those faces that always look slightly bruised. Either that or she's been crying.

Quinn whips out his warrant card and his suavest smile. 'Detective Sergeant Gareth Quinn. When do you expect him back?'

'He's at work. Late, I should think.'

She's about to close the door but he takes a step forward. 'Perhaps I could come in – leave him a message? We just wanted to apologize about how the news came out about his wife.'

She shrugs. 'Suit yourself.'

She turns and walks away and as he pushes the door open wider to follow her he realizes she has a glass of wine in one hand. A large glass.

The girl has already disappeared and Quinn finds himself alone in the sitting room. There's a handbag decorated with a clutch of different-coloured pom-poms on the sofa, and a wine bottle on a low table. It's almost empty. Quinn starts to check out the room; if she catches him he can always claim he was looking for paper and a pen, even though he has both in his inside pocket. A fairly expensive TV, a few books, mainly medical textbooks, framed prints in black and white. Quinn's never let a woman move in, but it does strike him that there's not much of the girl's stuff here. He goes back to the hall.

'Are you OK?' he calls.

There's a silence, and then the girl comes out of the bedroom carrying a suitcase gaping with clothes and dumps it on the sitting-room floor. She has jeans on now and a pair of very high-heeled ankle boots. There's an inch of pale skin between the top of her boots and the hem of her jeans. She perches on the sofa and tries to close the lid of the bag, her long hair falling across her face.

'Here,' says Quinn, rushing forward. 'Let me help you with that.'

She looks up at him, struggles with the zip for a few moments more, then gives up. 'Whatever.' She slumps back on the sofa and turns her face away, and it takes him a few moments to realize she is, really, crying.

He pulls the zip the last couple of inches and stands the case upright. 'Are you OK?'

She nods, pushing the tears away with her fingers. She still isn't looking at him.

'Do you need a lift or anything?'

A little gasp that might be a sob, then a nod of the head. 'Thanks,' she whispers.

Ten minutes later he's putting the case in the back of his car, and they're heading down the Banbury Road.

He glances across at her.

'Can't be easy for him. You know, all that —'

She turns to look at him. 'Yeah, right,' she says. 'All that finding your wife under the floorboards thing. But it was *two years* ago.'

Which is nothing, of course. But perhaps not at her age.

'Where will you go?' he says, after a while.

She shrugs. 'Dunno. Not home, that's for sure.'

'Why not?'

She shoots him a glance and he decides not to push it.

'The last few days — it can't have been easy on you either.'

'No shit,' she mutters, staring out of the window. But there are tears in her eyes again.

At the bus station he parks up and goes round to the boot to get the case. It's only when she reaches to hitch her handbag over her shoulder that he sees what he probably should have noticed before.

'How did you get that?' he asks quietly.

She flushes and pulls down her sleeve. 'It's nothing. I banged my arm on a door.'

He holds out a hand and she doesn't resist. The bruise is ugly, still red. The imprint of fingers dug into the delicate skin.

'Did he do this?'

She isn't meeting his gaze, but she nods.

'You could report him, you know.'

She shakes her head vehemently; she's struggling not to cry again.

'He didn't mean it,' she says, her voice so low he has to stoop to hear her. A London coach grinds past and Quinn can see people eyeing them curiously.

'Look, let me buy you a coffee.'

She shakes her head again. 'I have to find somewhere to stay.'

'Don't worry about that. I'm sure we can find you somewhere.'

Then he picks up the case and pushes it back in the boot.

*   *   *

The woman at reception at St Aldate's looks harassed. She checks her mobile three times in the five minutes it takes for the desk sergeant to haul himself out of the back office and down to the front.

'Yes? Can I help you?'

'My name is Lynda Pearson. Dr Lynda Pearson. I'm here to see William Harper. He's one of my patients.'

'Ah yes, we're expecting you. Can you take a seat? It shouldn't be too long.'

She sighs; she's heard that one before. She goes over to the line of chairs, then takes her phone out of her canvas bag. At least she can do something useful while she's stuck here.

'Dr Pearson?'

She looks up to see a solid man in a suit that's a bit too small for him. The buttons on his shirt gape slightly. Balding, a little out of breath. Halfway to high blood pressure. He looks forty but he's probably at least five years younger.

'DC Andrew Baxter,' he says. 'I can take you down to the custody suite.'

She gathers up her things and follows him down the stairs. 'How's Bill been?'

'As far as I know, he's OK. We've been doing our best not to put him in any stressful situations. Made sure he's getting food he likes, that sort of thing.'

'He's probably eating better here than he was at home. He's lost a lot of weight in the last few months. Has Derek Ross seen him?'

'Not since he was first brought in. Ross was the one who suggested we called you.'

They've reached the custody suite and Baxter nods to the sergeant at the desk. 'Dr Pearson to see William Harper.'

As they walk towards Harper's cell Lynda Pearson has a horrible sudden premonition that they're going to find the old man hanging from the window bars by a twisted shirt. But it must just be her tired brain overplaying all the TV cop shows she's seen over the years, because when the door opens Harper is sitting docilely on his bed, both feet on the floor. He looks thin but there's some colour in his cheeks that wasn't there before. The plate and cup on the tray by the bed are both empty.

'How are you, Bill?' she says, taking a seat on the only chair.

He looks at her narrowly. 'What are you doing here?'

'The police asked me to come. They wanted me to check you over. Make sure you're OK.'

'When can I go home?'

Pearson glances up at Baxter. 'Not yet, I'm afraid, Bill. The police have more questions they need to ask. You may be here a while longer.'

'In that case,' he says, in sudden clear tones, 'I want to see the officer in charge. I want to make a statement.'

*   *   *

'Is that really necessary?'

Walsh has gone from disbelief to irritation in the space of about three sentences. The former in response to the news, the latter to Gislingham's request that he accompany them to St Aldate's.

'Why on earth do you need me to do that? I have commitments — classes, marking, extracurricular activities to supervise — it's incredibly inconvenient.'

'I appreciate that, sir, but we need to take samples. DNA, fingerprints —'

He stares at them. 'What the hell for? I haven't been to that house in years.'

'Really?' says Somer. 'You weren't on good terms with your uncle?'

'My good woman, as your colleague quite rightly observed only a few minutes ago, we weren't actually *related*.'

Gislingham's eyes widen; if that was an attempt to get in Somer's good books it's a miscalculation of spectacular proportions.

'Mr Walsh,' she says coolly, 'we have already established that very few people have visited that house in recent years and you are clearly one of them. We need to eliminate you from our enquiries –'

His eyes narrow. 'Enquiries? You don't seriously think I could be involved in what he was doing? I can assure you that I had no idea what he was up to – I was as shocked as anyone else.'

Somer eyes him for a moment. '*Was?*'

He looks irritated. 'What?'

'You just said, "I *was* as shocked". That means you knew – you knew before we got here. You saw the news just like everyone else.'

'Look,' he says, taking a deep breath, 'I work in a school. A very *expensive* school. Do you know how much people pay every year to send their children to a place like this?'

She can guess. And it's probably more than she gets paid.

'The last thing I need in my position is to be associated with something like – like *that*.'

I bet you don't, thinks Somer, and all the more since you're clearly so far down the pecking order that you're stuck in a room in the overflow block with a grandstand view of the bins.

'We'll do our best to be discreet,' she says, 'but the fact remains that we need you to accompany us back to Oxford. Even if you haven't been to Frampton Road for a while we have fingerprints that are so far unidentified, and could have been there quite some time. And in any case, I'm sure a "school like this" would expect you to do everything in your power to assist the police.' She has him there, and he knows it.

'Very well,' he says heavily. 'I trust I can drive myself?'

Out in the car Gislingham turns to her. 'Blimey, you got him by the short and curlies and no mistake.'

'You know,' she says thoughtfully, 'I'm sure there are guidelines in the state sector these days about teachers being alone with pupils. I think you're advised to leave the door open.'

'What, are you suggesting something was going on with him and that kid?'

'No, not necessarily. But I think we should make a few enquiries. From what I remember this is the third school he's taught at in the last ten years. Might suggest something. Or nothing.'

'Worth checking though.'

She nods. 'Though we really do need to be careful how we go about it. If you're a teacher, a rumour like that can wreck your career. Even if it proves to be completely untrue.'

It happened to someone she knew. A quiet, inoffensive and – as it turned out – hopelessly naive man who got hounded out of his job after one of his Year 10s claimed he'd hit him. The last she heard, he was behind the till in Lidl.

Gislingham starts the engine and a few moments later they see Walsh's silver Mondeo emerging from the staff car park.

'By the way,' says Gislingham as Walsh comes towards them, 'what was that he was talking about – the sex mashing thing?'

For a moment she's completely nonplussed. 'Oh, you mean the *deus ex machina*? It's from Greek tragedy – it's when a writer gets his plot into such a complete horlicks the only way to fix it is to send in a god.'

Gislingham grins. 'Sounds like a great idea. We could do with one of those ourselves.'

'I thought we already had one,' she says drily. 'Under deep cover as Detective Inspector Adam Fawley.'

Gislingham laughs out loud this time, then puts the car in gear. The back of his hand brushes hers.

Just for a moment.

*   *   *

I'm writing this because I want everyone to know. If I die down here - if I never get out - I want people to know what he did to me.

I was on my way to look at a bedsit. One of the students had dropped out so they had a room free for a few months and it had to be better than where I was before. Only I'd managed to break my heel crossing the road so I was sitting there, on the wall, trying to fix it, when he came out. I thought he was going to ask me to get off his wall but he just looked at my shoe and said he had some glue that could fix it. It would only take a minute, he said. And I looked at him and he smiled. He had a tie on, I remember that. He didn't look like a psycho. He looked nice. Kind. Like someone's uncle. So I said OK and I followed him into the house.

He said he had to fetch the glue from the shed, and he'd just made some tea and would I like some. That's how he must have done it. The tea.

I thought it tasted a bit weird [material illegible]

. . . lying face down on the floor. I started yelling but no one came. He never came. And eventually I needed to pee and I started crying because I could feel my jeans getting soaked and it was so horrible. I don't know how long it was before I worked out I could crawl on my knees. I kept banging into things in the dark but I found the bed and the toilet and the boxes of junk. It all smells of old people. I think this room must be underground because it's so cold all . . .

[*one sheet illegible*]

. . . heard him outside. There was the sound of a key and then footsteps on the stairs and then a light went on. I could see it under the door. And then I heard him out there, breathing. Breathing and listening. I stayed really still and in the end he went away. But the light under the door is still there.

He's going to come down again, isn't he.

I don't want him to rape me. I've never done it before and I don't want it to be him that's the first.

Why doesn't anyone come?

[*two sheets illegible*]

. . . here again. He had water and he let me drink some, but most of it went down my top. I said I was

hungry too but he said I have to be nice to him
first. I tried to hit him and he slapped me. He said
I would play nice in the end because I wouldn't eat
until I did. I spat out the water at him and he
said suit yourself. You can drink out of the toilet
for all I care. You'll come round, you vicious
little bitch. You all do.

I keep wondering if anyone is looking for me. Those
people at the bedsit won't be bothered. Mum doesn't
know where I am and probably wouldn't care if she
did. She'd probably say it served me right for
being so stupid. That's what she always says.

I could die in here and no one would know

I don't want to die

Please don't let . . .

[*three sheets damaged*]

He raped me

He RAPED me

I don't know how long ago because I've been lying
here just crying and crying. Please, if you read
this, don't let him get away with it. Make him pay
for what he did.

He brought down more water but I think there was
something in it again because I started to feel

strange. As if I knew what was going on but I couldn't do anything about it. One minute he was sitting there smiling at me and the next he was taking my knickers off and then he was touching me with his horrible wrinkly hands and putting his fingers in me and asking if I liked it. He didn't untie me – I think he likes it that I'm tied up. He did it to me on my back then turned me over and did it to me again. And all the time I had my face in the dirt and it was hurting like he was ripping me inside.

I was sick, afterwards. There was blood running down my legs.

But he left the water and some food

And he put the light on

[*several sheets missing*]

. . . how long I've been here but I can't keep count because he took my watch and he took my phone. My period came today so it must be at least three weeks. I told him I needed things for it and he just brought me bog roll. He wouldn't even give me my knickers back, the mean bastard. He says they're dirty. And in any case he likes looking at me without them. Calls it my 'vagina'.

He sat there and watched while I stuck the paper between my legs. He had a strange look on his face.

As if he liked the blood. As if it made it even
better in his twisted screwed up mind. He said it
was a pity we couldn't have sex while I was
bleeding but he could do it to me from behind if I
want. It's like he thinks we have sort of a
relationship. I didn't think anything could make
this nightmare worse, but that does.

[*several sheets damaged*]

. . . nicer to me now. He says we can be a family
and he's always wanted a child and he hopes it will
be a boy. He let me have my pants back and he'd
even tried to wash them. He lets me have the light
on too. And more food. But when I said I needed to
see a doctor he laughed in a really nasty way and
said I was in the right place. Then when I asked
again he said women in the 19th century had babies
in the fields and went straight back to work. That I
was young and strong and he'd look after me. Me and
the baby.

But he must have been angry with me because he
turned the light off again after that. I lay here
in the dark. Feeling his kid in me. Eating me from
the inside.

[*one or more sheets missing*]

It's lying there now looking at me. When it cries
its face crumples up and goes red. He told me I had
to feed it but I turned my back on him. He wanted

to have it – he can feed it. He got milk and
managed to get the kid to drink some.

He took the dirty bedding away and gave me new
sheets. He kept saying he'd made sure everything
was clean and hygienic and I said I didn't care. I
didn't care if I died. Not any more. And he said I
had to live for the baby's sake and I just turned
my face to the wall and cried.

He said we were lucky I'm so young and the labour
was so easy. And I said 'Lucky? Lucky to be kept
prisoner down here? Lucky to be raped day after
day?' And he said it's not like that and I know it,
and I need to behave myself. That he's been lenient
because I was pregnant but things are going to
have to change now.

He says I've got to look after the baby and he'll
leave me alone if I do so it's in my interests. I
tell him to take it upstairs and look after it
himself but he won't. He says it's mine. Mine and
his. He says it's called Billy.

I'm not going to give it a name

Not down here

Not in the dark

He's looking at me now. The baby. He has blue eyes.
Dark hair just like mine. I'm trying to think of

him as mine. As just mine and nothing to do with
that horrible old pervert.

He doesn't cry much. He just lies there on the
blanket looking at me. It's over three months now.
The old man is still being 'nice' to me. I get
better food. Tampons. He even came back with some
clothes. He must have got them in a charity shop
but they could have been worse. He got some clothes
for the kid too. A T-shirt and some onesies.

Perhaps having the baby will be a good thing in
the end. Because he can't keep a baby down here
forever, can he. What if it got sick? He won't let
it die. He doesn't care about me but he won't let
anything happen to the baby.

Not his son

Not his Billy

       [one or more sheets missing]

THERE'S NO FOOD LEFT AND THE WATER IS RUNNING OUT I DON'T KNOW HOW
MUCH LONGER I CAN MAKE IT LAST

I CAN HEAR PEOPLE NEXT DOOR BUT HOWEVER LOUD I SCREAM NO ONE COMES

NO ONE COMES

                    * * *

Baxter calls me from the custody suite at 5.30 p.m. My head is full of words. The girl's words and the pictures my brain has made from them. I knew what he must have done to her but it's different – hearing it, watching it play out in my brain. I've an anger now that I know I'm going to have to be very careful of. And the most immense pity.

On the other end of the line, Baxter is waiting. 'Boss?'

'Sorry, miles away. What is it?'

'It's Harper. He's lucid. And he says he wants to make a statement.'

Time to count to ten.

'Right. Have you called his lawyer?'

'She's going to be at least an hour, I'm afraid, and I'm not sure we can afford to wait. Not in the state he's in – by the time she gets here we could have lost him again. His doctor's here though, so if you're OK with it she's willing to be the appropriate adult.'

'Fine by me. Bring him up to Interview One. Is Quinn around?'

'Haven't seen him.'

'You then. I'll be there in ten minutes.'

Harper looks me straight in the eye when I go into the room, which is definitely a first. His back is straight and he seems aware of his surroundings. The doctor is a capable-looking woman with tired grey hair and unexpectedly pretty eyes. I take my seat next to Baxter and look across at Harper.

'I believe you want to make a statement, Dr Harper?'

I sense Baxter glance at me; he can tell something's changed just from my voice.

Harper hesitates, then nods.

'And you are aware that this is a formal interview, and you are still under caution?'

Another nod.

'In that case, for the recording, I am Detective Inspector Adam Fawley. Also present besides Dr Harper are Dr Lynda Pearson and DC Andrew Baxter. So, Dr Harper, what is it you want to tell us?'

He looks at me, then at Baxter. But he says nothing.

'Dr Harper?'

He looks around at us all, slower this time. 'It's her, isn't it?' he says.

'I'm sorry?'

'You want me to talk about *her*.'

Baxter opens his mouth to speak but I put out a hand to stop him. I want to hear this the way Harper tells it. I've heard the girl's version; now I want to hear his.

He reaches for the cup of water in front of him, then looks up at me. His eyes are wet and streaked with tiny red veins. 'Have you ever wished you could put the clock back – even just for a single hour?'

My heart hammers and for a moment I don't think I can breathe. Whatever I was expecting, it wasn't this. The anger, it's still there, but what I'm feeling most now is loss. Not Hannah's, not Vicky's, not even the child's. My own. Because I wouldn't even need an hour; I'd give everything I have for five minutes. The five minutes I spent sorting out the dustbins the night Jake died. The five minutes that meant I was too late reaching him, cutting him down, getting life back into his lungs. That's all it was.

Five minutes.

Five bloody minutes.

'She haunts me, you know,' he says suddenly. 'That red

dress that made her look like a whore. Her cold little hands closing round my cock. I knew it couldn't be her – that she wasn't actually *there*. But it didn't stop. Night after night. She wouldn't leave me in peace.'

I lean forward. 'Who are you talking about, Dr Harper?'

'It was a moment of madness. That's what they say, isn't it? A "moment of madness". But you can't go back. Afterwards, I mean. You have to live with what you've done.'

He puts his head in his hands and rubs his eyes. 'These last few months, I know I've not been myself. The bloody booze. Blackouts. Seeing things. Waking up somewhere and not knowing how I got there.'

He sits back in his chair and his arms drop to his sides. 'That shit Ross wants to put me in a home. Says I'm fucking doo-lally. Perhaps he's right.'

I see Lynda Pearson glance at him and I think I know why. The swearing – it's like a warning light. A sign he's slipping. That we're losing him.

I open my cardboard folder quickly and take out a picture of the girl. It's the first time I've looked at her face since I read what Challow found.

'Is this the woman you're talking about?'

He looks at me blankly. Blinks.

'This young woman is called Vicky. She was found in the cellar of your house. With a little boy.'

I pass across a second picture. He pushes it away. 'Priscilla always was an evil cow.'

'This isn't your wife, Dr Harper. This is a young woman called Hannah Gardiner. Her body was found in your shed. She'd been missing for two years.'

I pull the photos together side by side, facing him. 'What can you tell me about these women?'

'I know what you're thinking but you're wrong. I am not a bad man. *She* probably told you I was. She probably said I was a pervert.' There is spit dribbling from his mouth now. 'One of those *paedophiles* the press get so uptight about. That's what she said. That I was a nasty twisted peedo and I ought to be locked up.'

'Who said that?' says Baxter. 'It was Vicky, wasn't it – when you were doing whatever sick things you were doing to her –'

Harper shrinks back. 'What's he talking about?' He turns to Pearson, louder now. '*What's he talking about?*'

I point to Vicky's picture. 'Dr Harper, we have evidence that you raped this girl –'

He starts to rock backwards and forwards, snivelling quietly. 'It's not my fault, it's not my fault.'

'– raped her and kept her locked up in your cellar for nigh on three years –'

He covers his ears. 'I don't go down there – not any more – there's something down there – I hear it – in the night – wailing and scratching –'

I lean forward, forcing him to look at me. 'What did you hear down there, Dr Harper? *What did you hear?*'

But Pearson turns to me and shakes her head. 'I'm sorry, Inspector, I don't think we can carry on with this.'

Outside, in the corridor, Pearson catches up with me.

'I think there's something you should know. I'd have said something before, but it's the first time I've seen that picture – there's been nothing in the press.'

'I'm sorry, I'm not with you.' If I'm a bit short with her, well, that's not going to come as any great surprise.

'That girl,' she says. 'Vicky. She's the image of Priscilla. The hair, the eyes, everything. I'm not sure what it means – or if it means anything – but it's something you need to know.'

'Was Mrs Harper your patient too?'

She shakes her head. 'No. She went private. But I met her a few times. Let's just say that she wasn't a very easy person.'

'According to our records, the police were called out twice to disturbances at the house. On both occasions it appears she was the aggressor. That she attacked her husband.'

She nods. 'I can't say I'm surprised. By all accounts she led him a dog's life. I remember Bill telling me he'd been to infertility testing because they were trying to get pregnant. It was only much later that he found out she'd had a coil fitted privately years before. He was furious. As much for the lie as for the fact that he'd missed his chance to be a father. He and Nancy had wanted kids but it never happened.'

I nod slowly. 'Anyone would be angry. That sort of deception.'

She sighs. 'I think he hated her, even before that. Because of what their affair did to Nancy. I tried to tell him the breast cancer would have happened anyway, but he kept blaming himself – saying that between them, he and Priscilla had killed her. Apparently, when he told Priscilla he would never leave Nancy, she went round to the house and told her what was going on. Nancy had no idea – she was very trusting. The thought of Bill being unfaithful would never even have occurred to her. She was diagnosed less than a year later and she only lasted six months after that. That's where a lot of the animosity is coming from now. All that fury he had to suppress while Priscilla was alive – the Alzheimer's is letting it all out. And then when you show him a picture of someone who looks so like her – well, it's small wonder he reacts how he does.'

'So how would he have reacted if he'd actually met her? If he'd seen Vicky outside his house?'

The doctor goes pale. 'Oh Lord – is that what you think happened? Is that what he meant about a moment of madness?'

I shrug. 'I don't know.'

She shakes her head sadly. 'That poor, poor girl. And that poor child. Do you know how he's doing?'

I could say something, but I don't. 'He's in good hands. At least for now.'

* * *

In the incident room, Somer is on one of the computers, scrolling down through batch after batch of images. One of the DCs wanders past behind her and bends to have a look. 'If it's furniture you're after you could try Wayfair. My girl-friend swears by it. I should know – I have to pay for all the bloody stuff.'

Somer is still staring at the screen. 'It's not for me. There's a particular type of cupboard I'm trying to track down.'

The DC shrugs. 'Suit yourself. I was just trying to help. We're not *all* after a shag, whatever you might think.'

She watches him walk away, her cheeks burning, wondering what she did wrong. Or if she did anything wrong at all. Then she sighs, knowing exactly what her sister would have said if she could see her now. But Kath was the most beautiful girl in the school from the first day she arrived: she got used to the cost of her looks very early on. Somer, by contrast, spent her childhood being told she was merely 'nice-looking', and the change, when it came, forced her into attention she had no idea how to handle. There are times, like now, when it feels as if she's hardly made any progress at all.

She turns back to the computer, and a few minutes later

she sits back, gazing at the screen. Then she logs on to the shared CID server and pulls up the photos taken in Frampton Road.

'Gotcha,' she says, under her breath.

*   *   *

Donald Walsh is sitting in exactly the same chair William Harper was sitting in half an hour ago, if he did but know it. In the room next door, Everett is watching on the screen. It's clear that Walsh is in full performance mode. He's making a great show of checking his watch every thirty seconds and looking around with an increasingly irritated expression. The door opens and Gislingham comes to join her. His face says it all.

'So you got something?'

'Yup. Walsh's prints are an exact match to the unidentified sets in both the cellar and the kitchen. They are *also* – and this is where it gets interesting – a match for some of those we found in the shed. But only on the paint tins and the garden stuff.'

'So you're going to interview him?'

Gislingham nods. 'He's deffo got some explaining to do.'

On the screen, the door opens to reveal Quinn, who looks around, clearly expecting Gislingham to be there already.

'Oops,' says Gislingham, 'I'd better go.'

Everett watches as he joins Quinn, taking his seat and pushing his chair back.

'Mr Walsh,' begins Quinn, 'I am Detective Sergeant Gareth Quinn. DC Gislingham you already know. For the purposes of the tape, I can confirm that you have already been cautioned –'

'Which is a preposterous bureaucratic overreaction, if you don't mind me saying so – I had absolutely *nothing* to do with any aspect of this ludicrous shambles.'

Quinn raises an eyebrow. 'Really?' He opens the file he was carrying. 'We've just had confirmation that some of the fingerprints we found at thirty-three Frampton Road are a match for yours.'

Walsh shrugs. 'That's hardly surprising. I have visited several times. Albeit not recently.'

'When exactly were you there last?'

'I'm not entirely sure. Perhaps the autumn of 2014. I came to a conference in Oxford that October and popped in to see Bill for a few minutes. To be honest, I pretty much stopped going after Priscilla died.'

Gislingham raises an eyebrow; that doesn't sound right, not with everything he's heard about her. 'So did you get on well with Priscilla then?'

'If you must know, I thought she was a terrible woman. A vicious bitch and a marriage wrecker, though I'm aware the latter is a rather old-fashioned concept these days. She turned my aunt's final years into a complete hell. I made a point of only going there when I knew she'd be out.'

'And how often was that, would you say?'

'While Nancy was still alive I used to go two or three times a year. After Bill married Priscilla, probably once a year at most.'

'So why did you stop going altogether after Priscilla died? Surely that should have made things easier between you and Dr Harper?'

Walsh sits back in his chair. 'I don't know, it just happened that way. There's not some ulterior agenda here, Constable.'

But Gislingham isn't giving up. 'So let me get this

straight – you stopped going to see him at the very point when he needed someone to look out for him? He's on his own, he's getting on, he's starting to show signs of dementia –'

'I knew nothing about that,' says Walsh quickly.

'Well, you wouldn't, would you. Since you'd stopped bothering to go and see him.'

Walsh looks away.

'It wasn't just that though, was it?' says Quinn. 'You two had argued. A major falling-out, from what we hear.'

'That's absurd.'

'Someone saw you.'

Walsh gives him a withering look. 'If you're talking about that old dear from down the road, she's hardly my idea of a reliable witness.'

There's a silence. Walsh is drumming his fingers on his thighs.

Then there's a knock on the door and it opens to reveal Erica Somer, with a sheaf of papers in her hand. She tries to catch Quinn's attention but he studiously avoids looking at her.

'Sergeant? Could I have a word?'

'We're in the middle of an interview, PC Somer.'

'I know that, Sergeant.'

Gislingham can see it's important, even if Quinn is refusing to. He gets up and goes to the door. Watching on the screen, Everett sees Quinn get increasingly irritated until Gislingham finally returns to the room. And this time, Somer follows him in. Quinn doesn't look up. And when she takes the chair in the far corner facing him, he still won't meet her gaze.

Gislingham puts the papers down on the table, then swivels one of the sheets round to face Walsh. It's a photograph.

'Do you know what this picture is of, Mr Walsh?'

Walsh looks at the paper and shifts slightly. 'No, not off-hand.'

'I think you know very well. You have one like this yourself.'

Walsh sits back and folds his arms. 'So? What's that got to do with anything? It's just a cupboard.'

Gislingham raises an eyebrow. 'Hardly. It's a very special type of cupboard, designed to hold a very special type of ornament. A type of ornament Dr Harper just happens to own. We know that, because they're right here –' he points at a second sheet '– on his contents insurance. Only strangely enough, I don't remember seeing any of them in that house. What I *do* remember, however, is seeing a cupboard just like this one in *your* front room.'

Gislingham is suddenly aware how hard Quinn is staring at him. And if there's one thing Quinn hates, it's being wrong-footed.

'So, Mr Walsh,' says Gislingham quickly, 'why don't you save us all a lot of time and tell us exactly what this thing is for?'

Walsh's mouth has set in a thin, irritated little line. 'My grandfather was a diplomat, and spent a number of years in Japan after the war. During that time he amassed a considerable collection of *netsuke*.'

Quinn puts down his pen and looks up. 'Sorry?'

Walsh raises an eyebrow. 'You haven't got a clue what I'm talking about, have you?' he says sardonically.

But sarcasm is rarely the best way to deal with Quinn. 'Well, in that case,' he replies, 'why don't you just go right ahead and enlighten me?'

'*Netsuke* are miniature carvings.' The voice is Somer's. 'They were part of traditional Japanese dress. A bit like toggles.'

Walsh smiles at Quinn. 'Your colleague seems to be rather better informed than you are.'

Quinn looks at him venomously. 'So this collection of your grandfather's – how much was it worth?'

'Oh, probably only a few hundred pounds,' says Walsh airily. 'It was more the principle of the thing – its sentimental value. My grandfather left them to Nancy, and when she died I thought they should revert to the family.'

'But Dr Harper didn't agree?'

A flicker of anger crosses Walsh's face. 'No. He didn't. I talked to him about it but he said Priscilla was very fond of them. He made it very clear she wasn't going to give them up.'

I bet she wasn't, thinks Quinn.

'I see,' he says, 'but after she died you thought, well, worth another shot?'

'As you so eloquently put it, yes. I went to see him again.'

'And he blew you off. Again. That's what the two of you were arguing about.'

Gislingham smiles drily; as he always says, when it comes to crime, it's love or it's money. Or sometimes both.

Walsh is really hacked off now. 'He had *no right* – those items were part of my family's history – our legacy –'

'So where are they now?'

Walsh stops abruptly. 'What do you mean?'

'As DC Gislingham just pointed out, there aren't any of those netsky things in the house. You, on the other hand, appear to have a cupboard specially designed to display them.'

Walsh flushes. 'I bought that when I thought Bill was going to be reasonable.'

'So you're saying that if we search your house we won't find any of the items listed on this insurance form?'

'Absolutely not,' he snaps. 'If they're not at Frampton Road I have no idea where they are. And that being the case I would like to report them missing. Officially.'

Quinn turns a page in his file. 'Duly noted. So, perhaps we could now turn to the issue of the fingerprints.'

'What?' Walsh looks at him blankly, distracted.

'The fingerprints I mentioned. So far we've found them in several different parts of the house. Some are in the kitchen —'

'That's no surprise, I must have spent most of my time in there —'

'And some are in the cellar.'

Walsh stares at him. Swallows. 'What do you mean, the cellar?'

'The cellar where the young woman and child were found. Perhaps you could explain how they got there?'

'I have no idea. I don't think I've ever been down there. And I want it noted that I absolutely and categorically do not know *anything* about that young woman. Or her child.' He looks from one to the other. 'Furthermore, I'm not prepared to answer any more questions until I see my lawyer.'

'You do, of course, have the right to do that,' says Quinn. 'Just as we have the right to arrest you. Which, for the avoidance of doubt, I am now doing. Interview terminated at 6.12 p.m.'

He gets up to leave, so quickly that he is out of the door before Gislingham is even on his feet. And when Somer comes out into the corridor he takes her by the arm and pulls her to one side. Her smile chills when she sees the look on his face.

'Don't you *ever* fucking do that to me again,' he hisses. 'Do you understand?'

She pulls back from him. 'Do what, exactly?'

'Make me look like a bloody idiot in front of a suspect – in front of fucking *Gislingham*, for fuck's sake.'

'I'm sorry – I was trying to help –'

He brings his face closer to hers. 'If that's what you call helping, then forget it. In fact, forget it, full stop.'

'Where's all this come from?'

But he's already gone.

*   *   *

The team meeting is at 6.30. And this time, I'm taking it. The room is packed and hot. But silent. Word has got around.

'OK,' I say, into the expectation. 'You probably know that Challow's team found something in one of the boxes in the cellar at Frampton Road. It's a journal, written by Vicky during her captivity.'

I step forward and turn on the projector.

'Some parts are missing or damaged but there's still no doubt what happened to her. This is a transcript of the key pages. But I warn you, it's painful reading.'

I'm silent as they read it. There are gasps, shakes of the head. Some of the women are really struggling, and I know the exact moment Gislingham gets to 'Billy'. I won't let myself look at him but I sense him stiffen, hear the intake of breath.

'We'll wait for the DNA,' I say at last, 'as formal proof, but I plan to charge William Harper with rape and false imprisonment by close of play today. We have enough now to make a case against him.'

There's a silence.

'Sir,' says Somer tentatively, 'I know I'm not CID and all that, but is it possible there's another way to read this? I haven't met Harper but I did meet Walsh, and I think *he's* the one she's talking about here. The man she talks about opening the door, that sounds more like Walsh to me.'

'Actually, she's got a point there,' says Gislingham quickly. 'The tie, the poncey way of talking. That's Walsh bang to rights. Harper's the one who goes out in the street in his vest.'

'This was at least three years ago. Harper was a very different man then.' But even as I'm saying it I'm starting to wonder.

'Yes, sir, but look,' says Somer, getting up and going to point at the transcript. 'He calls her a "vicious bitch". That's exactly what Walsh called Priscilla. This afternoon, when we interviewed him.'

Harper called his wife an evil cow, but it's Walsh who says vicious bitch. Words matter. Nuance matters. I walk towards the screen. Somer is standing in the light from the projector, Vicky's words trailing eerily across her face.

'This reference here,' she says, still half apologetic, 'to the doctor and Vicky being "in the right place". Yes, that could be Harper talking about himself, but it *could* also be Walsh, talking about Harper. About him being a PhD doctor but not a real doctor.'

'Either way, that's a pretty sick joke,' says Gislingham grimly. 'To a girl about to give birth without medical help.' He's bound to feel it: a man whose son only survived because of state-of-the-art equipment and a whole team of neonatal specialists.

I stand there, reading. Re-reading. I can hear them all behind me. The murmurs, the trying to work out which way it's going.

I turn back to face them. 'What do we have on Walsh?'

'Plenty, actually,' says Quinn as the energy in the room

shifts up a notch. 'We've got his fingerprints on some of the boxes in the cellar, as well as in the kitchen and on some of the items in the shed –'

'So how does Walsh explain that?'

Quinn shakes his head. 'Nothing doing. Insisted he's never been in the cellar and demanded to speak to his lawyer before he answered any more questions. We're still waiting for her to arrive. But when she does, we'll also be asking Walsh about a collection of *netsuke* Harper inherited from his first wife. You know, this sort of thing.' He holds up a page of images. An ivory hare, two entwined frogs, a coiled snake, a crow curled round a skull. Beautiful and tiny and perfect.

'Walsh wanted them back,' continues Quinn, 'but Harper refused. Only there's no sign of them in the house. There's a cupboard in the bedroom where Walsh says they were but it's empty.'

'So this collection – was it valuable?'

Quinn nods. 'Could be. Walsh told us they were only worth a few hundred but I happen to know rare examples can fetch a hundred grand or more. Each.' I see Somer glance across at him and the effort he makes to avoid her eye.

'Actually, sir,' says Somer, addressing herself rather pointedly to me, not Quinn, 'I saw a display cabinet on the wall in Walsh's house when we called there. It had quite a distinctive design – the sort of thing people buy for collections of *netsuke*.'

One thing I do know: her pronunciation is much better than Quinn's.

'My personal theory?' Quinn continues as if the interruption never happened. 'I reckon Walsh realized Harper was starting to lose it and took the opportunity to swipe the collection. Either all in one go, or gradually, so it wasn't so obvious in case someone like Ross was snooping around. That could mean he's been going to that house much more often than he's letting on. So he could have been there that day – the day Vicky was abducted.'

'But wouldn't someone have seen him if he'd been going there a lot?' says Baxter. 'There was only one neighbour who said she saw him and that was a good while ago.'

'I don't think we should take that as conclusive. Not in that part of Oxford. And in any case, he could have come at night. I doubt anyone would have noticed him in the dark.'

'Right,' I say, addressing the whole room. 'Gislingham – organize a search of Walsh's house. And let's remember, he only lives in Banbury. If he really is some sort of sexual psychopath, Frampton Road would have been the ultimate safe house – far enough away but not too far, only an old lady next door, a cellar with thick walls and no windows –'

'Christ, even better than the Loony Lock-up,' quips Gislingham to laughter that comes as a release of the tension. It's a joke we have – ever since *Prime Suspect* every TV serial killer seems to have his own private torture chamber. As Alex once drily observed, clearly all that's required to round up any currently operational serial killers is a systematic sweep of the nation's railway arches.

'And another thing,' I continue. 'When I interviewed Harper he said he doesn't go down to the cellar any more – that he'd started to hear noises coming from it. "Wailing and scratching" were the actual words. He appeared to be genuinely frightened. And that could make sense, if Walsh had locked Vicky down there without Harper knowing. The old man's getting confused, he drinks – it's not inconceivable Walsh could have got the girl into the house without him knowing. After all, he probably has a key.'

'Yeah,' says Gislingham, 'but isn't Harper going to say something like that, even if it's not true? He's bound to claim he never knew anything about it.'

'In theory, yes, but this came out towards the end of the interview, when Harper was starting to get more confused. I don't think he was faking that. It could also explain something else that's been bugging me about Harper. Kidnapping that girl, keeping her locked up – a crime like that doesn't come out of a blue sky. There's always something that leads up to it – some sort of escalation over time, even if that's only obvious in retrospect. But with Harper, there's nothing – or nothing we've found.'

'There's the porn in the house,' says Baxter.

'Yeah,' says Quinn. 'But what if that was actually Walsh's stuff? Let's face it, it'd be a safer place for a schoolteacher to stash it than in his own home.'

'Right,' I say. 'So let's get prints from it to be sure. And everything I said about escalation – that all applies to Walsh, just as much as to Harper. If it was him, there'll be something that led up to it. Some trace we can find if we look hard enough.'

'There was a kid in his room at the school,' says Gislingham. 'Poor little bastard looked terrified.'

Somer looks up. 'It's also the third school he's taught at in the last ten years. I ran the records. It would be worth checking if there's anything behind that.'

She's good, that woman. She's very good.

'OK, Somer – can you pick up the Banbury end. Work with Gislingham to liaise with the local force at both the school and the house.'

I see Quinn look at her, then me, then away. He's pissed off, but I don't care.

'Any news on the girl?' says one of the DCs at the back.

'She still hasn't said anything,' says Everett. 'But I'll be going back to the hospital in the morning.'

'And the kid?'

Everett glances at me, then across at the DC. 'He's OK. Better.'

I nod briefly to Everett. A nod of thanks. For her discretion.

'OK,' I continue. 'Now – Hannah Gardiner. Despite the appeal for witnesses, no one's yet come forward with any new information about Hannah's movements that morning –'

'Apart from the usual nut-jobs,' mutters the DC at the back.

'– but we *do* have two significant new facts. The first is that she often parked her car in Frampton Road. So if we're now looking at Walsh as a possible suspect we urgently need to check where he was that day – whether he could have met her on the street. Schools tend to keep pretty good records so we may get lucky.'

The noise level is rising and I raise my voice. '*However* – and there's a big *but* coming here, people – we also have a second new fact that points in a completely different direction. Baxter's spoken to Beth Dyer, who told him something that puts a rather different slant on the relationship between Hannah and Rob. Something Miss Dyer unfortunately didn't see fit to share with us two years ago. And which could also explain why we still haven't found any trace of a murder scene at Frampton Road.'

Baxter gets up and turns to face the group. 'Beth says she saw Hannah a few weeks before she disappeared, with a bruise on her face. Hannah claimed it was an accident with Toby but Beth didn't believe her. She thought it was Rob – that the two of them had been having problems. She skirted around that idea back in 2015 but she's come right out with it now. And she did say one thing that struck me – whoever it was who killed Hannah, how did they know where to dump her car? There weren't that many people who knew where she was going that day. Walsh wouldn't have, and Harper wouldn't either, for that matter. But Rob did. That's why Beth thinks Rob did it. That and the bruises.'

I nod, remembering. 'Jill Murphy said something similar back in 2015.' She was the DS on the case, and a bloody good one too. 'She always thought Beth had a thing for Rob.'

'Yeah, well,' says Baxter, 'I reckon she still does. Which could, of course, mean she's making all this up just to get back at him. It wouldn't be the first time.'

'Even so, we still need to take another look at Rob Gardiner. On the face of it the case for him as the killer is much stronger – that's by far the easiest explanation for the lack of other DNA in the car.'

Occam's razor. Always believe the simplest of all available explanations. We used to call it Osbourne's razor when he was still at Thames Valley, he said it so often. It's one reason we ended up so fixated with Shore: he was the easiest answer too.

'We discounted Gardiner in 2015 because we had sightings of Hannah at Wittenham, and the timings didn't add up. But now we know she never left Oxford so we're going to have to tear up that timeline and start again.'

I walk over and point to the timings Baxter pinned on the board. 'Gardiner has a rock-solid alibi from here, 7.57, when his train left Oxford, but what about before that? What about the previous day?'

'Hang on a minute,' says Quinn, pointing at the first entry on the timeline. 'Hannah was definitely alive at 6.50 that morning, when she left that voicemail message –'

'Have you listened to it?'

'Well, no –'

'I did. At the time. Over and over. And we played it to her friends too. The quality isn't great but they all thought it was her. But what if it wasn't? Is it possible it was someone else? Could Beth Dyer have been right all along – could there have been a mystery woman in the picture – someone we never knew about who gave Gardiner an alibi?'

I can tell they're sceptical, but I push the point home. 'All I'm saying is let's get it analysed again. Speech recognition software has improved massively, even in two years. And let's get Pippa Walker back in here too. Just in case there was anything odd about that call that didn't occur to her at the time.'

'Worth a shot,' says Gislingham. 'Especially now she's had that falling-out with Gardiner.'

I look at him with a question and he gestures towards Quinn, who's momentarily wrong-footed. 'I saw her at Gardiner's flat this afternoon,' he says, after a pause, glancing at Gislingham. 'She and Gardiner have had some sort of row and he's chucked her out. She had a bruise on her wrist. She said he did it.'

'Right, let's bring her in and get her to make a statement. I'm assuming you know where to find her?'

Quinn opens his mouth, then closes it again.

'And while we're at it, let's check Gardiner's past for any other suggestions of violence – talk to his ex-wife –'

'I tried,' says Baxter. 'She isn't returning my calls. And when uniform went round there no one answered.'

'So track down his old girlfriends, people he knew at university. Come on, you know the drill.'

I turn again to the timeline. 'If you take away the call at 6.50, Gardiner's whole alibi falls apart. He could easily have killed Hannah on the 23rd, buried her that night, then taken the car out to Wittenham early enough the following morning to make that train.'

'But in that case, how did he get back?' asks Quinn.

'He has a bike,' says Somer, not looking at him. 'One of those folding ones – he has it with him on the CCTV at Reading station. And Wittenham's only ten miles. He could do that in, what? Forty minutes?'

'What about the boy?' someone asks. 'Are you saying Gardiner just dumped him up there on the off-chance someone would find him? Could he really have done that to his own kid?'

It's a good question. 'I agree it's not likely – not on the face of it. But remember, Hannah's interview at Wittenham was originally scheduled for much earlier that morning. Rob couldn't have known Jervis had been delayed. He might have assumed the boy would be found much quicker than he actually was.'

'But that assumes he didn't have her mobile – that he'd already got rid of it by then.'

'Fair enough, but that's not impossible.'

'You'd still have to be a fucking psycho,' mutters Gislingham. 'To do that to a little kiddie.'

'That's the point,' I say. 'Perhaps that's exactly what he wants us to think – that only a psychopath could have done that to his own child. Either way, we can't afford to close down any line of enquiry until we're sure it doesn't lead anywhere. And if that sounds like a cliché, remember how a cliché gets to be a cliché.'

'*Because it's true*,' they mutter, sing-song. They've heard that one before. All except Somer, who grins suddenly, then hides it by pretending to make a note on her pad. She has a great smile; it changes her whole face.

'But what about the body, sir?' Baxter again. 'If Rob killed her, how did she end up in Harper's shed?'

'The two gardens back on to one another – Harper's and Gardiner's. And the fence at the bottom is pretty rickety – it wouldn't be that hard to get through it.'

'It's a bit of a stretch though, isn't it, boss?' interrupts Everett. 'I mean, Rob Gardiner burying his wife's body in the garden of *exactly* the same house where we found a girl in the cellar? I mean, what are the odds against that?'

I shoot a look at Baxter, who pretends I haven't.

'It's a good point, Ev. And you're right, I don't believe in coincidences. Usually. But if we reject the possibility of coincidence entirely there's a risk we bend the evidence to make it all fit. And I don't know about you, but the more we find out about these two crimes the more dissimilar they seem. So let's investigate them that way. At least for now.'

People start to stand up, shuffle papers, and I beckon Everett.

'Can you look into what Vicky says about herself in her journal – see if that helps us with an ID?'

'There isn't much, boss –'

'She talks about looking for a new flat and not being in the city for very long. So ask the job centre about girls called Vicky who were on their books two or three years ago and then suddenly stopped signing on without any explanation. And try the letting agents too.'

She's not convinced, but she's a pro. 'OK, boss. I'll see what I can do.'

'What is it?' I ask. Because there's something. Something she wanted to add, and didn't.

'I was just remembering how badly she reacted when

you wanted to put her picture in the paper. Have you any idea why?'

I shake my head. 'Right now, none at all.'

* * *

Janet Gislingham is asleep on the sofa when her husband gets back from work, and it's only when she rouses herself and goes to check on her son that she realizes he's home. Billy is dozing, nestled in his blue and white blankets, in his blue and white nursery, surrounded by soft toys and piles of clothes in a year's worth of sizes all still in their plastic packaging. There's no item of babyware Janet hasn't thought of, bought already or borrowed just in case. And above the cradle, a mobile Gislingham's equally football-mad brother made for his first nephew, hung with cut-outs of famous Chelsea football players. Drogba, Ballack, Terry, Lampard, rotating slowly in the warm air.

Gislingham is standing at the cradle, and Janet watches as he reaches down and gently strokes their baby's silky hair. Billy shifts slightly under his father's hand, making tiny dreaming noises, his little hands curling and uncurling. The love on the man's face is as painful as loss.

'Chris?' she says, her hand still on the door. 'Is everything OK?'

But he doesn't respond, doesn't move at all. All is still except for the baby's tiny mews. She's not even sure if her husband knows that she's there.

'Chris?' A little louder now. 'Are you all right?'

Gislingham starts, and turns to face his wife.

'Course I am,' he says, with his usual smile. 'How could I not be?'

But when he comes towards her and folds her in his arms, she can feel his tears wet against her face.

*   *   *

It's gone nine when I get home. I spent over an hour with Walsh and his story never changed: he's never been in the cellar, he knows nothing about either Hannah or the girl, and he didn't steal anything from the house. His only explanation for the fingerprints is that he helped Harper sort out some junk years ago and it must be those boxes that got taken downstairs. Stalemate, in other words. We've put him in the custody suite overnight, but we're going to have to bail him if we don't get something a lot better than what we have right now.

In this job, you get good at the unexpected. Spotting when even very little things aren't where they ought to be. But when I push open my front door at 9.15 I hardly need super-sensitive powers to realize something's changed. Lilies in a tall glass vase I haven't seen in months. Bryan Ferry on low. Even – and this really is a shock – the smell of cooking.

'Hello?' I call, dumping my bag in the hall.

Alex appears in the kitchen door, wiping her hands on a tea towel. 'Should be ready in ten minutes,' she says, smiling.

'You didn't need to wait. I could have shoved a pizza in the microwave.'

'I wanted to. I suddenly felt like making something for a change. Glass of wine?'

In the kitchen there's a pot of casserole on the hob. A Spanish recipe she used to make a lot. Memories of a weekend in Valencia. She pours the Merlot and turns to me, cradling her own glass. One of the last of the wedding present set.

'How was your day?'

That's different too. Alex doesn't really 'do' small talk.

I drink some wine and feel it go straight to my head. I think I forgot to have lunch.

'Horrible. It looks like it was Harper's nephew who imprisoned and abused that girl. We found a journal she wrote while she was down there. It's horrific, what she went through.'

She nods. Strictly speaking, I shouldn't be telling her any of this, but we don't speak strictly in this house. Just like we don't do small talk. 'I feared as much,' she says. 'And Hannah?'

'That's not good either. Her best friend just told us Rob may have been hitting her. He's right back in the frame.'

Her face is grim. Probably as grim as mine.

She turns back to the casserole. Garlic, oregano, a hint of anchovies. My stomach turns over. And I stand there, with my wine, trying to decide. Do I tell her what Vicky wrote about the boy? Do I tell my wife that she was right and I was wrong — that the boy's own mother once hated him — perhaps still does? That he's spent the whole of his short life imprisoned with someone who never wanted him? And if I do, will that only make it worse? Will it only make her even more determined to give him the love she thinks every child deserves — the love she still has but can no longer bestow?

'There's time,' she says, still preoccupied with the pan, 'if you want to go up.'

'It's OK, I won't bother to change.'

'I didn't mean that. I meant if you wanted to check on him.'

I knew he was here. Of course I did. The food, the music, the smile, the flowers. They're all because of him. But knowing that and going up there, seeing him —

'It's all right, he's fast asleep,' she says, mistaking my

hesitation. Perhaps deliberately. 'He went out like a light. I think he's completely exhausted.'

She looks round at me. It's a test. And I've never been able to bear failing Alex.

The landing light is on, even though it's not yet dark, and the door to the bedroom is ajar. I move forward slowly until I round the corner and see his head on the pillow. The dark curls, the teddy bear Jake loved when he was this age. The boy is curled up tight like a dormouse, the grimy toy still clutched in one hand. I listen to him breathing, like I used to listen to Jake, standing exactly where I am now.

*   *   *

The phone rings six times before Quinn picks it up.

'It's me,' Somer says. 'Are you in the car? I can hear the traffic.'

'What do you want?'

'To try to sort things out. To talk.'

'Not sure there's anything to talk about. It was OK while it lasted, but you know what they say about shitting on your own doorstep.'

'I didn't shit on you –'

'Yeah, right.'

'We have to be professional, at the very least,' she says. 'You're still running a lot of this investigation – and I'm still part of it.'

'*Part* of it? You seem to be doing a bloody good job of trying to take it over, as far as I can see.'

'Oh come on, that's not fair –'

'You know something? I don't give a fuck. All I care about is putting that bastard Walsh behind bars where he belongs.

If you can help with that, fine. If all you're interested in is building your own poxy career, then you can fuck off.'

He reaches across and jabs the phone off. Five minutes later he turns into the Lucy's development and parks the Audi in the underground car park. His flat is on the top floor, with a view that would justify even an estate agent's hyperbole. The sun is just sliding below the horizon and the air is milky rose. On the balcony, looking over the canal and across towards Port Meadow, is Pippa. She has a champagne flute in one hand. She turns at the sound of the door and comes towards him. She's wearing his dressing gown and her hair is wet.

'You didn't manage to find anywhere, then?' he says, trying not to sound as suspicious as he feels.

She shakes her head.

'You tried all those numbers I gave you?'

She shrugs; it obviously didn't feature very highly on her current list of priorities. 'You know Oxford. The place is always chocka.'

'Look, all I meant was you can't stay here – regulations – you know –'

'This place is amazing,' she says, interrupting him. She sweeps an arm round. 'This room – it's so *big*.'

Quinn dumps his jacket on the back of the sofa. 'Yeah, well, the rest of the flat is pretty small.'

And there isn't a spare room. Though he doesn't actually say that. But all the same, she's clearly guessed what's on his mind. 'Look, there's a couple of mates I could try later. I'm sure I'll find somewhere. I don't want to cause you a load of hassle. Not when you've been so nice to me.' She skips over to the bottle of wine and pours him a glass, then brings it over. 'It's only cava – I got it at that funny little offy on Walton Street. But it's still fizz, isn't it?' She's back at the window again. 'How long have you lived here?'

'Oh, eighteen months or so.'

'And all on your own?'

She hardly needed to ask that; she's had hours to go through his bathroom, his drawers, his wardrobes.

Quinn puts his glass down on the coffee table. 'Why don't you get dressed and I'll sort out dinner.'

Her eyes widen. 'You're going to *cook*?'

He grins. 'No chance. I'm going to order a sodding takeaway.'

And suddenly, they're laughing.

*   *   *

In the morning, I'm out of the house before Alex is awake. I'm not sure I'm ready for a shared breakfast. Or the bright new box of Cheerios that was on the worktop when I made my coffee. If that sounds craven, then that's probably because it is.

I'm walking across the car park when I get the call from Challow.

'My chance to redeem myself in the eyes of CID.'

'The DNA?'

'You'll have it later today.'

'Thank Christ for that.'

'I'm sending over those extra fingerprint tests we took from Frampton Road too.'

'And?'

'Harper's are in most of the rooms, no surprise there. Not much at all in the top floor but I guess it's a while since anyone's been up there. But we did find Walsh's on the banisters on the first flight of stairs. Which may or may not be useful. From your point of view, I mean. And that display cupboard — it's been wiped clean. Not a mark on it. There was one other interesting finding too.'

'Which was?'

'The cupboard wasn't the only thing with no prints. There were none on the porn either. Harper's prints are on the box, and Derek Ross's too. But on the porn itself – nothing. And I don't know about you but that strikes me as odd. Very odd indeed.'

*　*　*

When Quinn wakes he's already late, and there's a rick in his neck. He rubs his eyes with the heel of his hand and sits up, feeling the heavy ache in the front of his skull. Then he hauls on his dressing gown and goes out into the sitting room. A greasy box of pizza, a half-eaten slab of garlic bread, two empty bottles of wine. He can hear the sound of the shower. He goes up to the bathroom door and knocks. 'I'll need to leave in fifteen, but I'll come back and pick you up later so you can make that statement.'

No reply. He goes over to the kitchen and starts the coffee machine. It looks like the girl has beaten him to it. There's an empty mug on the counter, and next to it, her phone.

He stares at it for a moment. Then turns it on.

*　*　*

Phone interview with Christine Grantham
5 May 2017, 10.32 a.m.
On the call, DC A. Baxter

AB: Mrs Grantham, we're talking to a number of people who were at Bristol University in the early 2000s. I think you were there then, is that right?

CG: I was, yes.

AB: And I think you were also a friend of Robert Gardiner?

CG: So that's what this is about. I did wonder.

AB: You were his girlfriend, I think?

CG: For a while, yes.

AB: What was he like?

CG: That's not the real question, though, is it? You've found his wife's body and suddenly you're asking me about him. That can't be a coincidence.

AB: We're just trying to get a full picture, Mrs Grantham. Fill in the gaps.

CG: Well, 'gaps' is the word, really. When it came to Rob. I always got the feeling he was holding something back. He was a very private person – probably still is.

AB: Did he ever do anything that made you feel uneasy?

CG: Are you asking if he hit me? Because if you are, the answer is no. He's a caring person. And yes, he has strong views and he doesn't suffer fools gladly, and that can make him sound a bit abrasive sometimes. But to be honest, I don't think he even realizes he's doing it a lot of the time.

AB: What did you know about his background?

CG: He comes from somewhere in Norfolk, I think. Not a wealthy family, though. He had to work hard to get where he had. I always thought that explained a lot about him. The intensity, you know.

AB: Did you ever meet Hannah?

CG: No. We didn't keep in touch.

AB: And why was it that your relationship ended?

CG: [pause]

     I'm not sure that's something I'm happy
     telling you.

AB: This is a murder inquiry, Mrs Grantham —

CG: [pause]

     Look, I wanted a family —

AB: And he didn't?

CG: No, that wasn't it. He definitely did want
     children. He just couldn't have them himself.

*   *   *

'So you don't recognize her?'

Everett is in the job centre in the middle of town. Sofas, computer terminals, desks that are trying hard not to look like desks. There are bright hanging panels in yellow and green; shots of smiling models with great teeth and chirpy messages about being 'Here to help' and 'Ready for work'. In rather painful contrast to the people milling listlessly about the place, who don't look ready for very much at all. The woman sitting in front of Everett looks all but defeated.

She stares again at the picture on Everett's phone, then passes it back to her, shaking her head. 'There are so many — and they come and go so much. I probably wouldn't recognize her if she'd been in here three weeks ago, never mind three years.'

'What about your records — can you do a search for girls called Vicky or Victoria who were signing on here then? Say, January 2014 onwards?'

'OK. I can do that.'

She turns to her computer. There's a tired piece of cardboard stuck to the screen with Blu-Tack. *You don't have to work to be mad here, but it helps.* There's also a plastic troll with beady eyes and bright blue acrylic hair. Everett hasn't seen one of those since she was at school.

The woman taps the keyboard then sits forward.

'I have one Vicky and three Victorias on file here in January 2014. The Vicky is still signing on now and the three Victorias have got jobs, one with Nando's, one at Oxford Brookes and one with a cleaning firm. Though that probably won't last. Too much like hard work for most of them.'

'Is there any way our Vicky could have been claiming without being on that database?'

The woman shakes her head. 'No. She'd be in here somewhere.'

'Perhaps by another name?'

'Doubt it. She'd have had to show us two forms of ID. Passport, driving licence – you know the sort of thing.'

Everett sighs. How is it possible, in a digital world, to leave no trace at all?

*   *   *

Quinn clatters up the final few stairs to the flat and opens the door.

'Pippa? Are you there?'

But all he hears is the sound of his own voice. The congealing remains of last night's dinner are still on the table, but the bags that had been stacked in the corner are gone. The only sign she was ever there is a pair of black lacy knickers, draped over one corner of the widescreen TV.

'Shit,' he says out loud. 'Shit shit shit.'

* * *

When I look up at Baxter's face my first thought is that I've never seen him look so animated.

'Sorry to bother you, boss, but I've just come off the phone with Christine Grantham. Used to go out with Rob Gardiner when they were at university.'

'Oh yes?'

'There's something he hasn't been telling us. Something big.'

* * *

In Banbury, the local forensics team are in Lingfield Road. It takes them over an hour, but eventually they find the missing *netsuke* rolled up in a towel and hidden under a loose floorboard. The officer bagging them up looks at one more closely as she labels it. An otter, a tiny fish gripped between its teeth. You can almost feel the water on its coat. 'Are these funny little things really worth all that trouble?' she asks Somer.

'Oh yes, I suspect these are worth a good deal. Walsh probably hid them after he saw the news about Harper – he knew it was only a matter of time before we tracked him down.'

The woman raises her eyebrows. 'Just shows you. Looks like a load of old plastic tat to me. The sort of thing you used to get in cornflakes boxes.' She grins, sealing the bag. 'Showing my age. You probably don't remember that.'

Somer smiles. 'Actually, I do.'

'OK, that's the lot. I'll get them photographed for you.'

'Thanks – I'll need something to send the insurance

company. So we can prove exactly where these things came from.'

There's the sound of feet on the stairs and Gislingham appears with one of the other forensics officers. Between them, they're carrying a computer, swathed in plastic.

'Any luck?' asks Somer.

Gislingham makes a face. 'We've been through upstairs and the loft, and there's nothing. The computer doesn't even have a password on it, and deffo no dodgy images or porn sites in the browser history. If he's a paedophile he's got a funny way of showing it.'

'And that's definitely the only machine he has – no laptop or tablet?'

He shakes his head. 'Judging from the state of this thing our man is not exactly what I'd call a gadget geek. I mean look at it – it's probably fifteen years old. These guys are going to rake it over just in case. But if you ask me, this is a dead end.'

Two hours later, at the school, Somer is wondering whether that's going to be the theme of the entire day. Though perhaps 'brick wall' is a better analogy this time round. As she sits in the school secretary's office, watching her fiddle about with a computer that's clearly beyond her, she wonders, as she has many times before, what it is about schools and doctors' surgeries that makes their administrators such paradigms of the passive-aggressive. Is it the job that does it or is that sort of person attracted to the job in the first place? The secretary at the last school she worked at could be the clone of the woman she's looking at now. The same rigid hair, the same blouse and skirt and cardigan in shades of blue that don't quite match, the same glasses hanging on a chain.

'What date was it again?' asks the woman, poking at the keyboard.

'June 24th, 2015,' says Somer, for the third time, with the same smile she had for the previous two, though her jaw is starting to ache with the effort.

The woman looks over her glasses at the screen. 'Ah, here we are. According to the timetable, Mr Walsh had a double period with the third form that morning.'

'And what time would that have started?'

'Ten thirty.'

'Nothing before that?'

The woman looks at her. 'No. Like I said, he had the double period. Nothing else.'

'And he was definitely here that day – he wasn't off sick?'

The woman sighs audibly. 'I would have to check the absence records to tell you that.'

Somer refreshes her smile. Again. 'If you wouldn't mind.'

More tapping at the keyboard, and then the phone rings. The woman picks it up. It's clearly some immensely detailed query about the admissions process, and as Somer sits there, telling herself not to get pissed off, the door to the head's office opens.

Sometimes – just sometimes – the uniform is useful.

'Can I help you?' asks the man, coming towards her. 'Richard Geare, I'm the head.' And then, seeing her smile (a real one this time), he smiles in turn. 'It's not spelled the same way, before you ask. I guess my parents weren't to know. I tell myself it helps my cred with the kids, but I'm not sure it does really. They probably don't even know who he is. Now if it was Tom Hiddleston, that might be different, but I'm a good ten years too old to pull that off.'

'PC Erica Somer,' she says, shaking his hand. 'Miss Chapman is helping me with some information.'

'About?'

'One of your teachers. Donald Walsh.'

Geare looks curious. 'And why, may I ask? Is there some sort of problem?'

Somer glances at the secretary, who's still talking on the phone but trying to signal to the head. 'Perhaps we could go into your office?'

The room is surprisingly modern for a school that takes so much care to look traditional. Smooth pale grey walls, a vase of white peonies, a desk in dark wood and steel.

'You like it?' he says, seeing her looking round. 'My partner did it for me.'

'She has good taste,' says Somer, taking a seat. Geare does the same.

'He, in fact. But yes. Hamish has great taste. So, how can I help you?'

'I'm sure you've seen the news. The girl and young child who were found in a cellar in Oxford?'

Geare frowns. 'What on earth can that possibly have to do with Donald Walsh, of all people?'

'The house they were found in – it belongs to Mr Walsh's uncle. His aunt's husband, strictly speaking, they're not actually related.'

Geare puts his fingertips together. 'And?'

'We've been trying to establish who visited the house, and when. Miss Chapman was helping me with a particular date in 2015. Checking whether Mr Walsh was in school that day.'

'So that girl had been down there as long as that?'

Somer hesitates, just for a moment but long enough for Geare to register.

'We're not sure,' she says.

He frowns again. 'I confess I'm confused. Why do you

want to know about one specific day, unless you think that was the day the girl was abducted?'

She flushes slightly. 'Actually, it was the day Hannah Gardiner went missing. You may remember the case. We believe there may be a connection. And if there isn't, we need to rule it out.'

'And you think Donald Walsh could be that connection?'

'I'm afraid so.'

There's a silence. She can see him thinking.

'Obviously we don't want that information getting into the public domain.'

He waves a hand. 'Of course not. I understand that. I'm just trying to reconcile what you just said with the Donald Walsh I know.'

'And who is that?'

'Diligent, hard-working. A little tiresome if I'm honest. And a bit reactionary, which can make him seem hostile on occasion.'

She nods, wondering if the real problem was Geare's sexuality.

'And in case you're wondering,' he says, 'I've never made a secret of the fact that I'm gay. Either to the staff or the parents.' He sits forward, suddenly earnest. 'Look, PC Somer – Erica – I've only been in this job nine months and there are a lot of changes I want to make. This school may look like a museum piece but I have no intention of running it like one. This room,' he says, gesturing, 'is a better indication of the sort of school I want this to be than the crusty armchairs in the staff common room. Which is why I bring prospective parents here, long before I take them round the rest of the school.'

'Perhaps you should change them as well.'

'The staff?'

She smiles. 'The armchairs.'

'It's on the list. But yes –' more serious now '– it wouldn't surprise me if there were some changes in the staff too.'

Somer can't help herself glancing towards the door, and when she looks back Geare is smiling drily. 'Miss Chapman was already planning to retire at the end of this term. Sometimes it's best not to make too many changes all at once, don't you find? But some of the teaching staff may choose to move on of their own accord. Not everyone shares my vision of where we need to go.'

'And Walsh is one of them?'

'Let's put it this way, I suspect he'd probably have left already if he had another place to go. Or enough money not to care.'

'I was going to ask you about that – well, indirectly. I believe Mr Walsh has had three different jobs in the last ten years. This one is the longest he's had in that time. Is there anything you can tell me about that – about why he left the two previous schools?'

He frowns. 'I'm not sure how much I can say, what with data protection –'

'That doesn't apply in a murder inquiry, sir. But feel free to check if that would give you some reassurance. To be honest, it's in Mr Walsh's interests that we get as full a picture as possible. If it turns out he had nothing to do with any of this, the sooner we establish that, the better. I'm sure you know what I mean.'

Geare is silent.

'It would be especially important to know if there'd been any incidents with young women – any suggestion of sexual harassment. Or –'

'Or interfering with the children?' He's shaking his head. 'Absolutely not. The only reason I wasn't saying anything was because I was wondering how best to put it, that's all. Donald Walsh is a difficult man. A bit brusque on occasion. I often wonder why he went into teaching at all given that he clearly doesn't like children. All that irony – he'd no doubt call it wit but the kids just think he's being sarky. It makes them wary of him, so he struggles to build rapport. He's not much good at being part of a team either. Not "collegiate". That's a Donald word by the way. Personally, I'd just say "friendly".'

There's a knock on the door and the secretary puts her head round. 'Mr Geare, your appointment has arrived.'

Somer gets up and shakes his hand. 'Thank you. If anything else occurs to you that you think we should know, please get in touch.'

Down in the car park, Gislingham is waiting. The PC from Walsh's office is being loaded into the forensic team's van.

'I spoke to some of the teachers as well,' he says as she gets in the car and closes the door. 'They don't like him, but they don't think he's actually dodgy.'

'Richard Geare said the same. Broadly.'

Gislingham looks at her. 'Richard Geare? *Seriously?*'

She shakes her head. 'Poor sod. It must be the first thing everyone says.'

'So is he?' asks Gislingham, pulling on his seat belt.

'Is he what?'

He grins. 'You know, *An Officer and a Gentleman.*'

She smiles. 'If only you knew.'

* * *

The curtains are open on the first floor of 81 Crescent Square. Robert Gardiner can be seen moving about, talking on his mobile. At one point he stoops suddenly and lifts his son on to his shoulders. Quinn sits watching for a moment, then gets out of his car and walks across the street.

'Detective Sergeant Quinn,' he says, when Rob Gardiner opens the door.

Gardiner frowns. 'What do you want? Has something happened? Have you arrested someone?'

'For the murder – no. Not yet. It's your childminder. Pippa?'

Gardiner's eyes narrow. 'What about her?'

'Do you know where she is?'

'No bloody idea.'

'Can you give me her number then? You must have it on your phone –'

'I did but I've deleted it. And no, I don't have it off by heart, sorry.'

'What about an address for her family?'

'Nope, don't have that either.'

'*Really?*' says Quinn, openly sceptical now. 'She was looking after your child – didn't you check her out, take references?'

'Hannah hired her, not me. She met her at that Farmers' Market on North Parade. At one of the stalls. Pottery or artisan coffee beans or some such. Anyway, they met up a few times after that and she told Hannah she'd been training to be a nanny but the money ran out. Hannah took pity on her and gave her a chance. She was like that. Always seeing the best in people.' He stares at Quinn with undisguised hostility. 'What do you want Pippa for, anyway?'

'Don't worry,' says Quinn. 'It wasn't that important.'

*   *   *

Everett locks her car and walks back up to the Iffley Road; if Vicky was living in a bedsit, this is as good a place to start as any. She has a list of rented properties and the only way forward is to start knocking on doors. Though she has that sinking feeling of looking for a needle in a city-sized haystack.

She consults her map. The first house on the list is in the street opposite. A pile of bikes outside, wheelie bins stuck anyhow across the front garden. She rings the bell and stands, waiting, until the door opens.

'DC Verity Everett,' she says, holding up her warrant card. 'Could I ask you a few questions?'

*   *   *

Interview with Robert Gardiner, conducted at
St Aldate's Police Station, Oxford
5 May 2017, 2.44 p.m.
In attendance, DI A. Fawley, DC A. Baxter,
P. Rose (solicitor)

AF: Mr Gardiner, thank you for making time to come
     in. I apologize for the short notice. We
     wanted to talk to you because we have some
     additional questions in relation to the death
     of your wife.

RG: [silence]

AF: Mr Gardiner?

RG: I'm waiting to see what you have to say. I
     can't imagine what you could possibly ask
     that you haven't already asked me a hundred
     times over. The answers aren't going to be
     any different. But go ahead – knock
     yourself out.

AF: As you know, we constructed our timeline for
    that day based on the fact that several
    witnesses said they saw your wife at Wittenham
    that morning. We know now they were mistaken.
    Obviously this means we have to re-question a
    number of people about where they were.
    Including you.

RG: So that's it, is it - you're going to try to
    stiff *me* with this? What about that bloke -
    Harper, whatever his name is?

AF: We expect to prefer charges shortly in
    relation to the young woman and child found in
    the cellar at 33 Frampton Road. We do not, as
    yet, have any conclusive evidence to suggest
    there is a connection between those offences
    and the death of your wife.

RG: So in the absence of any other options you're
    going to have another run-up at me, are you?
    Just like last time?

AF: New information has come to light, Mr Gardiner -

RG: Right, so now you seriously think *I* killed
    Hannah? That I abandoned my own *son*?

AF: I didn't say that.

RG: You didn't bloody have to.

AF: Look, we're trying to find out what happened.
    And to do that we need your help. Your
    cooperation.

PR: My client is more than willing to assist you
    in every reasonable way. Although I take it as
    read that you are questioning him as a
    witness, not as a suspect, given that you have
    not cautioned him?

AF: For the present, yes. So, let's go over what
     happened again.

RG: How many *more* times. I left the flat at 7.15
     and caught the 7.57 to Reading –

AF: Not that morning, Mr Gardiner. The night
     before. Tuesday June 23rd.

RG: But you know Hannah was alive that morning.
     You don't even need to take my word for it –
     you heard her yourself on that voicemail. What
     difference does it make what happened the
     night before?

AF: All the same, I'd like you to answer the
     question.

RG: [*sighs*]
     As far as I remember I collected Toby from the
     nursery on my way back from work. Must have
     been about 5.00. So I'd have got home about
     5.30. I'd been in a meeting with some German
     investors most of the day so I was pretty
     knackered. We just had a quiet night in.

AF: Can anyone corroborate that?

RG: No. *Like I said*, it was just the three of us.
     Me, Hannah and Toby.

AF: Your childminder – she wasn't there with you?

RG: No. She left about 7.00.

AF: Was your wife in when you got back?

RG: No. She didn't get back till about 8.00.

AF: And how was she?

RG: What does that mean?

AF: Happy? Anxious? Tired?

RG: She was a bit preoccupied I suppose. She had a
     lot on her mind. The interview the following
     day – there was a lot riding on it.

AB: The interview at Wittenham? With Malcolm
    Jervis?

RG: Yes. You *know* that. We've been through it
    countless times. It was a big deal for her. A
    big story. She'd been working on it for months.

AF: So she'd been in Summertown that afternoon. At
    the BBC.

RG: As far as I know, yes.

AF: As far as you know?

RG: Look, what is this? Is there something you're
    not telling me?

AF: We're just trying to establish the facts,
    Mr Gardiner. There's nowhere else she could
    have been?

RG: She *told* me she was in Summertown.

AB: When she got back?

RG: Right.

AB: At eight o'clock.

RG: Right.

AF: So it would surprise you to learn that she
    left the BBC offices at 2.45 that afternoon and
    didn't go back?

RG: What are you talking about? This is the first
    I've heard about this.

AF: We had no reason to check before. As I said.
    Now we do.

AB: We have also ascertained that your wife's car
    was picked up by number-plate recognition in
    the Cowley Road at just after 4.30 that
    afternoon.

RG: [*silence*]

AF: Do you know what she was doing there?

RG: No, I don't.

AF: No other story she was working on?

RG: Not that I know of.

AF: There's also a call from a pay-as-you-go
     mobile to your wife's office line that
     afternoon. About an hour before she left. Do
     you know anything about that?

RG: No. I told you. And in any case it could
     have been anyone - some member of the public
     with a story. Anyone. One of those
     protesters at the camp. They all had that sort
     of phone.

AB: So why go to Cowley?

RG: How the hell should I know?

AF: I'm sorry to have to raise this, Mr Gardiner,
     but your son. Toby. He's not your biological
     child, is he?

AB: We've spoken to a witness who told us you are
     unable to have children -

RG: What? How dare you - that's *personal*. It's
     nothing to do with any of this.

AF: I'm not so sure about that, Mr Gardiner. If
     you're not Toby's father, who is?

RG: I have no idea.

AF: Your wife had an affair?

RG: [*laughs*]
     You're so far off it's pathetic. That's your
     theory, is it? That I beat my wife to death
     because I found out she had a mystery bit of
     rough on the Cowley Road who'd fathered her
     child? And then - presumably - I dumped Toby
     at Wittenham because he wasn't mine?

AB: Is that what happened - your wife had an affair?

RG: No, of course she bloody didn't. OK, yes, I
    can't have kids. I've never made a secret of
    that, though I don't go about broadcasting it
    on sodding Facebook either.

AF: Why didn't you disclose it to us in 2015, when
    Hannah went missing?

RG: Because a) it was nothing at all to do with
    it, and b) it was none of your bloody
    business. And both of those, incidentally,
    still apply.

AF: So Toby is adopted?

RG: No, he was conceived by donor insemination.
    Hannah had no problem with that.

AF: But it had caused problems with other
    relationships, hadn't it?

RG: You've been questioning my *old girlfriends*?
    [*turns to Mr Rose*]
    Are they allowed to do that?

PR: Is there anything else, Inspector? It strikes
    me Mr Gardiner has had more than enough for
    one day. He's still coming to terms with the
    discovery of his wife's body. In particularly
    gruesome circumstances.

AF: I'm afraid we're not through yet. Analysis of
    the blanket found wrapped round your wife's
    body bears traces of your DNA. Yours, hers and
    your son's. That's all. No one else's. Can you
    explain that?

RG: [*silence*]

AF: Can you explain that, Mr Gardiner? Did you
    ever own a blanket like that?

RG: I have no idea.

AF: It was dark green with a tartan pattern in red. In case that jogs your memory.
[*silence*]

RG: The only thing I can think of is the picnic blanket she used to have in the back of the car. I thought we'd got rid of it but it may have still been in the boot.

AB: What did that look like?

RG: I really can't remember. Some dark colour. Green maybe.

AF: There was also fingerprint evidence. When we found your wife's body there was tape wrapped round it. Packing tape.

PR: Is this really necessary, Inspector? This sort of detail is extremely distressing.

AF: I'm sorry, Mr Rose, but these are questions we have to ask. There were fingerprints on the tape, Mr Gardiner, but most of them are too smudged to give a clear result. But one of those is a partial match to yours.

PR: A *partial* match? How many points are we talking about here?

AF: Six, but as I said –

PR: Oh for heaven's sake, *my* prints are probably a six-point match. You'd need eight *at least* to even get to first base, Inspector. *As well you know.*

AF: Are you a violent man, Mr Gardiner?

RG: *What?* Not this again. No, of course I'm not *violent.*

AF: Your wife apparently had a bruise on her face a few weeks before she disappeared.

RG: [*laughs*]

      Who told you that? Beth bloody Dyer? Had to
      be. She's a right little stirrer - Dyer by
      name, dire by bloody nature. It was Toby, if
      you must know. He caught Hannah on the face
      with one of his toys. It was an accident. An
      occupational hazard with a small child. If
      either of you had a kid you would know that.

AB: Detective Sergeant Quinn also saw a bruise on
      your childminder's arm yesterday.

RG: Look, is she pressing charges or something?

AB: We will be bringing her in to make a
      statement. It's possible she may wish to take
      it further.

RG: [*silence*]

      I barely touched her. Really. She just pissed
      me off, that's all.

      [*silence*]

      Look, she'd just told me she was pregnant. She
      said it was mine - denied ever having slept
      with anyone else. Well, even you lot can put
      two and two together and make four on that one.

AB: So Miss Walker is your girlfriend.

RG: She's not my girlfriend.

      [*silence*]

      We slept together. *Once*. OK? Have you ever
      done anything really stupid when you were
      pissed and depressed and regretted it
      afterwards? No? Well, go figure.

AF: So when she tried to pass off the child as
      yours you lost your temper?

RG: I was angry. I don't make a habit of it.

AF: Really? It strikes me you have an unusually
     short fuse.

AB: Is that what happened in 2015? Did Hannah
     'piss you off'?

RG: Don't be bloody ridiculous.

AF: Or was it something else — did something
     happen to Toby — something you thought was her
     fault?

RG: [*silence*]
     I'm going to say this now, and then I am going
     to go home to look after my son, and unless
     you arrest me I don't think there's anything
     you can do to stop me. The last time I saw my
     wife was 7.15 in the morning on June 24th 2015.
     She was alive and well. I never hit her, I
     have no idea who killed her and I don't know
     how her body ended up in Frampton Road. Is
     that clear?

AF: Perfectly.

PR: Thank you, gentlemen, we'll see ourselves out.

*   *   *

Quinn is waiting outside when I leave. He was watching on the video feed. He seems jumpy. Uncharacteristically so.

'So what do you think?' he asks as we watch Gardiner and Rose disappear down the corridor.

'What do I think? I think he's angry, defensive and unpredictable. But I'm still not sure he's a murderer.'

Quinn nods. 'I can see him killing the wife in a fit of rage, but dumping the kid? That's a big stretch.'

'I know. Walsh or Harper, yes, but not Gardiner. But

Gardiner's the only one who definitely knew where Hannah was going that day.'

'Actually, boss,' says Baxter, coming out and closing the door behind him, 'I'm not so sure about that. I checked the spec of Hannah's Mini. She had satnav. She could easily have loaded the directions to Wittenham into the system the night before. In which case –'

Quinn throws up his hands. 'In which case any Tom, Dick or Harry who got into that car could have known where she was going. *Jesus.* Back to sodding square one.'

'Though in that case, my money would be on Walsh rather than Harper,' continues Baxter evenly. 'Harper's never even owned a PC as far as I can tell, never mind a car new enough to have satnav. He probably wouldn't know where to start.'

'OK,' I say, 'get on to Gislingham and ask him to check if Walsh has a satnav in his car. And ask him to cover off the Cowley Road angle when he gets back – see if anyone there recognizes Hannah. It's a very long shot after all this time, but it's a box we need to tick, all the same.'

'Right,' says Quinn, turning to go, but I hold him back and turn instead to Baxter.

'Can you do that?'

Baxter nods and starts off down the corridor, though not without a quizzical glance back over his shoulder.

Once he's out of earshot I turn to Quinn. 'Two things. First, where the hell is Pippa Walker – I thought you were bringing her in?'

He blinks. 'I'm on it.'

'Well, get a move on. And second, sort out whatever it is you have going on with Erica Somer. I don't particularly care what you do, Quinn, or who, for that matter, but I'm not having it getting in the way of this investigation. Don't make me say it twice.'

'Right,' he says. And odd though it sounds, it's almost as if he's relieved.

* * *

At 4.00 p.m. the Cowley Road is just getting into its stride. Stacks of exotic fruit in boxes, someone sweeping the pavement outside the Polish grocer's. Kids and bikes, mums and pushchairs, a couple of Rastas smoking cross-legged on the pavement, an old lady bent double over a floral shopping trolley, a mangy-looking terrier out on its own. Gislingham locates the number-plate recognition camera that picked up Hannah's car and looks back down the parade. Three betting shops, a 24/7 convenience store and half a dozen restaurants – Slovak, vegan, Lebanese, Nepalese, Vietnamese. He's prepared to bet most of them weren't here two years ago. But there's one place that was. The traditional family butcher that's probably been there a generation, never mind a decade. Pies and sausages in the window, an old-fashioned scalloped canopy and an even more old-fashioned life-size plastic butcher standing cheerily outside, hands on hips. Gislingham edges his way to the front of the queue and asks for a quick word.

'What's the problem, mate?' says the man, eyeing Gislingham's credentials as he trims a joint of beef, expertly turning, cutting, turning, cutting.

'No problem. No problem at all. I just wondered whether you'd seen this woman?'

He unfolds a picture of Hannah Gardiner. The one they'd used at the time. She's standing with her back to a gate; her long dark hair is tied in a ponytail, she's wearing a navy quilted jacket and there's a view of fields and sheep and mountains. Somewhere in the Lake District.

'I remember her – that's the woman who went missing, right?'

'You remember her – round here? When was that?'

The man looks apologetic. 'No, sorry, mate. I meant I remember that picture. It was all over the papers.'

'Do you think you ever saw her, though? Her car was picked up on the traffic cameras along here, the afternoon before she disappeared. The car was a bright orange Mini Clubman, but she may have come along here on foot as well.'

'But that's at least a year ago, isn't it?'

'Two, actually. June 23rd 2015.'

The man pushes the cuts of fat to one side and reaches for the string. 'Sorry, but no chance. Not that long ago.'

'Is there anywhere round here you can think of she might have been going? She was a journalist.'

The man shrugs. 'Take your pick. Could be anything. Have you looked at the paper for that week? *Oxford Mail?* Might give you a clue.'

Now why the hell didn't I think of that, Gislingham says to himself. 'Cheers, mate – really helpful.'

The man looks up. 'No worries. Always happy to help the police. Do you want some sausages before you go? On the house?'

Back out on the pavement, Gislingham tucks a packet of the house speciality into his jacket pocket and calls Quinn.

'Yeah, what is it?'

'I think I may have an idea on Hannah Gardiner. I'm coming back to the station to check it out.'

'OK, whatever.'

Gislingham frowns. 'You all right? You sound a bit off.'

There's a silence, then, 'Look, if you must know, I think I fucked up.'

So that's what it is, thinks Gislingham. Not the Erica thing. Or perhaps not just the Erica thing. He waits. Wouldn't do to sound too keen. Or too gloating.

'That childminder of Gardiner's,' says Quinn. 'Pippa Walker. You met her too, didn't you?'

For one horrible moment Gislingham thinks he knows what Quinn's about to say – but surely even he wouldn't have –

'You didn't – tell me you didn't.'

'No, of course I bloody didn't. It's something else. I let her stay.'

'What do you mean, you "let her stay"?'

'Gardiner had chucked her out. She had nowhere else to go so I let her stay.'

'At your *flat*? Jesus, Quinn –'

'I know, I know – look, nothing happened, I swear –'

'That's not the point though, is it? You need to get her out of there – pronto.'

'She's already gone. I went back just now and she wasn't there.'

'But she's still coming in to make that statement?'

'I don't know.'

'What do you mean, you *don't know*? You got her number, right – you can call her?'

Quinn sighs. 'The one she gave me is unobtainable.'

Gislingham's getting really pissed off now. 'Oh, that's fucking marvellous – so we now have no idea where she is, and no way of contacting her, and she could be the only witness we have against Gardiner.'

Quinn takes a deep breath. 'There's something else. I looked at the phone – her texts and stuff. It was just for a minute – she was in the shower –'

'Shit, mate, when in a hole, stop effing digging – you need permission to do that, you know you do. You could lose your sodding job over this –'

'I know that, all right?' snaps Quinn. 'It was just – *there* – and now –'

There's a silence.

'And now what?'

'Now I *know* Gardiner's lying. Pippa was texting him at least a week before Hannah's disappearance.'

'Yeah, well, that's not such a big deal, is it – she was looking after his kid – she was bound to text him sometimes –'

'Not like that, Gis. Trust me.'

Trust *you* to get us into this sodding mess, more like, thinks Gislingham. 'So what do we do now? They probably wouldn't give us a warrant for her phone even if we had the right number because we can't claim she's any sort of suspect – even if she *was* screwing Gardiner she has a rock-solid alibi for the morning Hannah disappeared. And we can't let on what we're really looking for because that'll just land you in the shit.'

'Look, are you going to help me or what?'

Gislingham sighs as loudly as he can. 'I don't have much of a choice, do I?'

*　*　*

It's just after five and I'm with Baxter at the tech firm who do our forensic voice-recognition work. We're in front of a bank of computer screens. I haven't got a clue what half this stuff is for. The analyst sitting beside us doesn't look much older than fifteen.

'OK,' he says after a moment, 'I've got the audio loaded now, so let's have a listen.'

24/06/2015 06:50:34
It's me. Where are you? I'll have to leave soon.
Call me, will you?

There's a muffled noise, some clicks and then the line goes dead. She sounds exasperated, on the edge of anger. The analyst goes back and plays it again, and Hannah Gardiner's frustration maps itself on to the screen in a series of peaks and troughs. Loudness, pitch, intensity. The analyst sits back, then turns towards me.

'The problem is she says so little. It's only fourteen words, and it's pretty distorted. But I cleaned it up as much as I can and compared it to some other material which we know is definitely Hannah Gardiner's voice. Reports on the BBC website, that sort of thing.'

He turns and pulls up more wave patterns on to the screen. 'See — all three of these are obviously the same person — you can tell that with the naked eye, even without doing the analytics.'

He drags the pattern made by the voicemail over and lines it up with the other samples. 'And here's your voicemail.' He sits back. 'Like I said, fourteen words isn't really enough to make a definitive match, but for my money, it's her.'

'So she was alive and well, in Crescent Square, at 6.50 that morning?'

He nods. 'Looks like it.'

* * *

'Quinn? It's me.'

Gislingham is out of breath, his voice coming in gasps. In the background Quinn can hear traffic.

'Where are you?'

'On the High. I was coming back from Cowley and I think I just saw Pippa Walker. If it wasn't her it's someone who looks bloody like her.'

Quinn grips the phone. '*Where* – where did you see her?'

'At the bus-stop by Queen's Lane. I'm there now – I came back as soon as I could turn round but she'd already gone.'

'Did she have bags with her – a suitcase or anything?'

'Not that I could see. Just a carrier bag, I think.'

'So if we're lucky she's still in Oxford.'

'I'll see if we can get some CCTV. We may be able to work out what bus she got on.'

'Cheers, mate. I owe you one.'

'Yeah,' says Gislingham heavily. 'I know.'

* * *

Sent: Fri 05/05/2017, 18.05
From: AlanChallowCSI@ThamesValley.police.uk
To: DIAdamFawley@ThamesValley.police.uk,
            CID@ThamesValley.police.uk

Subject: DNA results: 33 Frampton Road

I'm about to call you about this, but in case I don't get through, here are the salient points:

Shed
We double-checked the results for the blanket used
to wrap the body of Hannah Gardiner, and there is no DNA
from either Donald Walsh or William Harper. The only DNA
aside from hers was – as previously stated – that of her
husband, Robert Gardiner, and her son, Toby Gardiner.

Cellar
The young woman's bed yielded DNA from two males:
saliva from Donald Walsh, and both saliva and semen from
William Harper.

Child
We ran a DNA test on the samples obtained with the
assistance of Social Services, and cross-checked them
against some small blood spots found on the child's
bedding. The boy in the cellar is William Harper's son.

*   *   *

I've just got to the ward at the John Rad when the call from
Challow comes through, which earns me a disapproving
look from the nurse.

'You're supposed to turn those things off, Inspector.'

'I know. I'm sorry, but this is important.'

And it is.

'You're sure – no question?' I take a deep breath. 'Right.
I'm at the hospital. I'll talk to her. See if I can get her to confirm it.'

The nurse is looking at me with pointed impatience. 'Are
you ready now?'

'Yes, sorry.'

*

It's less than forty-eight hours since I last saw her, but Vicky looks a lot better. Someone's helped her wash her hair, and she's sitting in the chair by the window in a pair of jeans and a big jumper. There's a magazine on her lap and she suddenly looks re-attached to the world. An ordinary girl again. I tip my hat silently to whoever it was did all this, and when I catch the nurse's eye I know it was her. She smiles.

'I think Vicky's feeling a bit better today. We've even managed to persuade her to eat something.'

I gesture towards the chair by the bed. 'Can I sit by you for a few minutes, Vicky?'

She flashes me a look, then nods. I drag the chair a little closer and sit down.

'Have you been able to write anything down for us?'

She flushes a little and looks away.

'Vicky still hasn't been able to speak,' says the nurse. 'We think it's better not to push it. Take things slowly.'

'I think that's a very good idea,' I say, trying to look reassuring. 'But I've just had a call from our forensics lab, and if you think you're up to it I'd like to ask you a couple of questions. Would that be OK?'

She looks at me. Makes no movement.

'There's one thing we need to be really clear about: whether there was just one person who attacked you or whether there were two of them. We can't tell for certain from the DNA results we've had, and I'm sure you understand how important it is that we know for sure, one way or the other. So can you tell me, Vicky? Was it just one man – no one else?'

She stares at me a moment. Her cheeks are becoming flushed again. And then she nods.

I get out my phone, find the image and show it to her.

'Was it this man?'

She looks at me, then at the picture, then shakes her head.

I change the image.

'This one?'

She gasps a little, and puts her hand to her mouth. The tears come.

'Yes,' she whispers, her voice hoarse with long silence. 'Yes.'

*   *   *

> Quinn – found that CCTV from the bus-stop. Pippa was on the #5 towards Blackbird Leys. I've got the reg number so you shd be able to track down the driver. He'd prob remember her

>> Cheers Gis. Like I said I owe you one

> It occurred to me – the #5 goes via the business park – cd she have been going to see Gardiner?

>> Def worth asking him. Cheers mate

*   *   *

'So where are we now, Adam?'

Superintendent Harrison's office. Saturday morning. There are few good reasons to find yourself in here at the weekend, but on a scale of one to ten on the discomfiture scale this is probably only about five. And to be fair, he does need to know.

'Vicky identified Harper as her abductor, sir. And the forensic results back that up.'

'What about Walsh's DNA on the girl's bedding?'

'He did tell us he'd stayed over once or twice, and Challow says saliva could have got on the bedding if that had been on the bed he used. It's not impossible.'

'So the abduction was Harper acting alone. No collusion from Walsh at all.'

'It's looking like it. Vicky didn't recognize him.'

'All the same, this is a man who's never been violent before. Do you still think Harper's dementia was a factor – somehow triggered by her unfortunate resemblance to his wife?'

I take a deep breath. I'd been so sure it was Harper, but then the journal convinced me otherwise, and ever since then I've been thinking of Harper as a sad old man exploited by Donald Walsh for his own twisted ends. But he's not. He can't be.

'Actually, sir, I think it's a lot more complex than that. Harper may be showing signs of dementia now, but three years ago, it would have been a very different story. Look at Vicky's journal – there's no suggestion there that the man who imprisoned her was in a vulnerable mental state. I think he knew exactly what he was doing. And yes, Vicky's resemblance to Priscilla could have been a factor, but not out of confusion. Out of vindictiveness. Out of some perverted idea of revenge.'

'But didn't he say he was frightened of the cellar – that he could hear noises down there?'

'I suspect that's because the dementia is getting worse. He may even have forgotten the girl was there. That would also explain why the food and water were running out.'

Harrison sits back in his chair. 'I'm still struggling to get my head round this. On the face of it, Walsh seemed a lot more likely.'

'I know, sir. I thought so too.'

'But DNA doesn't lie. The boy is Harper's son.'

'Yes, sir.'

'Speaking of DNA, where are you with Gardiner?'

'We've questioned him again. We have the partial finger-print on the tape and some traces of his DNA on the blanket the body was wrapped in, but it's all just circumstantial – none of it would stand up in court. Though it appears he may have been violent to the childminder. We're trying to find out if it's part of a pattern.'

'*May have been?* Haven't you spoken to her about it?'

'Not yet, sir. She's proving hard to track down.'

I see him frown and I curse Quinn.

'But you're not ruling Harper out – it's still possible he committed both crimes – the girl in the cellar *and* Hannah Gardiner?'

'Yes, sir. That's still possible.'

'And would the CPS pursue a case against him, given his medical condition?'

'I don't know – we haven't got to that stage yet.'

'But he's in suitable accommodation, in the meantime?'

I nod. 'A secure dementia unit near Banbury. Whatever happens, he won't be going back to Frampton Road. The house will probably end up being sold.'

'Well, at least the Thames Valley Police will have one sat-isfied customer.'

'Sir?'

'That tosser who bought the pile next door.'

I'm starting to get the distinct impression that Quinn is avoiding me, and when I find him sitting in his Audi in the car park, eating a sandwich, I know I'm right.

I tap on the window. 'Quinn?'

He winds it down, hurrying to finish his mouthful. 'Yup. What is it, boss?'

'What are you doing out here?'

'You know. Lunch.'

I give him a 'yeah, right' look, and he does at least have the decency to look sheepish.

'Have you brought Pippa Walker in yet?'

'Ah, bit of a problem there, boss.'

So that's it.

'What sort of problem?'

'We can't track her down.'

I stare at him until he stops chewing and stuffs the sandwich back in its bag.

'I hear there are these things called mobile phones –'

He colours. 'I know – but we don't have the number. The one she gave me is unobtainable. Sorry. Sir.'

I don't usually get a 'sir' from Quinn unless he knows he's fucked up, so he appears to have decided to take his medicine on the chin. Mixed metaphor, but you get my drift.

'We took a statement from her in 2015 – there'd be an address on that.'

He nods. 'Arundel Street.'

'Well, start round there. It'd make sense she'd go back to somewhere she knew.'

'Right,' says Quinn, and starts his engine. 'Don't worry. It's my cock-up. I'll sort it.'

* * *

'PC Somer? This is Dorothy Simmons, from Holman Insurance. We spoke before, about Dr Harper's collection?'

'Ah, yes, thank you for getting back to me, especially at the weekend.'

'I've had a look at the photos you sent, and compared them to what we have on file for Dr Harper. And you're right – they're definitely some of the same items.'

'And are they valuable?'

'Oh yes. When Dr Harper had the collection assessed in 2008 it was worth somewhere in the region of £65,000. In fact, I've been trying to get him to have the valuation updated – I was worried he was underinsured. But he never seems to answer his correspondence.'

'That's really helpful, Miss Simmons. Thank you.'

'There was one more thing. I don't know how significant it is, but Mr Walsh only has some of the *netsuke*. Some appear to be missing.'

'Are they particularly expensive ones?'

'One is. But the rest are probably the least valuable of the lot. I don't know if that's significant.'

Quite possibly, thinks Somer. If Quinn's right and Walsh was only interested in filching the pricey ones. So much for 'sentimental value' and 'family legacy'. But all the same, it does raise one interesting question.

Where are the rest?

*   *   *

After a wild goose chase in Arundel Street Quinn's day is showing no sign of improving any time soon. When he gets back to the station at just gone three, the first person he sees in the corridor is Gislingham.

'Have you found that bus driver yet?'

Gislingham looks at him. It's your mess, he thinks, you

bloody fix it. 'No,' he says out loud. 'I've got stuff to do. *My own* stuff.'

Quinn runs a hand through his hair. He's proud of his hair and spends a lot on it. Which pisses Gislingham off even though he knows it shouldn't. Though the bald patch he's just started to notice in the bathroom mirror probably has something to do with that.

'Right,' says Quinn. 'Sorry. It's just I've got Fawley on my back.'

Yeah, but not half as much as you would if he knew the truth, thinks Gislingham.

He turns to the coffee machine and pretends to be debating between the cappuccino and the latte and chooses what he always has (which tastes the same as all the rest anyway). Then he turns to face his DS.

'Look, I'll help you out when I can, all right?'

Quinn looks at him; half of him wants to bawl Gis out, the other half is reminding him that he owes him. The second half wins.

'OK,' he says. 'OK. Thanks.'

* * *

'So do you think you'll be able to get back to them by close of play Monday?'

Alex Fawley switches her mobile from one hand to the other. It's one of her colleagues, chasing something for their most important client which should have been sent by Friday afternoon. Alex has been trying to avoid having to hand the case over to her assistant, but juggling her workload and a toddler isn't easy; it was bad enough when it was Jake, but now –

'Alex?'

'Sorry. I was just checking the diary. Yes, that should be fine.'

She must sound distracted though, because he asks her again; his doubt is audible.

'You're sure? I mean, we can always –'

'No, no. Really. It's fine.'

There's a crash then, from the other room. And a wail that spirals into a shriek.

'Jesus, Alex, what the hell was that?'

'Nothing – nothing. I have decorators in. They must have dropped something. Look, I'm sorry, Jonathan, but I have to go. I'll have the documents to you in plenty of time, I promise.'

*   *   *

In Interview Room Two, Donald Walsh is being formally charged. He's trying very hard to conceal it, but he's an angry man. Everett's drawn the short straw on this one, but she's grown a fairly thick skin for heavy irony. Which is probably just as well.

'Mr Walsh, you are being charged in relation to the theft of certain artefacts from Dr William Harper of thirty-three Frampton Road, Oxford. I believe your solicitor has explained your rights to you and what's going to happen next? Do you understand?'

'Given that it was in words of one syllable, I think I can just about manage it.'

'You have been given a date to appear at the magistrates' court as we have just discussed –'

'Yes, yes, you don't need to reel it all out again, Constable. I'm not *retarded*.'

Everett finishes filling in the form and hands it to Walsh, who snatches it away and makes a great show of signing it without reading a word.

'I still don't know what all the fuss is about,' he says tetchily. 'I was just looking after the collection. Any *reasonable* person would see at once that Bill's in no fit state to do so. Last time I was there one of the prize pieces had already gone AWOL. He could have flushed it down the bloody bog for all I know. And they'll come to me when he dies anyway – he has no children, who else is there? In fact it's a bloody miracle more of them weren't stolen long ago – anyone could have got into that place – the security was non-existent.'

'I believe my colleagues had to break the door down to get in.'

'Yes, well, if they'd used their *brains* and tried round the back they'd have found that the conservatory didn't even have a functioning lock. Half the windows were broken – even that bloody cat had got in – that Siamese thing – I heard it upstairs. No wonder items have been stolen. Something I will be insisting that you investigate, incidentally.'

Which, Everett thinks, is actually pretty rich, considering. But she has too much nous to say so.

Walsh tosses the form back at Everett. It slips across the table and falls on to the floor. 'Right, I *assume* I can go home now, if that's all right with you?'

*   *   *

It's 4.30 and Alex still hasn't done any work. It's raining hard and she's sitting in the kitchen with the boy at her feet. It was a nightmare, getting this extension built, but it's changed the whole house. Given it elbow room. And light. Even in cloud, light streams down from the roof lantern. She edges off the chair and on to the floor next to the child.

'Shall we play a game?'

He looks at her warily. He has a teddy bear in one hand. Jake's teddy bear. The one Adam bought for him before he was even born.

'It's easy,' she says. 'Look.'

She lies down flat and looks up, into the sky. Needles of golden rain catch the light before splintering in stars against the lantern glass.

'See? You can watch the rain coming down. It's like magic.'

The boy looks up, craning his neck. Then he raises his hands towards the light, laughing with a bubble of pure childlike joy.

*   *   *

Telephone interview with Terry Hurst, bus driver,
Oxford Bus Company
6 May 2017, 5.21 p.m.
On the call, DS G. Quinn

GQ: Mr Hurst, we're trying to track down a young
     woman who got on your bus at Queen's Lane at
     4.35 yesterday afternoon.

TH: Oh yes, what's all this about then?

GQ: It's a police inquiry, Mr Hurst. That's all
     that should concern you.

TH: So what did she look like, this girl?

GQ: About 5' 8", long fair hair. Green eyes. She
     was wearing a pair of denim shorts, a crochet-
     type top and sandals. And sunglasses.

TH: Oh yes, I remember her all right.

GQ: Do you remember where she got off? We think it may have been at the business park.

TH: Nope, definitely wasn't there. She was standing because we was pretty full, and I remember looking round to make sure everyone was getting off OK. She'd already got off by then.

GQ: You don't have CCTV in the bus?

TH: Not in that one, no.

GQ: So you have absolutely no idea where she got off?

TH: I didn't say that. As a matter of fact I think it was probably by the Tesco in the Cowley Road. Will that do you?

GQ: I suppose it's a start. If it's the best you can do.

TH: You're welcome.

    [*mutters*]

    Tosser.

*   *   *

It must be two or three in the morning when I wake. The sky is the deep blue never-quite-dark of early summer. The curtain is slightly open and I can feel a whisper of cool air.

I lever myself up on my elbows, blinking into the darkness. As I walk into his room he's standing there. In the cot. In the silence. The sheen of his eyes catching a sliver of light from the window. He has a finger in his mouth, and in his other hand, Jake's teddy bear.

'What is it? Did you have a bad dream?'

He stares at me, rocking slightly, then shakes his head.

'Would you like some milk?'

A nod this time.

I move closer. 'Do you mind if I pick you up?'

He looks up at me, then lifts his arms. I reach down and gather him up. It's the first time I've done it since he came here, and because of that, because it's dark and my senses are sharpened, I'm aware of him – of his physical presence – more acutely than I've been before. I know I've been keeping him at a distance, not just mentally but emotionally, and I know that this has kept me physically distant too. But now, for the first time, I have his skin against my skin, and his smell in my nostrils. Bath soap, milk, piss, that sweet biscuit scent little children always seem to have. He leans against my chest and I feel his heaviness shift in my arms. Alex always says there's a reason why women who have no kids have cats. Something warm and living that's just the weight of a baby – something you can lift and hold against you just as you would a child; there's a deep physiological pleasure in that, which goes beyond conscious love. And standing here, holding this boy against me, I feel it too.

In the morning, I'm up first, and when Alex comes down she finds us in the kitchen. The boy in the high chair with a bowl of mashed banana, and me at the dishwasher. I drive Alex mad re-stacking everything she puts in it, so I'm trying to finish before she comes down. The radio is on and I'm humming. Though I don't realize that until Alex comes in. She's in a pair of pale jeans and a white T-shirt, and her hair is down. With no make-up, she looks younger somehow. Perhaps I see too much of her in lawyer mode.

She smiles at me. 'You sound happy.'

She's staring at what I'm doing with the dishwasher, but

she's obviously decided not to mention it; she's determined not to spoil the mood.

'I shouldn't. I'm likely to have a grim day.'

She moves closer to the boy and puts her hand gently against his hair. 'Are you going to have to work all weekend?' Her tone is light; lighter than it usually is in circumstances like these.

'I'm sorry. You know how it is.'

She picks up the carton of juice and shakes it. 'Pity. I was hoping we might do something. Go somewhere –'

She stops herself but I hear the words all the same. *As a family.*

I turn back to the dishwasher and start stacking again, moving cups, shifting plates. Displacement activity in every sense of the word. 'Look, there's something you need to know.'

She pours a cup of coffee. Carefully, with exaggerated calm. 'Oh yes?'

'We had the DNA back. The boy's father. It isn't Donald Walsh.'

She leans against the worktop and lifts the cup to her lips. 'I see. So it was William Harper after all?'

'Yes. Vicky identified him.'

Her eyes widen slightly, but that's the only sign. 'She's talking?'

'A little. A couple of words. We can't afford to rush her.'

'No,' she says quickly. 'Absolutely not. That could do untold damage.'

I straighten up, feeling the pain in my knees. 'Look, Alex –'

'I know what you're going to say, Adam. That this is only for a few days – that I'm not his mother.'

I move a little closer, put my hand on her arm. 'I just don't want you to get hurt. I don't want you getting attached to him – or him getting attached to you, for that matter. It wouldn't be fair. Or kind.'

Her lips tremble. 'To him? Or to me?' And as her eyes fill with tears I pull her towards me and we stand there, my arms round her, kissing her hair. The boy looks up from his bowl and stares at us, his huge eyes locked on mine.

* * *

At 7.15, Gislingham has already been up for three hours. He eventually gave up trying to get off again and slid out of the bed, leaving Janet buried in a sleep even Billy hadn't broken. And now, his son nestling in the sling across his chest, he's moving about the kitchen, tidying up, warming milk, singing Johnny Cash.

'Who says men can't multi-task, eh, Billy?' he says, smiling down at the gurgling baby. 'But it's our secret, OK? Cos if Mum finds out she'll have the both of us with a list of chores as long as your arm. Actually, make that as long as *my* arm. Oi,' he says, seizing a chubby foot, 'that's some left kick you're developing there, lad. We'll have you playing at Stamford Bridge yet.'

'Oh no you won't,' says Janet, trailing into the kitchen in her dressing gown and bare feet. 'Not if I've got anything to do with it.' She slides heavily on to one of the kitchen chairs.

'You look done in,' says Gislingham carefully. 'Why don't you go back to bed for a bit?'

She shakes her head. 'Too much to do.'

Gislingham looks round the kitchen. 'I think I've done most of it. Washing's on, dishes are done, Billy's fed.'

She sighs then hauls herself up again and comes over, reaching to extract Billy from the papoose. The little boy starts to kick and then to cry, his face puckering into a red wail.

'He was fine,' says Gislingham. 'Really.'

'He needs changing,' she says over her shoulder as she bends to pick up a packet of nappies out of the carrier bag Gislingham brought home with him and then marches the still howling Billy out of the kitchen and up the stairs.

'Well, *I* didn't think he needed changing,' announces Gislingham to no one in particular. He unstraps the papoose and goes over to pick up the empty carrier bag. He scrunches it up for recycling, and then stops. Sits down at the table and gets out his phone.

> Just had a thought. That carrier bag
> Pippa had with her at the bus stop – I
> think it cd have been from Fridays Child.
> CCTV a bit fuzzy but I think I recog the
> logo. Its that place on Cornmarket

He presses 'send' and goes over to boil the kettle again. Upstairs, Billy is still wailing. He tips a teabag into a mug and hears the phone beep.

> That's only going to help if she paid by
> credit card

Gislingham makes a face at the phone and sighs. Do I have to do absolutely *every* bloody thing myself?

> I bought J's bd present there. They had
> a list at the till where you cd sign up for
> offers etc. You had to leave your name
> and number. Prob a long shot but worth
> a try?

This time the reply is almost immediate.

> Genius. Thanks mate will let you know.
> I owe you a beer.

Gislingham makes another face at the phone, then tosses it across the table and gets up to make that tea.

*   *   *

'The name is Walker. Pippa Walker. Are you sure there's nothing?'

The girl at the till rolls her eyes. 'I have *looked*, you know.'

The sign outside says FRIDAY'S CHILD . . . IS LOVING AND GIVING! but the girl at the till doesn't seem very keen on the latter, not when it comes to information, at any rate. She's chewing, her mouth slightly open, and there are studs through her nose and top lip. It's all rather at odds with the displays of sparkly pink and gold jewellery and girly accessories. Quinn takes a deep breath. Normally he's pretty good at dealing with women, but this one seems entirely immune. A dyke, he thinks. Just my bloody luck.

'Can you look again – or better still, can you let me do it?'

She looks at him suspiciously. 'Ain't there supposed to be rules about that? Data protection or something?'

He smiles. 'I *am* a police officer.'

Which is true. As far as it goes.

What goes a lot further, at least by way of distraction, is a group of Japanese schoolgirls, suddenly exclaiming over a rack of sequinned purses and flowery headbands.

Left alone at the counter, Quinn reaches across and swings the list round to face him. He scans down and finds

'Walker', only the initial looks more like a T than a P. But the number is very similar to the one she gave him – just with two digits transposed. Easy mistake to make. He gets out his phone and calls. Straight to voicemail. But it's her – it's Pippa's voice. He waits for the tone: 'It's me – Gareth. That statement we talked about – can you come into St Aldate's?' He pauses. 'Look, if you must know I'm really in the shit on this. So I'd really appreciate it, OK?'

* * *

At his PC, with a headache and a throat like gravel, Gislingham is scanning the pages of the *Oxford Mail* for June 2015, looking for some clue about what might have interested Hannah Gardiner on the Cowley Road. Everything and nothing, is the short answer. School fêtes, under-tens football, a new traffic scheme. All good and worthy but hardly riveting. Not in bulk, anyway. After twenty minutes he gives up and tries a different tack. He googles 'Hannah Gardiner' and 'Cowley Road', and comes up with a couple of stories she covered on the BBC and a smattering of photos. One of her reporting on a controversial planning application, and another a selfie at the Cowley Road carnival in 2014 that she posted on Facebook. There are dancers in feather plumes, a Chinese dragon, a man on stilts. And in the foreground, the family: Rob, Hannah, Toby.

He prints the picture then takes it along to the incident room, where Erica Somer is standing by the pinboard. She has a red marker pen and she's putting a ring round some of the *netsuke* on the sheet of photos.

'What's so special about those?' asks Gislingham, peering a little closer.

She turns and smiles briefly. 'Mainly the fact that they've

gone missing. Though there's one that's really rare, apparently – that one: *Ivory netsuke in the shape of a nautilus shell*,' she says, reading from a print-out, '*by Masanao, one of the great Masters of the Kyoto period. Height, five centimetres, length, six centimetres. Value, twenty thousand pounds.*'

Gislingham whistles. 'Who knew.'

Somer steps back from the board. 'Uniform are circulating these pictures to art dealers and antique shops. You never know, someone may recognize them. What have you got?' she says, looking at the paper in his hand.

'This?' he says. 'It's a picture Hannah Gardiner put on her Facebook page in August 2014. It's her and Rob at the Cowley Road carnival. I was looking for connections she might have had down there and found this.'

There's a noise behind them and Everett bangs through the door. She looks tired.

'The Banbury Road is backed up all the way to Summertown. On a *Sunday*,' she says, dumping her bag on a table. She turns to look at them, and at the picture Gislingham is pinning to the board. 'What's that?'

'It's a photo of Hannah,' he says. 'Look.'

He points and Everett comes over to join them.

'I'm trying to decide if she's really as happy as she looks or if it's just for the camera,' says Somer, turning to Everett. 'What do you think?'

But Everett is looking at something else.

Or rather, someone else.

*　*　*

When Quinn gets down to reception the girl is standing at the window, looking out on to the street. She turns to see

him and comes over but he takes her quickly back to the
window, out of earshot of the desk.

'Where the hell did you go?'

'Got a text from my mate saying I could sleep on her sofa
for a couple of days.' She looks up at him, smiling, all blue
eyes and come-on. 'Did you bring my knickers?'

Quinn looks over his shoulder; the desk sergeant is looking in their direction, clearly intrigued. 'You can't say things
like that,' he hisses. 'Not in here. You'll get me bloody fired.'

She shrugs. 'OK, I'll go then.'

He grabs her by the arm. 'No, don't do that. We need you
to make that witness statement – *I* need you to.'

She studies him, head on one side. 'OK,' she says eventually.

'I'll have to ask you other stuff too. Like what happened
the day Hannah went missing. And before that as well. It's
important you tell the truth, OK?'

'OK,' she says, frowning slightly.

'No, I mean it. *All* the truth. And there's another thing.'
He swallows. 'Give your address as that mate of yours' place.
Where you're staying now. Don't say anything about staying
over at the flat.'

She looks at him for a long moment, at the anxiety he's
completely failing to conceal, and she smiles. 'Sure. You
were only trying to do me a favour, right? Nothing actually
happened.'

'No,' he says quickly. 'Of course it didn't.'

*   *   *

I'm in the room next to Interview Room Two, watching a
video feed of Quinn questioning Pippa Walker. She seems

unperturbed by the surroundings or the heat. Quinn, on the other hand, is visibly sweating into his Thomas Pink shirt.

'Let's go over it again,' he says. 'When I saw you at Mr Gardiner's flat, you said you'd had a row and he'd caused the bruising you have on your wrist – that's right, isn't it?'

'Well, yeah. But I don't think he meant it. Not like *you* mean, anyway.'

Quinn shifts in his seat. 'It's still assault, Miss Walker.'

She shrugs. 'If you say so.'

'And you've been in a relationship, you and Mr Gardiner?'

She sits back and crosses one leg over the other. 'Yeah. Have been for a while.'

'Since before Mrs Gardiner disappeared?'

The girl looks taken aback. 'No. I mean, I think he fancied me, but nothing actually *happened*.'

She stares at Quinn, a tiny smile playing about her lips, and Quinn looks quickly away, fiddling unnecessarily with his papers.

'Are you absolutely sure,' he says, not looking at her, 'there was *nothing* between the two of you before Hannah disappeared?'

She looks blank. 'No. I just told you.'

He shuffles his papers again. 'On the day Hannah disappeared, she phoned you first thing in the morning.'

'Yeah, but I never got the message till later. Look, I told the police all this already.'

But Quinn isn't letting go. 'But when you *did* hear it, nothing struck you as odd?'

She shrugs again.

'Hannah sounds annoyed – why was that?'

She rolls her eyes, as if she can't believe he's so dense. 'I hadn't turned up, had I? I was throwing up. So she was going to have to take Toby with her for that interview she was doing. She hated doing that. She thought it was "unprofessional".'

'Mr Gardiner couldn't have taken him?'

'On the *bike*? I don't *think* so.'

'And even later, after you knew Hannah had gone missing – nothing struck you as odd about the call?'

She frowns. 'But all that happened later. She was OK that morning, wasn't she?'

Quinn sits there for a moment, then gathers his papers and leaves the room. The girl reaches down and gets her mobile out of her bag.

The door bangs open and Quinn comes in, chucking his jacket over a chair.

I glance over at him. 'What was all that about?'

He loosens his tie. 'Can't they just for once get the sodding temperature right in this place?'

'Quinn, I asked you what's going on. Between you and that girl.'

He puts his papers down. 'Nothing, boss. There's nothing going on, I swear. I just don't think she's telling us everything, that's all. I think she's hiding something.'

'Actually, boss, I think he's right.'

It's Gislingham, at the door. 'You both need to see this.'

He puts a photo down on the table in front of us.

'I found it when I was looking for reasons why Hannah might have been in the Cowley Road. It's her and Rob at the 2014 carnival.'

I stare at the picture. Hannah is smiling, holding the camera, Toby cradled against her. Rob is behind them, gazing into the middle distance, but with one arm close round her. It looks like love, but as I know only too well, pictures don't need to be photoshopped to deceive. Control can so often look like cherishing.

'There,' says Gislingham, pointing. 'At the back on the left.'

'The girl with the blonde hair?'

'It's a bit difficult to be sure with the shadow across her face, but I think it's her. I think *that* is Pippa Walker.'

Quinn whistles. 'Shit, you could be right.'

'And Rob Gardiner is staring straight at her.'

I look at the picture, and then at Gislingham. 'When did she tell us she first met the Gardiners?'

'I just checked her original statement,' says Gislingham, quietly triumphant. 'She said it was October 2014. Two months *after* this picture was taken.'

'Right,' says Quinn, and makes to go. But I hold him back. On the video feed, the girl is looking at herself in her make-up mirror.

'I want a woman in there with you this time.'

'What?' he says. 'Why?'

'Get Ev to sit in with you. And if she's not around, find Somer.'

He flashes a look at me, but he doesn't say anything. As for Gislingham, he could play poker with that face.

'Right, Quinn?'

'Right, boss.'

*   *   *

'But I need you here.'

'Sorry,' says Everett. The signal is breaking up; she's clearly in the car. 'I've got a whole list of antiques shops to see. Following up on those missing *netsuke*.'

Quinn can barely conceal his irritation. 'But that's a job for uniform, surely. It's just a poxy burglary.'

'Not my call, Sarge. Fawley said to –'

'Yeah, yeah, I know.'

'Why is it such a problem? Gislingham should be around, and Baxter –'

'Look, forget it, OK?'

Only 'OK' is clearly the last thing it is, and Everett ends the call none the wiser. Quinn meanwhile has a bullet to bite. Somer's not at her desk, but her sergeant suggests he try the canteen. Not without a smirk, though, which Quinn elects not to notice.

She's in the corner, with a coffee and a book. A huge book – some Penguin Classics thing. He'd forgotten, for a moment, that she was once an English teacher. When he gets to the table she sees his shadow fall across the page and looks up. She manages a smile. A slightly artificial one, but a smile.

'It's about a young woman kept captive and raped,' she says, indicating the book. 'It was published in 1747, but some things never change, do they?'

Quinn sticks his hands in his pockets. He's not making much eye contact. 'I'm going to interview Pippa Walker again. Fawley wants you to sit in.'

'Me? Why not –'

'He wants a woman, and Everett's not here.'

So it was Fawley's idea, not yours. The thought is clear enough on her face.

'So, are you free or what?'

She sits up and closes the book. 'Of course. Whatever you need. Sergeant.'

He flashes a glance at her, on the alert for sarcasm. But her face is smooth of all disdain.

'You want ten minutes to read the interview notes?'

'Already done. I've tried to keep up, even if I am "only uniform".'

She waits for him to make some barbed remark about using the investigation to further her career, but it doesn't come. She gathers up her stuff and follows him along the corridor and down the stairs to Interview Two, where he stops outside the door. They can see the girl through the glass panel. She's playing a game on her phone. She doesn't look up when they take their seats and sighs heavily when Quinn asks her to put her phone away. She looks at Somer warily.

'Who's she?'

'Constable Somer. She'll be sitting in on the interview.'

Pippa sits back. 'How much *longer* am I going to be stuck here?' she says, in that sing-song upper-middle accent this town is thick with.

'We just have a few more questions.'

'But I've told you everything I know.' She sits forward again. 'I've been *really* helpful, haven't I? You said I was.'

'You have,' says Quinn, flushing a little. 'But we have to be really clear what happened. So let's go back to the beginning again.'

The girl rolls her eyes.

'You met Hannah Gardiner in October 2014, at a stall in North Parade.'

She blinks. 'What's that got to do with anything?'

He pushes the photo of the Cowley Road carnival across the table. 'At the time this picture was taken – August 2014 – you said you'd never met either Rob Gardiner or his wife.'

She looks at the picture, then sits back and shrugs. 'There must've been hundreds of people there. Thousands.'

'So it was just a coincidence.'

She flashes a smile at him. 'Yeah. If you like.'

'And the fact that he's looking straight at you, that's just a coincidence too?'

She puts her head on one side and starts to twirl an end of hair. 'A lot of blokes look at me. *You* did.'

Quinn flushes, deeper this time. 'So at the time of this picture you and Rob Gardiner definitely hadn't met?'

'No –'

'You weren't having an affair?'

She smiles again. 'No, we weren't having an "affair".' She slides a glance up at him. 'Though as it happens, I do quite like older men . . .'

Perhaps this is why Fawley wanted a woman in on this, thinks Somer. Because I'm not falling for this winsome bullshit.

She pulls Quinn's file towards her and takes out a sheet of paper. 'You stated just now that you'd told us everything. Well, you certainly didn't tell us you were pregnant. Who's the father – because it isn't Rob Gardiner, is it?'

Pippa glares at her. 'Who told you that? It's none of your business.'

'You didn't know he couldn't have children?'

Pippa makes a face at her but says nothing.

'And those marks on your wrist – that's what happened when he found out? He hit you like he used to hit his wife?'

Pippa pulls down her sleeves. 'I'm not talking about that again.' But her tone has changed. The bravado has gone.

'Are you aware,' says Somer coolly, 'that you could end up in court if you lie to the police?'

Pippa's eyes widen and she looks at Quinn. 'What's she talking about?'

'Well –' begins Quinn, but Somer cuts across him.

'We are currently investigating Robert Gardiner as a possible suspect in his wife's death. That will mean going over every inch of his life with a fine-tooth comb. His phone records, his texts. Where he was and when. And *who he was with*. Do you understand?'

Pippa nods; her cheeks are red.

'And if we find out that you've been lying to us, you could find yourself facing a criminal charge.'

Quinn is staring at her, but Somer doesn't care. He might know she's pushing it, but the girl doesn't.

Pippa has gone pale. She turns to Quinn. 'You said *I* should think about bringing charges against *him*. You never said anything about arresting *me*.'

'Do you really want to have your baby in prison?' continues Somer. 'In fact, do you really want to have your baby at all, because I reckon Social Services will take the view that it'll be better off adopted by someone else. Perverting the course of justice carries a custodial sentence, did you know that?'

'*No*,' says Pippa, really frightened now. 'Please – don't send me to prison.'

'In that case,' says Somer, sitting back and folding her arms, 'you'd better start talking, hadn't you? And this time, we'd like the truth.'

For God's sake, don't say anything, Somer begs Quinn silently. Force her to confront it – force her to decide.

'OK,' says Pippa at last. 'I'll tell you. But only if I get protection. From him. From what he'll do to me when he finds out.'

An hour later, when they come out of the room, Quinn turns to Somer. 'Fuck, you can be a cold bitch when you want to be.'

Somer raises an eyebrow. 'All that matters is getting a

result. Putting the right bastard behind bars. Isn't that what you said?'

She turns to go but he calls her back. 'It was meant as a compliment. I'm sorry if it didn't sound like one.'

She looks at him; his usual swagger seems curiously deflated. In fact, he was pretty much silent the whole time they were taking the statement. 'Frankly, I'm not bothered either way,' she says. But as she walks off, she allows herself a small private smile.

*   *   *

STATEMENT OF PIPPA WALKER

7 May 2017
DATE OF BIRTH: 3 February 1995
ADDRESS: Flat 3, 98 Belford Street, Oxford

This statement, consisting of two pages each signed by me, is true to the best of my knowledge and belief, and I make it knowing that, if it is tendered in evidence, I shall be liable to prosecution if I have wilfully stated in it anything which I know to be false or do not believe to be true.

I started working for the Gardiners in October 2014. I never met them before that. That picture at the carnival really is just a coincidence.

I saw a lot of Rob. His wife was out a lot so we ended up spending a lot of time together. It was pretty obvious he fancied me so it was only a matter of time, really. He told me he wasn't happy with his wife and he wanted to leave her and be with me instead. He said he would tell her but he kept putting it off.

What happened on June 23rd 2015 was that Hannah found us in bed. She'd told Rob that she'd be in late but she actually turned up just after six. She completely lost it - started shouting at him, swearing, tearing up my clothes. Rob said Toby was in the next room and could hear it all but she took no notice. She dragged Rob out of the bed and started hitting him - he tried to push her off but she was crazy, screaming abuse at me, saying I was a slut and a whore and she never should have trusted me. He told me to get my stuff and go - that it would be OK and he would deal with it. So I did. The last I saw they were in the kitchen. I kept thinking Rob would call me, only he didn't, and when I texted him I didn't get an answer. So about midnight I went back over there. As soon as he opened the door I could tell at once something bad had happened. He looked really weird, and he didn't want to let me in.

He said it was all OK and they'd sorted it out and I should go home. When I woke up the following morning I was really sick, like I said before. That's why I never got that voicemail from Hannah till the evening, and by then it was on TV that she was missing. It didn't make any sense, that she'd still have wanted me to babysit Toby that day

after all those things she said to me the night
before. But I knew it was her on the message - it
was definitely her voice, though it sounded a bit
funny. Tinny. Not like when she usually called me.

My flatmate said I should go to the police but I was
really scared - I didn't see how Rob could have
killed her and what if they thought I had? What if
he told them it was me? My DNA would be in the flat
and he was a scientist - he'd be cleverer than the
police and could easily fake something. That's why
I never told the police we were having an affair. I
was scared they'd think I'd done it. That it would
give me a motive. And who were people going to
believe if it came down to him or me? And in any
case, I loved him. He could make me do anything he
wanted. I know he never meant to hurt me. And he
was always really sorry afterwards.

Pippa Walker

This statement was taken by me at St Aldate's
Police Station commencing 5.15 p.m. and concluding
6.06 p.m. Also present was Police Constable Erica
Somer. At its conclusion I read it over to Pippa
Walker who read and signed it in my presence.

DS Gareth Quinn

*   *   *

In the incident room, Quinn gets a round of applause, but he's a very long way from the parading general I'd expect him to be right now. In fact, he even has the (unaccustomed) grace to insist that the real breakthrough was Somer's. Though he looks so uncomfortable admitting it I wonder why he bothers saying it at all.

After a moment or two I cut short the congratulations. 'OK, everyone – let's keep this in perspective. Pippa's statement is a big step forward, but it's not enough – not on its own. It doesn't prove Gardiner killed his wife though it *does* prove he's been lying to us, and it *does* give him a motive. Neither of which we had before. But it still leaves us with a timeline that doesn't add up. If Hannah Gardiner died the night of June 23rd, how did she make a phone call at 6.50 the following morning?'

Baxter raises a hand. 'Actually, I have an idea about that. Leave it with me.'

'OK.' I look round the room. We've been on this six days straight. Everyone's flat-lining. 'Let's pick it up again in the morning. Rob Gardiner isn't going anywhere. All of you go home and get some sleep. That includes you, Gislingham. You look all in.'

Gislingham rubs the back of his neck. 'Yeah, well, babies. You know what it's like.'

An hour later I pull into my drive and sit there a moment looking at the house. The windows are open upstairs and the curtains are catching in the breeze. The sun is lowering and irradiating the house across the street against a brilliant blue sky. They call it the Golden Hour in Oxford. That brief slice of time where the sinking sun glows the stone like it's lit from the inside.

I turn off the engine and remember. How it used to be.

Before. Alex cooking. A glass of cold white wine. Jake playing on the floor at her feet or, later, kicking a ball about in the garden. Peace. Stillness. A golden hour.

The first thing I hear when I open the door is wailing. There's no food on. The kitchen looks like a war zone.

'Is everything OK?' I call as I dump my bag in the hall.

'Yes, it's fine. He just doesn't want his bath, that's all.'

When I push open the bathroom door I can see what she means. The boy is lying on his back screaming and there's water all over the floor, and a good deal on Alex too. She looks up, her face flushed. 'Sorry, I just seem to have lost the knack of this, that's all. He's been so good so far, he really has. But I had to put that toy of his in the washing machine and he's been impossible ever since.'

'You want me to take over?'

'Aren't you tired?'

'I think I can still deal with a toddler.'

'OK,' she says, getting to her feet in obvious relief. 'It'll give me a chance to get the dinner on.'

Once the door is closed the boy stops screaming suddenly and rolls over to look at me. There are smears of tears on his cheeks.

'Hello, mate, what's up with you then?'

When Alex comes out an hour later I'm in the garden, having a fag. The air is cool and the grass dewy but there is still a glow in the sky. She goes to turn on the lights but I stop her. Some things are best said in shadows.

She hands me a glass of wine and sits down next to me. 'He's asleep. Finally.'

She looks down the garden. 'Look at that lavender we planted last year – it's been alive with bees. I must bring him out here to look at them.'

I take a drag on my cigarette, letting the pause lengthen.

'Tough day?' she says lightly, letting me tell her if I want to. Or not.

'Every time I think I have this case nailed it turns into something else. Something even more horrific.'

'How can it possibly be worse than it already was? That poor girl imprisoned and raped. Hannah Gardiner beaten to death –'

'We're going to arrest her husband in the morning. The childminder gave us a statement incriminating him.'

Alex has her hand at her mouth. 'Oh my God –'

Then she stops. 'There's something else, isn't there.'

I grind out the cigarette. 'Yes. But not about the case. About us. The boy.'

'Oh yes?'

'It was when I had him on my lap in the bathroom – he started making these noises – moving against me – like – well –'

But I can see from her face that she knows exactly what I mean.

'You knew?'

She nods. 'That nice nurse. She warned me. Said he'd done it once before and I shouldn't be alarmed. That he must have been exposed to all sorts of terrible things down in that cellar that he's far too young to understand. His mother being – well, you know. She suggested I read that Emma Donoghue book – *Room*? It's been on my Kindle for ages but I never got round to it before.'

'Is it helping?'

She turns to me in the dusk. 'It's making me cry.'

Monday morning. Alex spends breakfast telling me all the things she's planning on doing with the boy. Feeding the ducks, going on the swings, walking along the river. It's as if she has a mental list – ticking off all the things we used to do with Jake. I can't do it. It's too close. And in any case, is it fair on that boy – to force him into the space made for another child? Or perhaps that's just me looking for excuses. Not that I need any. Not right now.

When I get to the incident room the voice-recognition analyst is already there, along with almost everyone else. And word must have got around because the place is electric with expectation.

'So what have we got?'

The analyst pushes his glasses a bit further up his nose. He clearly isn't used to such a big audience.

'Well, I looked at what DC Baxter suggested, and yes, it is possible. I can't *prove* it, but the spectral interference pattern could indeed indicate –'

'Hold on – in English, please.'

He blushes. 'The background noise – the quality of the sound – it's possible the voice on the call was a recording.'

There's certainly no background noise right now. You can almost hear people holding their breath.

'So, let's be clear,' I say. 'You think it's possible Gardiner played back an old message into the phone – something he already had on his own voicemail?'

The analyst nods. 'It's nowhere near one hundred per cent. But yes, he could have. It would account for the slightly hollow quality of the sound.'

'And remember,' says Baxter quickly, keen to capitalize on his coup, 'Hannah never used any names on that call and she didn't mention a time either – there was nothing that tied it to that particular day.'

I turn to the timeline again.

'OK, let's assume that's what happened. Gardiner kills Hannah the night before, after she finds him in bed with Pippa Walker. He buries the body in Harper's shed and when Pippa turns up again at midnight he doesn't let her in, presumably because he's still cleaning up the blood. Then the following morning he fakes a call to Pippa at 6.50 to make it look like his wife is still alive. But there's still a problem, isn't there.'

I turn to face them. 'That call was made from the landline at Crescent Square at 6.50, which means Rob Gardiner had to have been *at* Crescent Square at that time. We dismissed him as a suspect before because there wasn't time for him to get to Wittenham and back for the 7.57 train. And that's still true. It still doesn't add up.'

'It could do, sir.'

It's Somer. At the back. She gets up and comes forward. 'What if he wasn't on that train?'

Baxter frowns. 'We know he was. We have footage of him arriving at Reading.'

But she's shaking her head. 'We know where he got off. But we don't know where he got *on*.'

She looks to Gislingham, who nods. 'You're right. The Oxford CCTV was down that day.'

She turns and looks at the map. Wittenham, Oxford, Reading. She points. 'What if he got on here instead?'

Didcot Parkway. Halfway to Reading, and only five miles from Wittenham by road.

Gislingham's checking on his phone. 'The 7.57 from Oxford stops at Didcot at 8.15.'

'Right,' I say, picking up the pen and drawing a second timeline next to the first one, 'let's work it through. If he left Oxford just before seven, straight after faking that voicemail, he'd have got to Wittenham, when?'

Gislingham considers. 'By car, at that time in the morning, I reckon it'd only be half an hour.'

'Which would put him at Wittenham by 7.30. Perhaps 7.25. And he'd need to leave Wittenham by around 7.50, to be on the train at Didcot at 8.15. The question is, is that enough time? To dump the car, take the buggy up the hill, leave his son and go, all in less than half an hour.'

'I think so, sir,' says Somer. 'It would be tight, but it's possible. He could have done it.'

Gislingham is nodding. As is Baxter. There's only one person who hasn't said anything at all.

Quinn.

* * *

Outside the incident room, Gislingham gets hold of Quinn and pulls him into the empty office next door.

'What the fuck's going on? Have you got a death-wish or what? I saw Fawley giving you a funny look – it won't take long for him to rumble you if you keep going on like this.'

Quinn's standing with his back to him, but now he turns round slowly. Gislingham has never seen him look so haggard.

'What is it? There's something, isn't there?'

Quinn sits down heavily. 'She lied. Pippa – in her statement. Perhaps only about some of it, but I know she lied.'

Gislingham pulls up a chair. 'The text, I'm guessing.'

· Quinn nods. 'She said she texted Gardiner that night but I know she didn't. I saw all her texts to him. There was nothing that night.'

'Perhaps she deleted that one?'

'She's got the same phone as me. If you delete one it

deletes the whole thread. There *was* no text.' He puts his head in his hands. 'It's like a bloody nightmare. The more I try to sort it the worse it gets. Fawley's going to arrest Gardiner on the basis of a witness statement I *know* isn't reliable and yet I can't say anything without putting myself irretrievably in the shit.'

'OK,' says Gislingham, going into fix-it mode. 'We're just going to have to get that warrant to look at her phone records, aren't we? That way you'll be in the clear. We'd have had to verify that statement anyway, even without all this.'

'But the magistrate's bound to wonder why we haven't just asked her if we can look at the bloody phone – why we need a warrant at all if she's just a witness –'

'Yeah, well,' says Gislingham, 'you're just going to have to think of an answer to that one, aren't you?'

'But you know what'll happen the minute we put Pippa under any pressure – she's going to tell, isn't she? That she stayed in my flat – that we – you know.'

'Well, *did* you?'

'No. I *told* you.'

But he's sweating like a man who did.

'Look,' says Gislingham. 'If that's what she says you're just going to have to come clean. Tell Fawley you've been a twat and hope he doesn't want to take it any further. And in the meantime focus on something useful. Like trying to get that bloody warrant.'

'Right,' says Quinn, his voice lifting a little.

'And while you're at it, try to act a bit more like your usual irritating cocky sod of a self, would you? This give-due-credit-to-others stuff is giving me the willies.'

Quinn smiles bleakly. 'I'll give it a go,' he says.

* * *

Interview with Robert Gardiner, conducted at
St Aldate's Police Station, Oxford
8 May 2017, 11.03 a.m.
In attendance, DI A. Fawley, DC V. Everett,
P. Rose (solicitor)

PR: I have to say, Inspector, that this is veering
     perilously close to harassment. Do you really
     have adequate grounds for arresting my client?
     For *murdering his wife*? I fail to see what new
     'evidence' you can possibly have, and it's
     extremely inconvenient, given he currently has
     no permanent childminder.

AF: Yesterday afternoon, my detectives questioned
     Miss Pippa Walker. I imagine you thought she
     had left town, Mr Gardiner. Or hoped as much.

RG: [*silence*]

AF: But she's still here.

RG: [*silence*]

AF: She has made a full statement about your
     wife's disappearance.

RG: That's ridiculous. She can't have told you
     anything because she doesn't *know* anything.

VE: We also had our doctor take a look at that
     bruising on her wrist. The bruising *you* gave
     her.

RG: Look, it wasn't like that. I told you before. I
     found out that she was trying to pass off
     someone else's kid as mine - that she'd been
     screwing around -

VE: And that gives you licence to hit her?

RG: I didn't *hit* her. I *told* you. I just grabbed
    hold of her - probably tighter than I
    realized. If she's telling you something
    different then she's lying.

AF: [*silence*]
    I imagine it wouldn't go down well, would it?

RG: What are you talking about?

AF: With your employers. I don't imagine they'd be
    very happy about one of their senior managers
    being prosecuted for domestic violence.

RG: How many more times. It wasn't *domestic
    violence*. It was a *row*. There is a difference.

AF: It's not my place to advise you, of course, but
    I wouldn't rely on that by way of defence -

PR: Look, Inspector -

AF: But moving on. When did your relationship with
    Miss Walker begin?

RG: I'm sorry?

AF: It's a simple enough question, Mr Gardiner.

RG: What has that got to do with anything?

AF: If you could just answer the question.

RG: There is no *relationship*. I told you. We only
    slept together a couple of times. And it was
    after Hannah disappeared. Months after.

VE: I thought you said it was a one-night stand?

RG: Once, twice, three times - what difference
    does it make? It wasn't a relationship. It was
    just sex.

AF: So any suggestion that you are having an
    affair that began long before your wife's
    death is completely untrue. According to you.

RG: Of course it bloody well is – is that what she's been saying?

AF: So when did she move into your home? Exactly?

RG: Well, she was staying a bit, on and off. Look, I was all over the place after Hannah disappeared. Wasn't eating, couldn't even organize myself to do the washing – and I had Toby to think about. One day Pippa just turned up on the doorstep and said she was worried about me and did I need any help. I was on my way to work and when I got back the place was clean and there was food in the fridge and a meal on. She stayed over on the couch a few times after that, and when she said she was going to have to move out of her bedsit I said she could stay for a few weeks.

VE: So how long ago was that?

RG: I don't know. Three months. A bit more. She hasn't been able to find anywhere yet.

VE: I bet she hasn't.

RG: What's that supposed to mean?

AF: You should be aware, Mr Gardiner, that as a result of questioning Miss Walker, we have completely revised our previous theory about your wife's death.

RG: [looks from one officer to the other but says nothing]

AF: The broad outlines of the story go like this. By June 2015 you and Pippa have been sleeping together for at least six months. The fact that she is looking after your son gives perfect cover to the relationship. But on

Tuesday June 23rd your wife comes home early.
Unexpectedly. And what she finds is you and
Miss Walker having sex.

RG: Is that what she told you - that we were
having sex?

AF: She says there was a furious row, that your
wife was hitting you, and you sent Miss Walker
away, saying you would 'deal with it'. She
texted you and got no reply, and when she came
back again several hours later, you wouldn't
let her in.

RG: Absolutely *none* of that happened -

AF: We believe that in the course of that row your
wife received a heavy blow to the head.
Possibly an accident, possibly in self-defence.
Whatever the truth of it, you had a serious
problem on your hands. You fetched the rug from
your wife's car and wrapped her body in it,
securing it with packing tape. Then, once it
was dark, you took the body out the back of the
building and through the ramshackle fence into
William Harper's garden. A garden you knew -
having had a clear view of it from your flat for
several months - was almost never used.
Looking for something to dig a grave with, you
broke into the shed and found there was a
trapdoor in the floor. Scarcely able to believe
your luck, you stowed the body underneath. No
one would ever be any the wiser. Or so you
believed. The following morning you faked a
message to Pippa Walker using a voicemail you
had previously received from your wife. Then

you drove to Wittenham, where you left the car
and your son in his buggy, thinking – wrongly,
as it turned out – that someone was bound to
discover him within a few minutes. You then
went by bike to Didcot, where you boarded the
train to Reading. It was almost the perfect
murder. Almost, but not quite.

RG: [*silence*]

PR: Hang on a minute, I thought you were talking
about an accident? Self-defence?

AF: The initial blow may have been, but that
didn't kill her, as your client well knows.
What happened, Mr Gardiner – did she move? Cry
out in pain? Was that when you realized you
hadn't finished the job? Was that when you
tied her up? Was that when you *caved in her
skull*?

RG: [*gets up and rushes to side of room to vomit*]

PR: That's enough, Inspector. For the avoidance of
any doubt, Mr Gardiner absolutely and
categorically refutes this new version of
events. It is a complete fabrication from first
to last and you don't have a shred of evidence
to support it, as far as I am aware.

AF: We will be carrying out a full forensic search
of Mr Gardiner's flat –

RG: [*leaning forward*]
Well, you won't find anything, I can tell you
that for nothing –

PR: [*restraining Gardiner*]
You don't need to say any more, Rob.
[*addressing Fawley*]

My client had nothing to do with his wife's death, and he was *not* having a relationship with Miss Walker at the time his wife disappeared. It's not my place to advise you, of course, but I venture to suggest that that young lady has some serious explaining to do.

AF: Thank you, Mr Rose, your comments have been noted. Interview terminated at 11.34.

* * *

BBC News
Monday 8 May 2017 | Last updated at 12:39

BREAKING: Hannah Gardiner's husband arrested for her murder

The BBC has learned that Robert Gardiner has been arrested on suspicion of murdering his wife, Hannah, who disappeared in June 2015. Police now believe that Mrs Gardiner died on the evening of 23 June, after an argument at their flat in Crescent Square, Oxford. Mr Gardiner's son, Toby, is understood to be in the care of Social Services.

Thames Valley Police have confirmed that a 32-year-old man has been arrested in connection with the case, but have declined to release his name. They have also insisted that there is no evidence to link the death of Mrs Gardiner with the discovery of a young woman and a child in the basement of the house where Mrs

Gardiner's body was found, though 'enquiries are still ongoing'.

This breaking news story is being updated and more details will be published shortly. Please refresh the page for the fullest version.

*   *   *

'Fawley? It's Challow.'

There's an echo on the line – he sounds like he's standing in a drain.

'Where are you?'

'Crescent Square,' he says. 'Gardiner's place. I think you'd better come.'

When I get to the flat, the forensics team is in the kitchen, and Erica Somer's in the sitting room, checking the drawers, the shelves, behind the books. The kitchen is one of those Shaker jobs. Pale wood in some sort of Farrow & Ball off cream. Granite surfaces. Lots of chrome. And clean. Very clean.

'So what is it? What have you found?'

Challow's expression is grim. 'It's more a case of what we *haven't* found.'

He nods to the female forensics officer, and she closes the blinds and switches off the lights.

'What am I supposed to be looking at?'

Challow makes a face. 'That's just it. There *isn't anything.* We Luminol'd the whole floor and there isn't a trace of blood anywhere.'

'Gardiner's a scientist – he'd know what bleach to use –'

But Challow isn't buying it, and to be honest, I'm not either.

'This floor is wood,' he says. 'Even with the right chemical and a great deal of time you'd never get everything out of the grain. Not with the amount of blood she must have lost.'

'Could it have happened somewhere else in the flat?' More straw-clutching.

He shakes his head. 'The flooring is the same everywhere except the bathrooms. And we've found nothing so far.'

I go back out into the sitting room. 'Which room was Pippa staying in, Somer?'

'Through there, sir.'

It's Toby's bedroom. It looks just like Jake's. Not Jake's before, but Jake's now. Full of mess and life and boy smells. Toys across the floor, clothes anyhow on the back of the chair. And along one wall, a sofabed. So, Rob Gardiner was keeping Pippa at a distance. He might have been having sex with her, but he was giving her a message, all the same.

Back in the sitting room, Somer is going through the waste-paper bin.

'Photos,' she says, showing them to me. 'Looks like Mr Gardiner's been busily ridding his life of every last trace of Ms Walker.'

She passes the pictures to me one by one. Pippa lifting Toby in the air; Toby on her lap playing with a pendant round her neck; Toby in her arms, smiling at her, his little hands clapping.

'So what now,' she says. 'Does this get Rob off?'

I shake my head. 'Not necessarily. Just because she didn't die here, doesn't mean he didn't kill her. We just have to find where.'

'But all the same . . .'

Her voice trails off.

'What?'

'Nothing. I'm probably wrong –'

'So far, your instincts have been spot on. So tell me.'

'If Rob Gardiner really did get to Wittenham by 7.30 that morning, how come it took three hours for someone to find Toby? We have all those witness statements – there were loads of people about. Surely someone would have spotted that buggy sooner?'

And that fact snags itself against other things that have been bothering me. The tying up, for a start. I still don't see why he had to do that. Even if she was still moving after that first blow, I doubt she'd have been in any state to struggle. And I saw Gardiner myself the day Hannah disappeared and there wasn't a mark on him. No scratches, no grazes, nothing. If they'd really had such a violent row, I think I'd have spotted the signs.

There's a call then, on my mobile. The desk sergeant.

'There's been a message for you, sir. From Vicky. They've moved her to Vine Lodge. She wants to see you. Says it's important.'

'Tell her I'm on my way.'

Vine Lodge is a big four-storey Victorian house that would be worth as much as William Harper's if it was in North Oxford, rather than here, off the Botley Road, on the edge of the industrial estate with a view of the carpet showroom. They've given her a room on her own, which means it'll be small, but at least it's not – thank God – on the lower ground floor. Though three flights of stairs are an unwelcome reminder of how unfit I've let myself become.

'Don't worry, we haven't told any of the other residents who she is,' says the manager as we go up. He's a cheery shaven-headed bloke with an earring and tattoos up his neck. Perhaps it helps to look like the people you're supervising.

'And we're trying to keep her away from the papers and the news, like you asked. But I'm not sure how successful we've been.'

'How has she been – in general?'

He stops for a moment and considers. 'Better than I expected. Very quiet.' He shrugs. 'I guess that's not surprising. I think she'll be seeing the psych for a while yet.'

I nod. 'Has she talked about the boy?'

He shakes his head. 'Not to me, anyway. But when she arrived the TV was on downstairs and there was one of those baby adverts on. Pampers or something. She couldn't bear to look at it.'

We climb the rest of the stairs in silence. There's music coming from somewhere, and as we pass the windows on the landings I can see some of the kids outside. A couple are smoking. Two lads are kicking a ball about.

The manager knocks on the door at the top of the house, then clatters off back down. Vicky is sitting by the window, looking down at the kids in the garden. I wonder how long it is since she spent time with people her own age.

'Hi, Vicky, you said you wanted to see me?'

She smiles, tentative. She still looks painfully thin. The loose clothes only make it worse.

I gesture at the chair and she nods.

'You got everything you need? I hear the food's not bad. Well, perhaps "not as bad as it could be" is probably more accurate.'

She laughs a little.

I sit forward in the chair. 'So what did you want to talk to me about?'

She's watching. Still silent.

'You said it was important? Perhaps you want to tell us your full name? So we can find your family?'

She's twisting the end of her jumper in her lap. And when she speaks it's the first time she's said anything beyond a whisper. The first time I've really heard her voice. It's deeper than I expected. Softer.

'I saw the news. On the TV.'

I wait. But a thought is turning in my head.

There are tears now. 'When I saw it, I remembered. He said he'd got another girl and buried her in the garden. The old man. I thought he was just saying it to frighten me.'

'Did he say anything else – her name, what he did to her?'

She shakes her head.

'You've not remembered anything else?'

Again, she shakes her head.

It's enough. It's going to have to be.

I get up and when I stop in the doorway, she's gazing out of the window again. It's as if I was never here.

* * *

Phone interview with Rebecca Heath
8 May 2017, 4.12 p.m.
On the call, DC A. Baxter

RH: Is that Detective Constable Baxter?

AB: Speaking – can I help you?

RH: My name is Rebecca Heath. I gather you've been trying to reach me. I'm Rob Gardiner's ex-wife.

AB: Ah yes, Ms Heath, we did leave you some
    messages.

RH: I didn't get back to you because I didn't want
    to get involved. I'm trying to move on with my
    life. But I just saw the news. It said you've
    arrested Rob. For killing Hannah.

AB: An arrest has been made, but I'm afraid I'm
    not at liberty to discuss the details.

RH: Well, if it is Rob you've arrested, you've got
    the wrong man. I went round there that night -
    the 23rd.

AB: You spoke to Mr and Mrs Gardiner the night
    before she disappeared?

RH: No, not exactly. My mother had just been taken
    very ill and I thought Rob might want to see
    her. They were always very close.

AB: In your original statement, you said you were
    in Manchester the day Hannah disappeared,
    which I believe was verified.

RH: I was. That's where my mother lives. I got the
    first train to Manchester Piccadilly on June
    24th - it was stupidly early, 6.30 or something.
    But I was still in Oxford the night before.

AB: So you went to Crescent Square?

RH: I didn't want to phone and run the risk of
    getting Hannah, so I went round there. I was
    hoping I'd catch Rob on his own. But she was
    arriving just as I turned into the street.

AB: What time was that?

RH: Just before 8. Rob came out to help her with
    some shopping. She must have parked somewhere
    else, though, because I didn't see the car.

AB: How did they seem?

RH: Happy. He put his arm round her. She was smiling. It was all rather tediously lovey-dovey, frankly.

AB: So what did you do?

RH: I hung around a bit. Sat on a bench. They had the curtains open, so I could see them. They were cooking, I think. At one point I saw Rob carrying Toby on his shoulders.

AB: But you didn't knock at the door?

RH: No. I left after about fifteen minutes.

AB: Why didn't you tell the police this at the time?

RH: You never asked. And anyway, everyone was saying she'd been seen at Wittenham the next day. I didn't see how it mattered where she'd been the night before.

AB: Did you see the childminder by any chance?

RH: Well, I can tell you one thing - she *definitely* wasn't in the flat that night.

AB: What makes you so sure?

RH: Because I saw her on the Banbury Road when I turned off. I knew who she was because I'd seen her with Toby once or twice in town. She was sitting on a wall with a couple of lads. Students, probably. They all looked pretty pissed.

AB: Thank you, Ms Heath. Would you be able to come in and make a formal statement?

RH: If I have to. I couldn't stand Hannah, frankly. But it wasn't Rob who killed her. That I do know.

* * *

Back at the car, I get out my phone.

'Quinn? It's Fawley.'

'Where are you? I've been trying to reach you.'

'Vine Lodge. Vicky wanted to see me.'

'Look, Gardiner's ex-wife called. She actually saw Rob and Pippa that night. And if what she says is true, I don't see how he can have killed Hannah.'

'I know. Vicky's remembered something. She said Harper boasted about another girl. About killing another girl and burying her in the garden. That had to be Hannah. Hannah died in Frampton Road and William Harper killed her. These two cases – they've always been linked. And that link is William Harper. We just have to find some way to prove it.'

'OK –' he begins.

'And Quinn?' I say, cutting across him. 'Get the nanny – Pippa – in again. It's starting to look like she made up that whole cock-and-bull story about Gardiner, and I'm not about to let that pass.'

There's a silence. 'Are you sure?' he says eventually. 'I mean, she's only a kid. And she never actually *accused* him. She probably just wanted to get her own back –'

Fawley's law. Three lies and you're out. Or – in this case – found out.

'Since when did you get so soft, Quinn? She *lied* – in an *official statement*. Bring her in first thing and bloody well charge her.'

I can almost hear his anxiety. 'What with?'

'Arrant stupidity for starters.'

And something tells me she's not the only one round here who's guilty of that.

*

An hour and a half later I'm sitting outside my own house. In the car, closed in my own thoughts. Then a curtain moves inside and I realize I've been out here too long. She'll be worried. I get out of the car and drag my jacket out of the passenger seat. By the time I get to the door she's opened it, and is standing there in a pool of pale yellow light. My beautiful barefoot wife.

Inside, she pours me a glass of wine and turns to me, aware suddenly that my silence isn't tranquillity.

'You OK?'

'I saw Vicky today. She said Harper told her he'd killed before. That he'd abducted another girl and buried her in the garden.'

I can hear her breath come sharp. 'Hannah Gardiner?'

I nod.

'So Gardiner didn't do it.'

'No, Gardiner didn't do it.'

I take a gulp of wine and feel the warmth run through my veins.

'So why did that girl lie – the one who gave you the statement?'

'Gardiner had just thrown her out because she's pregnant with someone else's child. It may have been a cheap little attempt at revenge.'

Alex looks down the garden. ' *'Tis Pity She's a Whore.*'

'Sorry?'

She shakes her head. 'This whole case, it's turning into Jacobean tragedy.'

'Was that the play we saw – where was it?'

'Stratford. And it was actually *Women Beware Women.* But all those plays are much the same – vengeance, violence, mistaken identity. And gore. Lots and lots of gore.'

I remember that production now; I came out peppered with blood. Only this time, for once, it wasn't real.

Later, when I go out to collect something from the car, there's a movement at the window above and I glance up to see the boy, looking down at me. The changeling living in my son's place.

* * *

Rob Gardiner opens the door to his flat and closes it quietly behind him. His little son is asleep in his arms, and he walks across to the sofa and lays him gently down. Toby stirs a little and turns over, his thumb in his mouth. Gardiner gently caresses his son's hair then straightens up. The room is darkening in the twilight but he doesn't turn on the lamps.

He walks to the rear window and looks down at the garden. Then he closes the curtains and sits down heavily on an armchair. Opposite him, on the mantelpiece, the silver photo frames catch what's left of the light. He can't see the pictures but the images are etched in his mind. Toby and Hannah. The three of them. Hannah alone. The life he once had.

He gives a little gasp then, and puts his hand to his mouth, careful not to wake his child. And the tears that follow are silent, as he sits there in the dark, remembering.

Remembering.

* * *

First thing the following morning I brief the team on where we are. On what Vicky said, and Pippa made up, and Rob Gardiner didn't do.

'Which means,' I say at the end of it, 'that we revert to our original timeline: Hannah was alive at 6.50 a.m. when she called Pippa and left the flat for Wittenham around 7.30, taking Toby with her. The working assumption must be that she met Harper in the street a few minutes later when she went to collect her car and he lured her into his house. Just as he did with Vicky.'

There's a shifting of feet; a sense of being back where we started, and not much better off. Because we still have no evidence, and we still have no murder scene.

'So what next?' asks Baxter. I can hear the weariness in his voice.

'I want you to go back to Frampton Road and work with Challow's team on another search of the house.'

'But we've already been through the whole place – forensics analysed every room –'

'I don't care. There must be something we missed.'

When I emerge into the corridor the desk sergeant is waiting outside.

'That profiler is in reception for you, Inspector. Bryan Gow.'

'Really? I thought he was in Aberdeen or somewhere.'

'Seems not. Do you want me to tell him to come back later?'

'No, he wouldn't have bothered to come in if it wasn't important. Bring him up. And get someone to bring us coffee, would you? Decent stuff – not the crap from the machine.'

I get waylaid by the Super on the way back to my office, so Gow is already there when I push open my office door. And now I know what he's doing here: he has a photocopy of Vicky's journal on the table in front of him. As well as a take-out coffee from the café up the street.

'Where did you get that?'

He raises an eyebrow. 'The latte?'

'The journal.'

He sits back and crosses one leg over the other. His foot is jigging slightly against his knee. 'Alan Challow sent it to me. Said he thought I'd find it interesting. Which, of course, I do.'

I take a seat opposite him. 'And?'

'I have some preliminary thoughts.'

'Care to share them with a mere policeman?'

He smiles thinly. 'Of course. But I'd like to observe the girl as well. Is that possible?'

'I asked Vicky to come in and start on her statement. It was going to be tomorrow but we can call and see if we can bring it forward.'

Gow reaches over and picks up his cup. 'Perfect.'

I go out to find Everett and ask her to contact Vine Lodge, and when I return to the room Gow is leafing through the pages of the journal.

'It's the child that puzzles me,' he says. 'Or rather, the girl's relationship with the child. I gather they tried to put them together at the hospital but it wasn't a success?'

'She screamed so much they had to take the boy away. They said it would only make things worse, forcing the issue.'

'And since then? What contact have they had?'

'None.'

He frowns. 'You're sure? I mean, you wouldn't necessarily know –'

I bite the bullet. 'I would, actually. He's at my house.' I can feel the blood flooding my face. 'Just for a few days. While they find him a more permanent place.'

Shut up, Fawley. Just shut up.

Gow is staring at me. 'Well, that's not exactly standard protocol –'

'Harrison OK'd it. Before you ask.'

There's a long pause and then he nods. 'I see. And has the girl asked for him, as far as you're aware?'

'No. All I know is that she reacted badly to seeing TV footage of a baby.'

Gow sits back and puts his fingertips together. 'Anything else?'

'The trick cyclist at the John Rad said it could be PTSD. That she's blocking out what happened to her, and the child is part of that.'

Gow nods slowly. 'If the boy is the product of rape he will be a physical and ever-present reminder of that rape. If she's failed to bond with him, it may be no more complex than that.'

One thing I do know about Bryan Gow is that he chooses his words very carefully. '*If?*'

He turns to the journal again and flicks through the sheets. 'What we have here is a very clear psychological trajectory, in relation to the child. We move from her horror at Harper's sexual assaults, to rejection of the baby once it's born, towards a gradual acceptance of the child as her own. Here, for instance: "*I'm trying to think of him as mine. As just mine and nothing to do with that horrible old pervert.*"'

'So?'

'The point is, this is entirely at variance with how the girl is behaving now. The violent rejection of the child – the blanking him out. It's totally at odds with what we have in the journal.'

'OK, fair enough. But the bit you just read was before the food and water started to run out – perhaps her feelings changed because of the trauma she went through?'

But Gow is shaking his head. 'From what I've been told, she was giving what supplies they had to the child. That argues she was feeling a *stronger* connection to him by then. Not the opposite.'

'So how do you explain it?'

'I think it's possible there was some sort of collusion going on. Psychological collusion, I mean. A version of Stockholm Syndrome. That's why I want to see her for myself.' He sits back. 'When you interview her, talk to her about the child,' he says. 'But start neutrally – "birth" not "baby", for example. Keep the emotion out of it. Then gradually up the pressure. Let's see how she reacts.'

*   *   *

'How are you feeling, Vicky?'

'I'm fine.'

And she actually looks much closer to fine than I've yet seen. Though there are still dark circles under her eyes. The manager of Vine Lodge has come in with her, and she glances at him now and he gives her an encouraging smile.

'I also want to thank you for agreeing to come in, Vicky – it's going to be an enormous help.'

Everett and I sit down and I put my papers on the table. 'Bringing a case against the man who abducted you is a very complicated process, and we need to assemble a lot of detailed evidence. We'll probably need to talk to you several times over the next few weeks, and if it's OK with you we'll ask you to do that here – so we can tape the interviews and use them in court if we need to.' And so Bryan Gow can watch from the room next door. Though this, of course, I don't say. 'I know it isn't very nice in here, but it makes it easier for us. Is that OK with you?'

She looks at me steadily. 'Yes, that's fine.'

'And Mr Wilcox here has agreed to be what we call an "appropriate adult". That means he'll keep an eye on things from your point of view.'

She glances at Wilcox again and smiles.

'And you just tell me if you feel you need to take a break or if it's getting too much.'

I open my file. 'So can you start with your name, for the tape?'

'Vicky. Vicky Neale.'

'And your address?'

'I don't have one. Not any more.'

'Where were you living last?'

'A bedsit in East Oxford. I didn't like it much.'

'Which road?'

'Clifton Street. Number fifty-two.'

'What was the landlord's name?'

She shrugs. 'Dunno. He was Asian. Rajid or something. I was only there a few weeks.'

'And before that?' asks Everett, looking up from her note-book. 'Where's home?'

'Harlow. But it's not my *home*.'

'It would really help if we had an address.'

She glances at Wilcox, hesitant now.

'Don't you want your mum and dad to know where you are? You've been missing a long time –'

'My dad died. And my mum wouldn't care. Says I'm old enough to stand on my own two feet and she's got a new family to think about. She's probably moved by now anyway – she said they were thinking of going up north. Her and her new bloke.'

I know I bang on about Fawley's law, but in my experience three answers to one question is never a good sign. Still, the pain in her eyes is real enough.

'I think we should be able to track her down, all the same,' says Everett. 'I assume you don't mind us giving her a call if we do?'

Vicky opens her mouth, then closes it again. 'Suit yourself. But like I said, she won't want to know.'

'Even after she finds out what's happened to you – the ordeal you've been through – surely any mother – ?'

'Not mine. She'll probably say it was all my own fault. That I shouldn't have been so stupid.'

She's blinking away the tears, refusing to cry. I have a sudden image of how she must have looked as a little girl.

'So can you tell us how that happened?' I say gently. 'How Dr Harper kidnapped you? I'm sorry, I know it's upsetting, but we do need you to go through everything.'

She wipes her eyes with the heel of her hand. 'I was on my way to look at another bedsit, only I broke my shoe. I was sitting on his wall when he came out and said he could mend it for me. He didn't look weird or anything. He reminded me of Dad. So I went in.'

Everett looks up. 'When was this, exactly?'

'July 2014. The 5th. I remember because there'd been fireworks the night before and someone said it must be Americans.'

'And how old were you then?'

'Sixteen. I was sixteen.'

Everett passes across a photograph of Harper. 'Can you confirm that this is the man you're talking about, Vicky?'

She looks and looks away. Then nods.

'And he gave you tea,' I say. 'That's right, isn't it?'

'Yes. It was a really hot day and he didn't have anything cold. He must have put something in it though, because one minute I was sitting there in his horrible smelly kitchen and the next I was waking up in that cellar.'

'And he kept you down there – kept you and raped you?'

'Yes,' she whispers.

'I can't imagine how horrible that must have been.'

Her lip trembles and she nods.

I turn a page in my notes.

'Can you tell me about the food and water?'

She blinks, confused. 'What do you mean, the food and water?'

'I'm sorry, I know it's difficult, but the prosecution is going to have to explain things like that to the jury.'

She nods. 'OK. I see. He'd leave bottles of water. Food in tins. It was all old people's stuff. Peaches. Manky stew. I had a plastic spoon. My wrists were tied in front with those tie things. But I could eat. Just about.'

'And write,' I say, smiling at her. 'That's impressive. Not many people would have the presence of mind to do that.'

She lifts her chin. 'I wanted everyone to know what happened. If I died down there I wanted people to know what he'd done.'

'The same as he did to that other girl.'

'He boasted about it. About burying her in the garden. I didn't think it was true. I thought he just wanted to scare me. So I'd do what he wanted.'

'Did he tell you how he was supposed to have killed her? When it happened?'

Her eyes widen. 'I don't remember exactly, but I'd been in the cellar a long time by then.'

'And you were in Dr Harper's cellar for nearly three years?'

'I didn't know how long it was. Not till I got out.'

She gives a little gulp that's half a sob.

'And he still kept you down there – even when you were pregnant?'

She nods again.

'And what about when the contractions started? Surely you were let out then?'

She hangs her head. The eyes she raises to mine are full of tears.

There's a knock at the door and one of the DCs appears. I get up and go towards him.

'Sorry, boss,' he says in a low voice. 'But you're wanted. *Next door*.' He gives me a meaningful look.

When I turn back to Vicky she's leaning against Wilcox, crying silently.

'I'm really sorry, Vicky. I didn't mean to upset you. Perhaps we should stop for now?'

Wilcox looks up. 'I think that's best. She's had enough for today.'

'Tomorrow then? Tennish?'

He nods, and helps the girl to her feet.

I watch the two of them down the corridor and through the swing doors. At one point Wilcox places his hand lightly on the girl's shoulder.

When I open the door to join Gow he's scanning back through the interview footage.

'Here,' he says, without looking round. 'It's where you asked her about the food and water. She drops her eyes before she answers, then looks to the right. If you believe in Neuro-Linguistic Programming – which I do, incidentally – that's a big red flag for fabrication. But that's not the only thing. When you asked her that question, she repeated it. She doesn't do that anywhere else. She was trying to buy herself time.' He leans forward and points. 'And then she brings her hand to her mouth as she replies. Look.'

'So she wasn't telling the truth?'

'Certainly not the whole truth and nothing but the truth.' He sits back and turns to face me. 'I think I was right about the collusion – I think she came to some sort of accommodation with Harper. Something she accepted out of desperation at the time but now finds deeply shameful. Shame's a rather unfashionable sentiment these days: the modern world is always telling us we don't need to be embarrassed about anything we do – or think. But the shame response is still there, in the psyche – self-disgust, regret, revulsion. Those are immensely powerful emotions and all the more so when the subject is in denial. Whatever that girl did, she doesn't want to admit it – certainly not to you, and on the evidence I've just seen, not even to herself.'

He sits back and starts to clean his glasses. Which is his own particular 'tell', though I've never had the courage to say so.

'But that doesn't invalidate her whole story, surely?'

He puts his glasses back on. 'Of course not. It just means there's some element of what happened in that house that we don't yet know about.'

'So how do we find out the truth? We can't ask Harper – he's still claiming he doesn't know anything about any of it. That's when he's in a fit state to say anything at all.'

He can see the exasperation on my face. He checks his watch and gets up. 'You're the detective, Fawley. I'm sure you'll work it out.'

My phone goes. A text, from Baxter:

At Frampton Road. Somer thinks she
might have found something.

Gow, meanwhile, has stopped at the door. 'Might be
worth looking at the journal again. I can't point to anything
specific, but something about it doesn't quite ring true.'

*   *   *

At Frampton Road, there's a uniformed constable at the
door and the sounds of movement overhead. Whatever it is,
it's upstairs. The bathroom on the first landing has its floorboards exposed now and the ancient lino is rolled up in the
corner. The carpet's up in the master bedroom too. That
very faint smell Luminol has, that you don't even notice unless you've been around it many times.

They're on the top floor. Baxter, the forensics officer,
Nina Mukerjee, Erica Somer and another uniform whose
name I can't remember.

'So, what have we got?'

Baxter gestures at Somer. A gesture that says, as far as I'm
concerned this is a wild goose chase so if it goes tits up it's
down to her, not me.

'In here, sir,' she says.

The room at the front. It was probably a servant's bedroom
once, with its low window set into the roof and its small cast-
iron fireplace. She turns to me, more than half apologetic.

'You're going to think this is a crazy idea – that English
grad thing again –'

'No. Go on. We've run out of options. All we have left is
crazy ideas.'

She blushes a little; it rather suits her. 'OK, if we assume Hannah definitely did die in this house –'

'I think she did. I *know* she did.'

'OK, and yet forensics found absolutely nothing. That's just not possible.'

'It shouldn't be, no.'

'No,' she says, insistent now. 'It *isn't*. There must *be* evidence. We just haven't found it.'

'As Challow keeps reminding me, they Luminol'd every floor –'

'Exactly, so what if it isn't the floors we should be looking at?'

'I'm not with you –'

She turns and points overhead. 'Look.'

A dull brown stain, darker at the edges, curiously heart-shaped. The rest of the ceiling is blotched with damp and age, but this – this is different. Deeper. Heavier.

'It's dry,' she says. 'I checked. And I know it's crazy – I mean, how could she possibly have died up there – it doesn't make sense – but there's that scene in *Tess* –'

But I'm not listening – I'm already out on the landing. The loft hatch is directly above the stairs. The Victorians weren't constrained by such nice concerns as Health & Safety.

'Didn't someone check up here?'

Baxter makes a face. 'Uniform were supposed to, but it looks like someone dropped the ball. Sorry, sir.'

'Right, well, we'd better look at it ourselves then, hadn't we.'

Baxter finds a chair in the next-door room and I climb on to it. The hatch is stiff, and I have to force it to get it free. But I can't get all the way up from the chair.

'Do you have a torch, Baxter?'

'There's one in the car, sir. And there's a stepladder in the conservatory. I remember seeing it.'

'OK, fetch the torch and I'll get the steps.'

When he gets back I'm wedging the stepladder against the hatch.

'I'll hold it for you, sir,' says Somer quickly. 'You'd break your neck if you fell from here.'

I start up, pushing the loft hatch open until it swings back and bangs against the floor. I can feel a cold draught of air, and bits of dust and grit fall on to my face. Once I get to the top step I haul myself up until I'm sitting on the edge. I don't want to think about what I'm doing to my trousers. Somer hands up the torch and I turn it on and swing the beam round. Boxes, junk, old clutter; the same crap there was in the cellar. On the wall, the wiring for the old servants' bells. I can just pick out the labels. *Breakfast room. Parlour. Study.* On the far side there's a hole in the tiles the size of my fist.

I get slowly to my feet, stooped under the roof beams, and step carefully across the boards. Most aren't nailed down and they sway a little under my weight. Suddenly, out of nowhere, something moves. A looming in the dark, wings, something leathery in my face –

They must have heard me cry out.

'Are you OK, sir?' calls Baxter.

My heart is still hammering. 'Yes, it was just a bat. Startled me, that's all.'

I take a deep breath and get my bearings. Work out where the mark on the ceiling must be. And yes, there is something there. Shapeless, hunched somehow. I call down for Nina to come up and I train the light on it. When she edges across to join me I hold the torch beam on it as she snaps on a pair of

plastic gloves. And as she lifts the object carefully away we
can see the dark, spreading and long-parched stain.

*   *   *

It takes a while to open it out. The plastic is so dry and petri-
fied it cracks and won't lie flat on the lab table. The lab intern
makes a joke about it being like unwinding a Dead Sea scroll,
then realizes that's a bit crass in the circumstances and falls
quiet. They work in silence then, until the whole thing is
spread before them in the glare of the overhead lamp.

Nina Mukerjee picks up the phone and calls Challow.

'So,' he says a few minutes later as he slips on his lab coat
and approaches the table. 'Is it what we thought it was?'

Nina nods. 'A car cover. Probably seventies and probably
for that Cortina on the drive.'

They stand there, looking at it. No need for Luminol
this time.

'Jesus,' says Nina under her breath. 'He didn't even bother
to hose it down.'

*   *   *

The Botley Road, 7.00 p.m. The only sounds in Vine Lodge
are from the kitchen. Muffled voices, the clunk of the fridge
door opening and closing, laughter.

In the girl's room there is silence. But it is not the silence
of sleep.

Vicky is sitting up in bed, her arms clasped tight round
her knees, rocking a little. Then there's a noise on the landing and her head goes up. She slips quickly to the door and
tries the handle. It gives to her touch and she stands there

for a moment, breathing heavily, her fists clenched so tight that the knuckles show against the bluish skin.

* * *

Sent: Tues 09/05/2017, 19.35   **Importance: High**
From: AlanChallowCSI@ThamesValley.police.uk
To: DIAdamFawley@ThamesValley.police.uk

Subject: Urgent – Frampton Road

Just to say I think I may have found a way to test your theory about the journal. And the lab have run those other tests you asked for. One set of results didn't ring true so they ran them again. But there was no mistake. The room at the rear on the top floor – there are traces of meconium on the floor. You don't need me to tell you what that means.

* * *

'What's that smell?'

Gislingham turns to see his wife at the kitchen door. He's at the stove, pinny on, tea towel over one shoulder, spatula in hand. And he's bloody enjoying himself. On the other side of the table, Billy's in his high chair, and clearly far more interested in what his dad is cooking than the bland mush in his plastic bowl.

'Brunch,' he says. 'I'm not due in till later so I thought I'd make the most of it.'

Janet Gislingham comes over to the stove and stares into the pan. 'Sausages?'

Gislingham grins. 'A small token of appreciation from a

grateful member of the general public. Who just happens to be a butcher.'

'Careful – the powers that be might accuse you of taking bribes.'

Gislingham lifts his hands, mock-terrified, mock-Cockney. 'It's a fair cop, officer. You got me bang to rights.'

Janet raises an eyebrow. 'Shouldn't that be bangered to rights?'

Gislingham laughs out loud, then turns to the pan and cuts off a bit of sausage. 'Here – try.'

Janet hesitates a moment, but they smell just too good. She pulls the piece of meat off the end of the knife.

'Hey – that's hot!' she yelps, flapping her hand in front of her mouth.

'Fab, aren't they?'

She nods. 'Where'd you get them?'

'Cowley Road. Finest Old English.'

'I can't remember the last time I cooked sausages.'

Gislingham can't remember the last time she cooked anything at all, but it doesn't matter. She's smiling.

'You've got grease all down your chin.' He reaches out and wipes it away with his finger, then drops the spatula into the pan and folds his wife into his arms. Billy starts gurgling and Gislingham gives his son a wink.

It's going to be all right. Everything's going to be all right.

*　　*　　*

In the canteen, Quinn is on day six of his own private nightmare. He's giving off so much negative energy people are avoiding sitting with him, even though the place is always crowded at this time of day. He came in via Belford Street where Pippa said she was staying, but there was still no answer. He slams the phone down next to the plate of egg and bacon he's barely touched. She'll recognize his number now, so no surprises she's not picking up – he needs to get someone else to try, and right now, there's only one person he can ask.

He looks round the canteen. Where the fuck is Gislingham, anyway?

*　*　*

Just before 10.00, and Vicky and the manager of Vine Lodge are back in Interview One. Gow and I are watching them on the video feed. I took Wilcox to one side when they arrived and checked with him: she still hasn't asked about the boy.

Gow glances across at the papers I have in my hand. 'That was a shrewd call – asking Challow to run those tests on the journal.'

'It was what you said about it not ringing true. It was just a hunch.'

'That's what makes you good at your job. Gives you a problem now, though, doesn't it?'

I turn to him.

'Because you're going to have to disclose those tests to Harper's defence.'

I pull a face. 'I know. And we all know what they'll do with them.'

There's a knock at the door. Everett.

'Are you ready, sir?'

*　*　*

When Gislingham finally gets into the office he goes to find Quinn.

'Did we get those mobile records?' he asks, perching on the edge of Quinn's desk. Something Quinn usually hates. But when the cat's in the doghouse, the mice take liberties.

Quinn shakes his head. 'Magistrate said exactly what you said she would.' He looks, if anything, even worse than he did the day before. 'And now Fawley wants me to bring her in to charge her with giving a false statement. But the address she gave me – there's no one there. And she's not answering her phone.'

'She probably recognizes your number – let me have a go.'

Gislingham punches the numbers into his mobile and waits.

'Nothing doing,' he says eventually. Even his indefatigable optimism is taking a bit of a hit. Or perhaps not. Because Quinn's on the phone himself now, and he's gesturing urgently at Gislingham.

'You're sure?' he's saying. 'Definitely gave her name as Pippa Walker?'

His fingers clench into a fist. 'Woods,' he says, 'you are a bloody life-saver.'

*　*　*

'Thanks for coming back, Vicky,' I say as we take our seats. 'I've got DC Everett with me again, if that's OK. Just in case I miss anything.'

She smiles a little. Nods. She's playing with her jumper in her lap again.

'I want to start by thanking you, Vicky. After what you said about the other girl, we searched the house again. And we found something. A plastic sheet.'

She raises her eyes to mine. Her lips move but there are no words.

'There's blood on it. We believe it's from that other girl – the one who disappeared. So we think you're right. He did kill someone else.'

She closes her eyes for a moment. Then hangs her head.

I glance at Everett. She gives a tiny nod.

I take a deep breath. 'I'm afraid that wasn't the only thing we found, Vicky. On the top floor of the house there are three empty rooms. It didn't look like anyone had been in there for years. But we tested them all the same. Just to be sure. And in one, the smallest one at the back, we found traces of a very unusual substance. Only small traces, but you can never entirely remove a trace like that, even if you clean up really carefully. Not with the equipment we have these days. Do you know what that substance was?'

She's not reacting.

'It's called meconium. It's the waste matter babies have in their bowels when they're in the womb. It's unmistakeable, and it's only present for a few hours after birth. There's only one explanation, Vicky. A baby was in that room. In fact, a baby was probably *born* in that room.'

The girl raises her eyes to mine. Her face is defiant now.

'Why didn't you tell us?'

'Because I knew you'd start accusing me – just like you are now.'

'Accusing you of what, Vicky?'

'Of not escaping, of not getting away.'

'So why didn't you? Why didn't you try to escape?'

'Look,' she says, 'he only let me out when my waters broke. And he never left me alone up there. Not once. No way I could have escaped. *No way.*'

Everett looks up from her pad. 'How long were you up- stairs, roughly?'

She shrugs. 'A few hours, maybe. It was night. It was dark outside the whole time. Listen, are you accusing me of something here? That bastard raped me – did the most *disgusting* things to me –'

'We know that, Vicky,' I say quietly.

'Then why are you talking to me like I'm the criminal?'

'Look, Vicky, I'd understand – we'd *all* understand – you were just trying to survive. And if that meant coming to some sort of compromise with the man who abducted you, well, there'd be no shame in that – not as far as I'm concerned –'

'I'm not *ashamed*,' she says, staring me straight in the face, her hands flat on the table between us, 'because I never did compromise with that disgusting old pervert. Is that clear?' There are spots of dangerous colour in her cheeks now.

'OK,' I say quickly. 'Let's talk about something else.' I sift through my papers. 'Yesterday, you said Dr Harper brought down your food in tins, is that right?'

She rolls her eyes. 'Do we have to go over all this *again*?'

Wilcox shoots a look in my direction. A look that says, what the hell are you playing at, can't you see she's distressed?

And she is. But not for the reason he thinks.

'What about your baby, Vicky? Did Dr Harper get food for him? Your little boy?'

She flinches at the word. 'I was breastfeeding. I didn't want to, but the old man made me. He let me have my hands free while I did it and tied me up again after.'

'Ah yes, I remember that now. But there is one other thing that puzzles me.'

'Oh yeah?' she says, sitting back and folding her arms. Gow's always talking about the nuances of body language, but I don't need his help to interpret that one.

'That bag of rubbish in the cellar, there were some tins of baby food in there. So it wasn't just breastfeeding, was it?'

She starts looking at her fingernails. 'Yeah, he got the kid some stuff. Only recently though. When it got bigger.'

'So where did Dr Harper get the food from?'

'Don't ask *me*,' she snaps. 'I wasn't *there*, was I? Could be anywhere. There are shops all over the place round there.'

'Actually, there are surprisingly few. And even fewer within walking distance. Dr Harper hasn't been able to drive for at least a year, and with his arthritis, he's not very mobile. There are only two shops he could have got to on foot. Yesterday afternoon, DC Everett here went and spoke to the staff there.'

'And when I showed them Dr Harper's picture they all recognized him,' says Everett. 'They'd served him many times. Mostly beer, by the sounds of it. But none of them had ever sold him any baby items.'

'As you can imagine,' I continue, 'something like that would have stuck in their minds – an old man like him buying things like that.'

'Ah,' says Everett quickly, 'but there was the supermarket order as well, wasn't there, boss – perhaps that's where he got them?'

Vicky looks at her. And takes the bait. 'Oh yeah, I remember now.'

I glance down at my file. 'You're right. Some of the waste we found in the cellar did indeed come from Dr Harper's supermarket order. The trouble is, that's never included baby food. We checked. It was set up for him by his social worker and it's never varied.'

She glares at me. 'Look, I was *in the cellar*. I haven't got a clue where he got it from.'

'We took fingerprints from the baby food containers too. Yours are there, Vicky, and some others, mostly smudged. But there are none from Dr Harper. Some of the food tins have his prints, but there aren't any of his on the baby items – none at all. Can you explain that for me, Vicky?'

She shrugs. 'He's the one you should be asking. Not me.'

'Oh, we will. We definitely will. But to be honest, he's not in a good way –'

'*Good*,' she says quickly. 'I hope he rots in hell for what he did to me. Look, have we finished – I'm tired –'

'Not much more, I promise. But you're going to be asked for a lot of these details in court, so we need to hear what you're going to say. About the journal, for instance.'

She frowns. 'What about it?'

'I asked our forensics expert to look at it again. He's found something now he hadn't picked up before. Something that never occurred to him to check.'

She says nothing, but her eyes have narrowed. She's on her guard.

'He used a special piece of equipment called an Electrostatic Detection Apparatus. It's quite an old-fashioned piece of kit, these days.'

So old, in fact, that the machine in question has spent the last fifteen years stuffed in the back of a cupboard. It's the first time I've ever been grateful that Alan Challow is such a terrible hoarder.

'But it still has one very useful function,' I continue. 'It can give you a pretty good idea how much pressure has been applied to the paper. How hard the writer was holding the pen, in other words. Or whether they stopped and started at all while they were writing it. In that journal of yours, the pressure was remarkably even.'

'Yeah, and?'

'That's very unusual. I mean, with something written over more than two years. You wouldn't normally see that. It's much more likely to happen if all the pages had been written at the same time.'

Wilcox shifts a little in his chair. I can't imagine what he's thinking.

'The only sheet that was different was the last one. Where you talked about the water running out – about how desperate you were for someone to come –'

She bangs her palms down on the table. 'That's because I thought I was going to *die*. Don't you get that?'

'Oh yes, Vicky, I get that.'

Wilcox glances across at her. 'Perhaps we can take a break?' he says. 'This stuff – it's all pretty stressful.'

'OK. We'll get some coffee sent in and start again in about half an hour.'

The incident room is packed. Even Gow is there. The only ones missing are Quinn and Gislingham. I wonder in passing what exactly is going on there, because something sure as hell is. And now Gislingham's got dragged into it too.

'So Harper *let her out*?' says Baxter as soon as he sees us. 'Why the hell didn't she try to get away?'

'She had just given birth, Baxter –'

'Yeah, OK, but that doesn't mean she was completely incapacitated, does it, sir? Couldn't she have broken a window, called out to someone? There must have been *something* she could've done.'

Everett is looking thoughtful.

'What is it, Ev?'

'When Donald Walsh was being charged, he talked about hearing something upstairs in the house. He thought it was the cat from down the road. It's a Siamese. My aunt used to have one – bloody whingey thing. But you know what – it sounded unnervingly like a baby.'

Baxter is staring at her. 'What are you saying?'

Everett shrugs. 'How do we know she was only upstairs for the birth? Maybe he let her out more than once. Maybe she got that baby food *herself.*'

I turn to Gow. 'Is that feasible? You said there could have been some sort of collusion between them.'

He doesn't answer straight away; he always was one for the theatrical pause. 'Yes, it's possible,' he says eventually. 'That could have been the deal she made with Harper – he let her out of the cellar for periods of time, in exchange for some sort of concession on her part.'

'Like sex, you mean?' says Everett.

'That's the most likely. But a different type of sex to the rapes. She may have agreed to play along with him that they were in some sort of relationship. A family, even. There are hints of that in the journal.'

'I still don't know why she couldn't have escaped if he was letting her out of the cellar,' says Baxter. 'Especially if he was actually allowing her to go outside.'

Gow looks around the room. 'It's not uncommon, in these situations, for the abductor to separate the mother and child for fairly lengthy stretches of time. To weaken the attachment between them. Harper could have allowed the girl out occasionally, but kept the boy locked up. So the child was, in effect, a hostage. The girl couldn't escape without leaving him behind.'

Baxter shakes his head, strident now. 'No way I'm buying

that. I think she'd have left the kid there at the drop of a hat and good riddance.'

Gow smiles thinly. 'I'm just setting out the range of possibilities, Constable. Profiling isn't a sausage machine. You can't just press a button and out pops the answer. It's for CID to determine what actually *happened*.'

The door pushes open. One of the uniform PCs. He's carrying a tray with coffee and a can of Coke. He looks around the room then spots me. 'Your wife's here, sir. She says it's urgent.'

'My *wife*?'

Alex never comes to this place. And I do mean *never*. She hates it. Says it smells of lies. Lies and lavatories.

He looks a bit embarrassed. 'Yes, sir. She's in reception.'

Alex is sitting on one of the grey plastic chairs lined up against the wall. The boy is next to her, standing on the seat and looking out of the window. She has her hand on the small of his back, taking care he doesn't fall.

I walk towards her quickly. 'You really shouldn't be here,' I say in a low voice.

'I'm sorry, I know you're busy –'

'It's not that – Vicky's here. She's in the building. It could be awkward – I mean, if she sees the boy.'

The boy starts to bang on the window and Alex reaches up to grab his hands.

'Look, what is it, Alex – why didn't you phone?'

'I finished the novel. *Room*.'

It takes me a moment to remember. 'Right. OK. But I really need to get back – can you tell me tonight?'

'There's a bit at the end – after the girl is released. Her little boy has to adapt to a world he's never seen before.'

'I'm not with you.'

'He has to learn new things. Things he's never done before because he's spent all his life in one room. A room on
one level. With *no stairs.*'

I turn to look at the boy. He's banging on the window
again, shrieking with laughter. I try to remember – try to
picture him –

'He can do it,' she says, reading my mind. 'I've seen him.
Several times.'

'And he did it straight away?'

She nods. 'He had no trouble at all climbing the stairs.
Because he'd clearly *done it before.*'

* * *

Quinn parks the Audi along by the old prison quarter, now
prinked out as a swanky hotel and a paved courtyard with
bars and pizzerias. People are sitting outside, drinking coffee, talking, smiling in the sunshine.

'The store manager's been told to keep her there until we
arrive,' he says, turning off the engine.

'You were bloody lucky Woods overheard uniform radio-
ing in that shoplifting report,' says Gislingham, just a bit
resentful now that fate seems to have handed Quinn a get-
out-of-jail card. Or perhaps he just wanted to collect all the
available brownie points himself.

Quinn shrugs. 'He knew I was trying to track her down,
so I guess the name must have jumped out.'

'And it's deffo the same Pippa Walker?'

'I'm pretty sure – apparently this girl nicked a handbag
pom-pom. A pricey designer job. I've seen her bag – she has
loads of those things.'

'What the fuck's a handbag pom-pom anyway?' mutters Gislingham as he follows Quinn up towards Carfax, struggling at times to negotiate the unwieldy crowds, the people not looking where they're going, the small children who don't keep to the rules and lurch out at erratic angles; the shoppers, the idlers, the lost. The high-end fashion store is — appropriately enough — on the High. In the plate-glass window, chrome cubes display jewellery, shoes, bags, sunglasses.

Quinn points at one of the shelves as they push open the door.

'Right,' says Gislingham, 'so that's a handbag pom-pom when it's home. Who knew, eh — who bloody knew.'

The manager has clearly been hovering by the door on the lookout, and quickly ushers them away from a couple of extremely thin elderly Americans poring over leopard-print headscarves.

'So,' says Quinn, looking around. 'Where is she?'

'I asked her to wait in the office,' says the manager, lowering her voice. 'She was starting to get a bit, well, *loud*.'

I bet she was, thinks Gislingham.

'Can you show us?' says Quinn, clearly agitated now.

They follow her through to the back, which is dark, cluttered and pokey after the sparse over-white brilliance of the sales floor. The manager kicks a box of promo leaflets to one side and opens the office door. But there's no one there. Just a plastic chair, a computer and shelves stacked with paperwork. Quinn turns on her. 'You were supposed to be keeping her here — *where the hell is she*?'

The manager has gone pale. 'She can't have gone out the front — I'd have seen her. And Chloe's been back here stock-taking all morning — or at least she was supposed to be —'

There's noise then – a sound of flushing – and another door swings open. A woman comes out, sees them and blushes.

'Chloe – weren't you supposed to be keeping an eye on Ms Walker?' says the manager sharply.

The woman looks flustered, holding one hand to her stomach. 'She's in the office, isn't she? She was there a second ago. Honestly, I was only in the loo a minute – I held on as long as I could but you know what it's like when you're pregnant –'

Quinn throws up his hands. 'Shit – she must have bloody heard us.'

'Is there another way out?' interrupts Gislingham.

The manager gestures. 'There's a back exit on to the Covered Market, but we only use it for the bins –'

But the two men have already gone.

Quinn clatters out of the door into the market and checks each store as he passes. Sandwich shop, Thai takeaway, boutique, bakery. The place seems full suddenly of long-haired girls. Same voices, same clothes, same long blonde hair and expensive highlights. Faces that turn to his, startled, irritated, bemused. One of them even smiles at him. And then he's in the open space in the centre, seeing Gislingham racing down towards him from the opposite side. The two of them stand there, turning, scanning the alleys. Picture framer's, pie shop, cobbler's. The racks of plants outside the florist's, the noticeboard of posters for concerts and art shows and plays in college gardens. Avenues leading off in all directions. It's like looking for a rat in a maze.

'Can you see her?'

'Nope,' says Gislingham, his eyes on the crowds. 'We can't cover this whole place on our own – she could be anywhere.'

Quinn is breathing hard. 'If you were trying to hide in here, where would you go?'

Gislingham shrugs. 'Somewhere with an upstairs?'

'That's more like it – what's that place called – the coffee shop – ?'

'Georgina's,' says Gislingham, 'but I can never bloody find it –'

But Quinn has already gone, running now. '*This way.*'

He rounds the corner and crashes up the wooden stairs into the café, coming to a halt at the top and barely missing a waitress with a tray of coffee. Half the people in the room turn to look at him. But none of them is Pippa.

'Sorry,' he says. Then turns and goes back down, slower now. Where the hell is Gis?

His phone beeps.

'I've found her,' says Gislingham. 'Market Street. And move it.'

When Quinn emerges into the open air he realizes at once where she went. And why.

'Is she inside?'

Gislingham nods. 'Went in a couple of minutes ago. There's only this exit. All we have to do is wait.'

'Fuck that – let's go in.'

'It's the Ladies – you can't –'

But Quinn's already pushing past the queue of patient middle-aged women, flashing his warrant card.

'Police. Move aside please. Move aside.'

The women retreat, muttering and affronted, and Quinn starts to bang on the doors. 'Police – open up.'

One by one the doors swing open. An Asian woman in a headscarf scuttles out with a child, her face down, making no eye contact. An elderly lady follows, moving with difficulty. Then a sturdy woman in tweed who complains loudly about 'reporting this to your senior officer'. Until only the door at the far end remains. Quinn goes up to it. 'Miss Walker,' he says loudly. 'We need to speak to you. Open the door please or I'll have to break it down.'

His heart is beating hard with the running. Or the adrenaline. Hard to tell.

There's a silence, then the sound of the bolt drawing back.

* * *

When I was a kid I had a thing for those Escher pictures. You know the ones – all black and white and geometrical. There were no fancy websites then so all we had was paper, but I loved optical illusions and those were the best. I had one of the Escher pictures on my bedroom wall, *Day and Night*. You'll have seen it – it's the one where it's impossible to say whether it's white birds by night or black birds by day. And that's how I feel as I push open the door to the incident room. It's not what you're looking at, it's where you're standing that determines what you see.

The team look up. See my face. Fall silent.

And then I tell them what my wife said.

There's a long pause as they take it in, and then suddenly we're all looking at Gow.

'It's possible Harper was letting the child out too,' he says finally, taking off his glasses and pulling out his handkerchief. 'That the girl negotiated that.'

'But?' Because there is a *but* here. A big one; I can see it on his face.

'When she denied being ashamed of compromising with Harper, everything about her body language suggested to me that she was telling the truth. So whatever it is she's struggling with, it's not that. So how, I ask myself, are we to explain the fact that this child has clearly *not*, as Ms Neale alleges, spent the whole of his short life imprisoned in that cellar? Personally,' he says, putting his glasses back on and looking at me, 'I would tend towards the most obvious explanation.'

Occam's razor. The simplest answer is invariably right.

There's a ripple of incredulity as they work out what Gow is actually saying.

Surely not – surely she couldn't have –

But I think she did.

'She made it all up,' I say. 'The abduction, the imprisonment – the whole thing. It's all a fake.'

I can hear them draw breath. Gow glances at his watch and gets to his feet. 'I have a seminar to give in exactly thirty-five minutes. But you can call me later, if you need me.'

When the door closes behind him, people shift, change position. There's a sense of time shunting forward suddenly, after days of going round in circles.

'Makes complete sense to me,' says Baxter, folding his arms, thoroughly vindicated. 'There's no need to escape if you were *never imprisoned in the first place*. That girl has been camped out there all this time. Living in Harper's house. Eating Harper's food. No wonder the poor old sod has been losing weight.'

Somer turns to me. 'You really think she could have been living there for nearly *three years*? I mean, I know she was looking for somewhere cheap to live, but that's ridiculous. And in any case, surely *someone* would have noticed?'

I point to the photograph. 'I'm not so sure – look at that place. No one's used the top floor for years. The only neighbour was an old lady who wasn't likely to hear much through those walls. And the only person who visited didn't stay any longer than fifteen minutes and never went upstairs –'

'Walsh did,' interrupts Baxter, 'to steal those *netsuke*.'

'Exactly,' says Everett, 'and when he did he heard something he thought was a cat. But I bet you any money you like it was Vicky's baby.'

'But what about Harper?' asks one of the DCs. 'Both of my kids screamed the bloody place down when they were babies. Surely Harper would have heard *something* all those months, even if he was losing it?'

There's a silence. A silence that ends with Everett:

'Remember those sleeping pills forensics found upstairs? What if Vicky found them? She could have been drugging the old man to keep him quiet.'

'Not just him,' says Somer quietly. 'He wasn't the only one she wanted to silence.'

'I'll call Challow,' says Baxter grimly. 'Get him to run some tests on the samples from the boy. If that's what she was doing, they'll be able to prove it.'

Somer shakes her head. 'Even a small dose would be incredibly dangerous for a child that young. She could have killed him.'

Everett shrugs. 'From what I've seen, I don't think she'd have cared. There is absolutely *no* bond between those two. You see enough dysfunctional relationships in this job, but this is the first time I've come across a mother and child with no relationship *at all*.'

'But that's the real question, isn't it?' says Somer quietly. 'The child. Not the relationship between them. The fact that he even exists –'

Baxter turns to her, realization dawning. 'Because if it wasn't imprisonment it can't have been rape, either, can it? And the one thing we *do* know for a fact is that Harper is the father of that kid. So if he didn't rape her, then what? She actually *wanted* to have sex with him? That's just gross — I mean, why the hell would she?'

This time it's not Occam's razor I think of. It's Gislingham. Gislingham, who's still not bloody here, incidentally. Gislingham who always says that if it's not love, it's money.

I turn to the pinboard. And there it is: the answer. It's been right there in front of us from day one: 33 Frampton Road. Worth, even at a conservative estimate, somewhere north of £3 million.

'She's going to sue Harper,' I say. 'Accuse him of rape and false imprisonment, and then claim compensation. That child will give her a stake in everything William Harper owns. He's not a "child" at all; he's a money-making scam.'

I look around the room. Oddly enough, the women seem to be buying it more than the men. Though at the back, Somer is frowning.

'But could a girl like her actually *do* that?' asks one of the DCs, turning to Everett. 'I mean, would you?'

Everett shrugs. 'It's a lot of money. She might well have thought a couple of quick shags would be worth it for that sort of cash. Shut your eyes and think of England, and all that.'

Baxter gives a low whistle. 'Jesus,' he says. 'That poor old bastard —'

'OK,' says Somer, interrupting him. 'Let's get this straight. Somehow or other Vicky found out that Harper lives alone and sees pretty much no one from one week to the next. She moves in and starts living on the top floor – all without him noticing. She manages to get herself pregnant, also – if you believe Harper – without him noticing –'

'My money's on the turkey baster,' quips one of the DCs, to slightly embarrassed laughter.

'– and then she frames him for kidnap and rape by faking a journal of her captivity and locking herself in the cellar.'

Everyone's staring at her now.

'Only, she didn't, did she? Lock herself in, I mean. That door was bolted from the *outside*.' She looks around at the room. 'So who are we saying did that?'

I nod to Baxter. 'Did we get any prints off that bolt?'

He turns back to his screen, clicks on the forensics report and scrolls down. 'Nope. Just Quinn's. From when they rescued her.'

So someone could have wiped it. *Must* have wiped it.

'If you ask me,' says Baxter, 'it had to be Harper. He said, didn't he, that he was frightened because he could hear noises down there. He must have crept down one day, realized there was someone in that inner room and slipped the bolt. Vicky got trapped by her own scam – which would be pretty bloody ironic, when you think about it.'

Somer nods slowly. 'I guess that's possible, even though he doesn't seem to remember doing it –'

'He doesn't *remember* much at all,' snaps Everett. Which is really not like her. I see the same thought on Somer's face, and then Everett flushes a little when she catches my eye.

'Whether he remembers it or not, it's a plausible theory,' I say. 'So let's see if we can confirm it, shall we? And for now, send Vicky back to Vine Lodge. We need to get our facts straight before I talk to her again.'

*   *   *

Sent: Weds 10/05/2017, 11.50   **Importance: High**
From: AlanChallowCSI@ThamesValley.police.uk
To: DIAdamFawley@ThamesValley.police.uk,
        CID@ThamesValley.police.uk

Subject: Urgent – Frampton Road

This is to confirm that the blood, hair and particles of
brain matter found on the car cover are definitely from
Hannah Gardiner. The killer clearly used it to prevent the
leakage of body fluids on to the floor, which is why we
haven't been able to determine a precise murder scene
elsewhere in the house. The victim was probably rendered
unconscious then dragged on to the plastic before the
second and fatal blow. There are scrape marks on it that
would tally with that. The only fingerprints are those of
William Harper, which, of course, is only to be expected,
given it was on his car. If someone else handled it, they
must have worn gloves.

*   *   *

Interview with Pippa Walker, conducted at
St Aldate's Police Station, Oxford
10 May 2017, 12.10 p.m.
In attendance, DS G. Quinn, DC C. Gislingham

GQ: For the benefit of the tape, this interview is
     being conducted under caution. Miss Walker has
     been informed of her rights, including the

right to have a lawyer present. She has
confirmed that she doesn't want one.

PW: I don't need anyone. Rob's the one who's
guilty, not me. *I* haven't done anything.

GQ: But that's not true, is it? You've lied. A very
serious lie. And we can prove it.

PW: I don't know what you mean.

GQ: You gave us a statement three days ago,
claiming that Hannah Gardiner caught you and
Rob in bed, and there was a terrible row.

PW: So?

GQ: Our forensic scientists have done a thorough
examination of the flat at Crescent Square.
There's nothing to suggest Hannah Gardiner
died there. Nothing at all. Why did you lie?

PW: I didn't lie. It's *two years* ago. He's had it
redecorated twice since then.

GQ: That wouldn't make any difference. There would
still be something. You'd need a special type
of bleach and even then -

PW: Yeah, well, he's a scientist, isn't he. He'd
know what to do.

GQ: The point is, Miss Walker, that we now have
reason to believe Hannah died at 33 Frampton
Road, where her body was found. We have forensic
evidence linking her death to that house.

PW: [*silence*]

CG: What have you got to say to that?

PW: What's it got to do with me? I've never even
been there.
[*getting up*]
Look, can I go now?

GQ: No. Sit down, please, Miss Walker. You still
    haven't answered the question. Why did you lie
    about what happened at the flat?

PW: I *didn't* lie.

GQ: A witness has come forward who saw you on the
    night of June 23rd. You were with two young
    lads at a bus stop on the Banbury Road. At the
    same time as Hannah and Rob Gardiner were
    enjoying a peaceful and entirely row-free
    evening in their home.

PW: [*silence*]
    I was scared of him – he hit me –

CG: So you're admitting it – nothing happened at
    the flat?

PW: [*silence*]

CG: For the tape, Miss Walker, was there, or was
    there not, a violent argument at 81 Crescent
    Square such as you describe in your statement
    dated 7th May 2017?

PW: [*silence*]
    No.

CG: Did Hannah Gardiner come home that
    evening and find you in bed with her
    husband?

PW: No.

GQ: So you lied. Worse than that, you attempted
    to frame an innocent man for his wife's
    murder.

PW: He's not *innocent* – he's a bastard –

GQ: Do you realize how serious that is? The
    trouble you're in?

PW: [*turning to DS Quinn*]

Do you realize the trouble *you're* in? When I
tell them what you did – letting me in your
flat, having *sex* with me –

GQ: You know that's not what happened –

PW: Yeah, well, that's going to be your word
against mine, isn't it?

CG: I think a jury will be rather more inclined to
believe Detective Sergeant Quinn, don't you?

PW: [*pulls out her mobile phone and shows DS Quinn
a photo*]
That's *my* underwear in *your* bed. Who are they
going to believe now?

GQ: You staged that – it must have been while I
was out –
[*turning to DC Gislingham*]
She's lying – all of it –

PW: I want a lawyer. I can have one if I
want – yeah?

CG: Yes, as we have already –

PW: In that case I want one. Right now. And I'm
not talking any more until I do.

CG: Pippa Walker, I am arresting you on suspicion
of perverting the course of justice. You do
not have to say anything, but it may harm your
defence if you fail to mention when
questioned, something you later rely on in
court. Anything you do say may be given in
evidence. You will now be taken to the cells,
to await the arrival of your legal
representative. You will also be required to
hand over your mobile phone.
Interview suspended at 12.32.

* * *

'I still have reservations about this, Inspector.'

I'm standing in the kitchen doorway at Frampton Road with William Harper's lawyer. Looking down the hallway, I can see Harper's doctor helping him out of a police car. He looks shrunken. Shrivelled somehow. He stares around in terror at two or three passers-by who've stopped to watch from the other side of the road. We've done this to him. I know that. We didn't mean to, and we did it for the right reasons. But it's down to us all the same.

Erica Somer gets out of the driver's door and comes round, and she and Lynda Pearson support Harper slowly into the house. He stumbles on the step, bent half double, his hands outstretched before him as if he no longer trusts his eyes.

I turn to the lawyer. She knows what we're trying to prove by this exercise, but not why we're suddenly doing it now. 'This is in your client's interests. I'm sorry it has to be like this, but we need physical proof. I'm sure you understand.'

'What I *understand*, Inspector,' she says acidly, as Somer and Pearson ease Harper stiffly on to one of the kitchen chairs, 'is that you could have obtained this so-called "proof" right at the start, and saved a sick and vulnerable old man from enormous unnecessary stress, not to mention incarceration. I fully intend to make an official complaint.'

I see Somer glance at me but I'm not going to lose my rag with this woman. She's right. Or at least, partly so.

'You are free to do that, of course. But I'm sure you understand that we had no choice but to arrest Dr Harper when we did. Indeed, we would have been in derogation of our duty had we not done so, given the evidence we had at the time. And whatever the results of this experiment, it has no bearing at all on your client's physical state three years ago, at the time of the alleged abduction.'

She gives a little huffy sniff and reaches into her pocket for her mobile phone. 'Let's get this over with, shall we?'

I turn to Baxter, who's standing behind me with a video camera; the lawyer isn't the only one who's going to film this.

'OK, Dr Harper, are you ready now?'

He looks up at me, then lifts a shaking hand to shield his face, as if he fears a blow.

'There's nothing to be frightened of, Bill,' says the doctor. 'This is a police officer. He's not going to hurt you.'

Harper's watery eyes stare into mine. He shows no sign of recognizing me.

Pearson crouches down and puts her hand on Harper's arm. 'We just need to go down into the cellar for a minute –'

The old man's eyes widen. 'No – there's something down there –'

'It's OK, Bill. There's nothing down there now, I promise. And I'll be with you the whole time. As well as this nice police lady.'

She straightens up and exchanges a glance with Somer, who smiles weakly.

Baxter goes over to the door and pulls the bolt across, then leans in and flicks on the overhead light. Somer helps Harper to his feet and, between them, she and Pearson get Harper to the top of the flight of stairs.

'I'll go first,' says Somer. 'Just in case.'

'He has to go down unaided,' I say quietly. 'That's the whole point.'

'I know, sir,' she says, flushing. 'I just –'

Her voice trails off, but I know what she means.

'The video's running,' says Baxter behind me.

'Go on, Bill,' says Pearson gently. 'Take your time. Hold on to the handrail if you need to.'

It takes nearly twenty minutes, in the end, and he has to go down backwards, clinging to the banister with both hands, muttering and trembling with each step. Once or twice he nearly slips, but eventually we're all standing in the empty cellar. In the damp and the smell and the bleak, flickering light.

The lawyer turns to me. 'So what does this prove, Inspector?'

'It proves that Dr Harper is physically capable of accessing this area on his own, despite the fact that his arthritis has clearly deteriorated in the last few months.'

I catch Baxter's eye, and I know what he's thinking: Harper came down here and slipped the bolt on Vicky out of fear and confusion, condemning a young woman and a small child to a dreadful lingering death that only a chance coincidence prevented. But he'd had no idea that's what he was doing. He probably thought it was rats. It's not even attempted manslaughter, far less murder.

'Can we take Bill upstairs again now, Inspector?' asks Pearson. 'He's starting to get distressed.'

I nod. 'But he needs to do it on his own again, please.'

'Hold on a minute, sir.'

It's Somer, on the other side of the room, by the inner door. She looks up at the bolt at the top and reaches up to it.

She swivels round and looks at me. 'I can't get enough purchase on this to move it. Not without standing on something.'

The inference is obvious and the lawyer is on it at once. 'How tall are you, Constable?'

'Five foot six.'

'And my client can't be more than five foot seven even if he was standing up straight, and he has *very* limited mobility and hands crippled by arthritis.'

'Crippled' is a bit histrionic, in my book, but I appreciate that she's trying to make a point.

I turn to Baxter. 'Do you have the crime-scene photos on that thing?'

He shakes his head. 'Not on this camera. But I do have some on my phone.'

'OK, let's have a look.'

He scrolls back through. The inner room, the filthy bedding, the bag of empty tins, the repellent toilet. And then the room we're standing in. Broken furniture, cardboard boxes, black plastic sacks, an old tin bath full of junk. Nothing remotely robust enough to climb on.

'What about that stepladder?' I say in an undertone. 'The one in the conservatory?'

He shakes his head. 'No way. It was covered in spiders' webs and crap. No one had moved it for months. And Vicky can't have been in that cellar more than three weeks tops.'

And he's right. Of course he is. It would have been a miracle if the food and water we found had lasted even that long.

'Could you bring a chair down from the kitchen?'

He slides a glance at Harper. 'Well, *I* could, boss, but I don't think *he* could, if you catch my drift.'

'I don't think we need to submit my client to further humiliation by videotape, do you?' says the lawyer loudly. 'Assuming you have no objection, I'm going to take him back to the Council care home *your* actions have condemned him to.'

We stand and watch as she and the doctor help Harper

back up the stairs, and then listen as their footsteps retreat
down the hall and the door bangs behind them.

'I keep telling myself he was about to go into a home anyway,' says Somer, biting her lip. I know what she means.

'If it wasn't Harper who locked her in,' says Baxter eventually, 'the only other possibility is Walsh. OK, we know he
didn't rape Vicky, but he could easily have sussed she was
here. He admitted hearing that noise upstairs, didn't he –
and yes, he *claims* he thought it was a cat but what if that was
just a lie? What if he realized what Vicky was up to and decided to get rid of her – permanently? And he'd probably
have got away with it too – what with the DNA from the kid
and the old man in the state he's in. Everything would have
pointed to Harper.'

'What do you think, Somer?'

She pulls a tissue from her pocket and starts to wipe her
hands free of grime. 'If Walsh really did work out what Vicky
was up to, he had one hell of a motive to get rid of her. Her
and the child. Walsh said as much: he and his sister expect to
get Harper's money when he dies. I can't see him wanting to
share it with some grubby little teenage con artist.' She
makes a face. 'Which is exactly how he would describe her,
incidentally.'

'And you think he's capable of locking them in? Knowing
full well what that would mean?'

She sticks the tissue back in her pocket. 'Yes, sir, I do.
There's something cold-blooded about him. I don't think it's
an accident he lives alone.'

Baxter's clearly chuffed she agrees with him so conclusively. '*And* Walsh is deffo devious enough to remember to
wipe the bolt afterwards.'

I'm not about to argue with that one, either.

'In any case,' says Baxter, 'if it wasn't Walsh, then who?

There *isn't* anyone else. No one else has anything remotely close to a motive. Never mind opportunity.'

I take a deep breath. 'OK. Go to Vine Lodge and arrest Vicky. Attempted fraud.'

Baxter nods. 'And Walsh?'

'We know when Vicky was found and we know she can't have been there much more than three weeks. Let's find out where Walsh was in that time.'

*   *   *

'Where's Fawley?'

Somer looks up from her desk, surprised that Quinn should choose her to ask, given how many other people he could have picked on.

'In with the Super. I think he was wondering where *you* were.' *Because you've been AWOL most of the last two days. And because you look like shit.* But she doesn't actually say that bit.

Quinn rubs the back of his neck. 'Yeah, well, you know. Tough case.'

The door swings open and Woods, the custody sergeant, appears, scanning the room until he catches sight of Quinn and beckons him over. Somer sees the two of them confer, and then watches Quinn go quickly over to Gislingham. She can tell from their faces something's up. Whatever mess you've got yourself into, she thinks, I hope you're not dragging Gislingham down with you. She likes Gislingham, and he doesn't deserve to pay for Quinn's mistakes.

She gets up and walks over towards them, then pretends to be looking for something on the desk two bays down. Their voices are low, but she can hear what they're saying.

'She must have *something*,' says Gislingham. 'Credit card? Passport? Driving licence, then – we know she drives.'

'Woods says not,' says Quinn. 'He ought to know.'

Gislingham turns to his computer. 'OK, let's do a driving licence check.'

He types, then stares at the screen, chewing the end of his pen. Then he frowns and tries something else.

Then he turns to look up at Quinn.

'Shit,' he says.

*   *   *

Having briefed Harrison on where we've got to, I head back to the incident room. The place is humming with activity. Baxter is at the front, talking while he writes on a whiteboard.

DONALD WALSH

VICKY NEALE	*HANNAH GARDINER*
<u>*Motive*</u>	<u>*Motive*</u>
Money – Harper's estate, sexual?	Sexual Predator ? ? ?
<u>*Means*</u>	<u>*Means*</u>
Fit enough to commit crime / reach bolt	Access To: · Car cover etc · Possible murder weapons Fit enough to move body/ climb into loft unaided
<u>*Opportunity*</u>	
Known visitor to house with access to cellar	<u>*Opportunity*</u>
	Known visitor to house with access to loft/shed
<u>*Alibi ??*</u>	Could have met Hannah on the street
	<u>*Alibi ??*</u>

'Any luck on his whereabouts for the three weeks in question?' Baxter is saying.

'We're checking CCTV and traffic cams on the route between Frampton Road and Banbury,' says one of the DCs. 'But it's a big job. It's going to take time.'

'What about for 24th June 2015?'

'I'm still waiting to hear,' says Somer from her desk. 'The timetable has him teaching from 10.30 that morning, which would make getting to Wittenham and back virtually impossible. I did ask them to check if he could have been off sick that day, but when we started homing in on Gardiner I didn't chase it up. Sorry.'

'But Banbury CID are keeping an eye on him?'

'Yes – they're on the case. They know we'll be heading up there as soon as we have enough evidence to bring him in.'

Baxter turns from the board now and sees me. 'OK, boss?'

'What are you doing?'

'Working up the case on Walsh. Like you said.'

'I said to check his alibi for Vicky. I didn't say anything about Hannah.'

Somer glances at Baxter, then at me. 'It seemed the next logical step, sir. If Harper couldn't get on to a chair to open the cellar door there's no way on earth he could have got that car cover up into the loft, even if it was two years ago. You had enough trouble and you're thirty years younger and someone was holding the steps.' She's blushing slightly.

'And like I said,' interjects Baxter, 'who else is there? Walsh is the only one with both means and opportunity.'

I walk up to the board and stare at what Baxter's written under 'Motive'.

'We talked about it before, sir,' he says. 'How Walsh could have been using that house to prey on women. There's the stash of porn – no one's explained that, have they?'

'He's right, boss,' says Everett. 'If it's not Harper's, it has to be Walsh's.'

'Hannah's murder could easily have been sexually motivated, sir.' Somer again. 'We've no way of knowing how long she was in the house. He could have kept her there for days. And she *was* naked, as well as tied up.'

I turn to look at them. 'And all that time, Vicky was upstairs on the top floor, completely oblivious?'

Part of me wants to believe it, but we'd be in such wild regions of coincidence there'd be signs up saying 'Here be dragons'.

They're looking at each other. Not sure where this is heading.

'Look,' I say. 'I buy Walsh as the one who locked Vicky in. That adds up. And from his point of view it's the perfect crime: no blood, no contact – he doesn't even have to look at his victims. Just slip the bolt and walk away, with virtually no chance of ever getting caught. But Hannah – no. That's different. That's brutal and messy. Not to mention incredibly risky.'

'So what are you saying?'

I turn to look at the pinboard again. The maps, the timeline, the photos. There's a picture in my mind that's trying to come into focus.

'I think this crime was premeditated,' I say slowly. 'Planned down to the smallest detail by someone Hannah knew. Someone who tricked her to a place they'd prepared with everything they needed to get away with murder. The weapon, the packing tape, the blanket, the car cover. Someone who'd even worked out where they were going to hide that car cover afterwards. Someone, in other words, who didn't just want her dead, but *knew that house*.'

Somer's face is pale. 'But to do something like that —
they'd have to be —'

'A psychopath? You're right. I think the person who killed
Hannah Gardiner is a psychopath.'

'Boss?'

It's Quinn. At the door. With Gislingham.

'How nice of you both to pop in.' And yes, it did sound
that sarcastic. 'Are you two finally going to come clean about
what the hell's been going on these last few days?'

Quinn looks sheepish. 'It's all down to me, boss. Gis has
just been trying to help.'

The two of them exchange a glance.

'Can we go into your office?' says Quinn. I stare at him
and then at Gislingham.

'This had better be good.'

And it is. Though not for Quinn.

Half an hour later, everyone in the room stops what they're
doing as the three of us walk up to the front.

I turn to Quinn. 'Go on.'

He swallows. He's just endured the bollocking of his life,
and the shit he's in isn't over yet. Not by a long way.

'We brought Pippa Walker back in a couple of hours ago
to charge her with attempting to pervert the course of justice. But when the custody sergeant booked her, she didn't
have any ID. Claimed she doesn't have any. Which, of course,
has to be crap, so we tried to track her down via driving licence records. But —' he takes a deep breath '— there is no
Pippa Walker with a birth date matching hers.'

'You tried looking under Philippa?' asks Everett.

Quinn shakes his head. 'Nothing in that name either. We

looked under every name Pippa could be short for. Penel-
ope, Patricia –'

One of the DCs looks up from his phone with a mischie-
vous grin. 'Says here, Pippa means blowjob in Italian. Could
that be relevant, Sarge?'

There are stifled guffaws and I see Gis drop his gaze to
hide a smirk. Quinn is as red in the face as I've ever seen
him. I spot Somer watching him from near the back, caught
between irony and concern. I hope the irony wins out; she's
way too good for him. And Quinn's made his own bed on
this one. In every sense.

'What about a bank account?' says someone as the laughter dies down.

'Not that we've yet found,' says Quinn, still scarlet.

'Mobile phone contract?'

Gislingham shakes his head. 'It's a pay-as-you-go.'

'So she's using a fake name?' says Everett, clearly confused. 'Why on earth would she need to?'

And suddenly, I know what I have to do. I get up and pull
my jacket from the back of the chair.

'Where are you going?' calls Gislingham as I walk away.

'I'm going to find the answer to that question.'

*   *   *

'Next question: what links Mary Ann Nichols, Elizabeth
Stride, Catherine Eddowes and Mary Jane Kelly?'

There's loud laughter around the room and a couple of
good-humoured shouts of 'Fix! Fix!'

At his table by the fireplace Bryan Gow grins and writes
his team's answer on the sheet. Pub quizzes are one of his
fixations, along with trainspotting and quadratic equations.

And you think I'm joking. The other members of this particular team are an ex-lab technician and a retired professor of forensic pathology. They call themselves Criminal Minds, which I thought was quite clever until Alex pointed out, a little acerbically, that the TV series got there first.

This pub is Gow's regular on a Wednesday afternoon — used to be a dingy spit-and-sawdust for the workers at the coal wharf but in the last couple of years it's gone gastro glam. Log fires in winter, shades of paint in grey and teal, black-and-white floor tiles carefully restored. Alex loves it, and the beer's still good too. I gesture to Gow, asking if he wants one. He nods and when the current round of questions finishes and the sheets are being collected he gets up and manoeuvres round the tables to join me.

'What have I done to deserve this?' he asks wryly, picking up his pint.

'Talk to me about psychopaths. Sociopaths and psychopaths.'

He raises an eyebrow, as if to say, so that's where you've got to, is it? He licks froth off his upper lip. 'Well, some of the outer signs are remarkably similar. Both types are manipulative and narcissistic, they lie habitually, they're incapable of taking responsibility for their actions and they have virtually no empathy. All that matters — all that even registers — is their own needs.'

'And how can you tell them apart?'

'Psychopaths are much more organized and much more patient. Sociopaths tend to act impulsively, which means they make mistakes, and it's easier for people like you to catch them. In their case, there's usually some traumatic factor in childhood. Abuse, violence, neglect. The usual suspects.'

'And psychopaths?'

He makes a face. 'Psychopaths are born. Not made.' He's watching me now. 'Does that help?'

Behind him, the quizmaster is calling people back to their seats for the next round.

I nod. 'Yes. I think so.'

He picks up the glass to go, but I stop him. 'One more thing.'

'I didn't have you down as a *Columbo* fan, Fawley,' he says with a dry smile.

But when he hears what I have to ask, his face darkens.

* * *

When he unlocks the door and sees me his face is immediately wary.

'What do you want?' he says, not bothering to hide his hostility. 'Have you come to apologize? Because I should bloody well hope so.'

'Can I come in? It's important.'

He hesitates, then nods. And opens the door. Toby is asleep on the settee in front of a cartoon video, a toy dog clutched close to his chest.

Gardiner turns off the TV. 'Let me put Toby down and I'll be with you.'

The flat looks just as it did when I first came. There's a smell of cooking and he must have done a hell of a lot of cleaning too, because there's no trace of the forensics team. The only mess is happy-little-boy muddle. Gardiner is obviously doing everything he can to get his son's life back to normal. Just as I would, in his place.

He comes back in and sits on the sofa. 'Well?'

'I did come to apologize. For what you've been through these last few days. It doesn't bear thinking about.'

He gives me a dry look. 'Well, whose fault is that?'

'I'm sorry. But we had no choice. We have to eliminate all the possibilities. Pursue all the evidence.'

'Yeah, well, that's the point, isn't it? You didn't have any "evidence". Not against me. Just malicious lies.'

'That's the other reason I came. I wanted to talk to you about Pippa Walker.'

His face hardens. 'What about her?'

'That statement she gave us, we know she made it up.'

'Too fucking right she made it up.' His voice has risen and he corrects himself.

I sit forward slightly. 'But did she make *all* of it up? I believe you that there was no row that night, but were you actually sleeping together before your wife died? Look, I'm not trying to trap you – that's why I'm doing this here, not at the station. We now know she sent you a number of texts in the week or so before Hannah disappeared. Explicit texts. You must know what I'm talking about.'

Gardiner rubs a hand through his hair, then takes a deep breath and looks at me. 'OK, if you must know, we did it once. What I said about doing something you regret because you're depressed and pissed, well, that was it. She'd been making it pretty damn clear she was interested, and one night Hannah was away and I'd had one too many and it just – happened.'

'And this was just before your wife disappeared?'

'About a fortnight before. Hannah was in Nuneaton. Doing research on some of Malcolm Jervis's other developments.'

'And it was after that Pippa started texting you?'

His eyes are miserable. 'She wouldn't leave me alone. She

seemed to think it *meant* something. That we had some sort of future together – that I actually loved her. It was crazy. I deleted every single text – I never replied to *any* of them –'

'I know,' I say quietly.

'So I told her she was going to have to find another job – that it was just going to be too difficult.'

'And how did she take that?'

'She seemed to be being really mature about it. She was quiet for a bit and then she said she was sorry she'd misread the situation. That we could just carry on as if nothing had happened. Only I realized after a few days that it wasn't going to work, so I told her again she'd need to find another job.'

'What did she say to that?'

'She was fine about it – said not to worry, and she'd start looking.'

'How did you explain all this to Hannah?'

'I just said it was probably a good time for a change. Something like that. She agreed straight away.'

'And when did all this happen?'

'A few days before Hannah disappeared. I think I spoke to Pippa on the Friday.'

If bells weren't ringing in my head before, they are now.

'And why didn't you tell us any of this before, Mr Gardiner?'

He looks exasperated. 'Because I thought it would just land me in it – and that's exactly what happened, isn't it? As soon as you thought I was banging Pippa you lot put two and two together and assumed I must have killed my wife.'

'You still should have told us,' I say gently. 'It would have been better for you in the long run. And for us.'

'Sorry,' he says. He leans forward, his arms on his knees. 'I know. I'm sorry.'

We sit in silence for a moment.

'Did Pippa know anyone in Frampton Road, as far as you know?'

He shakes his head. 'She never mentioned anyone to me.'

'There's no reason you can think of why she might have visited number thirty-three?'

He frowns. 'No. I'm sure she didn't. When it was on the news — about that girl in the cellar — she asked me which house it was. What makes you ask that?'

I'm trying to work out how best to say it. But he's a scientist, as well as a father and a widower. He can cope with candour.

'You never thought Pippa could have been involved — with Hannah's disappearance?'

He stares at me. '*Pippa?*'

'It never occurred to you at all?'

He is clearly staggered. 'Of course not — you think I'd have let her live here — look after Toby — if I thought she'd killed my *wife*? Like I told you — after Hannah disappeared I was a mess — I needed someone to help — she was great at all that, and Toby liked her —'

His voice trails off. He swallows. 'I mean, yes, she was a bit full-on at one point — but it was just an infatuation. A crush. She got over it. You know what it's like when you're that age — one minute it's the end of the world and the next you can't even remember what all the fuss was about. She wasn't much more than a teenager, for Christ's sake. Not a bloody psychopath.'

* * *

'Only he was wrong.' I look around the room. If they were wondering where I went and why, they know now. 'I think that's exactly what she is. I think Pippa Walker killed Hannah, and she meant to do it.'

But I can see from their faces they're not with me on this – not yet. And I can't say I blame them – she's personable, nicely middle class, and she's only twenty-two, even now: would she really have been capable of the carnage that must have taken place in that house two years ago? So I tell them what Gow said. About how psychopaths are born, not made. And how – in his experience – the female of the species is even more narcissistic than the male, even more selfish, even more vindictive when crossed.

'The actual phrase Gow used was "hell hath no fury".'

'And I bet he told you where the quote comes from, too,' mutters Gis.

'The point is that someone with that personality type – everything revolves round them. Other people are merely obstacles to be eliminated. If she decided she wanted Gardiner, then a little thing like him having a wife already wasn't going to stop her.'

There was a scene I saw once on an old BBC cop show, *Waking the Dead* – one of the ones I did actually watch. The thing that stuck in my mind was what the profiler woman said about why people become murderers. She said men kill out of anger or for money, or words to that effect. But women are different. Women kill because something's standing in their way.

'And she got what she wanted, didn't she?' says Everett, her face grim. 'She ended up moving in with him. And if she hadn't messed up over getting pregnant Gardiner might even have married her.'

'Would a girl like her be strong enough to crush someone's skull?' asks Baxter. Pragmatic, as usual.

'That one could,' says Quinn, making a face. Some of the old Quinn is seeping back. 'And Hannah was hit from behind, remember. It probably didn't take that much brute force.'

'But what about moving the body – could Pippa really have got it into that shed on her own?'

'If you ask me, yes,' says Quinn. 'Hannah wasn't that big. And Pippa's young – she's fit –'

One of the DCs makes a 'yeah, right' face behind his back.

'– I reckon she could do it, as long as she had enough time.'

'And after that,' says Gislingham, 'it could all have panned out just like we said. Pippa could have driven to Wittenham, dumped the car and come back by bus. And she wouldn't have been that bothered about dumping the kid either – not if the whole point was getting Gardiner all to herself. I said, didn't I – only a psycho would do that to a little kiddie. Looks like I was right.'

'*And* they found her DNA in the car,' says Everett. 'Only it never raised any flags because we knew she often drove it.'

'So are we saying it was Pippa those people saw with the buggy?' asks Somer. 'But the hair colour's wrong, surely? Pippa's blonde, Hannah was dark.'

Gislingham shrugs. 'Wigs ain't hard to find. Not if she planned it all along the way the boss said.'

'Wait a minute,' says Baxter. 'Before we all get carried away. The murder happened in Frampton Road, right? We know Walsh had access to that house, pretty much whenever he wanted, but what about this Pippa girl? How the hell did she get in there?'

Everyone needs a devil's advocate, and Baxter has a kitemark from Old Nick himself.

'Actually,' says Quinn, 'I don't think it would have been such a big deal. You can tell the place is in a state, even from the outside. She could have gone round there – snooped round the back, found there was a broken lock –'

'Without Harper knowing?'

'He was getting a bit confused, he drinks, he was taking those sleeping pills – I reckon he was pretty much out of it most of the time.'

'OK,' says Everett, 'so let's say that's what happened. Just for argument's sake. Next question: how did Pippa get *Hannah* in there?'

Gislingham throws up his hands. 'Oh, that bit's easy: she waited for her in Frampton Road that morning. She knew Hannah parked along there so she just picked her moment. And she'd have known Hannah was going to Wittenham – in fact, she was one of the few people who definitely *did* know that. So she hangs around, then persuades Hannah down the path – I don't know, she says she's seen an injured cat or something. Then as soon as they're out of sight –'

'OK, fair enough,' says Baxter. 'But none of it *proves* she was in that house, does it? It's all just circumstantial. The CPS are going to want way more than that. And if we can't arrest her for the murder her lawyer will get her bail on the other charge and that'll be the last we see of her.'

There's a silence. The photos stare out at us. Hannah. Pippa. Toby. Toby who couldn't tell us anything about the bad man who hurt Mummy because there never was any bad man. Just his usual childminder taking him out for a nice ride in the car. I must have looked at these pictures a hundred times. Only now, for the first time, something is bugging me. Something about Pippa.

I turn to Baxter. 'This shot at the Cowley Road carnival –
we have an electronic version of that, right?'

'Yes, boss,' he says, going over to his desk and pulling it
up on the PC.

I go across and bend to look at the screen. Then point.

'The necklace. Can you zoom in on that?'

There's a low-level buzz in the room now, and people
start to gather round. They think I'm on to something. And
as Baxter enlarges the image and it pings into focus, they
know I am.

The chain is long and silver, and hanging from it, there's
an intricately carved object in the shape of a shell. Small and
beautiful and priceless.

It's the missing *netsuke*.

The noise starts to rise – the adrenaline of discovery, of
the pieces of the puzzle shifting suddenly into sense. Soon
there's only one person who isn't gathered round the screen.
Somer. She's at the whiteboard, staring at what Baxter wrote.

I get up and join her. 'What's on your mind?'

'It's what you said about Walsh, sir – that he couldn't
possibly have killed Hannah in that house without Vicky
knowing.'

I wait. 'And?'

'Doesn't the same apply to Pippa? I get it that she must have
planned it all really carefully, but however well-organized she
was, Vicky would surely have heard *something*, wouldn't she?
And there is *no way* Pippa could have got that car cover into the
loft without Vicky knowing, not if Vicky was camped out on
the top floor.'

I turn round and raise my voice. 'Quiet, everyone – you
need to hear this. Go on, Somer, say all that again.'

Which she does. Though not without blushing.

'So – what's your theory?' says Quinn. 'Vicky hears a noise, comes downstairs and walks straight into a bloodbath?'

'Why not?' says Somer. 'Only she can't go to the police without exposing her own little scam. After everything she'd gone through to get that money – having the baby, hiding out in that house – she'd risk losing it all.'

Quinn frowns, but it's a thinking frown, not a dismissive one. 'So you're saying they covered each other's tracks? Mutual assured destruction?'

Somer's got the bit between her teeth now and around the room I can see the thought taking hold. 'Think about it – the very *last* thing Vicky would want is the police sniffing round. *Both* those girls needed to do everything they could to divert attention away from the Frampton Road house. So they make a deal – Pippa agrees to keep quiet for Vicky, if Vicky helps cover up for Pippa. It's *Vicky* who helped move the body, hide the car cover, clean up the mess –'

'Whoa, whoa,' says Gislingham, leaping to his feet as he rifles through a pile of papers. 'Shit. Why the fuck didn't I think of it before.'

He finds the page and looks up, his face pale. 'That flatmate who gave Pippa her alibi in 2015? The one who said Pippa'd been throwing up that whole morning? Her name was *Nicki Veale.*' He looks around, drilling every word. 'Vicky Neale and Pippa's flatmate – they're the *same person.*'

*   *   *

An hour later Everett is looking for a parking place off the Iffley Road. When they divvied up the jobs she persuaded Quinn to let her do a recce of where Pippa was living in 2015.

He thought it was the arse-end of the tasks and said so, but Everett has a hunch that it could be the best chance they have to find out the girl's real name. But she wasn't about to say that in public, especially in front of Fawley. Or Somer. She's not envious of Somer, not exactly, but she is getting just a bit too much air time, especially for a uniform PC in a CID inquiry. And what with that and the way she looks, well, you'd be a sack of potatoes not to feel a bit out-shone. Everett tries not to remember her father describing her in exactly those terms when she was a child, and focuses on manoeuvring the Fiat expertly into a space that's only just longer than the car. Two years living in Summertown has some advantages.

She locks the car and walks up to the letting agent's. The young man inside is just shutting up shop, but relents and opens the door when she shows him her warrant card. He's wearing a Manchester United shirt and loose white cotton trousers.

'You were here last week, weren't you?' he says. 'You still looking for that girl? Vicky something, wasn't it?'

'It's a different girl this time. Do you have the records for the summer of 2015 – for twenty-seven Arundel Street?'

The young man flips open his laptop and scrolls down some files. 'Yup, what do you want to know?'

'Did you have a Pippa Walker as a tenant then?'

He scans a list, then, 'Yes, we have a Walker. Stayed until that October.'

'Pippa Walker?'

He makes a face. 'I dunno. My father was running the place then and he only used surnames. That's why we didn't have any luck when you were here last time – there wasn't enough to go on.'

'But people have to give you ID, when they take a tenancy?'

He flashes her a huge smile. 'Of course, Constable. We do things properly here.'

'You don't by any marvellous chance have copies of what she gave you?'

He makes a rueful face. 'Probably not. Not this long after. I can have a look, though it may take a while – my father wasn't exactly an early adopter when it comes to technology. Him and the scanner were in a state of perpetual armed stand-off.'

She smiles. 'No worries, I can wait.'

He gestures. 'We have a coffee machine.'

Everett glances at it then shakes her head quickly. 'I'm fine.'

He grins at her. 'Good choice. In my opinion, the coffee is rubbish.'

As he goes back through his files, Everett wanders around the office, looking at the sheets of property particulars pinned on the walls and marvelling at the prices even tiny bedsits in this part of town are now commanding. Commanding and getting too, by the looks of it – most have large red stickers saying 'LET'. A moment later she stops in front of one of them, then gets out her notebook and flips back through the pages. Quinn may have a tablet but humble DCs are still paper-powered. It pisses Gislingham off, all the time.

'This house here,' she says suddenly, swinging round. 'Fifty-two Clifton Street. That's one of yours too?' It's where Vicky told them she had been living when she claimed she was abducted.

He glances up and nods. 'Yup.'

'Can you look that one up for me?'

'2015 again?'

'No. The year before. Spring 2014 – before July.'

'OK,' he says. Then, 'Here we go. Who are you interested in?'

'Is there a Neale on the list?'

The lad nods. 'Yes.'

So Vicky was telling the truth about that, at least.

But then the lad glances up from the screen. 'You might want to see this, officer.'

Everett goes round the desk to stand next to him. He points at the computer screen. At the list of the other tenants in 52 Clifton Street when Vicky Neale was there.

Anwar, Bailey, Drajewicz, Kowalczyk.

And Walker.

'Forget the other ID,' Everett says quickly. 'That's the one I want to see.'

*   *   *

'I had a message to come here.'

The desk sergeant at St Aldate's looks up to see a woman in a denim jacket and skinny jeans. She has highlighted blonde hair and a strappy handbag with a pale pink monkey charm hanging from it. From the way she's dressed, she must look no more than twenty from behind. But face on, she's at least double that.

'Sorry, madam, you are?'

'I got a message about my daughter. From a woman, a Detective Constable Everton –'

'Everett.'

She raises an eyebrow. 'If you say so. So, can I see her? Vicky? I mean, I *assume* she's here.'

The sergeant picks up the phone. 'Let me ring the incident room and ask someone to come down and collect you. If you could take a seat, Mrs Neale –'

'It's Moran these days. If you don't mind.'

'Mrs Moran. I'm sure it won't be long.'

The woman looks him up and down. 'I should hope not. Because I've come all the way from Chester for this.'

Then she turns on her kitten heels, parks herself on the furthest-away seat and gets out her mobile phone.

* * *

```
Interview with Pippa Walker, St Aldate's Police
Station, Oxford
10 May 2017, 6.17 p.m.
In attendance, DI A. Fawley, DC C. Gislingham,
Mrs T. York (solicitor)


TY:  I asked you here, Inspector, to inform you
     that my client will be making a formal
     complaint relating to the conduct of Detective
     Sergeant Gareth Quinn.
AF:  That is, of course, her right.
TY:  I should also tell you that she has decided
     not to answer any further questions unless she
     is given some sort of immunity from
     prosecution.
AF:  Immunity from prosecution for what, exactly?
     She's already been charged with attempting to
     pervert the course of justice. That isn't
     going to go away.
TY:  My client fears she may be wrongly accused of
```

involvement in the death of Mrs Hannah
Gardiner.

AF: What makes her think that?

TY: Miss Walker has information pertinent to that
inquiry, but she is not prepared to divulge it
without the assurances I have mentioned. I
have discussed the advisability of this
position with her, and the likelihood of any
such immunity being granted, but she is
adamant.

AF: Investigations into Mrs Gardiner's death are
still ongoing. We are not yet in a position to
prefer charges –

PW: That's a load of crap. I'm not falling for
that –

TY: [*restraining her client*]
I take it you haven't found my client's prints
in the Frampton Road house?

AF: [*hesitates*]
No, we haven't.

TY: Or any other forensic evidence linking her to
the crime?

AF: [*hesitates*]
Full analysis of the crime scene has not yet
been concluded –

TY: Well then.

PW: [*pushing the lawyer's hand away*]
You want to know who killed her? Then give me
my immunity. Because I'm not saying *anything*
until you do.

* * *

'She's got balls, I'll give her that,' says Quinn, when I go back into the incident room. He was watching on the video feed. 'Did you notice, by the way, how it's not just the name that's fake? That upper-middle accent of hers has slid a notch or two as well.'

He's right. The mask has slipped. It's the same girl, but another person. White birds by night, black birds by day.

The door swings open behind him and there's a woman standing there with one of the DCs. Someone I don't recognize but who seems, all the same, somehow familiar. Someone who walks forward towards me then stops. She stares at the pinboard and then at me.

'What the hell's going on? They said on the phone that this was about Vicky.'

The DC steps forward quickly. 'This is Mrs Moran, sir. Vicky's mother.'

She looks at him, and then at me. 'Right,' she says, walking over to the board and jabbing it with a bright fuchsia nail. 'I'm *Vicky's* mum. So could someone please explain to me what you're doing with this picture of my Tricia?'

*   *   *

'Tricia,' says the Asian lad, looking up at Everett. 'Tricia Walker, that was the tenant's name. Here you are.'

He pulls up a scan of a passport page. The face, the expression — it's clearly her, even if the hairstyle is very different. And not just the hair: make-up, expression, everything about her now is sleeker, more precise, more expensive.

'Is that any use?' he says.

She grins at him. 'Absolutely bloody marvellous — can you print that?'

She gets out her phone and calls the incident room.

'Quinn? It's me. Everett. Listen, I know Pippa Walker's real name. It's *Tricia*. Her and Vicky, they didn't meet at Frampton Road like we thought. They *knew each other before*. They shared a house in 2014. And it's not just that — they gave the *same previous address* when they registered with the letting agency. Those two girls, I think they could be —'

'Sisters. Yeah, Ev. We know.'

*   *   *

'I'm not very happy about this, sir.'

The custody sergeant is looking uneasy; it can't be very often he gets a DI in here at eight o'clock at night.

'She should have her lawyer here — it should be taped —'

'I know, and I'll tell her all that and if she doesn't want to speak to me then I'll back off.'

He still looks unconvinced, but he gets up and collects his keys and we go down the passage to the cell. He opens the observation flap, checks inside, then unlocks the door and pushes it open.

'I'll be at the desk,' he says.

She's sitting on the narrow bed, her knees drawn up to her chest. She looks wan in the inadequate light.

'What do you want?' she says, wary.

'I shouldn't really be here.'

'So why are you then?'

'Because I want to talk to you. But you can have your lawyer here if you want.'

She stares at me for a moment. I can't tell if she's intrigued or just too tired to argue. 'Whatever.'

'They told me you didn't want to see your mum.'

Her eyes flicker at that, and I move a little closer.

'I expect you were surprised we tracked her down. She's moved twice in the last couple of years. Not to mention getting married.'

A shrug. 'I told you. She only cares about her new bloke. She doesn't care about me. Not any more.'

'Having spoken to her myself, I'm afraid I'm inclined to agree with you.'

Definitely a reaction now, but not one she wants me to see.

'I did explain to her that you're the girl who's been all over the newspapers for the last week, but I'm afraid it didn't make much difference. She seems to think you only have yourself to blame.'

Vicky puts her chin on her knees. 'I told you.' But there's a tremor in her voice now that wasn't there before.

'I also told her she has a new grandson, but I'm afraid that didn't get me very far either. Do you want to know what she actually said?'

Silence.

'She said, "If she thinks I'm being dumped with looking after it she's got another think coming."'

She still has her arms wrapped round her knees. But her knuckles are white.

'To be fair, she does have a baby of her own to look after now.' Vicky glances up. 'Didn't I say? It's a girl. Megan. A sister for you. Or half-sister, to be strictly accurate.'

I sit down on the end of the bed and open the file I've been holding.

'But you already have one of those, don't you? Tricia Janine Walker, to be precise. Born 8th January 1995. Her birth certificate is in her father's name, but your mother and Howard Walker never actually married, did they? And then within three years they'd split up and your mother married Arnold Neale. And had you.'

I let the silence lengthen. Thicken. And when I speak again I can hear my voice echo against the cold damp walls.

'Why didn't you tell us about Tricia, Vicky? Why didn't you tell us you had a sister living in Oxford all this time?'

She shrugs but says nothing.

'She could have come to see you in the hospital – you could have stayed with her instead of going to Vine Lodge.'

'I didn't know she was here,' she says eventually.

'I'm afraid I don't believe you, Vicky. I think you knew exactly where she was. She was in Rob Gardiner's flat. A flat you can actually *see* from William Harper's house.'

I dip my head, trying to make her look at me. 'Is that where she first saw him? From the top floor in Frampton Road? Because you were both there, weren't you? At least at the beginning.'

Her eyes narrow. 'You can't prove that.'

'We can, actually. Because Tricia stole one of Dr Harper's ornaments. She's wearing it in a photo of the Cowley Road carnival in August 2014, so we know she must have been inside that house by then. We didn't find her fingerprints anywhere, because the two of you have clearly spent a hell of a lot of time cleaning up, but Tricia just couldn't resist that *netsuke*, could she? Was it just by chance she chose that one or did she know how much it's worth? Did she know she could get over twenty thousand pounds for it?'

Vicky flashes me a look.

'I think she did know, Vicky. Because she's clever, isn't she? Much cleverer than she lets on. Cleverer than you, for a start. She uses sex to get what she wants from men who are too stupid to see they're being played. Cash, security, attention, control — the sex is just a means to an end. And if sex doesn't work, she's not unduly concerned. Because she has plenty of other options. I know. I've watched her in action, and I have to admit, she's good. She fooled Rob Gardiner and she fooled my sergeant. She even fooled me. But she fooled you and Hannah most of all.'

Women beware women.

Just like Alex said.

'You planned it together, didn't you? Moving into that house, having the child, getting Harper's money. She was in on the whole scam right from the start. And it was all going so well, until one day she sees Rob Gardiner and he becomes the only thing that matters. Too bad you were already pregnant with Harper's child. Too bad that, unlike her, you were trapped in that house. How was it all supposed to pan out, Vicky? With you dossing in the cellar for a few days to make it look real, then staggering up the steps when you knew Derek Ross was in the house? How were you going to explain your escape — make up some story about the old man losing it? Say he'd left the door unlocked by mistake?'

Vicky sits up suddenly and leans back against the cell wall. 'I'm not *stupid*, even though you seem to think I am. All of that you just said — it's a load of crap. I'm not falling for that.'

I smile. 'Funnily enough, your sister uses exactly the same phrase. If there's one thing police work has taught me it's that blood really is thicker than water.'

There's a tap at the door and Woods puts his head round. 'Just checking everything's OK, sir.'

I look at the girl, but she says nothing.

'We're fine, Sergeant. Perhaps Vicky would like some tea though?'

She nods, and Woods shuts the door. We can hear him bang open the observation flap of another cell a few doors down, and then voices. His. A girl's. Then his keys jingling all the way back down the corridor.

Vicky has stiffened. She recognized that voice. There's a strange expression on her face that in any other circumstances I'd call fear.

'Oh, didn't I say? Tricia is here. Just along the corridor. She's facing a criminal charge.'

Vicky's face has closed in again. She wants to ask me what the charge is but she won't give me the satisfaction. But that doesn't bother me. I'm going to tell her anyway.

'Three days ago she gave us a statement. About the death of Hannah Gardiner. She told us Rob Gardiner killed his wife during a furious row after Hannah found him and your sister in bed together.'

And there it is – in her eyes, that tiny quiver of doubt and surprise that I only see because I know what I'm looking for. That's not what she was expecting me to say; that's not what the two of them had agreed.

'But then *you* told us William Harper did it. That he'd killed another girl, then buried her in the garden, and boasted to you about what he'd done.'

She shrugs. Whatever.

'And that was Tricia's original plan, wasn't it? She wanted to make sure that when Hannah's body was found, the police would immediately assume Harper must have killed her. It was his house, who else was it likely to be? If you were lucky, we might not even bother looking for another suspect. And you know, it almost worked. So why, I asked myself, would Tricia suddenly put all that careful preparation at risk by telling us something completely different? Something she must have known we'd prove was a lie?'

She glances at me again. She can't work out if this is truth or trap.

I move a little closer. 'A couple of nights ago, my wife reminded me about a play we saw years ago. It was much more her thing than mine — she's always dragging me to stuff I'd never go to otherwise.'

She looks at me. Wary at where this is going.

'That type of play, it's called a revenge tragedy. And I think that's why Tricia changed her story. Revenge. She tried to frame Rob for killing his wife because he'd thrown her out when she told him she was going to have a baby —'

Vicky starts, then quickly drops her gaze. But not quickly enough to fool me: she didn't know her sister was pregnant.

'She just couldn't forgive Rob for dumping her, could she? She wanted her own back. Even if that meant getting him charged with murder. Even if that meant putting your whole scheme at risk. She betrayed you, Vicky. Just like she did when she left you at the mercy of a nasty piece of work like Donald Walsh.'

Her head comes up. 'Who's he?'

It occurs to me — as it probably should have done before — that she may never have known who it was who slipped that bolt and locked her in. She probably thought it was the old man.

'He's William Harper's nephew. We think he worked out what you were up to. He was stealing those *netsuke* too. It seems it really does take one to know one.'

Her head is down again, and a moment later I realize she's crying.

'Have you spoken to Tricia, Vicky? Have you asked her why she didn't come back — why she didn't realize something had gone horribly wrong? Those builders finding you when they did — that was a complete fluke. The last page of that journal — that was for real. You thought you were going to die. Down there, alone. In the dark.'

'It was a mistake,' she says sulkily. 'It must have been. She wouldn't have got any of the money without me.'

'Are you sure about that?' I pull out another sheet from my file. 'We've been having a look at your sister's internet history. What she's been looking at on her phone.'

I pass her the page and watch her read it. Watch the gasp and her hand coming to her mouth, and then the ferocity in her eyes as she crumples the paper in her fist.

There's a commotion suddenly outside and the door flings open with a clang. The custody sergeant is standing there, his chest heaving.

Jesus Christ —'

'You'd better come, sir. The other one — Tricia — Pippa — whatever her name is. I think she's having a miscarriage.'

I'm on my feet already. 'Have you called an ambulance?'

'On its way. DC Everett's going to go with her.'

'Have you got a number for the girl's mother?'

'I asked but she says she doesn't want us to contact her.'

'OK, but we'll still need two officers. See if you can raise PC Somer — ask her to meet Everett at the John Rad.'

I'm at the door when Vicky calls me back.

'You're sure about this?' she says, gesturing at the paper. 'It's really true?'

I nod. 'She even sent an email asking to speak to someone.' I pull out another sheet and give it to her. 'See. I'm sorry, Vicky, but there's no mistake. She may not have planned it that way at the start, but Hannah's death — that changed everything. Because you were the only one who knew what she'd done. The only one who knew her secret.'

*   *   *

The girl standing in the doorway hesitates. After all these months, now it's come to it, she's not so sure. The space is so small. So dirty. And it smells.

    'I've changed my mind. I don't want to do it after all.'

    'Oh, for fuck's sake, Vicky! What did you have that bloody kid for if you weren't going to go through with it?'

    Vicky bites her lip. 'That was all your *idea.'*

    'Yeah, and you know why. You won't get any of the money, you know, if you bottle it now. We've waited long enough — you've *waited long enough —'*

    'And whose fault is that?' snaps Vicky. 'We could have done this ages ago if you hadn't gone and ruined everything. I've been stuck in this bloody house for months on end while you swan about doing what the hell you want — bringing those bloody students in out the back. You do know, don't you, that the kid actually saw *you having sex with that Danny?'*

    Tricia laughs. 'I know, Dan looked up and saw him watching. Completely freaked him out. It was bloody hilarious.'

    Vicky says nothing. 'Look,' says Tricia, conciliatory now. 'I'm sorry you haven't had much fun lately, but we're going to go through with it now. We have to. You heard that social worker — he's going to put the old git in a home.'

    She reaches out and puts her hand under her sister's chin. 'I've cleared up upstairs and you have everything you need. I got you food, water, the torch. That diary thing for them to find. And it's only for a couple of days. Just to make it look real.'

She turns to the small boy kicking against one of the sacks of junk and picks him up. His dark hair curls on his shoulders. They made sure not to cut it.

'It's an adventure, isn't it?' she says brightly. The boy puts out his hand and touches her face. 'See? He thinks so too.'

Vicky reaches out and takes her son and holds him stiffly against her. She hesitates a moment, then steps over the threshold.

Behind her, the door clangs shut. And then there's the sound of a chair being dragged across the floor and the bolt sliding across.

Vicky rushes to the door and hammers on it with her fist, her heart pounding. 'Tricia! What are you doing?'

'I'm making it look real, you idiot. What do you think I'm doing?'

'But you never said anything about this —'

'Because I knew you wouldn't be up for it, that's why. But it's the only way — the only way to convince people you were really locked up down here.'

'Please — don't do this — open the door —'

'Look, it's only for a few days, right? Then I'll call the police anonymously and tell them I heard something and they'll come here and set you free. And we'll get the money. Just keep thinking about that — three million sodding quid. It's worth a couple of days of crap for that, right?'

'No — I don't want to — I can't — please —'

But then the footsteps retreat back up the stairs and the light under the door goes out.

The child she's holding goes rigid against her, his body contorted as he starts to scream.

* * *

Somer is already waiting outside when the ambulance pulls up outside the A&E entrance, and two nurses come out briskly to meet it.

'Possible miscarriage,' says one of the paramedics as she opens the back door. 'She's lost quite a lot of blood already.'

As they lower the trolley to the ground Somer can see that the girl is pale and visibly trembling, clutching at her stomach.

'OK, lovey,' says the nurse. 'Tricia, is it? Let's get you inside and take a look.'

* * *

Interview with Vicky Neale, conducted at
St Aldate's Police Station, Oxford
10 May 2017, 9.00 p.m.
In attendance, DI A. Fawley, DS G. Quinn,
M. Godden (duty solicitor)

AF: For the purposes of the tape, Miss Neale
      has previously been arrested on a charge of
      false representation and has been given
      police bail. She has now been arrested in
      connection with the death of Hannah Gardiner
      in 2015, and has decided, of her own free
      will, to assist the police by making a
      statement to clarify the exact extent of her
      involvement in this matter. That's right, isn't
      it, Vicky?

VN: [*nods*]

AF: OK, then. Why don't you tell us what happened.
      In your own words.

VN: Where d'you want me to start?

AF: At the beginning. When you first came to
      Oxford. When was that?

VN: 2014. April 2014. I came first and got that
place in Clifton Street. Then one day Tricia
turned up.

AF: Your sister, Tricia Walker. The young woman
currently using the name Pippa.

VN: [*nods*]

AF: But that wasn't the plan? You weren't
expecting her?

VN: I hadn't seen her for months. We'd had a huge
row and I'd walked out.

AF: From your mother's home?

VN: I was fed up living there anyway. Mum was
always at her new bloke's and I was bored with
Tricia telling me what to do all the time.

AF: What was the row about?

VN: [*silence*]
There was a boy I liked. Only, you know.

AF He preferred Tricia?

VN: She *took him off me*. She didn't even like him
that much. She just did it because she could.
It was the same with Mum's boyfriends. Tricia
was always walking about with hardly any
clothes on whenever they were there. It was
like she was daring them to come on to her.

AF: Did that ever actually happen?

VN: Once. Some bloke called Tony.
[*silence*]
Mum caught them in bed together. Tricia
claimed it was all Tony's idea. That he'd
been 'grooming' her or some crap like
that. He denied it, of course, but Mum still
threw him out.

AF: What did you think had happened? Did you
    believe Tony?

VN: Look, Tricia *never* does something she doesn't
    want to do, right? But she didn't *fancy* Tony or
    anything. She just wanted to prove she could
    get him if she wanted.

AF: How old was she at the time?

VN: Dunno. Fifteen, maybe?

AF: So what happened when she came to Oxford?

VN: She moved in with me. She signed on and I had
    some money my dad left me when he died, but it
    wasn't much. Trish always hated having no
    money. That was why she came up with the idea.
    All of it – everything that happened – it was
    all her idea.

AF: What, exactly?

VN: You know – all of it.

AF: You have to tell us, Vicky. We have to hear it
    from you.

VN: She'd seen a TV programme about that woman in
    the cellar in Germany. The one who had all
    those children. She said we could do something
    like that and get a whole load of cash. We
    just had to find the right person. An old bloke
    who lived on his own. Someone with
    Alzheimer's, that's what she really wanted.

AF: You couldn't just get jobs, like everyone
    else?

VN: I would have, but Tricia said she wasn't going
    to waste her time doing a crap job for
    rubbish pay.

AF: So how did you pick on Dr Harper?

VN: We went up to North Oxford on the bus.
    Everyone said that was the rich place - that
    there were a lot of old people living in
    huge houses up there. The second time we
    went we saw him. He was in the street on his
    own. He was in his PJs and he had a can of
    lager. Tricia said he was perfect so we
    followed him back to his house. We went
    back later after it got dark and got in.
    There was a broken lock round the back. He
    was in the front room, snoring. He'd been
    wanking off over this picture of a
    woman in a red dress. It was really
    disgusting.

AF: And you realized the rest of the house was
    empty?

VN: There was stuff in a bedroom on the first floor,
    but Trish said you could live up on the top
    floor and no one'd even notice. So we watched
    the house for a bit and realized the only
    bloke who came was the social worker and he
    was out of there in, like, ten minutes. It was
    after that I moved in.

AF: Just you - not Tricia?

VN: She stayed in the flat. But she'd visit
    sometimes.

AF: So when did she first see Robert Gardiner?

VN: I think it was a couple of months later. She
    saw him in the garden with the little boy. She
    was crazy about him. Rob, I mean.

AF: So she started stalking him. At the Cowley
    Road carnival, for example.

VN: It wasn't hard. We knew when they were going
      out - we could see straight into their flat from
      the top floor. One day we even saw them having
      sex. Tricia completely lost it about that.
      That was when she decided to get a job being
      their nanny.

AF: How did she go about doing that?

VN: She arranged it so she met the wife at the
      market, you know 'by accident'.
      [makes hooking gesture with her fingers]
      She wanted to make the wife think the whole
      thing was her own idea. Tricia is really good
      at things like that - getting people to do
      what she wants without them realizing. Like I
      said, she can really turn it on when she wants
      to. Especially with blokes.

AF: [glancing at DS Quinn]
      And was that when she started calling herself
      Pippa?

VN: She thought Pippa sounded more classy. She
      said things like that matter to people like
      the Gardiners. That they only like people who
      are like them.

AF: Was that the only reason?

VN: [hesitates]
      No. When we were at school she went for
      another girl's face with a fork. It was some
      stupid argument about her sitting in Tricia's
      chair. It was always like that - she'd go
      completely off on one if anyone tried to tell
      her what to do. Mum stopped bothering long
      before. Wasn't worth the hassle. But the school

went ape-shit - she got suspended and sent to
one of those counsellor people. She was afraid
that if the Gardiners checked up on her and
found out about it they wouldn't have let her
look after their kid.

AF: By the time she got that job you were
pregnant, weren't you? That was Tricia's idea
too, I presume?

VN: [*shifts in her chair*]
She said we'd get even more money that way.
That the DNA would prove the old man raped me.

GQ: And the journal?

VN: [*pause*]
She said people would believe me more if we
did that. That it'd look better in court. She
told me what to say.

AF: She dictated the journal to you?

VN: She made it up and I wrote it down. Then she
messed some of it up with water so it would
look more real.

GQ: And that was all when you were still living on
the top floor?

VN: [*nods*]

AF: But if having the baby was Tricia's idea, why
didn't she do it? That way she'd be the one to
get the money.

VN: She said I'd be a better victim.

GQ: She actually said that - that you'd be a
'*better victim*'?

VN: She said people were more likely to feel sorry
for me than for her. That no one would believe
she could have been that stupid.

```
AF:  But they'd believe that about you?
VN:  [bites her lip but says nothing]
AF:  What about the money?
VN:  She made me promise to share it with her.
     [in some distress]
     She said I owed her, after everything she'd
     done for me.
```

* * *

'You look fucking amazing. Just like her.'

Tricia stands back and admires her handiwork. The red dress, the lipstick, the hair. All perfect.

'What d'you think?'

Vicky looks at herself in the mirror. And Tricia's right. The resemblance is creepy. She shivers. She's not sure she likes looking like someone dead.

'Ready then?' Tricia is by the door, holding it open. 'Last I looked he was flat on his back. Off his face on that lager. Let's just hope he can still get it up. Or you can.'

'I'm not having sex with him, Tricia. Not real sex.'

Tricia makes a face. 'How many more times – you don't have to. Just toss him off. We'll collect the spunk and stick it in you.'

'And what if he remembers? What if he tells someone?'

Tricia laughs. 'Yeah, right. He's a spaz, Vicky. Talks fucking rubbish most of the time. No one's going to believe him. And anyway, that's what all this bloody get-up is for. He'll think you're his wife. That's why this is such an ace idea. If he says anything, people'll just think he's even more of a nut-job than he already is. The more screwed up they think he is, the better it is for us. Remember?'

Vicky shivers. This bloody house is always cold.

'Here,' says Tricia, holding out a bottle of Smirnoff. 'I got it down the road. Might help.'

The vodka burns down Vicky's throat.

'OK,' she says.

Down in the front room, William Harper is on the camp bed, snoring. Vicky hesitates at the door, but Tricia pushes her forward. She stands by the bed for a moment, then pulls back the bedspread. Harper is only wearing a vest. A vest and socks. His shrivelled genitals hang against his thigh.

'Go on,' whispers Tricia.

'It's disgusting – I'm not touching that.'

'Just get on with it, will you – he'll probably come in a nanosecond anyway.'

Vicky reaches out and takes Harper's cock in her hand. His eyes open at once and for a moment they're frozen there, staring at each other. His lips move, but no sound comes.

'For fuck's sake, Vicky,' hisses Tricia.

Vicky tightens her grip and Harper's eyes widen. 'Priscilla?' he whispers, cowering back. 'Don't hurt me. I didn't do anything. Please don't hurt me.'

Vicky drops his cock. 'I can't do this.'

Tricia comes forward and pushes her roughly aside. 'Oh for fuck's sake, do I have to do every *sodding thing myself?'*

Vicky retreats to the door as Tricia climbs on to the bed, straddling Harper's knees. She has a plastic bag in one hand.

'Right,' she says, 'you nasty old paedo. Let's see what you're made of.'

Vicky turns and goes out into the hall.

She can hear the old man crying out all the way up the stairs.

* * *

AF: OK, Vicky. Let's move on to June 2015. You're living in the house in Frampton Road, you're pregnant, and Tricia is working as Toby's

childminder. Tell us about Hannah. How Hannah
Gardiner ended up dead.

VN: It wasn't supposed to happen. None of it.

GQ: Don't try and bullshit us that it was some
sort of accident because I'm not
buying it - there were still bits of her
brain on that sodding car cover -

MG: That's quite unnecessary, Sergeant - my client
is being exceptionally helpful.

VN: I'm *not* bullshitting you. I'm telling the
truth.

AF: OK, so what was the plan? Because you did have
a plan, didn't you - you and Tricia? Hannah
didn't stumble into that house by chance.

VN: Tricia had sex with Rob one night when his
wife was away and she started saying that he'd
be with her if his wife was out of the way but
he was too decent to dump her. Stuff like
that. I didn't know what to do - I was worried
what would happen -

AF: What do you mean?

VN: I know what she's like. If she wants
something, she gets it. It doesn't matter who
she hurts.

AF: You were concerned enough to try to warn
Hannah?

VN: [*nods*]
But I was terrified what Tricia would do if she
found out. To me, I mean.

GQ: Hang on a minute - that call Hannah got the
day before she died - the one from the mobile.
That was from *you*, wasn't it?

VN: [*nods*]

     I didn't say who I was. I didn't tell her my
     name.

AF: So - what? What *did* you say?

VN: I didn't say anything about Rob. I just said
     that Pippa wasn't really called Pippa. I told
     her that she'd been living in Clifton Street -
     that there'd be people there who knew her real
     name, and she should check up on her. I was
     hoping she'd find out what Tricia did to that
     girl at school and they'd fire her.

AF: So that's why Hannah went to the Cowley Road
     that afternoon. To find 'Pippa'.

VN: [*nods*]

     But I don't think she found anyone to talk to.
     She can't have.

AF: So what happened the following day? What was
     your plan?

VN: I *told* you, there wasn't any plan. I didn't
     know anything about it. I was upstairs and I
     heard a noise and came down. And then - and
     then -

*   *   *

'Jesus Christ, Tricia, what have you done?'

    *Tricia is standing by the conservatory window. There's a hammer in
her hand, and at her feet, a young woman lying face down on the floor.
Blood is thickening her dark hair and she's making a terrible raw gasp-
ing sound. Her hands are moving – clawing at the air – and she's trying
to get up.*

    Vicky moves a step closer. 'Oh my God – that's Hannah *–'*

'I know that, you stupid cow – who else would it be?'

'But what's she doing here – what the hell happened?'

Tricia looks at her sister witheringly. 'I told you, you idiot. Remember?'

'You told me you wanted to get together with Rob – not that you were going to kill her.'

'Well, you know what blokes are like. They always say they'll leave their wives and they never do. This way, she's out of the picture. End of.'

She turns to the shelf behind her and picks up a pair of plastic gloves. There's a second pair of gloves, a roll of duct tape, a canister of industrial bleach, a dark wig. None of it was there yesterday.

'Jesus, Tricia, you planned all this?'

'Of course I fucking planned it. We won't get away with it otherwise.'

'What do you mean – we? I've got nothing to do with this – you can't make me –'

'Oh yes I can. Because if you don't help me I'll tell everyone about your nasty little scheme. That brat you're carrying – how you scammed that poor defenceless old tosser – you'll get three or four years at least.'

Tears come to Vicky's eyes. 'But that was all your idea –'

'Yeah,' she says, sardonic. 'But they don't know that, do they? So just stop fucking snivelling and help me.'

The woman on the floor groans suddenly and tries to raise her hand. Tricia bends down quickly and yanks her head up hard by the hair. There's blood coming from her mouth and she's staring – staring straight at Vicky.

'Right,' says Tricia, dropping her hold. 'She's seen you now, so you don't have a choice. So just fucking grow some, will you?'

'What do you want me to do?' says Vicky, her voice catching in her throat. Hannah is moaning softly. Calling her son's name.

Tricia reaches for the second pair of gloves and throws them across.

'Go out to the car and get the blanket out of the back. And bring the kid in with you.'

'He's out there? On his own? What if he starts screaming? What if the old man hears?'

Tricia laughs. 'The old bastard's dead to the world. As per fucking usual. I put more sleeping pills in his lager. I'll give the kid one too just in case.'

'You can't do that – he's only little –'

'Oh, stop bloody fussing, will you – I do it all the time. It's the only way I can keep him quiet.'

'But –'

Tricia stares at her. 'So are you going or what?'

* * *

AF: And you gave Tricia an alibi as well, didn't you? You rang Rob Gardiner and left a message saying she was ill. And later, when the police called you to confirm it, you gave your name as Nicki Veale.

VN: [*bites her lip*]
    Tricia was really angry about that. She said I should have chosen something different – something that didn't sound so much like my real name. That it was the only thing I'd had to do on my own and I couldn't even get that right.

AF: But that's the point, isn't it, Vicky? Tricia is a much better liar than you are. So what happens when she tells us her version of how Hannah died and it's much more convincing than yours – what then?

VN: *I'm* the one telling the truth. I didn't have
    any reason to kill her, did I?

MG: That's quite right, Inspector. My client didn't
    have any reason to kill Mrs Gardiner. Unlike
    her sister.

AF: I'm not so sure, Mr Godden. Tricia is very
    resourceful. I'm sure she'll come up with a
    very plausible story. I can hear it now:
    she'll say Hannah came snooping around that
    day – that she'd seen something out of the
    window of her flat and when she came to
    investigate she found a young woman, seven or
    eight months pregnant, living in a house
    supposedly occupied only by an old man.
    Hannah was a journalist: as soon as Vicky
    went public with the cellar story Hannah
    would have recognized her. I'd say
    that's more than enough motive for Vicky to
    kill her.

VN: But that's not what happened –

AF: But how do *we* know that? You can't possibly
    prove it. And all your sister's barrister has
    to do is create reasonable doubt –
    [*interruption – custody sergeant requests
    urgent discussion with DI Fawley*]

GQ: Interview suspended at 9.42 p.m.

* * *

'What the hell is it, Woods?'

'I'm sorry, sir.'

I follow him down to the custody suite, Quinn at my

heels. The cell door is still open and there's blood on the bedding and in the toilet bowl.

I turn to Woods. 'So?'

He gestures to the bed. Among the tangled blankets there's a small blister pack, just large enough for two pills. It's empty.

'Before you ask, she did *not* have those with her when we booked her in,' says Woods, red in the face.

'You definitely searched her?'

'Of course I did. Anyone with medication, it's the doc that administers it. I know the drill. I've been doing this bloody job long enough.'

And I believe him. But you'd be staggered at how devious people can be. At the things they've managed to smuggle in here, over the years. Two little pills would have been child's play by comparison.

Woods picks up the pack and hands it to me. I turn it over and read the name on the foil, and take a deep breath. 'The only way she can have got hold of this is on the internet. No legitimate doctor would have given it to her.'

'What is it?' asks Quinn.

I turn to look at him. 'It's misoprostol. To induce abortion.'

'Shit,' he says.

Woods' face goes from red to white and he sits down heavily on the bed.

'Get hold of Everett,' I say to Quinn. 'Tell her she can't afford to let that girl out of her sight.'

But he's anticipated me. He's already dialling.

'Ev? Quinn. Heads up – Pippa – whatever her name is –' He looks up at me, listening, then makes a face. 'OK, I'll tell him. Phone me if you get anything.'

'Too late,' he says, closing the call. 'She's gone. She was in one of those cubicle things and she must have got out the back somehow –'

'Jesus Christ, didn't one of them stay with her?'

'Apparently Somer was just outside. She thought the nurse was in there doing the examination, but she hadn't arrived yet. It was just a cock-up. We've all done it.'

Of course we have. He certainly has; I have. Just not when it mattered so much.

'Are they searching the hospital?'

Quinn nods. 'But she had at least ten minutes' head start. And you know what that place is like – it's a sodding rabbit warren.'

'Surely she won't be able to get far – not in the state she's in.'

Quinn makes a face. 'I wouldn't put it past her. After all, knowing her, she probably planned the whole bloody thing.'

I know. That's what I'm afraid of.

* * *

BBC Midlands Today

Thursday 11 May 2017 | Last updated at 17:34

BREAKING: Cellar suspect released without charge

Thames Valley Police have released a statement confirming that the owner of a house in Frampton Road, Oxford, who was suspected of abducting and imprisoning a young girl, will not be facing any charges. The police have not revealed the identity of the suspected

abductor, but he has been named locally as William
Harper, a retired academic in his seventies. There is
now speculation that Dr Harper, who suffers from
Alzheimer's, may have been the victim of a particularly
callous scam.

Detective Inspector Adam Fawley declined to discuss
rumours that the alleged abduction was connected in
some way to the 2015 murder of Hannah Gardiner, and
refused to be drawn on when charges might be brought in
that case. 'We have a suspect,' he said. 'But no arrest has
yet been made.'

*   *   *

Everett turns off the news. It's been wall to wall all day. TV,
papers, online. *'Fritzl fraud': Girl faked false imprisonment for
cash; Oxford case raises concerns about vulnerable elderly living alone.*
Journalists have been calling and doorstepping police officers, wanting a quote or access to the house or a picture of
Vicky. Fawley turned them all down.

She looks at her cat, curled on her lap.

'I'm going to shift you now, Hector. I need to make some
dinner.'

The big tabby blinks at her, clearly unconvinced that this
is a good enough reason to upend him. But then there's a
knock at the door.

'Off you go, Hector,' she says, lifting him on to the seat
next to her.

She gets up and goes over to the door.

'Oh,' she says when she sees who it is.

Erica Somer is smiling tentatively and holding a bottle of

Prosecco. She's in civvies: a pair of pale jeans, a black T-shirt, a ponytail.

'Sorry to surprise you like this. Your neighbour was just going out so he let me in.'

Everett is still holding the door.

'Look, I just thought that perhaps you and I – that we might not have got off on the right foot.' She holds out the bottle. 'Fancy a drink?'

Everett still hasn't said anything, but then Somer gasps, 'Oh, is that your cat?'

She crouches down and lifts the cat into her arms and starts to stroke him behind the ears. He closes his eyes and purrs loudly, cat-blissing.

'Careful – he'll be your friend for life if you keep doing that,' says Everett with a wry smile.

Somer grins up at her. 'I want a cat, but they don't allow pets in my block.'

Everett laughs drily. 'I only chose this place because it has a fire escape so he can have a flap. It was half the price again of the others I looked at. Everyone thought I was mad. And now the lazy bugger hardly ever uses it.'

The two women hold each other's gaze for a moment, then Everett steps back and opens the door.

'Didn't you say something about a drink?'

* * *

Three weeks later.

The garden.

My parents dressed stiffly in what they think you ought to wear for Sunday lunch with your son and daughter-in-law. Clothes that probably go straight back in the wardrobe as

soon as they get home. A table piled with food they'll probably only pick at. Smoked chicken, rocket salad, figs, rasp-
berries, pecorino. Alex is down at the bottom with my
mother and the boy, talking to next-door's cat, a friendly
ginger-and-white thing with a big plumy tail. Every now and
again the boy reaches out to try to clutch at it, and Alex pulls
him gently back.

My father joins me at the table.

'You always do a nice spread.'

I smile. 'Alex, not me. I think she bought the shop.'

There's a silence. Neither of us ever really knows what
to say.

'So did you find that girl you were looking for? The one
who killed that poor young woman?'

I shake my head. 'No, not yet. We've been monitoring the
ports and airports, but it's possible she's managed to leave
the country.'

'And what about the boy?' he says, pouring himself another low-alcohol beer.

'Toby? He's fine. His father's protecting him from all the
furore.'

'No, I mean *that* boy,' he says, gesturing down the garden.
'Is it really a good idea – having him here?'

'Look, Dad –'

'I'm just worried about you – after what happened with
Jake – it's not been easy, has it? For Alex, I mean. And you,
of course,' he adds quickly.

'We're OK. Really.'

It's what I say. What I always say.

'What will happen to him?' he continues. The boy has
started crying and Alex sweeps him up in her arms. I can see
my mother looking concerned.

'I don't know. Social Services will have to decide.'

Alex has sat down with the boy on the bench. He's still crying and my mother is hovering, not sure what to do.

'It's going to be tough for him, though,' says my father, staring at the three of them. 'Some day, someone's going to have to tell that boy the truth. Who he is, I mean. Who his father is, what his mother did. It won't be easy – living with that.'

I think about William Harper, who always wanted a son. Does he know yet, that he has one? Does he want to meet him? Or has the stress of the last few weeks pushed him further into the dark? Last time I drove down Frampton Road there was a *For Sale* sign outside. I try to tell myself he was on the point of going into a home anyway, but it's an aspect of this case that's never going to lie easy.

'Sometimes it's easier not to face something like that,' I say, forcing myself back to the present. 'Sometimes silence is kinder.'

He glances at me, and for a moment – just a moment – I think he's going to say something. That the time has finally come when he will tell me the truth. About me. About them. About who I am.

But then my mother calls us from the garden and my father touches me gently on the shoulder and moves towards the door.

'I'm sure you're right, son,' he says.

* * *

Late October. It's pouring with rain; that thin, mean-tempered rain that gets right into your bones. Rivers, canal, marsh: this city is ringed by water. In winter, the stone soaks up the damp. Along Frampton Road, some of the houses have Hallowe'en decorations in the windows – the family houses, anyway. Leering ghouls, Draculas, green-haired witches. One or two steps have pumpkins cut out in eyes and teeth.

Mark Sexton is standing under a golf umbrella in the drive of 31, looking up at the roof. No bloody chance of getting done by Christmas now. But at least the builders are finally back in. Or should be. He looks at his watch, for perhaps the fourth time. Where the fuck are they?

Almost on cue a flat-bed truck turns into the street and comes to a halt in front of the house. Two men get out; one is Trevor Owens, the foreman. The younger lad goes round to the back and starts unloading tools.

'Is it just the two of you?' says Sexton warily. 'I thought you said they'd all be back in today?'

Owens comes up to the door. 'Don't you worry, Mr Sexton. They're on their way. Just popped into the builders' merchants to pick up some materials. I came on ahead so we can take another look at that wee problem in the cellar.'

'Didn't look like a fucking *wee problem* to me,' says Sexton, but he turns and unlocks the door.

Inside, the house reeks of damp. Yet another sodding reason why he wanted to get it done in the summer.

Owens stomps down the hall to the kitchen and tugs open the cellar door. He flips the switch, but nothing happens.

'Kenny!' he calls back. 'You got that light, mate?'

The lad turns up with a large yellow plastic torch. Owens flips it on and trains the beam up at the light socket. There is no bulb.

'OK,' he says, 'let's see what we have here, then.'

He starts down the steps, but suddenly there's a crack and a shout and the sound of clattering.

'What?' says Sexton, leaning forward. 'What the fuck was that?'

He stops at the threshold and looks down. Owens is half-way down, on his back, clinging to what's left of the wooden steps.

'*Fuck*,' he says, his chest heaving. '*Fuck* – down there – *look*.'

The torch has fallen all the way to the bottom and the cone of light is glaring across the floor. The glitter of a dozen beady eyes in the dark, a scuttle of feet.

Rats.

But that's not what Owens means.

She's lying at the base of what was once the stairs. One leg twisted at an impossible angle. Long hair, now turning greenish, thin arms, black nail varnish. She's young. And possibly pretty once, but it's impossible to tell.

She no longer has a face.

*   *   *

Daily Mail

21st December 2017

VERDICT IN THE 'TWISTED SISTERS' CASE
Vicky Neale sentenced for 'cruel and unusual' scam
Still no charges in the murder of Hannah Gardiner

By Peter Croxford

'Cellar scammer' Vicky Neale was sentenced to six years in prison at Oxford Crown Court yesterday, after pleading guilty to attempting to defraud pensioner William Harper by accusing him of false imprisonment and rape. The court heard how Neale and her older sister, Tricia Walker, tortured and humiliated the old man, burning him several times on the gas cooker in the house, and planting pornography to incriminate him. Passing sentence, Judge Theobald Wotton QC condemned the 19-year-old teenager's behaviour as 'cruel and unusual', and a 'heartless and self-serving attempt to prey upon a frail and vulnerable old man who had done no harm to you'.

Speaking after the verdict, Superintendent John Harrison of Thames Valley Police said he was pleased that justice had been done, and confirmed that the police are preparing a file to submit to the Crown Prosecution Service in relation to the 2015 murder of BBC journalist Hannah Gardiner. Though many commentators doubt it will now be possible to determine the exact extent of Neale's involvement in that crime, after the discovery, two months ago, of Tricia Walker's partly decomposed body in the cellar of the house next door to William Harper's. The gruesome remains were found by the owner of the empty property, and police believe Walker was squatting there after absconding from custody by inducing a miscarriage. The postmortem concluded that she had fallen and broken her leg on the dangerous cellar stairs, after suffering blood loss and possible dizziness. The coroner's verdict was accidental death, due to dehydration. Only one mystery remains: what happened to the priceless Japanese ornament Walker stole from William Harper and wore around her neck? The silver chain was found broken on the floor, but there was no sign of the ornament itself, and an exhaustive search by the Metropolitan Police Art and Antiques Unit is believed to have found no trace of it.

Despite the fact that no charges have yet been brought in relation to the killing of Hannah Gardiner, some details of the terrifying circumstances of her death have since emerged. Tricia

Walker is thought to have planned the murder meticulously, stripping and tying up Mrs Gardiner's body to make it look like the work of a sexual predator. Vicky Neale has apparently denied any direct involvement in Mrs Gardiner's death, insisting that she only helped Walker cover up the killing because she was completely under her control, and feared for her own life if she did not comply.

Criminal psychologist Laurence Finch, consultant with the hit TV series *Crimes That Shook Britain*, says this is a classic example of a so-called *folie à deux* crime, committed by two people working together: 'In cases like that there is almost always one dominant partner, but it's more common for that to be a man imposing his will on a female partner, usually a wife or girlfriend. Look at the Moors Murderers, for instance. It's the fact that this particular killing involved two women – and two sisters – that makes it so unusual.'

Dr Finch also believes Tricia Walker was a rare example of a female psychopath: 'We're used to men committing crimes like this, but there are women who are equally capable, if the right triggers are there. Many potential psychopaths go through their whole lives without committing a crime, because they never find themselves in a situation where they can't get what they want. As long as they're not being thwarted or obstructed in any way these people can appear perfectly normal – perhaps rather manipulative but in many cases extremely charming. As one of the leading experts in the field once put it, a psychopath will show you a good time, but you'll be left paying a very heavy price.'

389 comments

Danielaking07

In my opinion Hannah Gardiner's husband and son are the real victims of those two vicious cows. That little boy is growing up without a mother – that's what I call a 'heavy price'.

Zandra_the_sandra

It's the old man I feel sorry for. How many more old people are going to be abandoned in their own homes before enough money is made available for social workers to do a proper job?

GloriousGloria

What I want to know is how two girls from a perfectly nice family can turn into such monsters? As far as I know they weren't abused or anything?

Otter_mindy1776

If you ask me, the internet has a lot to answer for. Bet they even took selfies of themselves abusing that poor old git.

FireSalamander33

At least Vicky's little boy will get a chance at a decent start in life now. I heard he's being adopted and Social Services have nicknamed him Brandon because of his dark hair. It means 'little raven'. That's so lovely, in't it?

Epilogue

The building is cold, despite the summer sunshine outside. It has the chill of somewhere not inhabited. The damp of no body heat, no warm breath. But that's an illusion, because sitting in one corner, among the empty cans of Coke, the half-eaten burger and the bag of sanitary towels, there's a girl. She's leaning against the wall, a jacket wrapped around her like a blanket. The jacket is navy. Quilted.

The door opens slowly and now someone is standing there, the face in shadow against the sudden glare of sunlight behind.

Tricia tries to get up, but grimaces. She's clearly in pain.

Vicky looks at her. 'They said you were losing the baby.'

'Yeah, well, the sooner I got rid of it the better. I only got pregnant because I wanted Rob. I didn't want the bloody *kid*. Just my luck the sad bastard was firing blanks.'

Vicky says nothing.

'What did you tell them?' says Tricia. 'The police?'

'Nothing. They don't know I'm here. I got bail.'

'How did you know where to find me?'

'I know how you think. I know *you*. The real you. Better than anyone.'

Tricia sneers. 'But all those people, they don't know *you*, do they, Vicky? You lied to them.'

'So did you. And *you* lied to *me*. I nearly died because of what you did. I *would have* died.'

Vicky closes the door behind her with a sudden bang; the sheets of newspaper on the floor shift in the gust.

'That Inspector – Fawley. He showed me what they found on your phone. Those websites you were looking at. About claiming the money.'

Tricia shifts her position a little. 'Yeah, well, we needed to start working out what we were going to do, didn't we?'

'But it wasn't *we*, was it?' Vicky's lips are trembling but there is something fierce and unforgiving in her eyes. 'It was just *you*. It wasn't just looking at stuff on the internet either – you emailed a law firm. You said you wanted to know how much you'd get if you sued someone for *killing your sister*.'

There's a silence.

'It wasn't a mistake, was it, Tricia? You wanted me dead. And you were going to say Harper did it.'

They stare at each other. Openly hostile.

'Where is it?' says Vicky, her voice hard now.

'What are you talking about?'

'You know damn well what I'm talking about. Hand it over.'

Tricia's eyes narrow. 'Why the hell should I?'

'Just give it to me and I'm out of here and you can go. Or –'

'*Or?*'

The question hangs in the air.

Unanswered.

Acknowledgements

There's a wonderful group of people now on 'team Fawley', all of whom have helped me make, shape and refine this novel. Most notably my fabulous, patient and supportive agent, Anna Power, and my two editors at Penguin – the equally delightful and insightful Katy Loftus and Sarah Stein. I also want to thank my fantastic PR teams, both in the UK – Poppy North, Rose Poole and Annie Hollands – and in the US – Ben Petrone and Shannon Kelly.

I also want to say a very big thank you to my expert advisers – Joey Giddings, CSI extraordinaire, who also drew up the crime scene sketches on pages 45–6; Nicholas Syfret QC for his advice on the legal side; and Detective Inspector Andy Thompson for invaluable help on police procedure. Also Dr Ann Robinson and Nikki Ralph. I have tried to make the story as accurate as possible, but as in all works of fiction there are a few places where I have exercised a degree of artistic licence. For example, the procedures involved in questioning vulnerable adults are very complex, and I do not pretend to have captured every single detail 100 per cent. Needless to say, if there are any errors or inaccuracies these are down to me alone.

Thanks too to my 'first readers' – my husband, Simon, and my dear friends Stephen, Elizabeth, Sarah and Peter. And also to my superb copy editor, Karen Whitlock.

And finally it seems odd to thank a city, but I couldn't have written this book without drawing on the special 'genius of the place' of Oxford. It's an endlessly inspiring and surprising town, and I'm very lucky to live there. However, needless to say, my characters are entirely the products of my imagination, and not based on any real individuals. Many of the places are my inventions too, though some are not. The Wittenham Clumps are real, as are the Cuckoo Pen, the Money Pit and the legend of the raven. The Iron Age remains of a man, a child and part of a dismembered female have indeed been discovered at the Clumps in recent years, and one theory is that the female was part of a human sacrifice. But there has never, to my knowledge, been a proposal to build a housing estate in the area.

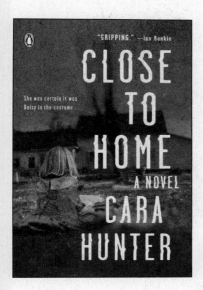